THE PIRATE'S KISS

"Like the gentle art of the fan with its multitude of meanings," Gabriel said, "a kiss may also mean many things. No doubt there's a proper way to kiss for which my life of piracy has not prepared me."

"That's a certainty," Jacquelyn replied, some of her vinegar returning.

"Then perhaps that's a bit of my training you'd care to take upon yourself."

"Well, we mustn't have you embarrassing yourself with improper and indiscriminate kissing," she admitted. "If a lady signals with her fan that she wishes you to kiss her, you might frighten off a perfectly good prospective wife if you fail to do it in a seemly manner."

"Then let us begin...."

Other *Leisure* books by Emily Bryan:

DISTRACTING THE DUCHESS

MORE PRAISE FOR *DISTRACTING THE DUCHESS*!

"As historical romances go, this is a cut above. The political intrigue, mysterious characters and a former spy struggling with dementia make this arresting tale thrilling, inspiring and sensual all at the same time. I won't forget this author's name..."

—Barbara Vey, *Publishers Weekly* Beyond Her Book Blog

"The characters are strong enough to appeal to the most ruthless romantic, and the story is edgy enough to hold your interest....There's humor....This was a very good read."

—Fresh Fiction

"*Distracting the Duchess* has everything this reviewer looks for in a historical romance, including drama mixed with humor and a believable story. The story line, the characters, but most of all Emily Bryan's writing are simply superb."

—Romance Readers At Heart

"*Distracting the Duchess* is an enjoyable read that will keep readers interested from page one! I appreciated how the author gave Artemisia's character strength and intelligence in contrast to Trevelyn's self-confident persona. Ms. Bryan has penned a great story and historical fans will want to pick this title up as it gives you a little bit of everything from intrigue to murder to love."

—The Romance Readers Connection

"*Distracting the Duchess* has a cast of characters that stay with you long after you close the book. Desire, sex, intrigue and betrayal...this book has it all."

—Night Owl Romance

"Reading *Distracting the Duchess* is like breathing in wonderful, fresh air."

—All About Romance

Pleasuring the Pirate

Emily Bryan

LEISURE BOOKS NEW YORK CITY

*For my dear husband. He doesn't wear an eye patch or say
"Aarrg" very often, but he's still my very own pirate!*

A LEISURE BOOK®

August 2008

Published by

Dorchester Publishing Co., Inc.
200 Madison Avenue
New York, NY 10016

ISBN 10: 0-8439-6133-3
ISBN 13: 978-0-8439-6133-1

The name "Leisure Books" and the stylized "L" with design are
trademarks of Dorchester Publishing Co., Inc.

Printed in the United States of America.

10 9 8 7 6 5 4 3 2 1

Visit us on the web at www.dorchesterpub.com.

Pleasuring the Pirate

Prologue

At His Majesty's good pleasure, this Letter of Marque is presented to one Captain Gabriel Drake. Be it known to all that the crimes of the aforementioned mariner are herewith pardoned. However, should the bearer of this Letter of Marque be hereafter found within the precincts of London, said pardon shall be void and the standing sentence to which Gabriel Drake is entitled shall be administered without trial and without further clemency on the part of His Royal Highness.

Duly signed and witnessed
this 12th day of June in the
Year of our Lord 1720.

Sir Cecil Oddbody
Keeper of the King's Privy Seal

Chapter One

The next time I decide to kill a man, Jacquelyn thought, *I really need to find better help.*

She struggled toward consciousness, but pain blocked her way. Jacquelyn sank back with dreamlike slowness, as though it weren't her body lying beside the dusty Cornish road. She lightly skimmed the surface of blackness, ready to plunge downward again, when the voices above her began to make sense.

"No more than a whelp," a deep baritone said with disgust.

"Dead?" another voice asked, the tone reedy and unabashedly cheerful.

Work-roughened fingers searched for the pulse point below her jaw line. "Not yet."

Jacquelyn hardly dared breathe.

"No blood so far as I can tell, but he took a wallop. Look at that goose egg. Still, we may get some answers from him." A booted foot nudged her hip. "Wake up, lad."

Lad. At least her disguise still held. Her eyes rolled in their sockets before she forced her lids open. A stab of sunlight made her squeeze them closed again. Her head pounded in tandem with her heart.

"Rum, Meri," the deep voice ordered, punctuated by a commanding snap of his fingers.

"There's no call to waste good rum on—"

"Whose rum is it, Mr. Meriwether?"

Jacquelyn peered from beneath her brown lashes. Grumbling under his breath, the one called Meri fished a silver flask from the gelding's saddlebag and handed it over. The other one, the one whose strong arms forced her to sit up, the one she loathed with every fiber of her being, held the drink to her lips.

"Steady now. Not too fast," he urged. "This rum's raw enough to put hair on your chest."

The spirits burned down her gullet. When she choked and sputtered, he pulled the flask away. She didn't dare look up at him.

He was coming to destroy her life and the lives of all she held dear. She didn't want to see his face up so close.

Not until she had a sword in her hand.

"Well, lookee there, Cap'n. He's still in the land of the living, after all. Must have just had the breath knocked from him, I warrant. Good. I like me boys' livers fresh." Meriwether flashed a wolfish grin. "Pity we've no onions to fry up with it."

She'd been warned the new lord and his minions were heartless and utterly without conscience. She felt the blood draining from her face, blanching white as a fish belly.

Damn her weakness! Why hadn't she been born a man?

"You aren't really going to eat my liver." She tried to sound sure about it, but her voice broke with a squeak.

"I won't," the captain promised. "But Mr. Meriwether spent longer in the Caribbee than I. He has peculiar tastes. If you tell me what I want to know, I'll make certain your liver stays where it is. Now what's your name?"

She needed time to gather her wits. Keeping her eyes downcast, she wobbled to her feet. A sword lay a bare five feet away, the hilt facing toward her.

"J-Jack," she stammered as she edged toward the weapon. "I'm called Jack."

"Very well, Jack," he said. "You were with that lot that tried to waylay us, but perhaps you can make amends."

With them? She'd tried to *lead* them, but her last fuzzy

memory was of one of the oafs clobbering her senseless with his sharp elbow as he drew his sword. The wretches had professed to be experienced assassins, and the royal seal they flashed about gave their claims the ring of truth. The ruffians must have grown wings after their initial assault failed. There was no sign of them now.

"I'm willing to believe you fell in with bad company sort of accidental-like," the captain went on.

"Aye, 'tis easy enough to fall in with villains, bad company being so much more pleasurable than good company as a general rule," Meriwether chimed in. "And who should know better'n you, Cap'n?"

"In any case, I've done you a good turn for an evil one," he said. "Will you help me then, Jack?"

She crossed her arms over her chest, pulling the ill-fitting smock shirt tight around her form, trying to seem as if she were weighing her options. She glanced at Meri, who was now picking rocks from his horse's hooves, totally disinterested in her since it appeared his captain wasn't going to let him cook her liver.

This might be her only chance.

"Aye, I'll help you." She dove for the sword and by some miracle came up with the hilt in her hand. "I'll help you on your way to hell." Remembering her training with Dragon Caern's master-at-arms, she brought the blade up in a glittering arc, trusting to surprise for success.

She only managed to graze his chin and knock off his hat.

Quick as an adder, his sword was out and facing her down. He was much bigger than she expected. He stood a hand's width more than six feet and carried fifteen stone in weight. Most of it looked to be in work-hardened muscle.

Jacquelyn swallowed hard. The folk of Dragon Caern depended on her to make good decisions. Clearly, this was not one of her finest.

She'd imagined the new lord would be whey-faced, powdered and perfumed, slightly effeminate in the manner of most courtly folk. But this man's face was bronzed the color of oiled cedar and there was nothing the least bit soft about him. Something inside her rebelled at the injustice. He had no right to such a strong-boned, handsome face. Not with as black a heart as he must possess. She felt a surge of triumph when a trio of red beads appeared on his smooth-shaven chin. He wiped them off and gave her a mocking bow.

"First blood to you then, Jack."

Meri chuckled. "And I was afeared life as a landsman would be dull."

Circling, the captain retrieved his fallen hat. The tip of his sword never dipped as he slapped the tricorn against his thigh, sending small clouds of dust puffing. The cockade and plume were decidedly the worse for wear, but he cocked the hat on his head at a rakish angle.

"You don't want to do this, boy," he warned.

The fine brocade frock coat and velvet breeches bespoke him a gentleman, but his dark eyes glinted beneath his darker brows, feral and cold as a dragon.

A dragon that would devour her world, the note with the royal seal had promised. She clenched her teeth and gripped the hilt of her sword all the tighter. "Oh, yes, I do."

"Me thanks to ye, Jackie-boy. Cap'n Gabriel swore anyone who wished him bodily harm was still sailing the Spanish Main." Meri settled on a rock to watch the combatants in comfort. "I recollect he wagered twenty sovereigns on the matter."

A wry grin lifted one corner of Gabriel's mouth.

"Apparently I lose." The smile faded. "But I warn you, Jack. I don't make a habit of it."

"Don't worry," Jacquelyn said with more bravado than

she felt. "I don't intend for you to live long enough to get used to losing."

She lunged at him, swinging her blade with all the spite she possessed.

Gabriel parried the stroke with economy of movement. "Bad form. Is it a lesson you're wanting then?"

"No, 'tis your head I'm after."

"Don't think I can accommodate you. I'm rather attached to my head." Despite the dirty face, there was no disguising the delicacy of Jack's features. Gabriel narrowed his eyes in speculation. Jack was definitely female.

A wickedly angry female.

She recovered from her initial blunder and launched a fresh assault that showed some skill with a blade.

"Better," he said as they danced with steel. He followed the praise with a rumbling chuckle. "Keep your knees bent."

"Keep your teeth together," Jack said hotly, cheeks flaming.

The livid blush made her pink mouth all the riper for the taking. Even with her spitfire temper, he wanted a taste of her.

A unique combination of strokes forced Gabriel to jerk his attention back to her blade. Her lips might look sweet as honey, but her sword arm carried a sting. Did she think hiding her sex under boy's rags would make it easier for her to attack him? Gabe would play along for the time being. Uncovering the truth of the matter might prove amusing.

"You take too many chances, Jack." He sidestepped her rushing blow and whacked her on the backside with the flat of his blade. Not hard enough to truly hurt her, but he knew a rap like that smarted like the dickens.

She yelped and rubbed her bottom with her free hand.

"I warned you." One corner of his mouth hitched up. "Perhaps when we're done here, I'll take you over my knee and warm your arse properly."

After all, she was attempting to kill him. The least she might expect was a paddling. He'd even try not to enjoy it too much.

"You truly are evil," she said in disgust.

"Did you hear that, Meri? Evil, Jack calls me."

"Evil, is it?" Meriwether's scrub-brush eyebrows rose. "Aye, well, he don't know ye like I do, else he'd not be so charitable."

Gabriel turned back to parry Jack's latest thrust. "I don't like being called evil when I've done nothing to warrant it. Not lately, at any rate."

"I've no care for your likes or dislikes." Her chin jutted upward in defiance as she raised her sword again. "All I wish is for you to die."

"You'll forgive me if I don't quake in my boots." Gabriel cocked his head and gave her a grudging nod. Perhaps he needed to change tactics if he hoped to expose her true colors.

"You know, Jack, you took a nasty blow. Might have cracked a rib or two in your fall." He bared his teeth in a wicked smile. "Best shuck out of your shirt so we can have a look-see."

Her eyes flared and she backed a step or two. "My ribs are fine."

"Don't be so sure. You were knocked senseless. A cracked rib might puncture one of your lungs. Nasty thing that. Have you bubbling blood in no time. Now, I ask you, would an evil man be so concerned for the well-being of one who tried to waylay him? Let me help you there."

Gabriel flashed his blade and, quick as thought, flicked the top button from Jack's shirt.

She squealed and clutched the shirt closed, but not before Gabriel was rewarded with a glimpse of the sweet meeting place between two tightly bound breasts.

There be a hidden treasure well worth finding. He smiled in satisfaction at having correctly divined one of Jack's secrets. *Two actually*, he thought as his smile deepened.

"Aw, Cap'n. Ye shouldn't frighten the lad so," Meri chided as he inspected the gelding's tack and cinched the girth tighter. "Sours the liver, it does. Makes 'em hardly worth frying."

"Steady on, Meriwether." Gabriel circled the girl slowly. She turned with him, her eyes spitting cold venom. "I think I've discovered a better way to loosen Jack's tongue than your threat to fry his liver for breakfast. Come now. Off with the shirt."

She shook her head with vehemence. "You're not just evil. You're a beast!"

"Freely admitted with pride." He lifted his tricorn and made a courtly leg to her. "You may dress him in lace and gold trim if you like, but dandy or not, there's a beast in every man."

"Don't tar others with your sins."

"No need, since I'm sure they have plenty of their own." With a deft movement, he caught her blade in his and whipped it out of her grasp. The sword turned end over end, but he caught the hilt cleanly. "But all men are part beast, the part that craves what it does not have and stops at nothing to possess. Now, Jack, if you value your skin, you'll stand still."

Gabriel stepped behind her and slashed the back of her long shirt in a deep upside-down vee, exposing the backside of her skin-hugging leggings and the muslin winding cloth she'd used to bind her breasts. She gasped but couldn't stop him from looking his fill.

"I must say, you're a forward-looking lad. Seems he's already bound his ribs, Meri."

Gabriel's gaze traveled lower.

No boy ever had such a bottom, the round mounds

shaped like an inverted heart. It was as snug a cove as a man could hope for.

The beast in Gabriel roared for a moment, tempting him with a vision of Jack bent over the nearest boulder, leggings twisted at her ankles. His mouth went dry and his breeches were suddenly uncomfortably tight. He'd been without a woman far too long, but he bridled himself.

Once, in another life it sometimes seemed, he'd been the son of a gentleman.

Perhaps he might be again.

"At least, an honest man will own up to his beast," he said between clenched teeth, as he tamped down the desire she stirred.

"An honest beast," she all but snarled at him over her shoulder. "So you make a virtue of admitting your faults."

"A man like me must take virtue where he may." He came full circle and deliberately strafed her form with a hot, knowing look.

Gabriel had never taken a woman by force in his life and wasn't about to start now, but Jack didn't know that. Let her think what she might. He needed answers.

"You'll pardon me for saying so, but you're not much of a fighting man, Jack. Why did the men who attacked me need you?"

Her lips clamped together.

He raised his blade. "You have more buttons."

"We were warned that a new lord was coming to take possession of Dragon Caern. One who'd bought and paid for the title and intended to turn out all the souls who shelter there now." She glared at him.

"And? What was your role in plotting my untimely demise?" His sword point teased another button.

"I was to lead a party of fighting men to a likely spot to catch you before you reached the castle," she admitted.

"A totally unnecessary plan, as I have no intention of taking possession of anything," Gabriel said. "Besides, I suspect my father would have a thing or two to say about being turned out. Rhys Drake may be getting on in years, but that old dragon won't leave the Caern till they carry him out feetfirst."

Jack's brows lowered, and she studied Gabriel through narrowed eyes. "Old Lord Drake is dead, God rest him."

She wielded no sword, but she couldn't have delivered a more ringing blow. A stone lodged in Gabriel's chest. He sank onto the nearest rock as he tried to wrap his mind around the thought of a world where his indomitable father was no more.

"Unless you're bastard born," Jack said, quick to follow up her verbal wallop with another telling strike, "Lord Drake couldn't have been your sire. The old lord only had two sons and they're both gone to God, too. The elder by a fever and the younger by the sea."

His brother dead, too. This was an ill-starred day all around. Gabriel dragged a hand over his face and looked up to find Jack staring at him quizzically.

"You can't be him." She swiped her nose on her shirtsleeve. A nice boyish touch, but it came far too late to fool him. "The younger son's ship went down with all hands."

"Aye, well, there's down and there's down," Meriwether explained. "When we poor mariners what sank the HMS *Defiant* found out Gabriel was a navigator trained, we sort of commandeered him, as it were."

"Mariners?" Jack's gaze swept the old rascal. "You mean *pirates!*" She turned back to glare at Gabriel. "And you went with them willingly?"

Gabriel snorted at her outrage. Had he ever been that cocksure about anything?

"They fished me out of the burning wreckage and offered me a choice. Turn to piracy or claim a watery grave then and there." Gabriel knew his father wouldn't have approved, even to save his skin. Not that Rhys Drake had ever approved of anything Gabriel did. He crossed his arms over his chest. "It was a compelling argument for a change of career at the time."

"And a brilliant career he made of it, let me tell ye—"

"That's enough, Meri."

"Aye, Cap'n," Meriwether said with a grimace. He lowered his voice conspiratorially. "But one who can claim to be the Dragon of the Caribbee—"

"That'll do, Mr. Meriwether."

A flash of recognition crossed Jack's face. "I've heard of you. The Cornish Dragon, terror of—"

"Just Gabriel Drake, if you please." He rose and sketched a mocking bow. "Your servant."

"Gabriel Drake," she repeated, her ears and cheeks going scarlet as she realized her error. He was no usurper. Gabe had every right to be here. Jack dipped in a quick curtsey, then remembered herself and returned his bow. She was doggedly determined to keep up her male disguise. "My Lord Drake." Then her eyes turned wary. "If that's who you are in truth."

Gabriel was suddenly weary of the game.

"I've no need to prove it to you. Let's away to the castle," he said as he lifted her up onto the gelding. The lass gave a startled squeak when Gabriel pinched her bottom. He swung himself up behind her with a satisfied nod. Jack tried to wiggle down, but he pulled her tight to his chest. "You can go upright or you can go flopped over the saddle with your bottom bouncing to the sky. In fact, now that I think on it, I believe I'd prefer you like that. But either way, you're going with me."

She went still as a hare in a thicket.

"That's better." He nudged the gelding into a sedate walk.

"To start, you might tell me what a young lady is doing traipsing about the countryside dressed as a lad."

"My lord, I'm not—"

"Spare me your denials, or I'll just have to finish unbuttoning that shirt to make doubly certain," Gabriel threatened. "I may have been at sea a long time, but I still know the feel of a woman's rump. Now talk."

He flicked open the top remaining button on Jack's shirt and moved down to the next one. Her bared skin was satin to his touch. A bit of meddling with this cheeky wench was just what he needed to ease the fresh ache in his heart. He suspected the best way to irritate Jack was to make sure she enjoyed it as well.

Since irritating her was the best idea he'd had all morning, he'd make certain of it.

He dipped his head to take her earlobe in his mouth and was rewarded by her sharp intake of breath. He bit down just enough to make her shiver and then released her.

His voice rumbled by her wet ear. "Who are *you* in truth?"

Chapter Two

Stop, for pity's sake, stop and I'll tell you." She grabbed at his hand to keep him from moving on to the next button. It was hard enough for Jacquelyn to breathe with her breasts bound so tightly. Being mauled by a bloody pirate made drawing breath even harder. "But in truth, my name *is* Jack."

"Wrong answer," Gabriel said, popping the next horn button right off.

A deep vee of flesh showed beneath her throat now as he parted the shirt. Where his fingers stroked her bared skin, a shiver trailed in their wake.

"Try again," he suggested as he toyed with a lower button.

"You, sir, are no gentleman," she said between clenched teeth.

"And neither are you, Mistress *Jack*."

His touch was maddening as he slid his fingertips over the bulge of her breasts. She forced herself to draw a hitching breath. Who'd have guessed his naked hand was more dangerous than his blade?

"You didn't really think I was fooled by your boy's rags, did you? You may have bound them tightly, but there's no disguising a ripe pair of pips like these," he rumbled, his tone husky as he continued to tease the tops of her breasts. "As fine a bosom as ever filled a man's hand."

Merciful heaven! He found the crevice between them and slid a broad finger into the tight space. Her nipples hardened at his hand's nearness and for a moment, she imagined him plunging beneath her binding cloth to cradle her breasts in his calloused palms.

A dark part of her wanted him to do just that, she realized in dismay. She struggled against him with renewed vigor.

"Is that supposed to be a compliment?" she demanded. "No gentleman would say such a thing."

"Steady on, lass. Since I've already admitted to being a pirate, the fact that I'm no gentleman goes without saying. A name, my sweeting. That's all I ask. Or perhaps you'd like me to start unbinding you next?"

Had he somehow guessed at her body's mutinous reaction to him?

"Wren. Jacquelyn Wren." She slapped at his hand as the gelding's jarring trot rattled her teeth.

"Well, Mistress Wren, it's pleased I am to make your acquaintance, to be sure." He buried his nose in her hair and inhaled. "I have been far too long at sea."

"Pity you didn't stay there."

He leaned down to whisper in her ear. His warm breath pricked the stray hairs that had escaped her boy's queue to stand at full attention.

"I love the gray swells of the sea, it's true," he said. "But these swells give a man even more pleasure."

His hand splayed across her bound breast. A jolt of something forbidden shot from her nipples to her groin.

This man was dangerous.

If only he didn't smell so wickedly good. . . .

"Let me go!" she demanded.

Instead he slid his arm down to her waist and cinched her tight against him. Her thighs rode on his muscular ones. Her bottom pressed against his groin where a hard bulge rose to meet her softness.

"So sorry to disappoint you, Miss Wren. I'm not in the habit of acquiescing to the requests of those who attempt to waylay me," he said with exaggerated politeness. "There. Was that gentlemanly enough for you?"

"You wouldn't know how to behave like a gentleman if your hope of heaven depended upon it!"

"You're probably right," he said agreeably. "The company of pirates tends to dull a man's higher sensibilities. But before you cast stones at me, Miss Wren, you might look to yourself. Leading a party of ne'er-do-wells with murderous intent, strutting about in breeches . . . you must admit your own behavior has been far from ladylike."

"But I was only trying to protect—" She stopped herself. The less this brute knew about those at the castle, the better. She might still be able to hide them from him. "I didn't join in the attack on you, more's the pity, but I did get a clout on the head for my trouble."

"For that you have my profoundest apologies," Gabriel said. "If I was the one who brought you down, it was purely unintentional. I was defending myself, you see, and didn't have time to notice your . . . finer qualities."

She wouldn't give Captain Drake the satisfaction of knowing that one of the men she'd lead there was responsible for knocking her senseless.

"I make it a policy never to strike a woman," he explained. "Not when there are so many more pleasurable things to do with one."

His voice was a rumbling purr at her ear, a beguiling summons to something dark and sinful. She squeezed her eyes shut against the fleshly possibilities his words conjured. So must the Serpent have sounded to Eve. Jacquelyn would not give in to her baser nature.

He urged his mount into a canter and the rolling gait forced her to move in tandem with him, her body rising and falling with his. The heat from his thighs radiated through the thin homespun of her breeches. Warmth pooled between her legs.

"If you don't release me at once, I will report you to the

magistrate," she threatened. "Lord or not, if you're a pirate, no doubt there's a price on your head. Squire Ramskelter will see you hanged at the next assizes."

"Beggin' yer pardon, but that were no good, Miss Wren," Meriwether said. "I'll warrant there's them what would like to see Drake the Dragon dance the hempen jig, but Cap'n Gabriel got himself a royal pardon. Him and all what sailed with him. His Royal Highness is content to let bygones be bygones. But Cap'n"—the aging sea dog turned a rheumy eye on her tormentor—"ye're still bound by the code same as ever ye were."

"A pirate's code?" Jacquelyn asked in horrified fascination. Were there proper rules for rape and pillage?

"Aye, Cap'n Gabriel drew up the articles himself, so he did. And every man jack of us signed on. Himself included!" Meriwether worried his scraggly beard like a dog chasing its fleas. Jacquelyn shivered in disgust. "And seems to me Article Number Nine goes something like—"

"I remember the bloody code, Meri." Gabriel Drake's grip around her waist eased by the tiniest of margins.

"Well, I don't," she said. "Pray, what is Article Number Nine?"

"Let me see if I can recollect it entire." Meri tapped his temple. "Ah! Here 'tis. 'If a man meets a woman of prudence and offers to meddle with her without her consent, the crew shall suffer that man to be done to death presently,'" Meriwether recited.

He gave his captain a pointed look.

Jacquelyn straightened her spine and held herself away from the broad expanse of Gabriel Drake's chest. A pirate's code was a small shield, but it was all she had.

"Thank you, Mr. Meriwether," she said, liking him better by the moment, despite his deplorable hygiene and recent threat to fry her liver. "Your code sounds almost civilized."

"Meri, what you forgot is that the code specifies the wench in question must be a woman of prudence. What about Jack here makes you think she fits that description?" Gabriel asked. "No proper lady would put herself forward as a lad."

"I didn't know the fellows I was meeting," Jacquelyn said, irritated that she must explain herself to this disturbing man. "It seemed more *prudent* to present myself as a boy than as a woman."

"Not necessarily, Miss Wren," Meri said. "There's places in this funny ol' world where a pretty little boy is at risk of buggery every bit as much as a pretty young lady." The old salt's ears turned bright red when he realized the wholly improper nature of what he'd just said. "But I reckon you've the right of it, in Cornwall at least. Seems a mighty prudent woman to me, Cap'n."

With a snort, Gabriel Drake slowed his mount to a walk and let his arm drop from its place around her waist. He rested his long-fingered hand on his own thigh. But she was yet wedged between the big man's legs, and no help for it unless he allowed her to dismount and walk. He'd left off manhandling her as if she were a common strumpet, but Jacquelyn was chagrined to discover her nipples still tingled.

She hastily refastened her remaining buttons, lest he change his mind.

"So let me understand this, Miss Wren. You were warned of my coming. How?"

"A note came to the keep bearing a royal seal."

She felt him stiffen behind her.

"So much for my pardon," he said. "Signed by whom?"

"There was no signature," she admitted. "But the seal spoke for itself, and the men were waiting for me with their own official orders."

"So, someone you don't know sends you a note telling you to meet some men, whom you also don't know, for the purpose of waylaying yet another man you don't know." The rich bass timbre of his voice rumbled along her spine. "I have to ask why a woman of prudence would agree to such a scheme."

"I don—"

"If you say you don't know, I shall have to rethink my policy about striking a woman," Gabriel warned. "An exception might be made for your bonny backside."

Her bottom warmed rosily at this suggestion. Perhaps she was more her mother's daughter than she wanted to admit.

"I was going to say that I don't take threats to those I love lightly." The tremor in her voice upset her even more than his nearness. She must not show weakness before this pirate. "The Crown has claimed several baronies in Cornwall in recent years. The usual excuse is that the lords were found to be secret Jacobites. The note wasn't signed, because the writer claimed to be a secret Catholic in King George's suite. He didn't want to see another Catholic barony fall into Protestant hands when it was plain we'd had no part in the Jacobite uprising. He said a new lord was coming to claim Dragon Caern. I couldn't allow that to happen."

"Neither could I," he said. "Dragon Caern Castle is my home, Miss Wren. Having made peace with my sovereign, I thought to undertake the harder path and make peace with my father as well. With my brother ever in favor, I never thought to be lord of the place. Last I heard, Rupert had married and was busily engaged in producing an heir." He fell silent for the space of several heartbeats. "I can't believe they're both gone."

She felt him take a shuddering breath. Was it possible for a pirate to feel sorrow?

"Did my brother leave no son?"

"No," she said softly. "His lady wife died in childbed trying to bring a stillborn boy into the world."

That much at least was true. Gabriel Drake didn't need to know everything.

"Then you won't evict your tenants and retainers to make room for your own people?" she asked.

They topped the rise and stopped to look down on the square tower of Dragon Caern Castle. Perched on a small spit of land overhanging the roiling sea, the weathered gray stone almost seemed to have grown there, instead of being built by man. Thatch-roofed cottages dotted the lowlands. As far as the eye could see, narrow brown roads stretched like spokes of a giant's wheel, leading to the safety of the keep.

"My own people," Gabriel repeated softly. "Since the pardon, my crew is gone, scattered to the four winds. Other than Meri here, I have no people."

He rested his hand on her shoulder for a moment. The pressure was light, but she sensed his bridled strength. When he withdrew it, she breathed a small sigh of relief. This man unsettled her thoroughly.

"I give you my word, Miss Wren. None who live here has aught to fear from me."

The way he set her insides quaking, she took leave to doubt it.

"Appears to me ye've made a well-placed enemy. Who do ye suppose at court didn't want ye coming home, Cap'n?" Meriwether asked.

"That seems to be the question, doesn't it? We'll have to satisfy ourselves on that point, but for now, I *am* almost home. A sad homecoming to be sure, but home nonetheless." He waved his arm expansively. "When you pulled me from the water, Meri, I never thought to see it again. You were my boon companion through dangerous seas. Welcome to Dragon Caern Castle, Joseph Meriwether."

"Ach! Don't take on so, Cap'n," Meri protested. "Ye saved me miserable neck countless times since."

Jacquelyn was surprised by the deep fealty between these two obvious scallywags. Who would have thought pirates capable of such ordinary feelings as friendship?

"Now that you're a man of leisure, whatever's mine is yours, mate," Gabriel said.

Meri's eyebrows shot skyward. "This castle o' yers have a wine cellar, by chance?"

Gabriel loosed a full, deep-throated laugh. "Used to be one of the best in Cornwall."

"Well, then." Meriwether drummed his heels on his horse's flanks. "I'll leave ye me opinion on it this evening," he called over his shoulder as he cantered down the hill.

Gabriel nudged his mount into a walk.

"We should go faster," Jacquelyn suggested. Mr. Meriwether's absence made her even more apprehensive about being so close to Captain Gabriel Drake. "Aren't you eager to be home?"

"Miss Wren, my mother died when I was born. My father and brother are both gone. There doesn't seem to be a need to hurry now, does there?"

His sense of loss seemed genuine, unlikely as that might be for a hard-hearted pirate.

The folk of Dragon Caern Castle had bitterly mourned the passing of Lady Helen, the hope of an heir dying with her. Then old Lord Rhys was gashed by a boar in a hunting accident. When Lord Rupert was taken by a raging fever a week later, folk spoke of curses coming in threes.

Since then, life had settled into a comfortable rhythm. The denizens of the keep rejoiced in the relative obscurity of their small corner of the world. It allowed them to continue in peace without interference from the Crown.

But the note warning of a new lord who would upset the natural order of things threatened all that.

Jacquelyn twisted around to look over her shoulder at Gabriel Drake. His gaze was fixed on the distant keep, his mouth drawn in a tight, grim line. Perhaps, just perhaps, he might not be too bad a lord for the folk of the Caern.

Then he looked down at her. A wicked smile tugged at his mouth.

"You know of course, Miss Wren, woman of prudence or not, I do intend to meddle with you."

"But the code—"

"Only requires that I have your consent." He traced his thumb across her lower lip. Jacquelyn froze like a coney caught in the gaze of an adder.

He lowered his face to hers and took her mouth, gently at first, then with more insistence. His lips were warm, and they slanted over hers with assurance. She knew she should pull away, but his mouth beguiled her.

The man is a pirate, for pity's sake.

Her mind reeled, but her heart pounded as if she'd just climbed to the top of the keep. Her mouth parted softly as his tongue invaded her, searching out her secrets and sending delight shivering over her. Everything inside her went soft and liquid. His warmth flooded her senses. She was drowning in this man.

And not caring one whit.

Then he stopped and pulled back to look down at her. A dark brow rose in satisfaction.

"I'll take that as consent, Miss Wren."

When he lowered his mouth to hers once more, she grasped a thin slice of sanity. Passion was her mother's curse, not hers. She took his lower lip between her teeth and bit him as hard as she could.

"There's my consent, Captain!"

"What the devil—" He loosed an oath that turned the air blue, but released his hold on her. She threw her leg over the horse's neck and slid off. Fast as her feet could carry her, she made for the keep, his string of profanities fading behind her.

She'd angered her new lord, but she didn't care. However much her body warmed to Gabriel Drake, she would not be taken for a trollop. He needed to know that Jacquelyn Wren was no man's plaything.

And certainly no pirate's.

She'd deal with his wrath later when they were on safer ground.

Her ground.

Dragon Caern Castle was her home, every bit as much as it was his. Surely, with the help of the folk of the keep, she could bring this new lord to heel.

She glanced over her shoulder, relieved to see that he had not spurred his horse into a canter after her. But just before she sprinted across the drawbridge, she heard him laugh. Rawtimbred and deep, the sound floated down the hill after her.

It did not bring her comfort.

After all, what a pirate wants, a pirate takes.

Chapter Three

Jacquelyn didn't slow her pace as she raced through the outer barbican and into the bailey. Like most castles, Dragon Caern started as merely a stone tower on a naturally defensible spot. Subsequent lords had added their own stamp to the estate, some with less than shining success. Over the years, certain parts of Dragon Caern were left to go derelict as the needs of its inhabitants changed.

In the scarcity of recent times, she'd judged it more important to try to fill the granary than to keep the defensive portions of the castle at peak operation. Now Jacquelyn bitterly regretted that the murder holes had been filled in and hot oil could no longer rain down on the approaching new lord.

"Mistress Wren! Thank the saints and angels you're here!" Mrs. Beadle said as Jacquelyn flew into the main hall. The housekeeper's round face flushed crimson in agitation. When her gaze swept Jacquelyn's bruised temple and boyish garb, Mrs. Beadle's brows lowered. "You're hurt. And what are you doing dressed in those rags, mistress?"

"I suspect it looks worse than it feels." Jacquelyn winced when the housekeeper put a hand to the bruise, then waved her away. If another blow would send Gabriel Drake back to the sea, she'd accept it willingly. "I was trying to stop something from happening, but it appears there is no help for it. Pray, don't ask."

Mrs. Beadle's curiosity faded in the heat of her own news. "Well, while you were gallivanting about the countryside dressed as an urchin, something's happened here right enough! You won't credit it, but there's a . . . a . . . a most unusual person demanding hospitality. I've never seen his like. I don't even know what to call him—"

"He's a pirate," Jacquelyn said helpfully.

Mrs. Beadle's mouth opened and shut wordlessly like that of a codfish. Her hands fluttered at her ample hips before she grasped the hem of her apron and clung to it as if it were a talisman against evil.

"Well, whatever he is, he's in the parlor demanding strong drink," Mrs. Beadle said, her eyeballs bulging. "Loudly."

"It's all right, Mrs. B. For better or worse, he's been invited here." Jacquelyn gave the housekeeper what she hoped was a reassuring pat on the shoulder. "His name is Mr. Meriwether. Promise him a bottle of the '08 if he agrees to take a bath. Where are the girls?"

"At their lessons, I expect."

"Good, that'll keep them out of sight for a while." Jacquelyn worried her lower lip for a moment. "At least, until I puzzle out what's to be done."

"Very sensible, what with that"—Mrs. Beadle gave herself a horrified shake—"that pirate lurking about the keep."

"He's rather an old pirate. I think he's mostly harmless."

Jacquelyn was nearly certain Mr. Meriwether hadn't really intended to eat her liver, and his strict adherence to the nefarious code actually saved her from Gabriel Drake's unwelcome advances.

She frowned. Even to herself, she couldn't abide a lie. His advances weren't all that unwelcome. Though her mind resented the liberties the new lord had taken, her body didn't resist one bit. It was a frustrating truth, and it would have to change.

"It's not Meriwether I'm worried about," Jacquelyn said, trying to banish the taste of Gabriel Drake from her lips. "Send Timothy to find Father and make sure he knows we need him right now, not next week. Any idea where he might be?"

In the parlor, Mr. Meriwether began croaking out a song about something called "keelhauling."

Horrified, Mrs. Beadle put a hand to her mouth.

"Please Mrs. B., trust me. I've a feeling Mr. Meriwether isn't as bad as he seems. At least compared to some." Jacquelyn took Mrs. Beadle's hand to steady her. "Now, where is Father Eustace?"

"Father will be praying in the chapel, as usual. Lot of good his newfound piety's done us." Mrs. Beadle rolled her eyes heavenward as if to plead for patience. "Pirates in the parlor! And old reprobates in the priesthood! Saints preserve us."

Mrs. Beadle waddled away, muttering under her breath. "Fine house this is. What with the mistress wearin' boy's breeches and pirates drinking up all the best wine. Next there'll be . . ."

Jacquelyn was grateful not to hear Mrs. Beadle's dire prediction. Whatever it was, it was surely not as bad as the fact that the real pirate was about to enter the gate.

And there was absolutely nothing Jacquelyn could do about it.

Gabriel took his time descending through the cultivated fields to Dragon Caern Castle. He didn't have the knack for agriculture his brother Rupert had developed, but even to his seafaring eyes, the weeds seemed to be beating out the barley for the best patches of arable land.

As he rode through the corbelled gate, he was amazed at how little the keep had changed. The portcullis still seemed to be rusted in the up position. The gargoyle at the postern still spat water into a trough for weary mounts, and an old dog still lay before the open stable door. The beast thumped its tail on the dirt in greeting but didn't bother to rise at Gabe's approach.

Probably old Rowdy's great-grandson, Gabriel mused. This dog was the spit and image of the deerhound he'd left behind when he went to sea all those years ago.

Lord, he'd been green as a beech in springtime.

He'd changed out of all knowing since then, but Dragon Caern Castle seemed frozen in time.

Then he remembered the two additional bodies interred in the chapel crypt—three, if he counted the sister-in-law he'd never even met. The changes at Dragon Caern went far deeper than mortar and stone.

This was all his now. To tend. To defend.

It was the last thing he'd expected.

The last thing he'd wanted.

Gabriel handed the reins of his mount to the nearest stable lad.

"A handful of oats for him," he ordered as he uncinched the saddle's girth and started to stride from the stable.

"Look here, sir. We're not a livery, ye know, and oats is in short supply. Miss Jack says we're not to be wasting oats while the grass is green," a gangly, pimple-faced youth said. "Who are ye to order me about?"

Gabriel rounded on the lad and flashed him a glare. "Not someone with whom you wish to trifle, boy."

"Uh, oats, ye said," the young man stammered. "Yes, sir. Right away, sir. But I'll not stand for the consequences if Miss Jack hears I done it."

Gabriel's threatening glance, dubbed by his crew "the Dragon's Glare," had averted more than a few brawls during his time in piracy and even as a landsman; it obviously had its uses. Once people of the keep knew who he was, there'd be no question that they'd obey him as thoroughly as his crew had.

All but the troublesome Mistress Wren.

He ran his tongue over his lower lip. It was swelling like a puffer fish, and he still tasted the coppery tang of his own blood.

Blow the wench to Bermuda.

He supposed he shouldn't have kissed her like that, but the little minx was asking for it. Prancing around in breeches, displaying the shape of her legs and round bottom for all the world to see. It reminded him of that doxy Meri was partial to back in Port Royal. The one who was always too drunk to remember to don her skirt.

And besides, there had been a moment when he was certain Mistress Wren enjoyed their kiss as much as he did.

Right up until she bit him.

Women were off the edge of the map as far as Gabriel was concerned. Pleasurable company at times, to be sure, but they should come with a cartographer's warning.

Here there be monsters.

Changeable as a nor'easter, unpredictable as a gale. Or if she wasn't a tempest, a woman might be doldrums that could suck the life out of any man who was unwary enough to get too close.

Gabriel was determined to enjoy, even savor the fair sex, but on his own terms. That meant keeping a weather eye out for squalls and being ever ready to up-anchor and make sail.

He stomped into the main hall, his lip still throbbing from Miss Jack's sharp little teeth. Where was a wayside tavern when a man needed one? A good brawl or a good tumble would cure his ills. At the moment, neither seemed likely to come his way.

"Is there no one here to greet their new lord?" he demanded in the voice that had carried from wheel to mains'l in a gale.

"It's midmorning, Your Lordship. Everyone is going

about their work just now," a familiar voice said from the top of the stairs. "However, if you wish me to call a halt to the operation of the keep solely for all to greet you as you seem to think you deserve, I shall, of course, oblige."

He forced himself to think of her as Jack, but it was difficult when she appeared on the landing in a snug-bodiced sac dress. No longer pretending to be a callow lad, she stood ramrod straight with an assurance that bespoke royalty, despite the humble homespun of her gown. The dirt of her boy's disguise was gone, but the bruise at her temple marred the pale oval of her face. Still, her face wasn't what captured his gaze.

Her lovely bosom curved above the low neckline. His fingertips tingled as he remembered the satiny feel of her skin. Her tiny waist was emphasized by the broad panniers on each side of her hips. Beneath that contraption of horsehair and wire, he knew there was a bottom as soft as a ripe peach. As she descended the stairs, he was treated to the fleeting sight of a well-turned ankle and her neatly shod feet.

How had he ever thought her a boy, even for a moment?

"Welcome home, my lord," she said with patent falseness. "No doubt this evening, the older servants who remember you will wish to pay their respects. But for now, I advise you to allow them to continue with their labors. Come December, we will all be glad we worked hard in July."

"I can see you've changed your feathers, Jack, but I'm still unsure what labor is fitting for a bird of your . . . talents." He let his gaze linger on the pearly flesh of her bosom before meeting her gray eyes. Her queue of auburn hair was tucked under a modest mobcap, but a few strands slipped out to tease her slender neck. He found himself wanting to yank off the cap and unbind the thick braid so he could run the silken tresses through his fingers. For a moment he imagined the reddish-brown cascade tumbled across his bare chest. Then he met her stony gaze. Miss Wren's sour expression wiped that pleasing thought from his mind. "Just what is your position here at Dragon Caern?"

"She's mistress of the castle, of course," a masculine voice said from behind him. "Has been ever since the Lady Helen passed. Keeps everything humming, too."

Gabriel turned to the newcomer. He wore the turned collar of a priest and the knees of his cassock were grimy with stains. Obviously a man of prayer. But his face was that of Gabe's dissolute, favorite relative.

"Uncle Eustace?"

The priest squinted at him and advanced uncertainly. "Aye. But to my shame, the Eustace you knew was not much of a man."

"Here's one who'd dispute that," Gabriel said.

"No, no, it's true. I wasted the strength of my best years in gaming hells with women of easy virtue and more drink than would fill an ocean," the priest said with more than a trace of wistfulness in his tone. "But I've renounced that life. Once I was 'Useless Eustace.' Now I'm Father Eustace. Who are you, son?"

"Father," Jacquelyn said, "this rogue claims to be your nephew, Gabriel. Word of his death came years ago, but if this man's story is true, it seems he left the Royal Navy under slightly different circumstances than we were led to believe." She let the threat to denounce him as a pirate hang in the air for a few moments. Then surprisingly, she allowed the opportunity to slip by. "However, if you don't know him, I'll turn the hounds on the miscreant and send him running."

She smiled at him. Like a tabby at a barn rat.

"Gabriel?" Father Eustace took another step toward him. "Is it possible?"

"Aye, Uncle, it's me."

"Same eyes," the priest said. "My nephew always had

eyes black as the pit of . . . but it's been so long. And Gabriel was but a stripling when he left us for the sea. I cannot be sure."

"Perhaps I can make it easier for you," Gabriel said. "Do you remember the night I sneaked out of the keep to visit the gypsy camp on the River Twyw?"

Father Eustace nodded slowly.

"I was surprised to find you already in the fortune teller's wagon," Gabe said. "A sloe-eyed beauty was . . . telling your fortune with vigor."

He cleared his throat in deference to Mistress Wren's presence and waggled his brows for his uncle's benefit. Gabriel had only been ten years old at the time, but the image of the gypsy girl's brown bottom merrily bouncing on his uncle's groin was burned into his brain. He remembered her berry-colored nipples disappearing into his uncle's hungry mouth and the way she'd tossed her mane of dark curly hair as she moaned in pleasure. It left quite an impression on young Gabe. His small willie had risen in lust for the first time and he half imagined himself in love with the brazen, exotic girl polishing his Uncle Eustace's cock.

Father Eustace swallowed hard and turned to Miss Wren. "My boyhood and youth were woefully misspent."

"Along with a good bit of your manhood as well," Gabriel said. "In any case, when you caught me peeping through a hole in the canvas, I ran off. I fell and gashed my knee." He turned back the hem of his breeches to expose a jagged scar. "You knew Father would beat me for sneaking out of the keep. So you patched up my knee and told me you'd keep my secret, if I kept yours."

"And it appears you did, until this day." Eustace's face split in a wide smile. His uncle folded him into a gigantic hug and thumped his back enthusiastically. "Welcome home, lad. This is indeed the answer to my prayers. A gift from heaven to be sure."

"I've been called many things, Uncle, but never a gift from heaven."

From the corner of his vision, Gabriel caught Miss Wren eyeing him with suspicion. No doubt she thought him a gift from Old Scratch instead.

"Rejoice with me, Jacquelyn," Father Eustace said. "Gabriel's homecoming will be the salvation of Dragon Caern."

"The Caern is doing well enough without the likes of a pirate."

Jacquelyn bit her lip and Gabriel suspected she'd intended to spare his uncle the truth of Gabe's piracy. In his day, Uncle Eustace had been enough of a bounder for ten pirates, but perhaps Miss Wren didn't know that.

A priest's robe does wonders for a man's reputation, Gabriel thought with a grin.

"A pirate? Oh, Gabriel, this is wonderful news!" Eustace said.

Jacquelyn flinched as though his uncle had slapped her.

"Don't you see, mistress? Spanish doubloons and prizes and all. If Gabe was a pirate, he no doubt has made his fortune!" Eustace turned an expectant eye on him.

"Well, yes, my crew did take its share of plunder on the Spanish Main," he admitted.

"There, you see!" Uncle Eustace flashed a triumphant grin at Jacquelyn. "I told you my prayers would be answered. Gabriel's treasure will save us."

"What do you mean?" Gabe asked.

"Forgive me, of course, you don't understand," his uncle was saying. "You've been sort of dead, haven't you? You may as well know we've had a string of thin years here in

Cornwall. Folk have been fearful, what with the Drake line ending, so we've lost a goodly number of crofters. A whole slew of them sailed off for the Americas as indentured servants rather than take their chances on whom the Crown might eventually send to run the place. And there was that year the rains failed completely.

"But the Drake line wasn't gone. Even without me, wouldn't the title revert back to the closest male relative?" Gabriel asked.

"Yes, to me, as it turns out." Eustace's lips turned up in a quirky smile. "However, I am without a legitimate heir."

Gabe suspected his wayward uncle had sired several illegitimate ones over the years. Bastards stamped with his bulbous nose and freckles sprouted like weeds over several Cornish shires.

"And since I'm bound by my vow of celibacy, I'm not likely to produce one now, am I?" his uncle said with a rueful expression.

Strange that nothing had been said to Gabriel about the disposition of the title when the king issued his pardon.

It certainly put this morning's attack on him in a new light.

Father Eustace clapped his hands together. "But now that Gabriel is back, the castle will remain and flourish in Drake hands."

"Surely Dragon Caern hasn't suffered because of your rule, Uncle," Gabriel said.

"I have enough trouble ruling my own soul, Nephew. I'd have run the estate to ruin in no time, though I'll not deny that even before Lord Rupert died, Dragon Caern's prosperity was in decline. But we've all managed to keep body and soul together at any rate. For that, we must thank Mistress Jacquelyn," his uncle said. "She stepped into the breach when our need was greatest."

Gabriel cast Miss Jack a quick, assessing glance. A likely lad in a pinch, a worthy chatelaine and a damn good kisser. Evidently a woman of many talents. He just wished she'd quit scowling at him.

"I've never been one for administration," his uncle admitted.

"You were never one for prayer either, as I recall," Gabe said.

"No, but when need arises . . . one comes to it eventually," Uncle Eustace said with a self-deprecating shrug. "And it seems my prayer has been effective. Pirate treasure. Truly, God works in mysterious ways."

"Father, however great our need, I doubt the Almighty had a hand in sending the ill-gotten gains of a pirate to cure Dragon Caern's woes," Jacquelyn said.

"Your exceedingly pure heart may rest easy, mistress," Gabriel said sardonically. "There are no gains, ill-gotten or otherwise. I had no doubt my father would take the same view of my acquired riches as you. So when I renounced piracy, I renounced my share of the spoils as well and divided my portion among my crew."

"You mean—" Eustace's mouth flopped open.

"There is no treasure," Gabriel finished for him.

Contrary to her previous pious statement, Jacquelyn cast him a withering glance that said plainly, *So you're not only a pirate, you're a useless pirate as well!*

"What about Mr. Meriwether?" Jacquelyn asked. "I assume he did not renounce his share of the spoils."

"No, he didn't, but it's gone just the same," Gabriel said. "Before we headed overland to Dragon Caern, Meri and I spent a week in Bath."

"And his share—"

"Is completely spent," Gabriel said with an evil grin. "We passed a very good time in Bath."

"Well, then Gabriel, you shall have to add to the Drake fortunes the old-fashioned way," Eustace said.

"By the sweat of my brow, you mean." Gabriel smiled. The thought of honest work, the kind that tired the body and eased the mind, made his heart swell. If he could sweat out the excess, the bloodiness, the sins of his years at sea, he'd do it gladly. "I'm not opposed to hard labor."

"No, son. I meant you'll make your fortune as all threadbare gentlemen do," Eustace said. "You must marry it."

Jacquelyn made a noise that sounded suspiciously like a snort.

"In order to assure that the Drake line continues, Gabriel must take a well-moneyed wife—and rather quickly, I should think," Eustace said. "Well, as quickly as these things can be done, at any rate."

"No," Gabriel said. "I've no wish to wed."

"Passing strange, I would have said you liked women," Jacquelyn all but purred at him. Her velveted claws didn't fool him one bit. She'd scratch him blind if she could.

"I like women fine, but I don't care to be trapped by one."

"Ah! I see." Her eyes darkened to gunmetal gray. "As long as you do the trapping, it's all well and good."

"Hold a moment, children!" Uncle Eustace interrupted, his gaze darting from one to the other, not missing the smoldering animosity between them for a moment. "We must find a way to save the Caern and make it thrive. Either Gabriel marries well and continues the Drake line, or the Crown will snap it up and who knows what will happen to those who are dependant upon us."

The sizzle went out of Jacquelyn's eyes at that dire prospect. "We can't let that happen."

"Passing strange," Gabe taunted. "I would have said you had little liking for Drakes or their lineage."

"Is that the best you can do?" She arched a russet brow at him. "Pity your wit isn't as sharp as your blade."

"Alas, mistress!" Gabriel gave her a sardonic bow. "Nothing is as sharp as your tongue."

"Would the two of you quit pricking each other? Our situation is dire enough," Uncle Eustace said. "Bald as an egg, here it is: Gabriel, you must wed, man. A lady of wealth and—please God!—fertility. It's our only hope of retaining this little patch of Cornwall for the people of Dragon Caern."

At that moment, five unidentifiable creatures, stair-stepped in height and covered with mud, ran screaming through the keep and up the stone steps with the long-suffering Mrs. Beadle huffing after them.

Gabriel had seen Caribs, members of a fierce tribe of cannibals on one of the islands. Those primitive people had nothing on the little savages that had just streamed past him. A long wail, a cry of the damned if ever he'd heard one, wafted through an open window.

Jacquelyn's lips went white. She looked more flummoxed than when he'd slashed the first button from her boy's disguise.

"Mrs. B., where is the girls' tutor?" she asked.

"Trussed up in the pigsty and promising to resign," the housekeeper said. "Honestly, mistress, you must do something. That's the third tutor in as many months."

Mrs. Beadle turned and hefted herself up the stone stairs after the fleeing barbarians.

"What on God's earth were those?" Gabriel demanded.

Jacquelyn turned her gray gaze on him. "Your brother left no son to hold the keep, just as I told you." She pointed after the retreating tribe. "Those are your nieces."

"Girls?"

"Aye, Gabriel, generally speaking nieces have to be girls," his uncle supplied unhelpfully.

"Girls," Mistress Jack affirmed. "Girls who've lost both their parents and will lose each other if Dragon Caern is forfeit to the Crown. They'll become wards of the king, separated and fostered out to God knows where. Imagine five pawns of noble blood for the Crown to use. The king will marry them off one by one to secure this alliance or repay that favor—"

"He'd have to bathe them first," Gabriel said uncharitably. He had enough trouble understanding women. Girls were another hornet's nest altogether.

"Perhaps you'd do well to concentrate on the problem at hand." Jacquelyn folded her arms over her chest and narrowed her eyes at him. "You must fight to hold Dragon Caern. You must wed a fortune and sire an heir, my lord. Otherwise your nieces and all the folk of the Caern will suffer. Now, will you honor your responsibilities or will you not?"

Gabriel had led his crew in countless skirmishes, but this was a fight with rules he didn't understand. In truth, he'd never felt more like hoisting all his canvas and running before the wind. But when Miss Wren looked at him as if he'd been weighed in the balance and found sadly wanting, he itched to prove her wrong.

"I've never yet run from a fight."

"I'll take that as *consent*, my lord," Jacquelyn said with a dangerous glint in her eye. "Very well, to business, then. Do you have a lady in mind to wed?"

"Miss Wren, I've been at sea—"

"Yes, and I'll try to make sure your time as a . . . a mariner doesn't prove a sticking point with your prospective bride. Given your recent behavior, I doubt you have any idea of the proper way to woo a lady."

"What makes you say that, Jacquelyn?" Uncle Eustace asked.

Jack's mouth flew open into a small O. Gabriel smiled. She'd been close to accusing him of manhandling her, but was finally caught in her own net. She couldn't denounce his boorish behavior without admitting her own unwise caper as a boy.

"She's right, Uncle. I've been absent from polite society for a number of years." Gabriel made her an awkward bow for Eustace's benefit. "Perhaps, Mistress Wren, you'd be kind enough to teach me the subtleties of courtly love."

He couldn't think of a better way to continue his campaign to *meddle* with the bothersome wench.

"It would be my pleasure to remind you of your forgotten manners." She glared at him. "But I suspect that is a task for which we have insufficient time. When would you like to leave for London?"

"London?"

"All the finest folk flock to London for the marriage season." She cocked her head at him as if he were a dunce not to know it. "Even with a few rough edges, a man with title and lands will find a wife of good family and generous dowry easily enough in London."

"No, not London," Gabriel protested. "I mean, I've just returned home. I've no wish to leave Dragon Caern so soon."

The less said about his real reason for avoiding the city, the better.

"Very well, but that narrows your choices considerably, my lord." She turned to go. "Tomorrow I'll start the process of finding a suitable wife for you from the daughters of the regional nobility."

"And my lessons in wooing as well," he reminded, tossing out the challenge as if throwing down the gauntlet. "Don't be forgetting that."

Miss Wren shot him a brittle smile. "Never fear, Lord Drake. I shall look forward to teaching you a lesson."

"You may find me a daunting pupil."

"And me a demanding teacher."

Aye, lass. I certainly hope so. Gabriel planned to have her far past demanding. He intended to see her beg.

"I trust you're capable of getting the heir Dragon Caern needs," she said with daggers in her voice. From the corner by the wine decanter, Eustace made a noise of surprise, like a pig bladder balloon deflating suddenly. Then the priest hid his urge to laugh with a quick drink. "Pressure can do strange things to a man, I'm told."

Gabriel swallowed his shock at her slight on his manhood. By thunder, he should have bent her over that boulder after all, the code be damned.

"I'll try to find a woman who pleases you, but no matter what, the needs of the estate must come first." She smiled at him sweetly, but he wasn't fooled for a moment. Miss Wren would happily saddle him with the first horse-faced daughter of a well-heeled and desperate father she could find.

"Now if you'll excuse me, Your Lordship, I believe Mrs. Beadle could use a hand." Miss Jack dropped a quick curtsey and started up the stairs in the direction of his shrieking nieces.

"Don't worry, Lord Drake. I'll see you wed by the end of next month," she called down to him. "You have my word upon it."

Gabriel watched her mount the stairs, temporarily robbed of the power of speech. His uncle pressed a glass of wine into his hand.

"She's an exceptional fine woman, our Miss Wren, but strong-minded as a mule," Uncle Eustace said. "I like my women more biddable—I mean, I did when I was allowed to like women, you understand. Make no mistake, Jacquelyn will do exactly as she says. She'd see you wed even if she had to marry you herself."

"Well, here's hoping it doesn't come to that," Gabriel said, swallowing hard.

He still fully intended to bed the little vixen, if only to put to rest her snide comment about whether he was capable of getting an heir. There were ways a man could torment a woman with pleasure before he took her, ways to reduce the wench to helpless pleading. It would do the indomitable Miss Wren good to be humbled before she fell.

And he was just the man to do it. She'd thank him in the end. He'd make sure of that. His cock twitched at the bare thought of subduing her.

But there could be nothing more between them. Miss Jack had a will of tempered steel. Like his uncle, he preferred his women on the softer side.

"No, I don't think she'll do," Gabriel said.

"Amen to that, Nephew. Of course, you couldn't marry Miss Wren in any case," Eustace said. "She's penniless in her own right and too proud to accept a dowry from her mother, even if Isabella Wren was capable of providing it, which I doubt, or inclined to offer, which is even less likely. Bless her heart, Miss Jack has no idea who her sire is. So our Jacquelyn is out of the running."

Uncle Eustace clinked the rim of his drink with Gabe's and knocked back the contents in one long swallow.

"Good thing, too," his uncle said. "The pair of you would kill each other within a fortnight."

Chapter Four

Midmorning sunlight streamed through the green glass windows of the solar. The shimmering threads in the ancient tapestry on the far wall fairly vibrated with color. Ordinarily, Jacquelyn loved this bright room. Now she prowled its perimeter, stopping every third circuit to tap her toe with impatience.

"Trust a bloody pirate to sleep away the day when there's serious work to be done," she grumbled.

The new Lord Drake and his nefarious friend Meriwether had gotten roaring drunk after supper. The pair had had every soul in the castle quaking in their beds, certain of impending mayhem. Jacquelyn had kept one ear cocked for the rasp of swords or splintering furniture, if the debauch turned violent.

Instead she was treated to a concert of raucous singing. Once, Jacquelyn even thought she heard Father Eustace's quavering tone join in on the fifth chorus of a particularly ribald song, but she dismissed that possibility as the fancy of an overwrought mind.

Gabriel Drake had her turning mental cartwheels.

The fate of the girls—indeed everyone at Dragon Caern—was now in the hands of a pirate. How was she to handle a man who'd willingly turned his back on the civilized world? And this man had not only stooped to piracy, he'd led a pack of the mad sea dogs.

For once, she wished she had her mother's ability to effortlessly bend a man to her will. A sought-after courtesan, Isabella Wren had been a renowned beauty, a regular bird of paradise. Even though she'd lost her protector years ago and hadn't bothered to acquire a new one, Jacquelyn's mother was still in demand in the most decadently fashionable salons. In the rarified air of that not-quite-respectable world, her stock-in-trade was now sparkling wit. When Isabella Wren entered a room, she claimed the space by right. Moving with polished grace, she drew all men in the room into her wake, panting to do her bidding. The wags who wrote for the London tabloids claimed she should have been named Swan instead of Wren.

But Jacquelyn was more like their dowdy surname, plucky and assuredly hardy, but not the sort of woman men fell over themselves to please. Jacquelyn sank into one of the heavy Tudor chairs, its oak now blackened with age. She sighed.

Her mother would know what to do with a pirate.

The scrape of a booted foot on the threshold brought her chin up. Gabriel Drake paused and leaned on the doorjamb, his broad shoulders filling the opening. He folded his arms over his chest and cast her a sideways glance. Barring his tousled hair and the shadow of a beard darkening his unshaven jaw, the Lord of Dragon Caern looked no worse for his late-night carouse.

By rights, he should be bleary-eyed and staggering, Jacquelyn thought crossly. *Perhaps the devil does look after his own.*

"Mistress Wren." He acknowledged her with a raised brow.

She rose to her feet and dropped a quick curtsey, though it galled her to do so. This man had done nothing to earn her respect except be blessed with the accident of his birth. "My lord."

"I was told you want me." He stressed "want" just enough to let innuendo sizzle in his sleep-roughened tone.

He probably wanted see if he could ruffle her dignity. She refused to rise to the bait. "If by that you're asking whether I sent Timothy to see if you had roused for the day, then the answer is yes."

"If you want to know if I'm roused, mistress, you should come yourself. If not, you can rectify matters." His mouth twitched with a repressed smile. "Then we'll see if your answer is still yes."

Heat crept up her neck. For a moment, she imagined him sprawled in his bed, his sun-bronzed skin dark against the linens. There was something so raw about the man, so primal; Jacquelyn could no more stop her belly from cavorting in response than she could stop the sunrise.

But he didn't have to know about it. She frowned at him.

"Perhaps that sort of remark is acceptable among women who regularly consort with pirates, but no well-born lady will find it so." She settled back into the chair and fiddled with the tea service on the low table to avoid his probing gaze. "I see a night's rest hasn't improved your manners."

"Nor your shrewish tongue." He strode forward and sat in the chair opposite her. "By all means, let us be mannerly. To that end, I wonder if you would satisfy my curiosity on one point."

She nodded cautiously.

"Granted, things may have changed in the years I was at sea." He leaned forward to balance his elbows on his knees. "Correct me if I am mistaken, Mistress Wren, but is it customary for one in your position to chastise the lord of the manor?"

She bit her lower lip. "Not ordinarily."

"So you didn't berate my father?"

"No, my lord." She would no more have spoken out of turn to the old baron than take a flying leap from the battlements.

"Then you must have taken my brother to task for every breach of etiquette."

"Lord Rupert committed no such breach."

"Oh, yes, I keep forgetting he was always the perfect one,"

Gabriel said. "Then it seems I am alone among my family in receiving the favor of your frequent tongue-lashing."

"So it would seem."

"You know, mistress . . ." He leaned back in his chair, a sinful smile lifting his lips. "That is not the best use of your tongue."

Jacquelyn stood and paced, trying to put more distance between them. "You have done it again, my lord."

"Done what?"

Set her cheeks aflame. Filled her head with forbidden images. Raised something dark to life. She wouldn't acknowledge the strange pull he exerted on her, so she grasped for the cover of indignation.

"Spoken to me in a manner that will do you no credit in polite society," Jacquelyn said icily.

He stood and moved toward her, like a wolf stalking a doe. "Yes, but we're not exactly polite society, you and I, are we?"

She flinched as though he'd slapped her and took a few steps back.

"I see someone has seen fit to speak to you of my background." She didn't have to feign anger this time. "My lord, we are not all blessed in the matter of our birth. I may not know who my father is, but that does not mean I must wallow in debasement."

"Now hold a moment—"

"I have made every effort to rise above my heritage." He continued to advance toward her and she gave way till her spine met cold stone. "You, however, have done just the opposite."

"Mistress Wren, I didn't mean—"

"You were born a gentleman, and yet you threw it away," she said as he trapped her against the wall with his long arms, his hands braced near her shoulders. There was no place left to retreat. "Do not, I beg you, deride me for aspiring to be a lady."

He leaned toward her, close but not touching. His warm masculine scent crowded her, breaking down her will to resist. His mouth, that devilishly tempting mouth, curved in a languid smile. If she so much as tilted her head, she was certain those lips would be on hers again. It took every ounce of willpower she possessed not to move.

"Are you finished?" he asked.

She clamped her lips shut.

"I'm not in the habit of having to explain myself, but for you, I'll make an exception," Gabriel Drake said. "When I said we were not polite society, I intended no slur on your parentage, mistress. What I meant was that you and I both seem to have a healthy disregard for the rules when it suits us to flout them. Can you deny it?"

She met his direct gaze. Dragon Caern was the only home she could claim and her orphaned charges her only family. She'd dare nearly anything to protect them. After all, she wasn't above leading a party of highwaymen in boy's garb to do just that.

She shook her head.

"No, my lord, I'll not deny it. But in this case, if you hope to wed soon, you must follow the rules. And you may as well start with how you address me."

"I suppose you're right." His bold gaze wandered down her form, leaving a trail of heat in its wake. "Would it make any difference if I told you I'd be more pleased with the study of undressing than addressing?"

She drew a deep breath, preparing to deliver a scathing setdown, when suddenly she realized that was exactly what he was angling for. The beastly man enjoyed seeing her discomfited.

She'd spent precious little time with her mother in her formative years. Jacquelyn was boarded at a fine school and raised by gentlewomen, with only occasional low passes from her flighty mother. But now Isabella's voice rang in her head, clear and true.

The art of handling a man is knowing when not *to give him what he wants.*

Usually Jacquelyn tried to push her mother from her mind, but in this instance, perhaps a courtesan's advice was exactly what she needed.

She allowed herself to smile at him.

"If you follow my lead, my lord, you'll be undressing your new bride soon enough."

A surprised chuckle rumbled deep in his belly. "Very well, Mistress Wren. I place myself in your very capable hands."

Jacquelyn resisted the urge to imagine what she'd do with him actually in her hands. She ducked under his arm and escaped to the table where tea was laid.

"In that case, let us begin. Allow me to pour your tea and we'll practice conversation—civilized conversation—designed with procuring a wife in mind."

He eyed her through narrowed lids, looking for some trick. Then he shrugged and followed her over to sit.

"You're sure there's no other way?"

"These lessons were your idea, my lord. However, if you like, I can make a selection for you from the available ladies in the region and you can meet your bride at the altar," she said. "Contracted matches are just as valid as courted ones. It would certainly save time. And money."

"Given your aversion to me, I shudder to think what sort of woman you'd choose." He waved the specter away. "No, thank you."

Aversion wasn't how she'd describe her feelings for him. Appalled fascination was more apt.

"How do you take your tea, my lord?"

"As I take most things, however and whenever I please," he said, still obviously hoping to goad her.

She merely arched an eyebrow at him.

"One lump," he said with a sigh.

A thrill of power rushed through her. Her mother was right for once. The key to handling a man was surprise. All she need do was anticipate what he was expecting and do the opposite.

With little resistance, she led him through a conversation about the weather and the condition of local crops, all perfectly innocuous and very respectable.

"That was excellent, my lord. Now, we need to decide how we'll handle the matter of your piracy," she said as she tidied the tea tray.

"What do you mean?"

"Well, you were believed dead. Your reappearance will be startling to some. Once you rejoin society, people will want to know where you've been. You can't very well regale your guests with tales of your buccaneer friends and the delights of keelhauling," she said. "What do you intend to say about your time at sea?"

"I don't think anything but the truth will serve. A man is defined by his choices. My ship was overpowered and went down," he said. "I chose to live."

"But surely you don't intend to admit to piracy—"

"Mistress Wren, whether we like it or not, we all have to admit what we are," Gabriel said. "If we don't, we are only fooling ourselves."

He leaned over and caught her hand in his. "For example, you can pretend to be outraged that I'm about to kiss your hand, or you can be yourself and enjoy it."

Jacquelyn's arm went rigid. "What makes you think I'll enjoy it?"

He fingered her wrist in light, feathering strokes. "Right here, I can feel your heart beating. It's taken a decided jump."

He turned her hand palm down and drew a thumb over her knuckles. The tension drained out of her.

"Your skin is warm."

He lifted her hand but didn't brush her knuckles with his lips. Instead, he inhaled.

"And fragrant," he said. "You use rose water to bathe, don't you?"

"It's not seemly for a gentleman to comment on a lady's toilette."

"Lye soap works as well as a perfumed one. If you didn't want me to notice, why go to the trouble?"

"You think I bathe just for your pleasure? Of all the conceited, puffed-up—"

He pressed a finger to her lips.

"Remember whom you're fooling, mistress. I assure you, it's not me." He turned his attention back to her hand. "Now, I can just buss my lips over your skin like so."

He brushed the back of her hand with his mouth. It was a perfect kiss, expertly done with just the right amount of pressure and respectful deference.

"Or, I can take my time."

He brought her hand back to his lips and peered at her over her knuckles, waiting for a reaction.

He wanted her to rebel. If she objected, he'd win.

Jacquelyn closed her eyes, willing him to get it over with.

His warm breath stole over her fingers and up her wrist. He brushed the back of her hand against his rough chin, then drew his slightly open mouth over her knuckles and across her fingers.

"Some people say that certain parts of the hand trigger sensation in other parts of the body," he murmured. He nuzzled the crevice between her forefinger and middle finger. "Do you suppose it's true?"

A downward spiral started in her groin. Jacquelyn's eyes snapped open. Gabriel's eyes were closed when he planted his lips over the spot. The tip of his tongue massaged the joint between her fingers.

A jolt of longing, an empty ache, streaked to her womb. She gasped.

Gabriel opened his eyes and released her hand. She folded them on her lap to keep them from trembling.

He rose to his feet. "Thank you, Mistress Wren, for satisfying my curiosity on that point."

Speechless, she watched as he strode to the door. He turned at the portal and looked back over his shoulder.

"I believe our lesson is concluded for the day," he said, his voice strangely tight. "Unless you have further need of me."

Need—yes, by heaven, she had need, but she wouldn't give him the satisfaction of admitting it. He'd already pulled back the carefully constructed lie she presented to the world and showed her for a sham. Priests always talked about the sins of the fathers being visited on their children. As it turned out, her mother's sins were her own as well.

Jacquelyn didn't trust her voice. She shook her head and averted her gaze.

As his footsteps retreated down the corridor, she realized her mother's advice was worthless. Even a courtesan wouldn't be able to handle a pirate.

There was no dealing with a man who took whatever he wanted.

And made her like it.

Chapter Five

$\mathcal{M}$eriwether pushed back from breaking his fast, loosened his belt and let fly a satisfied belch.

"Hot mince pie and goat cheese whenever I like. A wine cellar handier than mother's milk. And comely serving wenches, to boot."

He ogled the little parlormaid as she swept his empty plate from the long table and headed back to the galley with it. The formidable Mrs. Beadle waddled toward him to shield the girl from his gaze, frowning like a kraken.

Meriwether shivered and turned his attention back to his host.

"Aye, 'tis a most agreeable berth ye've secured for us, Cap'n."

He sneaked a glance at Mrs. Beadle, who was still regarding him with narrowed eyes.

"Mostly agreeable, that is."

"Maybe for you, Meri." Gabriel speared a plump sausage with his knife and bit off a hunk. "You're not the one who's about to be fed to the wolves."

Mistress Wren had sent out invitations to a ball to be held at Dragon Caern a fortnight hence. The stack of acceptance notes on the sideboard grew daily. The Cornish nobles were a buzzing hive of curiosity and more than ready to satisfy themselves about Gabriel Drake's return from the dead. And if in the process they might marry off one of their daughters to the new Lord of Dragon Caern, so much the better.

"Ah, well, there's worse ends than a marriage bed," Meri said. "In Kingsport, back in '85, they caught this poor piker meddling with the governor's wife. And she weren't screaming all that loudly till her husband bursts in, if you take my meaning. I heard tell the governor turned the fellow over to a band of wild Caribs still running free in the mountains. Word was they had the fellow's balls for breakfast."

Meri reached under the table and scratched his own in sympathy.

"And the rest of him for dinner," Gabriel finished for him. "A cautionary tale for lonely mariners everywhere."

"Weren't no tale. I got it straight from a bloke what was there. Rum way to go, if you ask me," Meri went on. "Course that was long before your time. Back when the ocean between the Caribbee and merry ol' England was ever so much wider than it is now. There ain't no more islands left where the girls swim out to the ship wearing nothing but a smile." He sighed wistfully. "The whole Spanish Main's gone and got itself civilized."

"Given the old bill of fare, that's probably a good thing. Though I'm always in favor of smiling wenches with nothing to hide," Gabriel added with a wolfish grin.

Timothy, the stable lad, sidled into the dining room with hunched shoulders and a long face. Meri squinted at him.

"Looks like a hound that just peed in the parlor, don't he?" Meriwether said.

"Beg pardon, my lord." The lad doffed his cap and twisted it nervously.

"What is it, Tim?" Gabriel asked.

"Mistress Wren sends her compliments and asks if Your Lordship be ready for your lessons?" Timothy tugged at his collar. "She says to tell you . . ." The lad fidgeted with his top button and gave the cap another twist.

"Out with it, man."

"She says she'll be waiting for you in the garden when you've a mind to see to your duties." Timothy bit his lower lip. The message was saucy, just shy of insubordinate, and poor

Tim knew it. Obviously, he was hoping his lord wouldn't blame the messenger.

Meri glanced over at Gabriel. As captain of the *Revenge*, Gabriel Drake had never let a challenge go unanswered. It wouldn't be healthy to tolerate defiance. The least disrespect merited swift and certain punishment. The crew liked it that way. Made 'em feel better to know the man who led them could handle himself. And them.

"I see." A muscle ticked along Gabriel's jawline.

That didn't bode well for Mistress Wren.

"I've already mastered the art of balancing a teacup on my knee without spilling more than a drop or two, and I'm prepared to say any number of witty things about the blasted weather. What more could there be to this business of courting?" Gabriel demanded. "Did she tell you what my *duties* might entail this day?"

"My lord, it seems you're to learn the language of the fan this morning."

"The language of the fan? What kind of dandy does she take me for? God's teeth! That woman will be the death of me." Gabriel rolled his eyes and crumpled his linen napkin at the side of his barely touched plate. "Apparently, Meri, there are still those who want a man's balls for breakfast."

He rose and left the room without a backward glance.

"And yet, ye hop to at her first bidding. Ah, Cap'n, I'm afeard for ye," Meriwether muttered after Gabriel's retreating back. Then he pulled the captain's plate in front of him. He popped a link of sausage into his mouth and sighed in pleasure, heedless of the lovely grease trickling into his beard. "Any man who lets a good English sarnie go to waste over a woman is in a sorry state indeed."

Gabriel stormed through the keep. In the past week, Jacquelyn Wren had put him through more interminable sessions with tea and finger sandwiches than a ship's hull had barnacles.

And never alone with him, either.

All his lessons were carefully arranged to include the brooding presence of Mrs. Beadle or the gawky Timothy. There was never an opportunity for another attempt at seduction.

At least this day he'd been able to order Timothy to the stables to shoe his horse, and he'd left Mrs. B. scowling at Meriwether. He'd have Jacquelyn to himself for once.

After all his lessons, Gabriel was certain of one thing: polite society was vastly overrated.

Most of the rules seemed designed to make sure a man made a fool of himself with the least amount of effort on his part. Granted, things had changed since he put to sea, but how had the system of manners been brought to such ridiculously elaborate heights? Surely the whole of English manhood hadn't lost its collective mind in the spate of years he sailed the Caribbean.

What in perdition was "the language of the fan"? It sounded like the worst sort of feminine silliness.

He stopped short at the open doorway and looked out on the garden. It was a little triangle of green festooned with blooms around a central fountain. An herbarium rioted in one corner. The space was designed as a refuge, sheltered on all sides by the gray stone of the castle.

Jacquelyn was seated on a stone settee, looking as cool and inviting as a shady cove. She was wearing a fetching sac dress, the best one he'd seen her wear. It was not too ostentatious in ornamentation, and made of sturdy muslin, but an open panel displayed a ribboned petticoat. Her pointy-toed slippers peeped demurely beneath her hem.

No stolen glimpse of an ankle this day, Gabriel thought with regret.

The costume bespoke her position as chatelaine. Her erect posture proclaimed her every inch a lady. A shining russet curl escaped her cap and coiled over her shoulder. She drummed the tip of her fan on her other hand.

She thought to teach him the language of the fan? No need for interpretation of that gesture. She was already agitated.

Then she flicked the fan open, and it tremored before her breasts. The motion drew his eye to the sweet hollow between them even quicker than usual.

Maybe that's why Englishmen put up with such fripperies. A grin tugged at his lips as he stepped into the garden.

"Mistress Wren." He made an elegant leg to her, turning his toe out to better show the musculature in his calf as she'd instructed.

"My lord." She hopped up and dropped a curtsey. Her gaze darted behind him. "Where is Timothy?"

"He has duties elsewhere. I can't imagine he has much to offer on the subject at hand," he said. "Now what have you to teach me about fans besides how enticing your bosom looks behind one?"

She flicked the fan closed.

"My lord, you may wish to make light of—"

"Miss Jack, I would never make light of your bosom."

Flame kissed her cheeks.

Good. He liked her all the better when she was enraged or embarrassed. He'd settle for either.

"Indeed, I hold your bosom in the highest possible esteem," he assured her. "That is to say, I would like to hold them"—she punched his stomach with the butt of her fan, and air exploded from his lungs—"in the highest possible esteem," he finished, rubbing his flat belly gingerly. "At a guess, that fan signal means you wish to gut me."

"I was improvising," she said between clenched teeth.

"That's not an acknowledged fan gesture, and I doubt you'll receive it from another lady unless you continue in boorish behavior."

She settled back on the settee and arranged her skirts artfully on either side of her hips, hips that he knew were nowhere near as broad as her panniers made them seem.

"I fear you are not taking your responsibilities seriously, my lord."

"Since when is knowledge of fans such a serious responsibility?"

"Your goal is to marry and marry well," she reminded him. "When your female guests arrive for the ball, your future wife may well be among them. Wouldn't you like to be able to correctly read the subtle signs she sends you?"

"As opposed to your not-so-subtle ones?" When she glared at him, he threw up his hands in mock surrender and settled beside her. "I am clay in your capable hands, Miss Jack. Mold me into the fashion most suitable for feminine approval."

"Very well." She nodded, mollified for the moment. "We'll start with the basics. A wealth of information can be conveyed with a few simple movements. Now, if a woman touches the tip of her fan to her right cheek, it means yes." She brought the fan up to demonstrate.

"And the left cheek means no, I suppose."

"Exactly." Her lips curved in a fleeting smile. He suddenly wished he knew how to coax one to stay.

"My left or your left?" he asked.

"It's always the woman's left."

"Why am I not surprised?" He leaned toward her. Even in the midst of a wildly blooming garden, he caught a whiff of her rosewater scent. It swirled around his brain and nudged his groin to aching life. "But why go to so much trouble? How hard is it just to say yes or no?"

"This may be difficult for a pirate to grasp, but sometimes

a situation calls for delicacy. In a crowded drawing room, wouldn't a subtle *no* be preferable to a bald-faced one?" She hitched herself away from him on the settee.

"Actually, a *yes* would be preferable."

Her lips were mere inches away, softly parted. Sweet and moist, he could nearly taste them. The pulse point at the base of her throat fluttered faster than her fan.

"There are some men who will not hear a *no* even if it is shouted from the battlements," she said.

Her pointed little tongue darted out and swept her bottom lip.

"Maybe that's because we're not the dolts women take us for." He closed the distance between them, intent on claiming her mouth. "A man can tell when a woman is saying no with her fan and yes with everything else."

She shoved the fan between them right under his nose. It was nine inches long and had ivory spines webbed with stiff, itchy lace.

"Another improvisation?" he asked.

She arched an eyebrow at him.

"You seem to have a gift for it." He rubbed his upper lip when she finally lowered her weapon.

"I fear you are not attending, my lord." She snapped the fan shut and pressed the tip to her left cheek. Her gray eyes flared at him. "What does this mean again?"

He pulled away from her. Strategic retreat was often the path to victory, the old sea dogs claimed.

He'd wager none of them had ever crossed fans with Jacquelyn Wren.

"It means no," he admitted.

"That's right. Kindly remember it."

She held the closed fan away from her body and twirled it slowly, like a witch stirring her cauldron. He had to admit the graceful motion was enchanting. His mouth fairly watered to sample the thin skin at her wrist where the tiny veins showed blue beneath the pale, smooth surface.

"Now if a lady twirls her fan in the left hand," she explained, "it means 'We are being watched.'"

Gabriel frowned, wondering how such a signal might come in handy.

"Ah!" He slapped his thigh. "As in, 'Don't look now, but my husband is coming this way'?"

"No," she said testily. "If a lady is married, she will fan herself slowly."

He cocked his head. "A languid movement like that could be considered an invitation, I suppose."

"It's meant as a warning *not* to pursue a liaison." Her tone was straying upward, a sure sign she was exasperated. She flapped the fan open and shut with a loud pop.

"What's that mean?" he asked.

"That you are cruel," she accused.

"Truly?"

"Truly," she affirmed.

"I'm not the one shoving ivory and lace up someone else's nose." He folded his arms across his chest.

She unfurled the fan again and snapped it shut, her lips a tight line across her face.

He leaned forward, resting his elbows on his spread knees. He'd surveyed the feminine battlements and determined there was no way to breach the walls Jacquelyn had erected between them. Maybe it was time to concede defeat.

"I don't mean to be cruel, Jack. Not to you."

She laughed. It was not a pleasant sound. "Then why do you insist on making everything so difficult?"

"Maybe because it is," he said to the grass sprouting between his feet. "My homecoming has been nothing like what I expected. I never meant to be lord here, you know."

Amazingly enough, he sensed her softening beside him.

He glanced at her without turning his head. She unstiffened ever so slightly, her knuckles less white where she gripped her fan.

Was that the secret to winning a woman's confidence? All a man need do was confess his doubts? It sounded absurd, but what about women ever made sense?

He decided to test the idea.

"And I had no wish to marry, assuredly not like this." He waved a hand uncertainly. "Under duress, as it were."

"It is necessary," she said with uncommon gentleness.

"I know, but that doesn't make it easier."

Did he imagine it, or did she move toward him on the stone settee just a bit?

"Why *did* you come home?" She was definitely leaning toward him now. When he didn't answer immediately, she prodded. "I mean no disrespect. Please, my lord, I'd like to know."

"Truly?"

"Truly." Her tone was mere wisp.

Her question struck close to the bone. Still, in for a penny, in for a pound.

"When I was captain of the *Revenge*, I was dead to my old life." He shrugged, in hopes the gesture would render his words less significant. "The longer I was away, the more I came to know a man can't stay dead forever. At least, not if he would remain himself. I hoped to be my father's son once more."

"And you returned to find him gone," she finished for him, her tone laced with sympathy.

Her slim white hand rested lightly on his forearm. He didn't move lest he scare her off.

"I'm sorry for your loss," she said.

Slowly, he turned to her. Jack's eyes were moist beneath her russet brows. He realized his losses were hers as well.

Except she'd actually been here when his family died. Perhaps it had been even harder for her.

He tried to smile at her, but he found himself adrift in the gray sea of her eyes. Her chin trembled. Without seeming aware of it, she brought the handle of her fan up to brush her lower lip.

His brows came together. "There's a new one. What does that mean?"

Her pink lips formed an O and the whites showed all the way around her eyes. "Forgive me, my lord. I . . . what I mean is . . . oh, never mind."

"That is a real fan gesture, isn't it?" He seized upon her gaffe like a deerhound on the last shank. "Surely you wouldn't withhold such important knowledge from me. Not when it will aid Dragon Caern. Come now. What does it mean when a lady touches a fan to her lips?"

She avoided his gaze. "It means she wants a kiss."

Chapter Six

She wants a kiss.

"Does it indeed?" He'd guessed as much, but hardly dared hope. "I begin to see the benefits of this fan language. A man could grow to like it after all. Just to make sure I remember this very important signal, I think you've forfeited a kiss to me."

"My lord, I don't—"

"Like the gentle art of the fan with its multitude of meanings," he continued, sensing approaching victory, "a kiss may also mean many things. No doubt there's a proper way to kiss for which my life of piracy has not prepared me."

"That's a certainty," she said, some of her old vinegar returning.

"Then perhaps that's a bit of my training you'd care to take upon yourself."

"Well, we mustn't have you embarrassing the Caern with improper and indiscriminate kissing," she admitted. "If a lady signals that she wishes you to kiss her, you might frighten off a perfectly good prospective wife if you fail to do it in a seemly manner."

"Then let us begin. Shall I try another kiss on your hand?"

That was a tactical blunder. Her cheeks flamed with remembrance of the deeply sensual interplay. For a brief moment in the solar, when he'd slid his tongue into the crevice between her fingers, it was as if he'd invaded another, far-more-intimate cleft. Her discomfort now proved she'd been as moved by that sinful kiss as he. It might be time for another judicious retreat.

"No matter. We seem to have covered hand kissing with thoroughness. But suppose I should kiss you like so—"

He moved toward her, but she straight-armed him.

"Trust me, Jack. It's not a kiss you should fear."

She relaxed slightly while he cradled her cheeks and planted his lips on her forehead.

"There," he said as he released her. "In the language of kisses, what does that tell you?"

"That you think I'm a child."

"I think you fear to spend time alone with me," he said. "But I'd never think of you as a child."

"What a ludicrous idea. I have no fear of you, my lord."

"Perhaps you should."

She slanted a look at him. "At least your last kiss showed respect."

"Indeed," he said. "But surely there are other kisses which also qualify as respectful."

"Do you think so? Truly?"

"I do. Truly. Allow me to demonstrate."

She didn't move when he pressed a lingering kiss on the hollow of her cheek. He didn't think she even breathed.

"There," he said when he strained to pull back. His insides rioted, but he forced himself not to push forward. "What do you suppose that kiss meant?"

She turned her lips inward for a moment as if to hide them from him. "It felt as if . . . as if you wished to give to me. Not take."

Surprised, he realized she was right. With everything in him, he wanted to give her pleasure. He wanted to give this woman the sweetest kisses the world had ever known.

"Then let me, Jacquelyn." He cupped her cheek. "Let me give to you."

She looked up at him, her gray eyes enormous in the soft

light of the garden. Her little tongue traced her top lip this time, but she didn't say a word.

He took her silence as consent.

He brushed his lips on her temple and her eyelids fluttered shut, the thick lashes trembling on her cheekbones. Featherlight, he kissed her just below her eyebrow.

"Repectful?" he asked.

"Mmm," she murmured.

He dropped a playful peck on her slightly upturned nose.

She made a noise that sounded suspiciously like a giggle. Who'd have thought he could bring the woman who'd set out to kill him not long ago to genuine laughter?

He pressed his lips to the corner of her upturned mouth. It was such a sweet spot, half smooth, warm skin, half moist intimacy, that he lingered, inhaling her fragrance as he kissed her. Her breath hitched and her lips parted, but she didn't resist.

He drew back to look down at her. Dewy and soft, she was a feast a man might never tire of sampling. His cock swelled to life. His pirate's heart would have had him plunder her mouth. To thrust in with fierceness, demand her surrender and give no quarter.

She opened her eyes and held his gaze. The fragile trust he read in them made him hold himself in check.

Slowly, with as much care as if he were piloting his ship up to an unfamiliar dock, he closed the distance between their mouths. He stopped a finger's width from his goal.

She swallowed hard and, amazingly, her gray eyes closed in submission.

A plainer invitation than a fan signal, and one he recognized in a blink.

He covered her lips with his, holding steady for a few heartbeats. Then he slanted his mouth over hers, delighting in her moist sweetness. She was all that was soft and pliant and woman.

And she made him desperately hard.

He slid one hand behind her head to steady her and prevent her escape. But Jack didn't seem to want to escape. She turned her head so their lips slanted the other way, almost as if his mouth was a new garment and she was testing the fit.

Gabriel slipped his fingers under the mobcap to bury them in her thick tresses. Gently, he kneaded the nape of her neck.

Her lips parted under him, but he didn't rush in. Instead he took her lower lip between his and sucked once before releasing it. When he did it again, she reciprocated with his top lip. He stifled a groan.

Lust roared more urgently in him, demanding release. He wanted to pull up her skirt and find her slit, wet and swollen with need. He wanted to yank down her bodice and suckle her nipples till she pleaded for him to take her.

He wanted to rut her blind.

Instead, with Herculean effort, he released her mouth and pulled back from her. Another strategic retreat, but it cost him dear.

His cock throbbed in protest, the pleasurable ache blurring toward shrieking pain.

Jack opened her eyes, searching his face for a moment. Then to his surprise, she palmed his cheeks and brought his mouth back down to hers.

Wonder of wonders.

She kissed *him*.

Chapter Seven

Jacquelyn knew the exact moment sanity deserted her. It was when she saw her own reflection in his dark eyes—all flushed and wanting and unable to care about the things she was certain were so terribly important, but at the moment wouldn't spring to mind.

She tumbled with him into the void.

The world he led her to was a slick, wet place, far different than the kisses he'd forced upon her that first day they met. A warm, sweet rush of mingled breath and soft gasps, of little nips and harder love bites, of dueling tongues and hands that roamed forbidden places. Pleasure pressed at her from all sides, more than she could take in at once.

The pleasure demanded she give as well. She responded with joy. He groaned into her mouth when her hand slipped inside his jacket and discovered the hard expanse of his chest. When her fingertips dipped lower to his belly, she was rewarded with a feral male growl.

Instead of scaring her, his involuntary response sent a thrill of power surging through her. Warmth settled in her groin and smoldered, ready to burst into flame.

She suckled his tongue. He stole her breath.

Here was a world where anything was possible and the only law was delight. He made her want so many things for which she had no name. This was madness, of course, but somehow he'd wrapped her in a space that made the insanity safe.

Here she might be more than Mistress Wren, the keeper of the keys and chatelaine of Dragon Caern. In the world of Gabriel Drake's kiss, she soared free, giving and receiving this strangely pleasing ache without care.

And wasn't that the oddest thing? How could a dull throb feel so good? It must be part of the madness of the place, she reasoned dimly.

In the circle of Gabriel's arms, Jacquelyn might be anyone she wished. A lady of noble birth, someone's beloved, someone's naughtiest dream, or all three at once.

She'd seen it in his eyes.

She tore her lips from his and looked at him again.

For a blink, Jacquelyn was sure she saw her mother's reflection. Isabella Wren smiled at her with kiss-swollen lips.

Reason rushed back into her. There was no magic here. Only animal lust.

And the betrayal that follows in the wake of its satisfaction.

"No!" she gasped.

Jacquelyn tore herself from his arms and ran from the garden.

"Jack, wait." Gabriel stood and took a step after her. Then he stopped himself. What was he going to do, force her?

Yes, damn it! his cock demanded.

Everything was going so well. Far better than he'd hoped. He wasn't sure what he'd done to set her off, but he'd give anything to call the moment back.

Anything but his pride.

Gabriel sank back onto the bench with an explosive sigh. If she didn't want him, he bloody well wasn't going to chase after her.

The deuce of it was, he was sure she *had* wanted him. Wanted him very much. What on earth had he done to change that?

He clenched his fists and studied the silver buckles on his shoes for the count of ten. If he lived to be a hundred, he'd never understand the dizzying fizzle that went on in a woman's brainpan. He dragged a hand over his face and looked up.

Into the faces of five women in miniature.

Five pairs of green eyes that looked suspiciously like feminine versions of his brother. They all stared at him accusingly.

"Ah," he said in sudden comprehension. "The Misses Drake, I presume."

His nieces stood in a semicircle before him, arms crossed over their girlish chests, pale brows lowered. From smallest to tallest, they formed a neat staircase of feminine disapproval.

"Why you bite Miss Jack?" the littlest one demanded. Clear-eyed and towheaded, she couldn't have been much more than four years old. "Mrs. B. tan your bottom if you bite somebody." She rubbed a hand on her own posterior as if it still stung from a paddling she'd received for an infraction of the "no biting" rule.

"Hush, Lily," the tallest hissed.

She leaned down to frown at the child, then straightened to her full height to glare at him. The crown of her head probably wouldn't reach Gabriel's armpit, he decided. Her little bodice was snug over breasts like ripe figs. More than a child, but not yet a woman, she held the promise of beauty. She'd be a handful in a few seasons for whoever was responsible for guarding her purity.

With a start, Gabriel realized that "whoever" was *him*. As Lord of Dragon Caern, he was in charge of his nieces' upbringing, making sure their education and accomplishments matched their station. Ultimately, he'd have to see them wed. These girls were under his protection now. Short of locking them in their chambers when they began attracting men, he had no idea how to go about it.

The oldest one looked down her pert nose at her siblings.

"He wasn't biting her," his niece explained. "He was trying to com-pro-mise her. That's what Mrs. Beadle would call it." She narrowed her eyes at him in a perfect imitation of the housekeeper at her scowling best.

Perhaps he'd lock this one up sooner.

"You think you know so much, Hyacinth," the second tallest jabbed her older sister with a sharp-looking elbow. "Just because you caught Timothy with Mary the dairymaid when they didn't know you were in the loft. If you hadn't interrupted them, you'd have learned far more. For your information, His Lordship would have to do a good bit more to compromise Miss Jack than kiss her." She tapped her pointed chin with her finger. "Looked to me like they were just dallying a bit."

"Dallying? Daisy, where did you hear such language? As if Miss Jack would stoop to willingly consorting with a pi—" Hyacinth stopped herself, her face reddening. "He was kissing her to beat thunder and Miss Jack had to run off to get away from him."

"He wants a paddling," Lily said with a pout.

"He shouldn't be paddled." Hyacinth shook her head. "He should be horsewhipped."

"No, that wouldn't be fair. I think Miss Jack liked his kisses," Daisy said, her lips screwed to one side as if she were considering the evidence. "In fact, it looked like she was kissing him back, too. For awhile, at least."

Gabriel smiled at this most astute observation. Daisy was obviously the brains of the outfit. He guessed her to be around ten. He turned his gaze to the next two, a pair as like as two bookends, with thin, blond braids dangling to their waists.

"How about you two?" he asked the twins. "Lily thinks I need my bottom tanned. Hyacinth wants me horsewhipped. Daisy may be willing to give me the benefit of the doubt." He tossed that most amiable niece a quick wink and she beamed back at him. "Would you two like to express an opinion?"

The twins faced each other and Gabriel could almost see the silent conversation that went on between them. Then they turned back to him, solemn as judges, and shook their heads in unison.

"That's Poppy and Posey," Daisy said helpfully. "They don't talk much. Except to each other."

"Well, let me see if I have you all straight." Gabriel pointed a finger at each girl as he ticked off the names. "Hyacinth, Daisy, Posey and Poppy—"

"No, that's Poppy and the other one's Posey," Daisy corrected.

Gabriel squinted at the twins. They were identical to the last eyelash. "How can you tell?"

"Poppy is the oldest, of course," Daisy said as if the information was stamped on their faces.

"Of course. A grave oversight on my part." Gabriel nodded at the twins. "I crave your pardons, ladies."

The pair blinked at him and shot him gap-toothed grins.

He cocked a brow at them and waggled his finger to Daisy, motioning her forward. "And just how do you know which is the oldest?" he said in a stage whisper.

The twins giggled.

"Poppy always stands on Posey's left." Daisy cupped her hand at her little bow of a mouth and matched his whisper. "Mrs. B. says it's how they started out and like to be how they'll end up."

"And they never switch places just to fool people?"

"Oh, they try sometimes," Daisy admitted. "But then they think they're so clever, they can't keep from smirking a little and it gives the whole thing away."

Gabriel added sharp eyes to Daisy's sharp mind in his tally of her attributes. He was already imagining his difficulty in trying to find a man to match her when she came of age. Most men shied away from women with too much in their noggins.

Until he'd met the confounding Jacquelyn Wren, he would have counted himself in their number.

"They'll probably get better at switching places as they get older," Daisy said. "But by then, I'll figure out another way to tell them apart."

"No doubt," Gabriel said, already lightheaded from a vision of twin debutantes. A squall on the horizon if ever he'd seen one.

Why hadn't his brother Rupert left at least one son?

The smallest sister toddled over and patted his knee with her pudgy hand. She still had little baby-fat dimples on each knuckle.

"You forgot me," she accused.

"No, I didn't," he said. "You're Lilac."

"No, I'm not."

"Lavender?" He pulled a face to make her laugh.

She squealed with pleasure. "I'm not Lavender. My name is—"

"Wait a moment." He snapped his fingers. "I have it. Your name is Licorice."

"You're silly," she said with a grin.

"No, I'm your Uncle Gabriel," he said, lifting her onto his knee. "And you're Lily."

Lily snuggled close, her babyish smell wrapping an invisible hand around his heart and giving it a squeeze. Barring Uncle Eustace, the rest of his family was gone, but for better or worse, at least he had these girls. He needed to let them know they had him as well.

"I'm new at this uncle business," he admitted.

"We noticed," Hyacinth observed coolly.

"However much it pains you, Niece, we seem to be stuck with each other," Gabriel said.

Hyacinth had obviously conceived an intense dislike for him, but he seemed to be making inroads with the younger ones. The twins were rocking on their heels, grinning at him, and Lily was investigating his pockets, hoping to find a sweetmeat. He made a mental note to make sure he was better provisioned next time.

"What do you suppose an uncle might do for his nieces to prove his goodwill?" he asked.

"You could be my pony," Lily suggested. "We could ride around the garden."

The twins approved, hopping up and down and clapping their hands.

"Pony rides it is, then. Up you go." Gabriel leaned forward so Lily could crawl onto his back and wrap her arms around his neck.

"Don't be ridiculous," Hyacinth said. "If you were truly concerned for us, you'd suggest riding lessons on real ponies, at the very least." She turned a sly expression toward Daisy. "A proper uncle would be more interested in helping us with our studies."

"Oh, that's right," Daisy said with a nod. "Especially as we are without a tutor at present."

Gabriel realized later that warning bells should have gone off in his head at this point. Hadn't the girls' previous tutor left shortly after he arrived, under less than pleasant circumstances?

But at the moment, Gabriel was more interested in gaining some allies in Dragon Caern. Jack thought the sun rose and set on these girls' golden heads. What better way to soften Mistress Wren's heart than to earn his nieces' trust?

"Quite right," he said. "Being a naval man, I have some

expertise with mathematics and astronomy related to navigation and such. What have you been studying?"

"We were learning about the Colonies," Daisy said. "More specifically about the aboriginal peoples they call American Indians."

"I've put in to a few Colonial ports," Gabriel said. "I may be able to help you with that subject."

"I'm sure of it." Hyacinth bared her teeth at him in a feline smile, then under her breath, she said, "Daisy, get the rope."

Chapter Eight

Gabriel had survived the death of a ship. Before that, he'd acquitted himself admirably in dozens of skirmishes in defense of king and country. And once he'd turned pirate, his sword arm put the fear of his wrath into the heart of every member of his buccaneer crew.

But for the life of him, he couldn't figure out how to defend himself against his nieces. Not without harming them at any rate. They seemed so fragile. It was the chivalrous chink in his armor the little vixens were counting on, and they weren't disappointed. They swarmed over him in a tangle of arms and legs.

Without knowing precisely how it happened, he found himself gagged with an embroidered handkerchief and bound tightly to the stone settee. His nieces were doing a fair imitation of an Algonquin war dance in a circle around him. Daisy appeared briefly in his field of vision with a leering grin and an armful of kindling.

She disappeared beneath the settee for a few minutes.

He wasn't able to raise his head, but he thought he smelled sparks from steel and flint. What a fool he was. He'd been sure Daisy liked him.

Obviously, he didn't understand women at all. Even fledgling women.

"Captain, what be the meaning of this caterwaulin'?" Meriwether's voice boomed from the castle door.

Salvation! And just in the nick. A wisp of smoke drifted from under the settee.

"My lord, what devilry is afoot?" Mrs. Beadle's voice came next.

Gabriel tried to answer, but only managed a few disjointed sounds. The hanky made a deucedly effective gag.

"Ach, Cap'n. Ye shouldn't teach the children to play with fire. Might burn the wee dears' fingers," Meri said as he kicked the small blaze from under Gabe and stomped it to embers.

Mrs. Beadle caught the two eldest by the ears. "No, no, missies. None of your running off or it'll be the worse for you, I swear it," Mrs. B. scolded, her round face flushed with exasperation. "You stay right here and take your medicine, you little imps. Poppy and Posey, untie that gag you've stuffed in your poor uncle's mouth."

Their nimble fingers freed his lips as quickly as they'd bound him. Gabriel ran his tongue over his teeth trying to get the starchy taste of the hanky out of his mouth. The twins fumbled with the knot by his ear and finally gave up, shoving the rope that immobilized his head toward his hairline, taking a layer of hide from his forehead with it.

He was able to turn his head now as the twins scrambled back to join their siblings. Mrs. Beadle had released her captives and his nieces were standing in their deceptively sweet semicircle, hands folded before their bodies fig-leaf fashion, eyes demurely downcast.

"I din't bite him," Lily said quickly.

"Maybe not, but it's not nice to cook people either. Not at all the done thing," Mrs. Beadle said, with a shake of her jowls.

"Aw, Mrs. B., these little mites weren't out to cook the Cap'n," Meriwether said. "Appears to me this whole thing was just a bit of high spirits what got out of hand."

Gabriel's eyebrows shot skyward, but Meri tossed him a warning glance.

"Looks like a lesson gone awry. As a master mariner, the Cap'n has plenty to teach his nieces about knots and such."

His first mate leaned down to inspect one of the rope mazes still binding Gabriel to the settee. "First-rate double clove hitch there."

"That one's mine," Daisy said modestly.

"And a right good job ye made of it, darlin'," Meriwether said as he pulled out a frog sticker and slashed Gabriel's bindings. "Now as no blood was let, I don't see as there's any call to punish the poppets. I reckon ye're of the same mind, aren't ye, Cap'n?"

Gabriel sat up and rubbed his wrists, casting a dark glance at the girls. Hyacinth arched a cynical brow at him and looked away. Daisy gave him an apologetic shrug. The twins blinked owlishly and edged closer to each other. Mr. Meriwether's excuses notwithstanding, Gabriel was about to demand punishment for the little heathens when Lily's chin started to quiver.

He might as well give himself up for lost right now and be done with it.

"No, Mrs. Beadle, Meri's got the right of it. We were just having a bit of fun. No harm done." He waved the housekeeper off. "The girls and I are fine."

"Well, then, my lord, if you're certain . . ." Mrs. B. said, not sounding the least certain herself. She dropped a shallow curtsey. "I'll be off with myself then. There are cherry pies in the oven that need tending."

Meriwether watched her go with a look of naked admiration on his craggy features.

"What's this?" Gabriel demanded. "Are you ogling my housekeeper now? I didn't think you and Mrs. B. were getting on so well."

"Aye, not yet we're not, but she's a widow, ye ken. Oh, she's strong-minded and a bit broad of beam. Not that I ever held extra flesh against a woman," Meriwether admitted. "But I've been smelling those pies all morning. She's a goddess in the kitchen, is Mrs. Beadle. A man can overlook quite a bit if there's cherry pie in the offing."

Gabriel chuckled, and then turned back to his nieces, who were still standing there hanging on the exchange.

"Perhaps you'd better thank Mr. Meriwether," he advised them. "He's the one who saved you from Mrs. Beadle's wrath. If it had been left to me . . ." Gabriel let the threat dangle unspoken.

One by one, the girls murmured their thanks as they eyed the old pirate with horrified fascination. Meri ignored them, cleaning his snaggled nails with his dirk.

Even Gabe had to admit that his first mate was an unlikely savior. With his gold tooth glinting and the honorary tribal tattoo sagging the leathery skin of one cheek, Joseph Meriwether must have seemed a fantastical creature from the ends of the earth to his nieces. Even the intrepid Daisy was too aghast to speak much above a whisper.

"It's passing strange that you should be their champion, Meri," Gabriel said. "I would have said you weren't fond of children particularly."

"Oh, I like children fine," Meri said with a pointed look at the girls. "Boil the pith out of 'em for an hour or so and they make a right tolerable stew."

The girls' squeals of terror as they hoisted their skirts and ran almost made Gabriel's near roasting worthwhile.

"Is he following us?" Hyacinth demanded as she hunkered behind the stables with the twins beside her.

"No, of course not," Daisy said, putting Lily down to wobble on her own pudgy legs. "He was just shining us on. I'm certain of it."

She glanced over her shoulder. "Almost certain."

"Don't act so superior, Daisy. You were screaming as loudly

as the rest of us," Hyacinth accused. "That horrible Mr. Meriwether. I can't imagine what possessed our uncle to bring him here. What absolute beasts! Both of them."

"Still, he did keep us from a whipping," Daisy said. "And Uncle Gabriel, too. He didn't have to let us go so easily, you know."

"Have you forgotten the way he was bedeviling Miss Jack?" Hyacinth said with a sniff. "If we don't do something, he'll be after her again."

"I'm not sure that isn't what she wants," Daisy argued. "Besides, Miss Jack can fend for herself. I think I like Uncle Gabriel."

"I like Unca Gabrul, too," Lily chimed in.

The twins nodded.

"But not that other. He a bad man," Lily pronounced. "He eat children."

"Mr. Meriwether eats children just as much as we intended to truly roast our uncle. He was only trying to scare us, booby," Daisy said, obviously feeling much braver now that Meriwether wasn't actually close by. "Don't you worry, though. We'll get even with him."

"How?" Hyacinth asked.

"We could put a toad in Mr. Meriwether's bed," Daisy suggested.

"I got a toad," Lily offered, pulling a flat amphibian from her grimy pocket.

"That old pirate has the personal habits of a boar," Hyacinth said, wrinkling her nose. "He probably wouldn't even notice a toad between his sheets. We must think of something else."

Pepper in his tea, a cow pie in his boots—one of the twins even suggested a spider in his coffee, but no one wanted to actually handle a spider, so that excellent idea was shelved.

"Pity we've no brother," Daisy said. "It's times like these when one would come in handy."

"If we had a brother, we'd have no problem," Hyacinth said, basking in the glow of superior knowledge. "Uncle Gabriel wouldn't be lord if one of us had been a boy."

She ended the debate with a clap of her thin hands.

"That's it. It's not Mr. Meriwether we need to fix. It's Uncle Gabriel. Since he got here, Miss Jack is in a state and Mrs. Beadle is after us constantly to behave and not mess the house because of the ball that we aren't allowed to attend," Hyacinth said. "If we make Uncle Gabriel go back to the sea, he'll take old Mr. Meriwether with him and everything will go back to the way it was. Then all we'll have to manage is how to rid ourselves of the next tutor."

Daisy shook her head, mutinous for the first time. "No, Hy, whatever you're planning, I won't be part of it. I like Uncle Gabriel and I want him to stay."

Hyacinth narrowed her eyes at Daisy. "Fine. I will manage without you. Come, girls."

The twins consulted each other briefly, then sidled over to stand by Daisy. Lily sniffed, torn between her older siblings.

"I like Unca Gabrul," she finally said. "He smell good and he give good hugs and he play pony."

Hyacinth rose from her crouch before Lily with a regal shake of her head. "So be it. I will do it myself." She glared at them. "Don't think for a moment I won't."

Daisy folded her arms over her chest. "You've no clue how to proceed. Admit it, Hyacinth. You never had an original idea in your life."

"Well, I've got one now," she lied. "And it's brilliant. And when it works and there are no more pirates in Dragon Caern, you'll all thank me. See if you don't." She pursed her lips in an expression she was sure made her appear wise beyond her years. "And I'll have no more of your sauce, Miss Daisy."

Daisy rolled her eyes. "I'll not be holding my breath."

Chapter Nine

Dragon Caern's armory was on the upper floor of one of the many round towers within the castle's curtain walls. Shields emblazoned with the barony's coat of arms hung at intervals and several ancient suits of armor stood as silent sentinels. Abundant light from countless arrow loops flooded the space and the ancient oak floor was polished with age to a glassy sheen. Through the centuries, countless squires and knights had exercised and honed their skill in the space, but this day only four feet trod the smooth planks.

"You will find this smallsword very much more suited to your hand than what you've been using, my dear," Father Eustace explained to Jacquelyn as he presented the new weapon to her hilt first. "Shorter than the rapier, light enough to wield one-handed with ease, it should answer any defensive need a lady might encounter."

Surely Father Eustace knew that a sword wouldn't cure all defensive needs. Not if the woman wasn't so sure she wanted to defend herself. Jacquelyn shook off that weak-minded thought and tested the blade with a few thrusts.

"The balance is perfect."

"It pleases me to hear you say so, mistress," he said. "But in these times of peace, I should be counseling you to turn to plowshares instead of swords."

"You know I value your counsel, but I value your sword arm as well. Dragon Caern couldn't ask for a better master-at-arms. Thank you for teaching me." She flexed her knees and adopted a classic pose. "After all, before you turned to God, you were the best swordsman in Cornwall."

"Only because my brother had hung up his spurs and

Gabriel was at sea," he said with modesty. Father Eustace turned a sheepish eye on her. "I fear I honed my skill fighting my way out of more married ladies' bedchambers than I can count. Husbands *will* come home when one least expects them."

Jacquelyn looked askance at him. "Surely, you exaggerate."

"Surely, I understate." He shook his head ruefully. "You didn't know me in the old days. Second sons tend to grow up without many expectations, you see. I certainly had none beyond the next pint or the next skirt. You have my apology if my candor shocks you."

"Remember whom you're talking to, Father," Jacquelyn said, still trying to imagine Eustace as the rakehell he claimed. "The fatherless daughter of a courtesan can't afford to be easily shocked."

"In a perfect world, the accident of your birth would not be held against you." He sighed deeply.

"Alas for the Fall," she said with a wry smile before she struck the pose of challenge. "En garde."

"Alas, indeed." Father Eustace saluted her with his sword and adopted a defensive posture. "Yet, even the imperfect world is filled with wondrous surprises. Who would have thought a reprobate like me would live to such an advanced age, let alone spend the pleasant hours of my dotage training a young lady in swordplay?"

"You're no dotard." She lunged forward. "And I'm no lady."

Father Eustace parried her stroke with an approving nod. "In all the ways that count to the folk of Dragon Caern, you are."

"And in all the ways that matter to the world, I am not," she murmured.

If a wellborn second son had few expectations, a bastard

girl had none. Her mother had paid handsomely for Jacquelyn to be educated in an exclusive school. To her fellow students, the headmistress passed Jacquelyn Wren off as a noble orphan with a secret benefactor and kept Isabella's visits to a strict minimum. Jacquelyn acquired all the polish and accomplishments of a lady, but without the necessary pedigree she was unable to take her place among the nobility when she came of age.

She might as well have been reared to be an illiterate milkmaid.

The position of governess for the Drake girls brought her to Dragon Caern. It was as high a perch as she dared reach. When the Lady Helen died and Jacquelyn took over the duties of chatelaine in such an effortless manner, it seemed not to matter to the grieving residents of the castle that she couldn't name her sire.

But since she couldn't, and since she had no dowry to bring to a marriage, Gabriel Drake wasn't allowed to even consider her for his baroness. He would marry, and another would take her place as mistress of the Caern. For a fuzzy moment, she couldn't decide which bothered her more. That her position as chatelaine would be forfeit to another . . .

Or that the new lord would take another lady to wife.

"Concentrate, mistress." Father Eustace's voice called her back to the moment. "Your guard is spotty."

It certainly was. Whatever had possessed her to return Gabriel's kiss with such abandon in the garden? The taste of his mouth rushed back into her unbidden and she was shamed to find her lips tingling.

Father Eustace's smallsword tip slipped under her guard, pressing against her padded shoulder. "Touché. If your purpose for study is self-defense, you are sadly in want of attention this day."

"Perhaps it's because she feels no real threat from you, Uncle," Gabriel's voice interrupted them.

Why had she allowed herself to think on him at all? *Call up the devil and he will come.*

When Jacquelyn turned to face him, he was already drawing his blade.

"Well, Jack, once again we meet where swords are crossed," he said, running a thumb along the edge of his foil. "You've been schooling me right enough these past few weeks. Pinky out, napkin tucked, and let us not forget, the rarified language of the fan. Time for turn and turn about. What say you to another chance to gut me?"

"It would be my pleasure, my lord."

"No, no, none of that, children." Eustace hastened between them, corking the tip of both blades. "If you're to practice, you'll do it safely."

"I'm not sure Miss Jack likes to play safely," Gabriel said, his dark eyes snapping. He raised his sword and she lifted hers in answer. "In fact, even if I withdraw, I suspect she's likely to rush in."

He spread his arms to the side, baring his chest to her in an attempt to provoke an attack.

She suspected he was making a bald reference to that blasted kiss she'd pressed upon him. And the deuce of it was, he was right. He had pulled away from her lips in almost a gentlemanly manner, but something dark flared to life in her belly and, come wrack or ruin, she'd had to kiss him again.

It was convenient to blame her mother for her loose behavior.

Unfortunately, it was not just. Even if Jacquelyn's lustiness was an echo of her heritage, it was not Isabella Wren who forced herself on Gabriel Drake. Isabella would have been too cunning for such a blatantly wanton display.

The trick, darling, she'd always say, *is to make the man believe that he is taking the lead.*

Gabriel seemed to be leading right now, but it was none of Jacquelyn's doing. He lifted a dark brow in question, daring her to engage him.

"Defend yourself, my lord," she said in a silken tone laced with spurs.

"No, Nephew. Not without proper padding," Eustace said. "I'll not have it."

"You've nothing to say about it, Uncle. This is between Mistress Wren and me. I may not be able to defend myself from those little hellions everyone assures me are my nieces, but if the day comes when I can't face down an armed woman intent on doing me harm, I'll slice my own throat."

"Gabriel, caution is always wise," Father Eustace began in a conciliatory tone. "As the Good Book says, 'Pride goeth—'"

"And so do you, Uncle. Right now." Gabriel cast him a black frown.

Eustace tossed an apologetic shrug to Jacquelyn, signed a benediction in the air between them and shuffled to the door. He paused with his hand on the knob.

"If the pair of you forces me to administer last rites this day, I'll see that you both spend a hundred years in purgatory—at the least!" The door slammed behind him.

"Father Eustace is right," Jacquelyn said. "Suit up or I'll concede and you'll never know if you could have bested me."

"I'll take my chances. Besides, mistress, give me credit for knowing you a little bit. It's not in your nature to concede. Let's make this interesting, shall we?" Gabriel said as he drew nearer. "A wager?"

"And what might I have that you care to win?" She circled slowly, looking for a weakness. "Last time you disarmed me, you seemed to think you had the right to carve up my clothing and unbutton my shirt. I suppose this time you expect I'll forfeit my maidenhead."

As soon as the words left her lips, she wished she could pluck them from the air and unsay them.

His brows shot upward. "An interesting idea, but no. The rare gift of a maidenhead is something that can't be forfeited. Such treasure must be given or there'll be no pleasure at all in the exchange for either of us." His mouth spread in a slow, wicked smile as he mirrored her circular steps. "However, it pleases me to no end that your thoughts are running in that direction."

She growled low in the back of her throat and lunged. He parried her thrust and danced back a step.

"Tsk, mistress. You're rushing your fences again. Much as there is to commend unbridled passion, there's more to be said for control." He loosed a string of light blows that had her giving ground, though she turned his blade each time.

She drew a deep breath and returned his assault in a more measured and effective way.

"Much better," he said with a smug grin. "I'm delighted to find you so apt a pupil."

"Perhaps it is you who will be schooled, my lord," she said with a deft flick of her blade that he barely managed to meet. "What is your wager?"

"First touch on the torso wins. If I manage to penetrate your defenses, all I demand is the truthful answer to one question," he said.

She narrowed her eyes at him. Something about the way he said "penetrate your defenses" made all sorts of unsuitable images spring to her mind. The kind of images that tingled her nipples. "And what might that question be?"

"Where's the fun in that?" His sinful smile would tempt a saint. "Not knowing is part of the wager. Do you accept?"

She nodded warily. "And if I win?"

"What do you want most?" his silky baritone rumbled through her.

You, a dark part of her being clamored. His black eyes sent forbidden thoughts rushing through her brain, and heat flared in her belly. An image burned across her vision . . . of the unpredictable, utterly male Lord Drake pressing her against the ancient stone walls . . . with her skirt hiked to her waist. She shook off her inner wanton and forced a scowl. Of the all men in the world for her to lose her battle with lust over, why must it be this bloody pirate?

"If I win," she said, schooling her voice into bland evenness, "I want you never to seek private speech with me again."

"An acceptable wager. Besides, speech is highly overrated," Gabriel said. "There are plenty of things we can do with each other that don't involve talking at all."

"You are purposely misunderstanding me," she accused.

"No, I understand you far better than you think, mistress."

That's what she feared most.

"In earnest, then." Gabriel Drake brought his sword before his face in salute. "Defend yourself, Miss Wren, for however much I might enjoy communicating with you without benefit of speech, this is a contest I don't intend to lose."

Chapter Ten

In the flurry of steel that followed, Jacquelyn barely held her own. Through monumental concentration, she managed to turn his foil tip at the last possible moment whenever it chanced to slip beneath her guard.

"Bravely done," he conceded after a particularly well-executed feint and riposte.

"Not yet," she murmured through clenched teeth. "Your gut is still intact."

He laughed. "Good thing I like bloody-minded little minxes, Jack."

She clamped her lips tight. He was trying to rattle her with conversation, when all her attention needed to be on his naked blade.

"Not so sure I like calling you Jack, though," he said as he turned with her as smoothly as if they were doing the minuet in a ballroom. "Not with a bosom such as yours. Nothing remotely Jack-like about you."

"My bosom is none of your concern," she said. Tingling heat crept up from her bodice to spread over her neck and cheeks. "Jack is my name. Jacquelyn, Jack, it's evens or odds. Perhaps you should settle on Mistress Wren, my lord. Though once I win, you'll not need to call me anything at all, since you will not be speaking with me except in public."

She launched a hail of blows that had them both breathing hard.

"No, Jacquelyn doesn't suit either," he said, ignoring her more proper suggestion as he parried her thrusts. "Jacquelyn is far too buttoned-up for your sort."

"My sort?" She drew in a panting breath. "What's that supposed to mean?"

"Jacquelyn is a hard, brittle sort of name, and even though you try not to let it show, you've much more softness about you than you want to admit." He paused, the tip of his foil waving before her like an adder poised to strike. "Has no one ever called you Lyn?"

"Never."

"Then I'll be the first. Lyn." His tone caressed the name and a strange warmth stirred in her chest. "I want to be the first for you. In everything."

He moved so quickly, her eye couldn't follow the blur, but suddenly her smallsword was flying across the room. It clattered to the floor and rolled to rest at the feet of one of the suits of armor.

She stood before him defenseless, his foil poised for the win. Her chin jutted up a notch.

"A gentleman would allow me to retrieve my sword so we could continue."

"No doubt a gentleman would. But such a chivalrous thought would never enter the mind of a pirate," he assured her. He closed the distance between them and slid an arm around her waist, pulling her tight against his hard chest. "I win."

"There's been no touché," she protested. "Your foil has not touched my torso."

He pulled open her protective padded jacket, exposing her décolletage. Her nipples hardened beneath the lace of her bodice. Jacquelyn couldn't bring herself to move as he lowered his mouth. He pressed his lips to the tender skin over her collarbone. She trembled like a beech in a breeze.

"I didn't say it had to be a foil touch." He let his rapier drop and splayed a possessive hand over her right breast. "Touché, Lyn."

She'd lost. Anger flare inside her. She drew back her arm and struck him across the cheek with all her strength.

He blinked in surprise, but didn't release her. Instead he grabbed both her wrists, lifted them above her head and pinned her against the stone wall. She'd had a wicked fancy of him doing just such a thing, but the action was less romantic and far more frightening in real life.

And far more rousing than she would have believed.

With her arms raised, her bodice pushed her breasts up even more than usual. She suspected one or both of her pebble-hard nipples peeped from behind the Brussels lace at her neckline. The panniers that held her skirt away from her bare thighs usually gave her a sense of freedom of movement. Now, she felt acutely aware that, barring the stockings that were gartered at her knees, she was naked from the waist down beneath her broad skirt. A dull ache started at the apex of her thighs.

"Don't your scruples give you pause before you strike your lord?" he asked.

"No more than yours stop you from ravishing your chatelaine."

"So you think I'm about to ravish you?" The fierce hunger in his face when his gaze swept down her neck to her breasts made ravishment seem a foregone conclusion. "Good idea, but no. When I take a woman, it's because she wants to be taken." He met her eyes with a smoldering gaze. "You're close, Lyn, but you're not there yet."

"My name is Jacquelyn," she said.

"And yet to me, you're Lyn," he said in an almost tender rumble. He nuzzled her neck and stopped when his lips neared her ear. She tried to squirm away from him, but his one-handed grip on her wrists high over her head was firm. "Settle yourself, girl, and it will be done with all the sooner. Time for the question."

"Go ahead, then." She'd almost forgotten her forfeit was the truthful answer to this unknown question. His warm breath sent shivers of pleasure down her neck, but she willed herself to stand perfectly still.

"It's about what happened in the garden—"

"I suppose you want to know why I ran away."

"No, I already know the answer to that." He pulled back to look her squarely in the eye while his free hand traced the edge of her neckline, stopping when his fingers brushed an exposed nipple. He drew deliberate slow circles around her sensitive areola with his thumb. "You were afraid."

"I'm not afraid of you." The ache between her legs throbbed steadily.

"I hope not," he said. "But in the garden, you weren't afraid of me. You were afraid of yourself."

Her snort of derision made her breasts jiggle and his eyes flared at their movement. She silently cursed herself for making things worse. He slid his hand down her bodice and came back out cupping her breast in his hot palm. He lowered his mouth to her taut nipple and teased it with his tongue.

Jacquelyn gasped. The lust in her groin shot from an ache to white-hot pangs. She caught herself arching her back, the better to present her needy breast to his mouth. She bit her lip to keep from pleading with him to suckle her and be done with it. Anything to stop the torment.

The question. He had a question for her. It might be her salvation.

"What did you want to know?" she managed to ask as she ground her teeth. "Your question . . ."

That brought his head back up and she nearly cried out at the sharp longing in her nipples. If she didn't feel his mouth on them again, tugging and demanding soon, she might go mad.

At least he pacified her breast with his hand, flicking the

taut flesh as he leaned in to touch the side of her nose with his. His eyes were closed and his mouth was so close.to hers, his breath feathered across her lower lip.

"I need to know why," he said, his tone ragged. "After I let you go, why did *you* kiss *me*?"

Because I'm insane. Because I've inherited my mother's lack of judgment about men. Because . . . A dozen answers sprang to her mind, all of them perfectly plausible. But only one of them true.

"Because I couldn't bear not to."

She felt his cheek lift in a smile. "Do you think you could bear to do it again?" he whispered.

"That makes two questions, my lord."

"Who's counting?" When he drew back and lifted an eyebrow at her, she knew she was lost.

She raised herself on tiptoe, found his mouth and slanted hers across it. For a moment, he seemed content to let her set the pace, and she embarked on a leisurely exploration of his lips. But when she slid her tongue into his open mouth, the kiss changed.

Command of their carnal odyssey shifted to him and he took possession of her mouth as if by right. To her surprise, Jacquelyn didn't mind. She surrendered to his plundering tongue, gasping for breath when he released her mouth to trail his lips over her jaw, down her neck and straight as a plumb line back to her aching nipple.

Far from stilling the need, his mouth at her breast made her want all the more. Outlandish things. Wicked, indecent things. Things her mother had told her about. She never dreamed she'd actually want a man to do them to her, but now they suddenly sprang into her mind. A second heart-beat pounded between her legs and she felt a spurt of moist warmth.

She groaned. She could no more control the helpless

little noises of distress coming from her throat than she could stop the torrent of wanting that washed over the rest of her.

"Ah, Lyn, that's it, lass."

He released her wrists so he could palm both her breasts. She was free, but passion rooted her to the spot where her spine pressed against the cold stone. Instead, she buried her fingers in his hair, kneading his scalp, whispering urgent encouragement in disjointed sounds. It was no language known to man, but he seemed to understand her perfectly.

He yanked the front of her skirt up. Cool air breezed over her heated flesh as he draped the yards of fabric on the wire and horsehair shelf of her panniers.

Gabriel stepped back and looked down at her triangle of coppery brown curls. She stopped breathing.

"You're beautiful," he said with reverence. Then he cupped her sex with his whole hand.

She whimpered with longing as he spread her swollen folds and drew a fingertip along her delicate inner lips. When he dropped to his knees before her, she swayed unsteadily. Only his arms around her hips and his hands on her buttocks kept her upright as his mouth claimed her secrets.

Had he somehow climbed inside her mind and seen her most wicked fancies?

Jacquelyn was drowning in a sea of sensation with only a pirate to throw her a lifeline. She nearly wept with relief when he stood and unbuttoned the front of his bulging breeches.

He kissed her again while he hooked an elbow under her knees and lifted her, spreading her wide to receive him. She pressed down on his shoulders to help him. Just the tip of him slid between her throbbing vulva.

To her dismay, he stopped.

"I want you so bad, it's like a sickness, but I have to be

certain," he said, his voice hoarse with passion. "You're a maiden and once done, this is a thing that cannot be undone. Do you want me, Lyn?"

His question echoed in her mind. *Do you want me?* Not just ease for her demanding body, did she want *him*, his past piracy and impending marriage be damned? God help her, she did.

"Yes—oh, yes," she almost sobbed. The world dulled to a hazy gray around them and all that mattered was this man, this moment, this unassailable longing. She couldn't think beyond her next heartbeat.

He kissed her again as he lowered her, his shaft gently invading her moist flesh. When he reached her maidenhead, he paused for a blink and she moaned softly. Then he rammed himself home and pain shrieked through her.

He held her perfectly still. Then the pain sizzled away and she felt his full length embedded in her, hot and hard and throbbing with its own rhythm, his heartbeat in tandem with hers. One salty tear streaked her cheek.

"Now, there'll be only pleasure between you and me," he assured her as he kissed away the tear. "No more pain, I promise."

"I believe you," she whispered.

Slowly, he began to move and the world faded to nothing.

Until the door behind him swung open and Father Eustace burst in.

"Gabriel, lad, you must come right away. We've royal compan— Oh!"

Chapter Eleven

By thunder," Gabriel roared over his shoulder, trying to shield Jacquelyn from his uncle's view. "Does no one ever knock in this cursed place?"

Eustace's eyes widened as he realized he'd interrupted Gabriel and Jacquelyn in the very act. The priest whirled around, faced the door and banged his knuckles on the worm-marked oak.

"Your pardon, Nephew." The set of his uncle's shoulders told Gabriel that Eustace was upset by the scene he'd interrupted, but his voice was commendably even. "But Sir Cecil Oddbody is on your doorstep waiting to be announced."

"Who the hell is he?" Gabriel's tone was decidedly less even.

Though he was still inside her, Gabriel straightened his arms and let Jacquelyn slide her legs down so her feet rested tiptoe on the floor again.

"One of the king's counselors. Unless memory fails me, Oddbody is the courtier whose signature is on that pardon you're so proud of," Uncle Eustace said. "Shall I tell him you'll meet him in the solar directly or that you're too busy defiling Mistress Wren to attend him at present?"

"I'll be along," Gabriel said.

"I hardly think—"

"I said, I'll be there. Now go!"

"The lord of a castle wields great power. But power is seductive. It consumes all who use it. Be careful yours does not consume you, Gabriel." Eustace slammed the door behind him.

Gabe twisted back to Jacquelyn to find her stuffing her

breasts back into her bodice, her cheeks flaming. The moment was definitely lost. He felt himself wither and slip from inside her.

"I didn't want it to be this way," he said softly, tucking an errant lock of hair behind her ear.

She smoothed her skirt back down without meeting his eyes. Her lips trembled in a mirthless smile and if he hadn't known how strong-minded she was, he might have feared for her senses. There was certainly nothing to smile about.

He reached for her again. "I'm sorry if—"

"No need, my lord." She held up a forbidding hand, careful to keep her eyes downcast. "Now if you will excuse me, your duties take you elsewhere. As do mine."

She tried to push past him, but he grabbed her arm.

"We're not finished with this," he warned. "Not by a long stretch."

"On the contrary," she said, her tone brittle. "Your goal is achieved. You have added my maidenhead to your collection. But take heart, my lord. No doubt a new trophy will arise on your horizon presently."

"It wasn't like that, and you know it."

"No, it wasn't. It was my own fault. I should have known a pirate would not stop until he'd—"

"I did stop."

"Yes, you did," she admitted. "But only when you were certain I was incapable of it. Now, Lord Drake, if you will release me, I will see to your guest's refreshment."

"Lyn—"

"Kindly refer to me as Mistress Wren, if you please."

Her eyes glistened with unshed tears, but there was fire behind them. He found her fury strangely comforting. Familiar, at any rate.

"It's not much to ask," she said. "I think I've given service enough this day to warrant at least that small consideration."

He inclined his head slightly. She wished to shelter behind distant courtesy, did she? He'd allow it.

But only for a short while.

He watched her walk to the ancient door, a pang of conscience lashing him when she wobbled slightly and her shoulders shuddered before reaching it. She left him without a backward glance.

He wished with all his heart that Uncle Eustace had made his appearance very much later.

Or, if it would've spared her this pain, a few moments sooner.

"Good workmanship, this," Cecil Oddbody said as he inspected the ancient tapestry in the solar. In the early morning, the golden threads shot through the piece would be shimmering glory, but now as the sun sank into the sea, they were nearly invisible in the soft light shafting through the room's green glass windows. "Lovely pattern in the goldwork. And certainly not the only gold hidden in Dragon Caern Castle, if your claim is correct, Curtmantle."

"It is," Hugh Curtmantle said. "Time out of mind, the rumor has circulated that back in the glory days of Good Queen Bess, the Lord of Dragon Caern was one of her privateers. She pardoned his crimes, and he filled her coffers with Spanish gold. But the old pirate also filled his own. And it's here someplace. I'm sure of it."

"Let us hope so," Oddbody said. "Else a good deal of effort will have been wasted for naught. It's not so easy a thing to have a title declared in abeyance, you know."

Cecil spared a glance for Baron Curtmantle. The man had inherited the barony to the north of Dragon Caern and was within a pinch of running the estate into bankruptcy.

Hugh sat a good horse and was reputedly a wicked swords-man, but the man had the imagination of a gnat.

In the large scheme of things, he was nobody.

However, at present, he was a very useful nobody. After all, a string of convenient deaths was difficult to arrange this far from London.

"My lord, you know I appreciate your endeavors on my behalf," Hugh said.

"And well you might." Cecil was no lord. He'd merely been invested with a knighthood when he was given charge of the king's privy seal. With the power he wielded, it appeased his vanity to be called lord in any case. "Until the resurrection of this friend of yours, this Gabriel Drake, you were well on your way to being named protector of Dragon Caern once the title devolved to the Crown and thence to me. What do you intend to do about it?"

"Do?" Hugh seemed puzzled. "What can I do?"

"Think, Curtmantle." Oddbody sighed. It was difficult to believe this toady traced his lineage back to the first Tudor kings. Perhaps more than one of Hugh Curtmantle's illustrious ancestors was cuckolded by a stable hand with a big cock and a small brain. "A man who returns *from* the dead can just as easily return *to* the dead. See what you can do to manage such a journey for the new—"

Cecil stopped in midsentence when the guard cleared his throat from his position at the arched doorway. Gabriel Drake filled the space, his expression stony. He was followed by a priest, whose face looked only slightly less harsh. This was hardly the grateful welcome Sir Cecil expected.

"Ah, Lord Drake, there you are," he said, extending his bejeweled hand so the king's seal flashed importantly.

It was ever so handy to have a monarch who spoke little English. It forced the Hanoverian king to rely heavily on his advisors. Cecil was careful to maintain and embellish the trust George I invested in him. He would ever guard the Crown's interest.

So long as the king's interest didn't run too contrary to his own.

"We were on our way to Bath," Cecil said majestically, "and wished to satisfy ourselves that you are settling well into your new role."

"We?" Drake looked at Cecil's extended hand and then ignored it. "I thought only kings used the royal *We*. Perhaps you should stick to *I*, unless of course, you have a mouse in your pocket."

"Gabriel, your manners," the priest muttered, then in a louder voice. "Welcome to Dragon Caern, good sir. I'm Father Eustace. A blessing on all souls here."

The priest took his hand and pressed a quick kiss to the king's seal. Not exactly protocol, Cecil supposed, but he appreciated the gesture. Oddbody had studied the family tree of the House of Drake. This must be the new lord's uncle.

"I'll be thanking you for Gabriel's pardon," Father Eustace said.

"I earned my pardon, Uncle," Lord Drake said testily, "in service rendered to the king. His Majesty was grateful to have his cousin returned unharmed from the French buccaneers who'd abducted him. Oddbody here is just the clerk who signed the papers."

"I am Keeper of the King's Privy Seal," Cecil said, tight-lipped. He shot a glance at the priest, who visibly cringed. "Perhaps, Father, you should remind Lord Drake that I also have the king's ear. What His Majesty so graciously gives, he may also take."

"My apologies, sir," Father Eustace all but stammered. "Gabriel has been a long time at sea. I trust your forbearance to excuse his lack of . . . polish."

"It wasn't the sea that ruined Gabriel Drake," Hugh said

from his place in a shadowy corner. "He was well on his way to hell before that."

"Hugh Curtmantle, I didn't notice you skulking there in the dark." A look of genuine pleasure flashed in Lord Drake's eyes. "Is it really you?"

"In the flesh."

"And considerably more of it than the last time I saw you. Come here, man."

The Lord of Dragon Caern drew Hugh into a back-slapping bear hug.

"So I guess you've forgiven me for stealing Catherine Uxbridge from you?" Curtmantle said. "After all, losing her is what sent you running off to the sea."

"Probably did me a favor," Gabriel Drake conceded. "I haven't given the matter a thought in ages. The girl was beautiful, but cold as a witch's teat. The years are never kind to harpies. Whatever became of her?"

"I married her."

"Ah, you have my apology, Hugh." A wry smile crossed Drake's face. "And perhaps my condolences."

Hugh took a feigned swipe at his friend and the two fell to easy conversation of old acquaintances and days gone by. Cecil nodded his approval. Perhaps Curtmantle was more cunning than he gave him credit for.

Oddbody settled back into the carved oak chair and watched his underling work. While he followed their byplay, he calculated the wealth represented in Lord Drake's solar. The tapestry was the only remnant of the estate's glory days, but the fireplace along one wall was large enough to roast an ox whole. The heavy candelabra on the serving table was fashioned of pewter, not silver. A sideboard sat empty, as if the best pieces had already been sold. Tales of the barony's financial troubles were true, then.

But there was treasure untold hidden somewhere in

Dragon Caern Castle. More than would satisfy even Cecil's avaricious dreams. Such luxury would be wasted on a pirate.

Well, it wouldn't be wasted on him for long. Not if Cecil had anything to say about it.

And he always had his say.

Cecil's attention was captured by the slip of a girl who carried in a tea tray. She was small, barely more than a child, but with ripe breasts budding in the first blush of young womanhood. Her oval face was innocence itself, only lightly brushed by the corrupting knowledge that she was attractive.

Just the way he liked them. Cecil was a slight man with less in the way of masculine attributes than he wanted to admit. Children or diminutive whores always made him feel bigger. A wellborn woman-child would be even more gratifying to bend to his uses.

"Hyacinth, what are you doing here?" Lord Drake demanded of the girl. "Where is Mistress Wren?"

"She asked me to tell you she's indisposed, Uncle," the child said with a not-so-childish smile.

Her wide eyes flicked around the room, and Cecil read an unmistakable invitation in them. The young ones always wanted his attention. Every one of them.

"Miss Jack asked if I'd pour out for you and your guests," the girl explained.

"Who is this charming creature?" Cecil asked.

"This is no charming creature. This *child* is one of my nieces," Lord Drake said with a scowl. "Very well, Hyacinth. You may serve, but that had better be sugar lumps you've got there."

She blinked at Drake, her thick lashes fluttering on alabaster cheeks. "Of course, dear Uncle. What else?"

What an insufferable bully he was! Cecil was doing this

child, the entire household in fact, a gigantic favor in masterminding his removal.

Her smooth white hands were poetry in graceful service as she poured out the steaming brew and stirred in the sugar and milk. As he sipped his excellent tea, an idea came to Cecil. Curtmantle complained loudly enough of the chill in his beautiful wife's boudoir. Cecil hadn't missed the glint in Hugh's eye when he accepted his tea from the girl's hand.

Cecil would plant the seed and then continue to Bath, trusting that Hugh would see the benefits of the plan. It should be easy enough to tempt the oaf into imprudence once Cecil was on his way. In fact, it would be better for Oddbody if he heard the sordid details second or third hand and at a safe distance.

The one fly in the ointment was that this plan would give someone else the first taste of her. The girl was delectable, after all. Cecil so loved to initiate innocents into carnal delight. He'd have to satisfy himself with taking the poor soiled dove under his wing after the fact. That idea took firm root. Perhaps there were pleasures he'd not experienced before in administering penance to a ruined girl. It would be worth exploring.

But Gabriel Drake was an imposing figure. Cecil had no desire to meet the Lord of Dragon Caern on a field of honor and Drake was not the sort to forgo satisfaction. So if the girl was to be used to incite an incident, it could not be by Cecil.

Hugh Curtmantle was Drake's match for height and probably carried a stone or two more of weight. If Hugh defeated Drake, that would answer nicely.

If not—well, Drake's already tarnished character would not withstand another scandal. What wellborn, well-moneyed lady would consider wedding a man who would murder his childhood friend? The reason for the fight would surely be hushed up to protect the girl, and it would thoroughly destroy Drake's reputation among the nobility. If Gabriel Drake didn't succeed in wedding and producing an heir, then the outcome would still be the same. The Dragon Caern barony would lapse. It would just take longer. Delicate maneuvers such as these required patience.

And Cecil was nothing if not patient.   ●

Chapter Twelve

On the night of Lord Drake's ball, Curtmantle's coach-and-six pounded along the narrow road that led from his threadbare barony to Dragon Caern.

"This velvet is abominably worn." Lady Catherine Curtmantle fingered the offending upholstery.

"No one else sees it," Hugh said.

"And it doesn't matter to you if my sensibilities are offended."

He grunted. "Madam, since you've consented to aid me in advancing our cause this evening, I fear your sensibilities are already sadly lacking."

She slanted her cat-eyed gaze at him, loathing burning in the back of her throat. Since he had shared the plan he and that horrid Oddbody had hatched, Catherine could barely stand the sight of her husband.

Not that she'd been overfond of him to begin with.

If he'd just done it, she could wink at his indiscretion, order herself a new wardrobe—for which he could not complain—and be done with it. She certainly didn't care where Hugh took his ease as long as it was not in her bed. She'd given him an heir, and one confinement was definitely enough. There were things one could do to avoid another child, but she didn't care enough about her husband to make the effort.

But now he'd made her an accomplice in the seduction of a near child.

And she hated him for it.

But she wouldn't try to stop him. They needed the wealth hidden in Dragon Caern. She was sick to death of scrimping and patching and trying to keep up appearances. If she had to wear this tired old gown one more time, she'd have a fit. Once they had control of Dragon Caern's treasure, she'd never have to do without again.

She looked out the window as they bumped along. The Caern winked in the distance like a star. But for a wee misstep years ago, she'd be mistress there, married to Gabriel Drake. Hugh was a charmer back then, and she'd succumbed to his wiles. She'd been lusty and curious in her youth, and Hugh had a big, willing cock. Of course, the fact that he stood to inherit while Gabriel was merely a second son might have played a part in the debacle as well.

Now Gabriel was master of the estate and, if Hugh's tales were true, blessed with a hoard of gold he didn't even know existed.

Fate was indeed cruel.

Folk still counted Catherine Curtmantle a beauty. She wondered what Gabriel looked like now and if she'd enjoy his bedplay more than Hugh's. Perhaps she *should* look into ways to refrain from conception, just in case.

She sneaked a glance at her husband from beneath her lashes. He'd grown broader in the last few years, and there was just the hint of a double chin, but Hugh was still considered a fine-looking man. When he set himself to it, he could still charm anything in skirts.

Except her, of course. She knew him too well.

Which made the plan all the more despicable.

"Are you sure about this, Hugh?" she asked. "You said Gabriel was looking fit."

"He is, but I could always best him with a blade," Hugh said. "Don't worry, Cat. Just make excuses if anyone misses me and before you know it, you won't worry over worn velvet ever again. You'll be able to buy a new coach if you like. Dragon Caern will be without its baron and Oddbody will hush up the scandal and see me named protector."

"And Gabriel's niece? Poor despoiled child. What will become of her?"

"That's incidental."

"Try not to enjoy it too much," she said. "Besides, you'd better save your strength. Gabriel Drake's swordsmanship may have improved over the last fifteen years."

Hugh grasped her chin and forced her to look at him. "And if it has, will you weep for me, Cat?"

"Terribly," she said, willing herself not to cringe. She hated Hugh when he manhandled her like that, but if she made a fuss, he only did it more often. She decided to make light of it. "I may have to let Lord Drake console your grieving widow."

She forced a laugh so he'd think she was joking, and he joined her.

Privately, she thought the idea had merit.

Torchlight blazed from the battlements. Banners snapped in the breeze overhead. Every hoarded bit of silver was polished, every stone scrubbed. They might face weeks of gruel to make up for this night's excess, but Mrs. Beadle had moved heaven and earth to create as sumptuous a feast as might be found on the king's own table. All the folk of Dragon Caern were turned out in their best. The arriving nobility with their marriageable daughters in tow were warmly received by Father Eustace and ushered into the little-used ballroom where the string ensemble was tuning up.

Everything was going exactly as planned. Jacquelyn had worked tirelessly to make Lord Gabriel Drake's reentry into society a brilliant success.

Of course, it would help if she knew where he was.

She'd successfully avoided being alone with him since "it" happened. Even to herself, she wouldn't give their encounter a name. She only knew that in order to keep "it" from happening again, she must keep her distance from Gabriel Drake.

She was fairly certain she needn't worry about bringing a bastard into the world. There hadn't been time to do that much damage.

Just quite enough.

Jacquelyn rarely allowed herself to think about "it," but when the memory rushed back unbidden, she was surprised that the loss of her maidenhead didn't cause her more grief.

Rather, she mourned the loss of that incredible connection when she held him inside her, when she and Gabriel Drake joined deeply. For that earthshaking moment, when he rechristened her Lyn, she'd felt anything was possible, that something entirely wonderful was taking place and her life would never be the same. Even if they'd taken a tumble from the battlements in their conjoined state, she had no doubt both Lyn and Gabriel would have sprouted wings.

But now she was just Miss Jack again as if "it" had never happened.

Gabriel must not have given "it" much thought since. He certainly hadn't sought her out, and his demeanor toward her before others was stiltedly polite. No furtive glances. No sly innuendo. He had even allowed her to teach him the minuet without so much as a fingertip where it didn't belong.

The man was positively maddening.

He was also nowhere to be found.

Jacquelyn searched his chambers, the stables, the armory— she even took a candle down to the wine cellar, but only found Mr. Meriwether, sprawled mournfully amid the sad remains of the last empty bottles of the '08.

No one had seen Lord Drake.

The musicians were starting a shaky bit of Purcell just

to warm up their strings, and still the host of the gala was absent.

"Where the devil could he be?" Jacquelyn stepped out into the bailey, beside herself with worry. Since Meriwether was still in residence, she was reasonably certain Gabriel hadn't absconded. She was ready to admit defeat and have Father Eustace make some sort of apologetic announcement to their guests, when she noticed a lone candle shining through the chapel windows.

She didn't suspect for a moment that Gabriel Drake was a praying man, but it did seem like a good spot to hide— certainly the last place anyone might look for him. Jacquelyn lifted her skirt and sprinted across the courtyard.

There was no one kneeling at the altar, but the door leading down to the crypt was ajar. She stopped on the third step from the bottom. Gabriel Drake was standing, head bowed before his father's tomb.

Even in the dimness of a single candle, he was resplendent. Despite a number of loud disagreements over the subject, she'd been unable to convince him to don a wig for the festivities.

"The blasted things are nothing but French foppery," Gabriel had insisted. "I will dance like a dandy. I'll be as charming as Lucifer himself. For the sake of Dragon Caern, I'll even wed one of the insipid little twits you've arranged to come to this bloody ball, but I'll be damned if I'll wear a wig."

Now the way his own hair glinted blue-black in its neat queue made her realize he'd been right on this point.

But she was right about his new suit of clothing.

"In order to marry money, you must appear not to need it," she'd argued. The cut of his brocade jacket did justice to the width of his shoulders, and the golden frogs and epaulets winked in the candlelight. Old Lord Drake's ring, a twisted convolution of twin dragons swallowing each other's tails, gleamed on Gabriel's forefinger. His green velvet breeches displayed his muscular thighs and the bulge of his maleness made her mouth go dry. She jerked her gaze back to his troubled profile.

Even without his darkly handsome face, he'd be dazzling in the ballroom. With it, Jacquelyn predicted a string of swooning maidens in short order, especially if, as promised, he set himself to be as charming as Lucifer. She swallowed the lump that formed in her throat.

She almost spoke when he extended a finger and traced his father's name engraved in the stone slab.

An invisible hand squeezed her heart. She shoved the unwelcome emotion aside. She dared not allow herself to care for this man. There was no other option. He must marry well. Wasn't she responsible for filling Dragon Caern's keep with his potential wives? No matter what had passed between them, she must not succumb to the tenderness welling in her chest. It was the path to madness.

She cleared her throat. "My lord."

His lips lifted in a fleeting smile when he looked over at her. "Trust you to find me, mistress."

"You led me a merry chase," she admitted. "What are you doing here?"

"Just basking in my state as the prize of the evening," he said sardonically.

"Prize? You're thinking mighty highly of yourself."

"Not at all," he said. "In my years at sea, occasionally I've seen more than one pirate crew go after the same prize ship at the same time. A Spanish galleon filled with gold or a heavy French frigate is a tempting morsel, after all. If there's more than one buccaneer captain after her, you'd think she'd fall easily. But more often than not, the prize is accidentally put to the torch in the melee and goes down in flames." He tossed her a weary glance. "I'm less than pleased about being the prize."

"I know this is difficult—"

"No, this is nigh impossible, but you'll not let me out of it, will you?"

"You act as though this were my doing," she said. "It's not my will that you wed."

He raised an eyebrow at that. "Nor mine, but there seems no help for it."

He rested his hand on the cold stone again as if he would draw strength from his father's bones interred within. "What did my father say when he was told I had been lost to the sea?"

"I wasn't here yet when the news came that your ship had gone down with all hands, but Mrs. Beadle told me about it once. Your father took it very badly. Old Lord Drake didn't speak for a month—not even to your uncle. Everyone went about on tiptoe for fear of upsetting him further."

Gabriel snorted. "Aye, fear was always his strong suit. Rhys Drake was a hard man."

For the first time, Jacquelyn wondered if she might not be blessed in not knowing her father.

"And yet, I miss him. Oh, not just because I'm in this kettle of brine, though Lord knows I'd give anything to be someplace else this night. It's just . . ." He sank down onto the cold stone floor, heedless of his fine garments. "On my way home, I had it all planned out. What I would say. What he would say . . ." Gabriel's eyebrows tented on his forehead. "And somehow, I thought everything I'd done, what I'd become . . . well, it wouldn't matter so much anymore."

"Laying aside the past is not always possible." She knew she'd never be able to put away the heat and the ache and bliss of holding him. If she lived to be a hundred, the memory of his mouth on her would still make her belly clench. But she forcefully thrust aside the remembrance now.

"Perhaps, just coming home is enough," she said.

Jacquelyn crouched beside him and rested her palm on his forearm. Heat from his body radiated through the brocade to her hand. She was seized by the desire to feel his bare skin beneath the fine fabric, but she reined herself in and drew her hand back. She should be helping him face his duty, not make things more difficult. If peace with the old lord would ease his heart, she'd share what little she remembered of his father.

"I know your father was hard on you, but he was proud of you, too," she said. "I heard it in his voice every time he spoke of you."

"Proud? Of me?" The corner of Gabriel's mouth twitched. "Was he?"

"Oh, yes. He was. Quite proud," she assured him.

Gabriel studied the stone between his feet for a moment, looking very much younger than his years. Then he glanced back up at her. "Well, that's something then, isn't it?"

He gave himself a small shake and Jacquelyn realized her brief glimpse behind his self-assured facade was over. Gabriel stood and offered her his arm.

"Enough of this, now. Thanks to your hard work, I believe we have a ball to attend, and somehow I have to pick a wife from among our guests." When she slipped her hand under his elbow, he closed his other hand over it. "Lyn, I wish—"

"Mistress Wren," she corrected. Then, against her better judgment, she added, "or Jack, if you like. I can't see the harm when it's just the two of us."

His smile crinkled the edges of his eyes. "Well then, Jack, perhaps as the night progresses, you'll do me the honor of a minuet or two."

She knew it was the worst sort of foolishness. He needed to dance with his prospective brides. But when he smiled at her, she couldn't help smiling back.

"Perhaps, my lord, if you promise not to tread on my toes."

"Hyacinth, you're making yourself look ridiculous."

Daisy flopped belly-first on her bed and rested her pointed chin on her knuckles. Hyacinth had been preening in the room they shared all afternoon. It was enough feminine folderol to make Daisy want to invade the twins' adjoining chamber. Or even the little room Lily shared with Molly, the sweet-natured, simple girl who'd been engaged to nurse the motherless Lily. She'd stayed on to dote upon the littlest Drake girl as if she were her own. Daisy had been the picture of forbearance over Hyacinth's silliness, but wearing their mother's jewelry was over the line.

"You put those back," she warned, "Or—"

"Or what?"

Hyacinth fingered the ear bobs she'd pilfered from their mother's jewel box. She wasn't supposed to know where Mrs. Beadle had stashed it for safekeeping, but there wasn't much that went on in Dragon Caern Castle that she and Daisy didn't know. She turned her head from side to side to admire the effect of the bobs in the silvered glass.

Daisy reluctantly decided they really did make her look older, but she wasn't about to give Hy the satisfaction of telling her so.

"Miss Jack gave me permission to dance till the supper is called," Hyacinth said with a gloating grin. "You're just jealous because you're stuck here with the children this evening while I'm down there dancing with the rest of the adults."

Daisy rolled her eyes.

"Just don't do anything stupid, Hy."

"Whatever do you mean?"

"Act your age. Just because you're all dressed up, don't forget you're only twelve."

"I'll be thirteen in two months." Hyacinth patted her neatly coiffed hair. She'd worked on it for over an hour to pile it up on her head like that. "It's a pity Miss Jack won't let me wear a powdered wig, but my own tresses are pale enough, I suppose. Maybe in the ballroom with the swirl of lovely dresses and shining crystal, no one will notice the difference." Hyacinth picked up her fan and flirted with her reflection, batting her lashes and trying to look as haughty as possible. "And besides, nearly thirteen isn't that young. There was that girl in Dover who married at fourteen."

"And everyone whispered about her, too." Daisy sighed deeply. "Don't act like some simpering ninny."

"I'm sure I have no idea what you're talking about." Hyacinth stood and smoothed the front of her gown. It had belonged to their mother and Hyacinth had sewed like a demon taking it in. Though the dress wouldn't be mistaken for the latest thing from Paris, it really was quite fetching, Daisy decided. But Hy didn't need to hear it. She was already so full of herself it was a wonder she didn't burst at the seams. Hyacinth twirled, dipped in a deep curtsey and made a moue at her reflection.

"Like that, for instance," Daisy said. "No one really smiles like that."

"Like what?"

"Like a cat with milk on its whiskers." Daisy folded her arms across her flat chest. Just because Hyacinth had sprouted a pair of bumps, she thought she was some high-and-mighty, grand lady now.

"Well, the look on your face would sour the milk," Hyacinth said with another pursing of her lips. "Don't be such a pickle, Daisy, and I'll tell you all about it later."

"You promise?" Daisy extended her pinky.

"And hope to die." Hyacinth locked little fingers with her.

"Stick a needle in my eye," they recited together. Then the sisters turned aside in unison and spat on the floor.

"Did you get some on my skirt?" Hyacinth demanded.

"Only a little," Daisy admitted. "No one will notice. Here, let me wipe it with my hanky."

"Not that one. You never have a clean hanky. Go get one from Posey—" Hyacinth froze when the strains of a violin wobbling over a particularly difficult passage of triplets wafted into the room. "Oh no! The ball has started without me!"

In a flurry of satin, Hyacinth rustled out the door and down the long staircase with haste worthy of a blooded colt eager for its first race. Daisy followed and watched her descent from the landing. Near the bottom step, Hy threw a slipper and had to stop to cram her foot back into the shoe Daisy had told her was too small. Hy's feet had grown along with the rest of her in the last month or so, but she wouldn't give up the intricately beaded pair.

"Her feet'll be so covered with blisters she won't be able to walk tomorrow," Daisy predicted grimly.

Even though Hyacinth had pinky-sworn to tell all, she probably wouldn't feel like talking either. It would be just like her to have a grand adventure and then keep all the juicy details to herself. Well, there was a remedy for that, right enough.

Daisy slipped off her own shoes and tailed her sister down the stairs, silent as a cat. She was quick as a blink and she knew all the good hiding places. As long as Miss Jack didn't spot her, this plan would work. Daisy would go to the ball along with Hyacinth.

She'd just have to hide under a few tables to do it.

Chapter Thirteen

When Jacquelyn and Gabriel reached the ballroom, parallel lines of ladies and gentlemen were forming up. She noticed Hyacinth already on the dance floor, her painted cheeks flushed even brighter with excitement. The gangly youth from Essex with whom she was paired looked as if he were being led to the pillory instead of the dance floor. Fearful of treading on her toes, no doubt.

"What's Hyacinth doing here?" Gabriel asked.

"The quadrille, I believe."

"You know what I meant. How could you allow my niece to attend?" Gabriel asked. "She's just a child."

"A child who will soon be a young lady. Perhaps I shouldn't have," Jacquelyn admitted, "but I couldn't dash her hopes. Hyacinth pleaded so eloquently to enjoy her first taste of merriment. Heaven knows there's been little enough of it here in recent years."

Now the castle itself seemed to shake off the old gloom as the fresh sounds of laughter and music rattled the ancient stones.

"You spoil those girls," he said.

"Mrs. Beadle says the same." Gabriel and Mrs. B. were probably right. Jacquelyn suspected she coddled her motherless charges because there'd never been anyone to spoil her when she was a child. Her earliest memory of her mother was of a sumptuously dressed, sweet-smelling stranger who didn't want Jacquelyn to soil her gown with sticky fingers.

She brushed away the old hurt as the glittering ball gowns of the candidates for Lord Drake's affection caught her eye.

"That's Lady Millicent Harlowe of Doud over by the punchbowl. She's the daughter of a viscount," Jacquelyn whispered to Gabriel. "It's reported His Lordship will settle a handsome dowry on her. And with her father's connections at court, she's considered no end of a catch."

He grunted noncommittally. "It would have to be a monumental dowry."

"I know," she agreed with his unspoken objection. *Pity Lady Harlowe resembles a carp.*

Musical laughter floated toward them, and Gabriel's head turned like a foxhound scenting his quarry.

"Miss Elisheba Thatcher," Jacquelyn said, her belly tightening with an emotion she didn't care to name. Pale and pink, the girl was as lovely as an English rosebud, her petals just beginning to unfurl. "Her father boasts a *Sir* before his name thanks to some exemplary service to the Crown, but no hereditary title. Just lots and lots of tawdry money. He's in trade."

For reasons Jacquelyn had never understood, money a man inherited or married was regarded as respectable, while a fortune earned by his wits or hard labor deserved society's scorn.

"Obviously hoping his daughter's good looks and a generous dowry are the tickets to permanent nobility for his grandchildren," Gabriel said. Elisheba's laugh came again, this time more shrill than musical and followed by a definite snort. Jacquelyn felt him wince.

One by one, she searched out and found the eligible young women she'd invited for Gabriel's consideration. Lady Rosalinda Breakwaithe from Plymouth, Lady Calliope Heatheridge from Bath, Miss Penelope Fitzwalter from Falmouth—Jacquelyn whispered the pertinent facts about each of the potentials in Gabriel's ear. She tried to swallow her satisfaction when he seemed not to prefer any of them.

Yet they had all come. She shook her head in wonderment. Though rumors of Lord Drake's piracy had probably traveled even faster than the news that he was seeking a wife, the nobility seemed more than willing to offer their daughters to the new baron. Amazing what a title and land would induce folk to overlook.

"A man's sins are easy for the world to forgive," her mother had told her once. "But a woman's indiscretions? Never."

The world was patently unfair.

Jacquelyn shoved aside this glaring understatement and turned to the pirate whose arm she still held. The world offered little hope for a courtesan's daughter, but if she could see Gabriel Drake suitably wed, perhaps she could help balance the scales for the rest of the folk of the Caern. She had to try.

"This is beginning badly," Jacquelyn said. "We shouldn't be standing here weighing the graces and deficiencies of your choices as if we were judging cattle at auction."

"A fairly apt comparison, when you get down to it," he said with resignation. "Perfumed and pomaded, but breeding stock just the same."

She frowned at him. "I hope you'll keep that less-than-gallant sentiment to yourself."

He ignored her, smiling and nodding to an acquaintance across the room.

"You said it first," he reminded her in a half voice. Then he looked down at her, a wicked smile spreading across his face. "Actually, I rather like the idea. It makes me the bull standing at stud."

She dug a sharp elbow into his ribs. "But unlike the bull that has a whole harem, you, my lord, must content yourself with one cow. So choose wisely." She narrowed her eyes at him. "And let me remind you that bulls who prove too unmanageable often find themselves gelded."

He laughed. "Trust you to keep me from feeling too full of myself, mistress. By all means, manage away at me."

She rolled her eyes at him. "If you were at all manageable, you'd have been available to greet your guests as they came in, instead of gawking at them once the dancing has already started."

"Then I'll just have to give a little welcome speech over supper," he said smoothly. "I'll have a captive audience then. With their mouths full of my mutton, no doubt my remarks will be found even more amusing."

"Have you decided what you'll say about your . . . your time at sea yet?" She'd fretted for naught that his stint at piracy would turn away the best, most eligible potential brides. Still, society might be willing to ignore only what was kept from its view. If the bare truth were confirmed, the arbiters of correct behavior might feel compelled to shun Lord Drake.

"The less said about my former career the better, but I'll not deny it, if that's what you're angling for. As you say, laying aside the past is not always possible. Looking forward seems the most prudent course," he said. "And right now, I'm looking forward to taking a turn around the floor with you."

Country manners allowed for a relaxation of the normal stratification of class. And Jacquelyn was the chatelaine of Dragon Caern—a position of authority normally filled by the wellborn lady of the household. But noble blood did not flow through Jacquelyn's veins. Not acknowledged nobility at any rate.

"It's not seemly that your first dance should be with me, my lord."

The corner of his mouth lifted in a half smile. "When did a pirate ever concern himself with what's seemly?"

"This night you are Baron Gabriel Drake, Lord of Dragon Caern and no pirate," she argued.

"If, by the admission of your own lips, I'm your lord, then

my will is to be obeyed," he said, his pleasure evident at having caught her neatly in the web of her own words. "Come, mistress. I'll not be denied. It's not a minuet, but you did promise me a dance."

Jacquelyn felt all the eyes in the room fastened on them as he led her onto the dance floor. Continued argument would only create more spectacle, so she went with him quietly, the picture of demureness.

"Ah, Drake. You finally decided to join us," the man next to Gabriel said as they bowed in unison.

"Hugh, it's good to see you." Gabriel nodded to the man. "Mistress Wren, I'm sure you know Baron Curtmantle. Hugh, this is Jacquelyn Wren, Dragon Caern's chatelaine."

The baron cast a dismissive glance her way. Jacquelyn had never met him, but she knew of Dragon Caern's neighbor to the north. Given his reputation for deflowering serving girls, she wouldn't have invited him and his wife to the ball, but Gabriel had requested it.

"You remember my wife, Lady Catherine," Curtmantle said as the woman beside Jacquelyn dipped in a low graceful curtsey.

"Charming as always, my lady," Gabriel said in a tone that told Jacquelyn he found Baroness Curtmantle neither charming nor a lady. The woman gave no outward sign of understanding Gabriel's subtle message. Perhaps Jacquelyn was more attuned to his meanings than most.

She observed the woman from the corner of her eye as they moved through the precisely prescribed movements of the dance. Catherine Curtmantle had all the marks of fashionable beauty, long-necked grace and even features.

But the permanent cleft between her brows warned of an evil temper.

Gabriel may be friends with her husband, but the baroness would make a formidable enemy, Jacquelyn decided.

The two couples joined hands to form spokes of a rotating wheel.

"We've heard you're planning to wed, Lord Drake," the baroness said, the arch of her elegant brow turning the statement into a question.

"All these lovelies lining up for a chance to warm your bed," Lord Curtmantle said. "If I had your choice before me, man, I'd have made damn sure to be here on time."

His wife glared dirks at him.

Perhaps she has reason for the frown mark between her brows, Jacquelyn allowed. Of course, hadn't Gabriel just likened the women in the room to cows waiting to be serviced by a bull?

Maybe Mrs. Beadle was right. "All men are swine, dearie," she'd said. "We may like bacon well enough, but just remember there's no telling where it's been wallowing."

All adults are addlepated, Daisy decided, propping her chin on her fist while she peeped from beneath the long tablecloth. The whole Caern had been atwitter about this blasted ball for weeks, and for what? She squirmed under the serving table that held the big punch bowl, trying to keep the people she knew in sight. For the last hour, nothing remotely exciting had happened, except when someone dropped their dainties plate in front of her table and she managed to snag a sweet, sticky petit four.

Miss Jack didn't dance after that first quadrille. She wandered among the guests, chatting and smiling, but Uncle Gabriel tripped the light fantastic toe each time the music started afresh. Daisy was no judge of male grace, but she thought he was quick enough on his feet without being overly silly looking. He changed partners each time the music stopped—even giving a bow and dancing a somber sarabande with that poor girl whose thin face, pursed lips and buggy eyes made her look like a fish.

Uncle Gabriel really must be pretty nice, she decided, even though folk whispered that he'd been a bloody pirate. If it was true, Daisy bet he was a nice bloody pirate, for all that.

She couldn't understand why Hyacinth had decided to dislike him so. Uncle Gabriel was certainly better than that big fellow, Baron Something-or-other, who kept wanting to dance with Hy. Daisy shivered each time. The man was old—as old as their uncle—and there was a woman with a pinched face who kept staring at them each time Hyacinth danced with him. The woman didn't look at all happy.

Hyacinth, on the other hand, had this sort of squishy expression on her face. Like she was a dish of butter left in the sun and part of her was melting.

Daisy wanted to slap Hy till her teeth rattled.

She wasn't completely certain of the proper etiquette for a ball, but surely it wasn't right for a man to dance with the same girl that often. She didn't see any of the other men singling out one dance partner to the exclusion of the others.

Not even Uncle Gabriel, who was supposed to be picking out a wife, for pity's sake! His face was exactly the same, no matter who was leaning on his arm. The only time he'd looked the slightest bit different was once or twice when Daisy caught him sneaking a glance at Miss Jack. Then he had this sort of wooly-headed, dazed expression that made him seem quite a bit less bright than Daisy knew he was.

She wondered if he was thinking about that time he kissed Miss Jack in the garden. Judging from the wooly-headed, dazed expressions she saw on some of the other dancers' faces, adults probably thought about that sort of thing a lot.

When the gavotte tottered to a stop, Miss Jack tinkled a little bell at the far end of the ballroom.

"Dinner will be served directly, but before we retire to the banquet, Lord Drake begs your indulgence while he says a few words—"

"Blah, blah, blah," Daisy muttered. Miss Jack went on for several more minutes about how grateful the folk of Dragon Caern were to have the son of the house returned from the sea and all that gushy rot.

Daisy stopped listening. Even when Uncle Gabriel started talking, Daisy's attention was riveted on her sister. Judging from the little shakes and nods of her head, Hyacinth seemed to be in silent communication with someone across the room. Daisy followed the direction of Hy's gaze and found that horrible Baron Who's-his-face.

He gestured and waggled his eyebrows back at her sister, even though he was standing behind that other lady. He leaned down and whispered into the frowning woman's ear and then slipped behind one of the curtained alcoves that led into the garden.

How rude! And while Uncle Gabriel's still talking, to boot!

Of course, Daisy wasn't attending one bit to her uncle's speech either, but then she wasn't even supposed to be here, so her rudeness didn't count.

Then Uncle Gabriel's booming voice ceased and the revelers began moving slowly in the direction of the dining hall like a herd of cattle toward its feeding trough. A wide assortment of silver-buckled boots and ornate slippers shuffled past, stirring up a low-lying cloud of dust that tickled Daisy's nose and made her fight off a sneeze.

It also blocked Daisy's view of Hyacinth. She pressed her cheek to the hardwood and tried to follow the progress of Hyacinth's too-small, but oh-so-cunningly-beaded pair of pantofles.

Daisy's eyebrows nearly met over her pert nose in consternation. Hyacinth was going the wrong way.

Oh, wait. That's right. Miss Jack had only given her permission to attend the first set. When the rest of the guests retired for supper, Hyacinth was supposed to retreat to the nursery.

Where she belonged.

Wouldn't she be disappointed when she discovered Daisy already knew everything that had happened and Hy would have no captive audience for tales of her exploits?

Serves her right for trying to act so grown-up and superior.

Daisy was just about to scramble from her place of concealment when she realized Hyacinth wasn't on her way to the stairs that led to their room. She watched in horrified fascination as her sister's beaded slippers disappeared into a curtained alcove.

The same curtained alcove that awful baron had sneaked into earlier.

Once she was sure the rest of the guests were gone, Daisy bolted after her sister. There was no one in the alcove, but the door to the garden beyond was open a tiny crack. Daisy stuck her head out and peered into the moon-washed night.

Hyacinth was nowhere to be seen.

Chapter Fourteen

Gabriel had never felt less like eating. He remembered most of the older folk at the festivities. Though many had gained flesh and lost teeth, he was able to call them by name. They treated him with every courtesy to his face, but he'd lost count of the number of times conversations came to an abrupt halt whenever he joined a group. Obviously, his past was grist for the gossip mill and the wags found it an even tastier dish than the delicacies created by the excellent Mrs. Beadle.

Not that he gave a ship rat's arse what the nobility thought about him. But it seemed to matter a great deal to Lyn. He'd come to think of her by that secret name, though she didn't want it to pass his lips. What she wanted had come to mean a great deal to him.

A very great deal indeed.

So somehow, he'd get through this interminable evening without embarrassing her if he could help it. He'd court one or more of the women she seemed to think would make a good baroness. God help him, he'd even marry one of them.

But how he was going to bed one when Lyn was just down the hall, he had no clue.

The first course of jellied eel and stewed kidneys was just being laid out. He looked down the long table. Since Lyn hadn't seated herself at his side, he hoped she'd at least be at the foot of the table where he might catch a glimpse of her from time to time.

He should have known she'd be too crafty for that.

Uncle Eustace was in the place of honor at the foot of

the table, and Gabriel suspected Lyn was seated on his right. He couldn't be sure because the beefy vicar from Salisbury on her right hid all but her dainty hands.

Like most of Lyn's decisions, the placement was probably wise. He'd have had a hard time conversing with anyone if she was in his line of sight all evening. If Jacquelyn Wren sat opposite him, it might signal to his prospective brides that she was making a certain proprietary claim on the workings of the estate, at the least.

He wished she'd assert a claim on him.

But she wouldn't.

Most women wouldn't put the needs of an estate before their own. Just his luck that he'd found one made of sterner stuff.

Uncle Eustace raised a glass toward him in silent salute. Even though Gabriel had forestalled any priestly scolding from Eustace, he knew his uncle was still furious about what had passed between him and Lyn. Eustace's mute toast warmed him. At least someone was pleased with his performance this night. No doubt Lyn would give her critique of his deportment later, whether he welcomed it or not.

A bite of fresh, crusty bread was halfway to his mouth when he saw Daisy skitter into the banquet hall. Her little face taut with worry, his niece made a beeline for Miss Jack.

Very convincing, he thought. Daisy could have a bright future on a London stage, if it wasn't too scandalous an occupation for a wellborn lass to consider. Whatever devilry the little imp had dreamed up, Jacquelyn could handle.

But she shouldn't have to, he snorted in consternation.

On this night of extreme manners, successfully negotiating the shoals of society was plague enough, and the last thing Gabriel needed was trouble from his brother's brood of she-vipers. Sometimes he imagined Rupert was enjoying

Gabriel's trials from the comforts of heaven. Perhaps his perfect brother might someday tumble off one of those fluffy celestial seats for saddling him with this little pack of fiends below.

Gabriel was jerked back from his musings when Jacquelyn stood and flashed him a wide-eyed glance. She rushed from the banquet hall with Daisy at her heels.

He didn't need further prompting. He'd read genuine concern in Lyn's eyes. Without so much as a by-your-leave to the viscount at his side, he rose and strode after them.

There had better be a real emergency, he thought disgustedly. If Daisy was crying wolf, he'd tan her bottom so well, she'd need to carry a pillow to sit on for the next month.

And she was his favorite.

He caught up to Daisy and Jacquelyn in the long arched corridor.

"And then I couldn't see her anywhere!" Daisy finished miserably.

"What's amiss?" Gabriel narrowed his eyes at his niece.

Instead of wilting under the Dragon's Glare, Daisy nearly knocked him over, wrapping her thin arms around his waist and clinging to him. The child was trembling. Not even Daisy was that good an actress.

"Oh, Uncle Gabriel, you have to find her."

"Hyacinth's gone missing," Jacquelyn said, panic creeping into her voice. "With a man. From Daisy's description, I think it's your friend Baron Curtmantle."

"Damnation."

"Indeed, but more to the point, what do we do? Dragon Caern is a veritable rabbit warren. We have no idea where they've gone, and if we raise a general alarm, Hyacinth's reputation and yours by association is ruined."

"Hang my reputation," Gabriel growled. "Damn that Hugh. Not again."

"What do you mean?"

"Just that this isn't the first time I've gone looking for a girl Hugh's seduced." Gabriel snapped his fingers. "That's it. I know where they are. Hugh would think it clever to use the same spot."

Gabriel sprinted out the nearest alcove and into the garden. In the far corner of the open space, an exterior staircase wrapped around one of Dragon Caern's many turrets. Gabriel mounted the steps two at a time, fingering the hilt of his sword.

The sword was meant to be decorative, Jacquelyn had explained, as much an ornament as the silver on his shoes or the golden lace at the wrists of his frock coat. She insisted it was quite the done thing that he wear a weapon on the dance floor. Now he was grateful he'd demanded that it be functional as well. The hilt might be crusted with cut glass hoping to pass as jewels, but the blade was honed to a killing edge.

As he neared the top of the tower, an eerie sense of history repeating itself stole over him. The last time he'd climbed this tower, he found Catherine, his betrothed, with her heels in the air and his friend Hugh grunting between them.

He'd left for sea the next morning without a word to anyone. It was the only way he could avoid the urge to gut his childhood friend and denounce his fiancée for a light-skirt.

Rage roared through him. By God, if he found Hugh rutting his niece, he'd not hesitate this time. He'd hang the man by his own entrails.

His bloody thoughts were interrupted when he heard Jacquelyn and Daisy clambering behind him.

"Go back," he stage-whispered. If there was carnage in his near future, the last thing he needed was this woman and child to witness his savagery.

"No, if Hyacinth is there, she may need me," Jacquelyn said.

"Me too." Daisy piped from behind her.

Gabe was about to object more strenuously when he heard Hyacinth's voice from above.

"Oh, please, let me go. I want to go back. I want to go back," her reedy voice chanted in despair.

"Hugh!" Gabriel bellowed as he flew up the remaining steps.

When he threw open the door to the top of the tower, he found his niece hugging her knees and making herself into a very small ball. Hugh was standing a few feet from her. He hadn't had time to rebutton both sides of his drop-front breeches, but he'd been forward-thinking enough to draw his blade when he heard Gabriel's shout.

"You bastard," Gabriel said, his voice low and crackling with menace. He heard Jacquelyn's gasp behind him. Then she and Daisy hurried over to wrap Hyacinth in their arms.

"Oh, Miss Jack!" Hyacinth wailed.

"Come, Drake. Surely you understand. The girl taunted me all evening," Curtmantle said. "If you lay out such a tasty morsel, you can't blame a man for wanting to take a bite. After all, you were a pirate. Lord knows you've done your share of taking."

"Not if the lass was unwilling or young enough to still be in the schoolroom," Gabriel said. "Even a pirate has certain standards you seem to be sadly lacking."

Hugh laughed unpleasantly. "You may have me there. So, Drake, what do you intend to do? You ran away rather than challenge me last time."

"I'll not run now."

Gabriel roared and launched a blistering assault. The world spun around him, a disjointed blur of shrieks from the girls, the musty scent of old rushes on the stone floor and the ever present metallic rasp of blade on blade. A spurt of red shot across his vision as one of them drew first blood. Wounds were never felt in the heat of battle. He wasn't sure whether the blood was his or Hugh's.

It didn't matter. A red haze settled over his eyes. Hugh drew a dirk from his boot and sliced at Gabriel in a windmill of flashing steel.

Gabriel parried and gave ground. Then in a neat trick not taught by gentlemanly sword masters, he disarmed Hugh with a couple of maneuvers that would have been labeled unsportsmanlike in any fencing master's school. But since he and Hugh were trying to kill each other, the rules could go hang. At the very least, the flat of Gabriel's sword across Hugh's groin would ensure he'd sire no bastard this night.

He grabbed up Hugh's dropped dirk, shoved his onetime friend to his knees and pulled his head back to expose his throat.

"Wait!" Hugh pleaded when Gabriel laid the cold steel to his neck. "I didn't do anything. The girl is yet a maid! On my hope of heaven, I swear it."

"If Heaven lets the likes of you in, I hope to be bound for hell," Gabriel growled.

"Gabriel, stop!" Jacquelyn stood. "He's telling the truth. Tell your uncle, Hyacinth."

"Well?" he demanded. "What did this scum do to you?"

Hyacinth swiped her nose on her fancy sleeve and sniffed. "He told me I was pretty and then he kissed me, and that wasn't so bad." Her little face crumpled in misery. "But then he stuck his tongue down my throat."

"Ew!" Daisy shuddered.

"And that's all?" Gabriel demanded, the dirk still poised for a killing slice.

"There wasn't time for anything else," Hugh said honestly.

He swallowed hard and a thin ribbon of red trickled down his neck. "Think, Gabriel. Surely, you can't mean to kill me over this trifle. Not with your banquet hall filled with guests."

"Your concern for my guests is touching." Gabriel spat the words through clenched teeth.

The dirk bit into Hugh's flesh, no deeper than a hair's breadth. Sweat beaded his old friend's brow and Gabriel caught a whiff of urine.

The old wound in Gabe's heart ached once or twice. He'd never have left Dragon Caern if not for Hugh and Catherine's betrayal. He'd never have turned pirate, never have become the beast he was trying so hard to tame. Within him, all that longed for peace and civility ordered him to put down the blade. Yet the beast whispered to him, tempting him with the thought that it would be so sweet to let his dirk drink its fill of this coward's blood.

"My lord . . ." Jacquelyn's voice called him back from the brink of murder. "Please."

With effort, he lowered the dirk. But he kept a firm grip on Hugh's shoulder, forcing him to remain on his knees.

"You're right, as always, mistress," he said. "Let there be decency and decorum this night."

Hugh slumped forward in relief.

A totally wicked thought occurred to Gabriel, and he was unable to resist this one. "I will not kill you as you deserve. However, penance is required for your crime."

Jacquelyn held him with her gaze over the sobbing Hyacinth's shoulder. "My lord, if you demand redress in a public fashion, the damage to Hy—"

"I would never do anything to harm my nieces," Gabriel assured her. "In fact, I shall see to it that Baron Curtmantle helps them. The girls have been studying the practices of the noble savages who populate the wilderness in the Colonies.

Hugh, you're going to aid their study in exactly the same way I did a few days ago."

He winked at his niece.

"Daisy, get a rope."

Chapter Fifteen

Gabriel made one more circuit of his chambers, then climbed back into bed. He sank into the feather tick. It was certainly more comfortable than his narrow captain's berth aboard the *Revenge*, but he still missed the sea's constant rocking, whether it was gentle or tossing him about. He willed his mind to give up and let his body find sleep.

It was a losing battle.

He laced his fingers behind his head and stared up into the damask bed curtains. At least, the evening had been declared a rousing success. Supper was heartily enjoyed by all. The string ensemble was nearly inexhaustible, playing one reel after another as his guests reveled in exuberant country dancing after their oh-so-proper, courtly steps earlier.

And almost everyone had left him at the door exclaiming over the delightful comedic farce presented after the meal.

His lovely nieces had played an Algonquin war party and one thoroughly humiliated Baron Curtmantle served admirably as their victim. Jacquelyn made Gabriel step in, acting as "His Majesty's loyal militia" to rescue the poor baron before the flames got too high. Hugh was covered with sweat and smoke, but without a singe on his miserable hide, more's the pity.

After making a spectacle of Baron Curtmantle, Gabriel had called Meriwether up from the wine cellar to stitch the shallow flesh wound Gabriel had given Hugh during their sword fight. Meri told him later the baron whimpered throughout the procedure, especially since Meri forbade him a drink of spirits to dull the pain.

Of course, nothing had kept Meri from taking a nip or three while he stitched.

Gabriel sighed. *So much for turning the other cheek.*

He really intended to let the past stay there. His pain over Hugh bedding his betrothed was so far dissipated by time, it was as though it had happened to someone else. Gabriel had actually been pleased to see him again. He'd been willing to overlook Hugh's sins since he had plenty of his own to atone for, but damn his eyes! The man had to try to seduce his niece. If Gabriel were still Captain aboard the *Revenge*, he'd have run up the red flag and given Hugh no quarter.

The loss of Hugh's friendship was no great thing, but now he'd made an enemy of him. Who knew what Hugh might do? Part of him wished he'd followed his instinct and spilled all Hugh's blood in the tower.

There was much to be said for a clean kill. A wounded boar was more likely to take down his hunter than a healthy one. Humiliated and alive, Hugh was more dangerous than ever to all Gabriel held dear.

But Jacquelyn had stayed his hand.

For this night at least, seeing the quiet approval in Jacquelyn's gray eyes was worth whatever danger the future might hold.

"Lyn . . ." His deep voice wrapped her in its velvet timbre, but it gave her no peace.

The aching wouldn't stop. Every muscle in her body clenched in concert with her throbbing vulva. There was an emptiness inside her that cried out for filling, a longing that knew no surcease.

His mouth on her breasts was heaven. Her nipples drew up tight and tender. She arched her back as his tongue flicked over them, teasing them into demanding little points.

"Gabriel," she whimpered his name over and over as if she were

chanting a prayer. Finally he suckled her, flooding her being with pleasure.

But the pleasure was sharp edged. Far from satisfying, he only whetted her hunger. She grabbed a fistful of her linen sheets when his lips trailed over her sweat-slick ribs and belly to delve into her inner secrets.

She cried out when his mouth parted her, loving her sensitive mound of flesh with his lips and tongue and—good Lord!—his teeth. Jacquelyn teetered on the edge of some precipice, but couldn't seem to fall. She rubbed her breasts with the flat of her palms, trying to still their complaint at being left wanting.

The scent of her own arousal filled her nostrils, and still the ache wouldn't stop. She was too far gone for shame to matter anymore.

"Please," was all she could manage before he raised himself to claim her mouth. His tongue sweetly invaded and she tasted herself on him as his weight settled on her.

Then in a sudden rush, he was inside her, swollen and potent. She expanded to receive him with joy. They moved in tandem, slick and wet, skin on skin, but the ache went on. Each thrust only sharpened her torment.

"Gabriel," she moaned. "I can't . . . I can't . . ."

"Lyn, what is it?" His voice washed over her, rumbling and true.

She thrashed to one side, trembling with need. His hand brushed her temple and slid down to cradle her cheek.

"Wake up, Lyn. You're dreaming," he said softly. "And though I've no hope of heaven, I'd give a year in paradise to know what this dream is about."

That brought her bolt upright. She jerked her sheets to her chin. Had he been bedding her as she slept?

No. Her nightshift was bunched at her waist, but it was still there beneath her sheets. And Lord Drake was fully clothed. In her dream, they'd both been splendidly naked.

"What are you doing here?" she demanded, louder than she intended.

Gabriel clamped a hand over her mouth. "Easy, now. There's no cause for alarm." He settled beside her on the bed and lowered his hand.

"I wake to find you in my chambers in the dead of night. How can you say there's no cause for alarm?" When she inhaled, she was dismayed to find that a little muskiness from her dream lingered in her bedclothes. "We narrowly avoided scandal earlier tonight. If anyone saw you enter . . ."

"No one saw me enter."

"How can you be sure?'

"Because I didn't come through the door," he said, his teeth flashing white in the light of a single candle. Behind him, she noticed a gaping hole in one of her walls. "This old castle is more riddled with secret passages than a block of Swiss cheese. You didn't know?"

Jacquelyn shook her head. If he scented her arousal, at least he was gentleman enough not to mention it. Her groin still throbbed.

"Come. I'll show you." He stood and offered his hand.

She didn't dare touch him. Her skin prickled all over, charged and sensitive. She was dry tinder waiting for a single spark to burst into full flame. If she touched so much as a fingertip of him, a dark, wanton part of her might pull him back into bed with her to finish the madness her dream had started.

Instead, she wrapped a sheet around herself as an extra layer of protection from him and climbed out of bed to inspect the opening. Cool air from the dim, secret corridor shivered over her.

"Rupert and I used to play in these passages when we were children," he said, his tone both wistful and boyishly excited. "They go everywhere—from the battlements to the lowest dungeon."

"Really?" She peered into the void. "Are all the chambers connected this way?"

"No." He shook his head. "But the corridors all seem to lead eventually to mine."

She took the candle from him and stepped into the passage. There was plenty of room for her, but the musty space was barely wide enough for his broad shoulders to pass through and only a hand's breadth taller than Gabriel himself. It was festooned with cobwebs, but otherwise seemed clean and dry, leading off in both directions.

"How did you know this particular hidden doorway led to my chamber?" A sudden naughty thought seared her brain. "There aren't peepholes, are there?"

The idea that he might secretly have watched her sometime as she dressed and undressed or bathed in her little hip bath was at once horrifying and beguiling. If she'd known, would she have lingered at her task, stretching naked for his consideration? Might she let the soap bubbles slide longer than necessary down her limbs or take sly pleasure in spreading herself with her washing cloth, hoping to hear his sharp intake of breath through the wall?

A wicked tingle settled between her legs. She pulled the sheet tighter around herself and gave a little shake, trying to slough off the last wayward urges of her wanton dream.

"A peephole? No," he said with sorrow in his voice. "But the idea has merit! I could certainly see to it, if you'd like."

"Absolutely not!" Her cheeks burned. He seemed to sense her lurid reaction to the thought of him spying upon her. "Then if you couldn't see me, how did you know this is my chamber?"

"I didn't. Just fortunate, I guess," he said with a grin. "I couldn't sleep. I remembered the old system of passageways and thought I'd do some exploring, just to see if my memory of them was correct. When I heard someone call out my name, I nearly jumped out of my skin."

"Someone called out?" She shriveled with embarrassment. In her dream, she'd fairly sung his name.

"Imagine my surprise when it turned out to be you, mistress." He took a step closer to her. "I wasn't able to find solace in the arms of Morpheus this night, but from the sounds you were making as you slept, it seemed you certainly found someone's arms. Since you called my name, dare I hope they were mine?"

"I rarely have any recollection of my dreams," she said as she handed him the candle. This dream, however, was fresh, and stark as a full moon on a cloudless night. "A night phantom is of no import and when one wakes from it, the vision flees like the vapor it always was."

But most dreams didn't leave her with such a heavy, dull ache in her groin. It was almost enough to make her believe Father Eustace's warning that there were such things as incubi, malicious spirits intent on driving women mad with desire as they slept.

Except her particular incubus definitely bore Gabriel Drake's face.

"Now, since you have no business in my chamber, would you please be so kind as to leave the same way you came?" she demanded, waving a hand toward the opening in the wall.

"I can understand your desire to return to that dream," he said. "Sounded like you were having a wonderful time."

Part of her knew she should be affronted, but another part couldn't condemn him for the truth. Her dream was wonderful.

And frustrating.

And terrifying.

She didn't know how much more of it she could bear.

"I doubt very much that I can go back to sleep now." The pulsing between her legs would probably torment her for hours. "Would . . . would you like some company in your explorations?"

His grin almost outshined the candle.

"Nothing would please me more." He cocked a sugges- tive brow. "Well, almost nothing."

Jacquelyn glowered at him. She might dream of wild abandon with this man, but in the real world, she had to help him do his duty to Dragon Caern.

"If you are coming with me, you might wish to change your mode of dress. Not that I don't find you delectable *en déshabillé*," he hastened to add. "But no one has used these passageways for years. I'd hate to see you soil your night- shift."

"One moment then," she said as she padded to the trunk that held her belongings. "I still have Timothy's clothes. They're little more than rags anyway. Especially since you nearly ruined the shirt. But maybe I can tie it closed in the back."

"Pray, don't trouble yourself on my account," he said as she pulled out the boy's garments. "There are so many cobwebs in the tunnels, no doubt you'll want me leading the way. So if your backside is a bit exposed, I'll never know." His lips twitched with suppressed amusement. "But I can dream."

"Then by all means, my lord, dream on," she said. "And while you're about it, turn your back so I can dress."

He complied with deceptive meekness.

"You won't turn around until I say?"

"Mistress, you have my solemn promise," he said. "Wild horses could not drag me from this exact spot."

Eyeing his broad back, Jacquelyn reached down and grabbed her hem. She pulled the nightshift off in one smooth motion.

Did she imagine it, or did he just suck his breath in over his teeth? As promised, he hadn't moved an inch, but his fingers balled into fists at his sides.

She leaned forward, her breasts swinging free, to slide her legs into Timothy's old breeches.

Was she hearing things? She could have sworn Gabriel made a low groan.

She straightened and wiggled the breeches up over her hips. Carefully, she fastened first one side, then the other of the drop front, concealing her triangle of curls.

He couldn't see her unless he had eyes in the back of his head, but just having him in the room while she was nearly naked made her feel utterly wicked. She fisted her hair and pulled it up off her neck, letting the cool air from the passageway tickle her nape. She arched her back in a stretch.

He coughed and sputtered as if he'd just choked on a pumpkin seed.

"Are you quite finished?" he asked, his voice tight.

"Almost." She pulled Timothy's shredded shirt on and began doing up the few buttons Gabriel had left on it the last time she wore it. She'd never thought to wear it again, just to use the fabric for patches, so she hadn't replaced them.

"Bloody pirate," she muttered.

"What was that?"

"Nothing," she said, irritated when she couldn't seem to close the shirtfront decently. Her nipples still peeped out at her.

This is exactly what he'd like, no doubt. She shook her ribs to make her breasts bounce.

Another noise, almost a sigh came from Gabriel's direction.

Strangely enough, even if he couldn't see them, it pleased her to think of her breasts bare with him so close. Her nipples tightened and she glowed rosily, flushed with guilty pleasure. She tried so hard to be a lady, but at her core, she was a creature of passion. Jacquelyn truly was Isabella's daughter, after all.

Maybe that is no bad thing, provided I keep things in check, she decided as she knotted the shirt in front and left her back bare. The ache in her groin had dulled to a pleasantly tolerable level.

"Very well. I'm ready," she announced.

The tension drained out of his shoulders and he turned to face her, tight-lipped.

"My lord, I'm very impressed," she said. "You were a perfect gentleman in a trying circumstance."

"You've no idea." He took up the candlestick and disappeared into the passageway. "If you'll follow me, mistress."

"Lead on, my lord," she said cheerfully as she started to close the secret doorway behind her. Her smile faded when she looked back into the room.

And noticed the placement of her looking glass.

Gabriel stifled a chuckle. "Very trying circumstances indeed."

Chapter Sixteen

Jacquelyn gnawed the inside of her cheek in embarrassment. He'd had a full view of her the whole time. He'd seen every bit of her skin, even down to the delicate folds between her legs that still pounded with aching fury. And worse yet, an exceedingly naughty part of her was actually glad he'd seen her.

What possessed her?

Gabriel Drake.

That had to be the explanation. Since he'd taken her maidenhead, she'd felt stripped of every sense of decency. He'd claimed her, changed her somehow. During the ball, she caught herself watching him as he danced, enjoying the display of masculine grace. She admired the cut of his frock coat and the snug fit of his knee breeches.

And imagined what he'd look like without them.

The old Mistress Wren would no more have entertained such notions than she'd have screamed obscenities in the chapel, but *Lyn* seemed overflowing with wicked thoughts.

Even now, as she trailed him through the dark corridor, part of her couldn't help noticing the way his breeches hugged his buttocks and muscular thighs. Her fingertips tingled to slide up under his shirt to trace the indentation of his spine.

This is so wrong. Jacquelyn knew she should go back, but when she glanced over her shoulder at the dark void behind her, she realized she could wander this labyrinth for days without finding her chamber again. For better or worse, Gabriel Drake was her guide.

"My lord—"

"Shh!" he cautioned, stopping to turn and place a finger on her lips. The silence was severed by a loud snort on the other side of the wall, then followed by the deep rhythmic buzz of a snore. "If we are to explore together, you must call me Gabriel. *My lord* makes me feel far too . . ." his whisper trailed away to nothing as he searched for the apt word.

"Lordly?"

"I was going to say old. Reminds me of my father, but I'd accept *lordly* if it meant you were inclined to obedience," he murmured into her ear. His warm breath on her neck set her skin dancing.

"And how would you have me obey you more thoroughly?"

He made a sound she couldn't decipher, almost like a low growl in the back of his throat.

"Have I displeased you?"

"No." He inhaled deeply and she thought he muttered something about Ulysses only being plagued with Sirens, while he . . . Here she lost the thread of his thought.

"Gabriel?"

"We must be quiet. If we can hear them, they can hear us."

The wheezing on the far side of the wall grew louder.

"That must be Mrs. Beadle," she whispered back to him.

He shrugged. "Or Meriwether. His snore could wake the dead."

"And Mrs. Beadle could make them long for the quiet of the grave," she said with a grin.

"God forbid Meri and Mrs. B. ever call a truce and admit to fondness, then."

Jacquelyn choked on that thought. "You think such a thing might be possible?"

Gabriel's shoulders hitched upward. "God knows. Meri's half convinced himself into high regard for her on the strength of her excellent cherry pies." He shook his head.

"Only the very wise or a total fool would claim to understand why some folk fancy each other."

"I don't think it's a matter of choice," Jacquelyn said as they moved on. If she had a say in the matter, she certainly wouldn't have a twitch in her loins for a prodigal pirate. "I'm coming to believe passion isn't a thing that may be chosen."

"And yet, a choice is what you've foisted upon me."

" 'Tis not my doing," she said. " 'Tis simply a thing that must be done. Besides, from what I've heard of marriage among nobility, passion is not a requirement in any case. What matters is that the match be deemed suitable and profitable for both parties."

The passageway led them steeply upward until they came upon a door that led out onto a small, private balcony overlooking even the battlements. After the confinement of the narrow passage, Jacquelyn breathed a sigh of relief as the heavens opened above them. Stars winked overhead, brittle pinpricks in the inky sky.

"Life is filled with choices," Jacquelyn said. She chose to fill her lungs with the crisp night air rather than throw herself upon the man at her side as she wished. "Some choices are just harder than others."

"And somehow you expect me to choose a baroness from the eligible young ladies you trotted before me this night."

" 'Tis not my fault you were born to the title," she said, leaning on the stone crenellations to peer down into the dark bailey. "All I'm trying to do is help you keep it."

"Ah, mistress, there's somewhat else I'd rather have you help me keep. My sanity, for one."

He pinched off the candle flame and set the candlestick down. Then he turned back to her. She stood perfectly still as he reached up a hand and ran a finger from her temple to her jaw. Then he cupped her chin and lowered his mouth to kiss her softly.

She should run, she knew. Whether she could find her way out or not, she should bolt down into the blackness. But she couldn't bear to tear herself away from the sweetness of his mouth on hers.

When he pulled back, he brushed her lower lip with his thumb. "A title isn't everything. What if I decided I didn't want it?"

"You must," she said miserably, turning her face away from him. "For the sake of everyone in the Caern."

"Dragon Caern was old when my father's father came into this barony," he said, releasing her to lean on the balcony rail. "It will continue when I am gone."

"The estate will survive under different leadership, yes, but it will change out of all knowing," she said. "And what of the girls? You must protect your nieces' interests. Can you honestly think they'd be better off in the Crown's keeping?"

"So far, they're not doing so well in mine. Hyacinth was nearly ravished this night."

"And would have been but for you," she said. "You were right. I shouldn't have let her attend the ball."

"You couldn't have known what would happen." He waved off her confession. "Even the perfect Mistress Wren cannot see all ends."

She decided to let this little jibe pass unremarked.

"I've yet to thank you for what you did." She'd been afraid Gabriel would be hurt during the sword fight with that vile Baron Curtmantle, but she was unable to look away. Muscles tense, sword arm swinging, his face etched with the fury of an avenging angel, he was too spectacular for her to miss a moment. "I've never seen the like. You were magnificent and terrible at the same time."

"Bah! The day I can't best Hugh Curtmantle I may as well turn up my toes," he said.

"Still, you shouldn't take chances with your life. Your nieces need you, Gabriel," she said.

"And what of you, Lyn?" He rested his warm palm on her shoulder and then let it slide down her arm. Their fingers twined of their own accord. "Have you no needs?"

"I need . . ." The back of her throat felt suddenly thick. A host of erotic longings assaulted her, beginning with where her wicked dream left off. Ignoring the clamor of her body, she called upon her will. "I need for you to stop calling me Lyn."

His mouth tightened into a hard line, but he gave her a grudging nod. "Mistress, I wish to heaven you weren't stronger than I am."

"I'm not," she said, suddenly angry with him. "Can you not see that I'm dangling by a thread? You stupid, stupid man. Do you think I don't want you?"

"Frankly, I don't know what to think," he said, backing half a step from her, stunned by her outburst. "First you give me your purity, then push me away. You fill the castle with other women for me to court, then call out my name in your sleep. You're all I can think of, and yet your first thought is always for the Caern. Except when you're ripping off your nightshift and shaking your teats at me. You're a right puzzlement, Mistress Wren."

She covered her face with both hands and heaved a sigh. "I'm a puzzlement to myself as well." Her voice shook. "My looking glass shows me a face I don't recognize these days. I don't know what's come over me."

"I do." He gently took her wrists and pulled her hands away from her face. His smile was both gentle and wickedly sensual at the same time, and Jacquelyn couldn't figure out how he managed such a feat. "Don't blame yourself and don't blame the mirror. I have an exceptionally high opinion of that looking glass just now."

"Oh, you beast!" She tried to swat at him, but he held her wrists tight. "You know what I meant."

"Yes, I do," he said, suddenly serious. "You've discovered a part of yourself you didn't know exists. Perhaps you'd rather not admit to your passionate nature, but it won't change the facts. You're not the first to discover you are something other than what you always thought. I was born the son of a gentleman. Do you think I enjoyed waking up every morning and shaving the chin of a pirate?"

"According to Mr. Meriwether, you weren't given much choice."

His smile inverted slightly. "I wish I could believe that, but I must live in this skin. I know the truth. The truth is the pirate was in there all along, just waiting for the opportune moment." His smile turned suddenly wicked again. "There were times when I enjoyed shaving a pirate very much."

"So you're saying that I've always been a whore, but I just didn't know it?"

"No, not at all," Gabriel said. "For a bright woman, you're singularly gifted in mistaking my meaning. I find you the most exciting, the most passionate woman I've ever known. Certainly no whore. And I want you to know I've never regretted taking your virginity."

She scoffed. "Is that your idea of an apology? Of all the——"

He silenced her with a searching kiss that warmed her to her toes.

"That's just the pirate in me," he admitted when he released her mouth. "I can't regret what I've taken from you, Lyn. But I've suffered untold pangs over having taking your maidenhead so badly."

She digested this astounding admission. "It wasn't so bad," she said in a small voice. "I suspect it would have gotten better. You must admit, we were interrupted at an untimely moment."

"Granted." His lips twitched in a suppressed grin as he looked around. "Since no one but we knows of the secret passages, the likelihood of our being interrupted again now seems remote."

She closed her eyes, only to see an image of the two of them clinging together in grinding passion burned on her vision.

"But I'm not wellborn or well-moneyed and you must—"

"Yes, I must do my duty for Dragon Caern," he finished for her. "And God help me, I will. But I'm only a man. And not a very good one at that. I'll do what needs doing for the sake of the Caern, but I can't bear the thought of not ever making love to you, Lyn. I don't think I can live that way."

He pressed a lover's kiss into her open palm.

"Please don't make me," he whispered.

She shuddered with need. "Oh, Gabriel . . ."

"I'll take that, mistress, as consent."

Chapter Seventeen

Gabriel bent and scooped her in his arms. She was light as a child, but her soft curves quickly dispelled the comparison. No longer the prickly chatelaine, she was pliant and willing, pressing her lips against his throat as he ducked back into the secret corridor. He left the door open behind him, hoping the moonlight would shaft down enough for him to see. He couldn't bear to put her down long enough to re-light the candle.

"Where are we going?" she asked between planting feverish kisses on his neck and nipping his earlobe.

"To my chamber."

He didn't make it a question. There was no going back. She wanted him. He wanted her. Damn tomorrow, they'd have each other this night.

But as urgently as he needed to bury himself in her sweet flesh, he was determined not to rush things this time. In the armory, his world had turned to heat and irresistible longing in a blink. It had taken everything in him to stop long enough to make sure it was her will, too, before he deflowered her. If she'd said no, he hoped he'd have been able to pull back, but he wouldn't have laid money on it.

Now there was no question of stopping. Lynn draped her lithe arms around his neck and laid her head on his chest as he sidestepped down the dark passage. When they'd passed this way before, the smell of decades-old dust had filled his nostrils. Now he was drowning in the scent of this woman, all warm and musky in his arms.

His eyesight adjusted to the dimness, and he traced his

steps by distant memory back to the lord of the manor's suite. It seemed an eternity before he was able to kick open his chamber door, which he'd left ajar. He stood stock-still for a moment, trying to quell the hammering in his chest. Lyn made him weak and strong at once. He was tempted to give in to the rutting beast inside him, but he was determined to love her well this time.

He kissed her as he lowered her feet to the ground. To his delight, she molded herself against him, her softness against his hardness. Her fingers curled around his lapel, tugging him ever closer.

Part of his mind screamed this was a heartache waiting to happen. He would still have to wed another. She would see to it. There was no turning Jacquelyn from her purpose when she set her mind to something, and she was fiercely determined to save his barony for the sake of his nieces. He might only have her this one time.

There was so much that needed saying.

Yet when her tongue dove between his lips, no words would form in his mind. Surely she must know the way of things, that their joining would be as ships chance-met on the high seas, an exchange of mail and messages and then parting to continue their separate voyages. Jacquelyn seemed set upon having him in any case. With a groan of pleasure, she met his passion with her own. Her fingertips fluttered over his bared throat and upward, twining his hair, kneading his scalp.

He fondled her breast, but she gently pushed his hand away.

"You've had your time to explore, Captain, and may yet again," she said with a devilish grin he'd never have believed if he hadn't seen it with his own eyes. "But this is my time."

He would have argued, but she unbuttoned his shirt and slid her hands inside, caressing, teasing, her fingers splayed across his chest. So she wanted her hand on the tiller, did she? He'd allow it for now.

He contented himself with cupping her cheeks and making love to her mouth as she touched him unhindered. As their kiss deepened, her hands drifted lower to tug at the waist of his breeches and fumble with the buttons on either side of the drop front. In her haste, she popped one right off. It hit the floor with a plop and rolled out of sight.

"Oh, dear," she said as she reached into his breeches to cup his scrotum in her warm smooth palm. "You seem to have lost a button."

He was near to losing control. His cock ached for her touch. The way she kneaded his balls sent his groin into a frenzy of pleasure and agony in equal measure.

"Shall I stop to find it?"

What is she talking about? Oh, the damn button.

"Not for all the gold on the Spanish Main," he said between clenched teeth.

Lyn grazed his member with her palm, her touch a glancing caress. She looked up at him, her eyes enormous. She stroked him again, harder this time while never taking her gaze from his, questioning, watching for his reaction.

He'd made love to a number of women. This was the first time a woman made love to him. He'd always had to take his pleasure with the others, but Lyn was intent on giving.

Waves of sensation rolled over him, engulfing him, nearly taking him down. When she pressed a shy kiss beneath one nipple, he drew in a shuddering breath. Lyn nipped him and sent desire surging to his swollen cock. She began trailing kisses down his chest to his navel and dropped to her knees before him.

If she lost her nerve now, he thought he might die. But Lyn was no coward.

If there was such a place as heaven, surely it couldn't

hold more exquisite bliss than the sweetness of her mouth on him.

He groaned low again, a rumble of male strength reduced to incoherence. A thrill of power coursed through Jacquelyn as she licked his full length. When he invaded her with his mouth in the armory, she'd lost herself. Since the madness of that time, she'd wondered what it would be like to turn the tables on him.

Her imagination hadn't come close.

She was sure she was doing it all wrong, that she was using her tongue when she should take him into her mouth, that she stopped to kiss him when he wanted her to suckle, but somehow her inexperience didn't seem to matter. He was powerless before her, trembling with need, and she reveled in enslaving him with pleasure.

Strangely enough, giving to him sent shivers of delight over her. Warmth pooled between her thighs and the ache that was becoming all too familiar to her began its incessant drumbeat. He caressed her head with both his big hands, gently threading her locks through his fingers. She flicked him with her tongue in random feathery strokes. His breathing hitched as he sucked air over his teeth.

He fascinated her. She'd known how men were fashioned. At least she had a good guess after overseeing the breeding of the broodmares at Dragon Caern. She'd assumed men were just smaller versions of stallions.

But Gabriel's cock was a wonder, all smooth and hard and hot. She loved the way it moved of its own accord, arcing toward her, veins bulging. She closed her lips around him and laved her tongue over the bit of rougher skin just below the tight head. His ballocks drew up into a snug mound.

He made a strangled sound and pulled her away from him.

"Did I do something wrong?"

"No, you were doing everything very right." He took her hands and raised her to her feet. "But if you continue, this will be over far sooner than I wish it to be. And I want to give you a full measure of pleasing before I take my own."

"I gave you pleasure, then?"

"More than I dreamed possible." Gabriel swore softly as he cupped her cheeks. "Far more than I deserve."

"Let me be the judge of that." She smiled up at him. The fire that started in her exceedingly naughty dream now threatened to erupt into a full blaze, but she banked the flames. Drawing out the torment only seemed to increase it. "I'll wager you can bear a good bit more. Besides, it pleases me to give you pleasure."

"Truly?"

She nodded.

"What would you have me do, Lyn?"

"To begin with, I would look at you. All of you."

He spread his hands in surrender and she reached up to shove his shirt off his shoulders. He toed off his shoes as she hitched his breeches down over his muscular thighs. He stepped out of them and stooped to pull off his stockings. Then he straightened to his full height and held her in a smoldering gaze. Faint light from the banked fireplace kissed his frame, accenting the mounds and indentations of his muscles.

Hard and strong, he was everything that was male. All that was female in her answered him with soft moistness.

So this is how a woman crosses over to the dark and becomes a courtesan. Is this how it was for Mother? This thundering need to be with a man, devil take tomorrow?

She shoved away all thought but Gabriel.

"If I live to be a hundred," Jacquelyn said, "I'll never see anything finer than you in the altogether, Gabriel Drake. Not ever in my whole living life."

He chuckled, his belly and cock jiggling. "Apparently, you've led a sheltered existence up till now, mistress."

"Then unshelter me." The ache between her thighs was making her a terrible wanton, but she was powerless to stop it. "I want to know everything about you. Everything that pleases you."

He closed the distance between them and gathered her into his arms. "All you need do is look in the mirror, then. You are what pleases me, Lyn." He bent to kiss her, taking his time, his lips sweet and almost chaste on hers. Then the kiss changed, deepened, and he stole the breath from her lungs.

His hands roamed over her body, sending sparks across her skin. He parted Timothy's shirt and bared her breasts. Her nipples hardened as they grazed his chest. He pulled down her boy's breeches so their bare bodies could press against each other, skin on skin. She kicked off her slippers, reveling in the feel of him, warm and solid and wanting.

He cupped her bottom and lifted her off her toes so his cock spread her opening just a bit. Her gut clenched, waiting for him to enter her. To her dismay, he lowered her back down without joining with her.

He released her mouth and shot her a wicked grin. Clearly he planned to draw out the torment as well. "Speaking of mirrors, the sight of you changing clothes in yours this night was a treasure I'd not trade for a chest of doubloons. If you would truly please me, Lyn, all you need do is shake those lovely breasts at me again. My view in the mirror wasn't as clear as I'd have wished."

Embarrassment heated her cheeks, but she'd asked what he wanted. Isabella's daughter would never do anything by halves.

She raised her arms above her head in surrender and bounced twice on her toes. "Like that?" Then she cupped her breasts and offered them to him. "Or like this?"

"Oh, Lyn." He took them in his calloused palms as if they were more precious than gold and bent to claim a nipple with his lips.

Her whole being thrummed with life. She felt each pulse of her heart twice, once in her chest and once between her legs. She arched into him, hooking her knee around his thigh and pressing her wetness against him. Anything to appease the ache.

He groaned in response to her arousal, scooped her up and carried her to his big feather bed. They tumbled into it in a tangle of limbs, kisses that fell where they may, hands that sought and massaged the neediest of places.

His head disappeared beneath the sheet and she felt his hot mouth on her, probing and teasing. A coil strained in her belly. She was wound tighter than the eight-day clock in the parlor. At any moment the spring might break under the tension.

"Please, Gabriel," she said between shuddering breaths.

"My every intent, Lyn," he said as he mounted her, sliding his full length home in a rush of need. Her womb contracted once in greeting and he stilled, willing them both into control. The ache subsided only a little.

There was no pain this time. Only the wonder of holding him inside her. They moved as one, sinuous and slow. The pressure bubbled up inside her again, like a pot ready to boil over.

Gabriel thrust deep and held her head between his hands, holding his weight on his elbows. He said her name with tenderness as he looked down at her. "Lyn," the secret name he'd given her, low and rumbling. One more thrust and she began to unravel.

Rolling contractions bucked her frame. Her limbs were no longer her own, shuddering in spasms of joy. Then she felt his release, pulsing hot and steady in tandem with her own. She held him tighter, welcoming him into herself, accepting all of him.

Spent and gasping, they clung to each other. She kissed his sweat-dampened temple, savoring the saltiness of his skin. He covered her mouth with his in a soft kiss. A kiss that said she had given him a gift and he was grateful.

As he laid his head beside hers on the pillow, still joined, unwilling to sever their connection until it was absolutely necessary, she realized he'd gifted her as well. The giving and receiving of pleasure was a paradox, the most selfish *and* selfless thing she'd ever done. The more she gave, the more she received.

They'd been lifted out of themselves for that blissful moment, transported to a place of delight she'd never dreamed existed. A part of them would always be joined in that secret place.

"That was . . . extraordinary," he said as he finally rolled off her. She started to rise, but he pulled her back into his arms, snugging her against his body. "Don't go, Lyn. Please. Not yet."

"For a little while," she agreed.

"You feel so wonderful. I . . ." He breathed a deep sigh of contentment and was asleep before he could put together another two words.

Her lips lifted in a smile before she dropped another kiss on his forehead. It would have to be enough. She'd pleasured a pirate. And good heavens, but he'd pleasured her in return. Her smile faded.

Tonight she might lie abed with the pirate, but tomorrow she would still have to help the baron find a wife. Once his breathing told her he was deeply asleep, she slipped from his bed, donned her boy's rags and crept out into the hall.

She hoped to heaven no one would catch her wandering about like this before she reached the safety of her own chamber. The outlandish garb she might be able to explain.

The tears streaking her cheeks were another matter altogether.

Chapter Eighteen

Gabriel woke with her scent still in his nostrils. He almost always rose with a swollen cock, but this morning his erection was more insistent than usual. He was disappointed to find himself alone in the big bed. He didn't remember Lyn leaving him, but the rest of his memories from last night were both vivid and fantastic. The old secret passages, the brittle stars overhead on the battlements and the hot, slick romp he and Jacquelyn had shared.

She'd been wondrously wanton. And adventurous. And far more passionate than he'd ever expected from a woman who prided herself on dignity and decorum. He wondered for a moment if the wild, loving Jacquelyn in his mind was just an erotic night phantom.

The long strand of ruddy brown hair on his pillow convinced him she was no dream.

"You little minx," he said softly, remembering the heart-stopping bliss of her mouth on him.

Such a woman could bind a man to her so tightly, he'd never wish to be freed.

He wound the hair loosely around his finger and stared at it. Had she already wound herself around his heart?

Mayhap, but it wouldn't matter, he told himself. Jacquelyn Wren might be a veritable Aphrodite by moonlight, but she was all Hera by day. The needs of the household would always come first.

Gabriel swung his legs out of bed, secreting the strand of hair—a small, tangible reminder of their night of passion—in the pocket of his breeches before he tugged them on. Jacquelyn tried to insist he have a valet, but he'd been dressing himself without assistance for so long, he had no patience for anyone fluttering about in his chamber.

Now if Lyn wants to volunteer for the position, I might be persuaded, he mused. No, that wouldn't work. Aside from being scandalous, he was much too keen on being *undressed* by her to submit to a daily ritual of having her put *on* his clothing.

He knew she'd arranged for at least one potential bride to come for tea later today. With a grimace of resignation, he decided to make the best of things. He'd sip from his cup correctly and make inane small talk till he was ready to burst out of his skin, but he refused to let reality dampen his spirits.

Somehow, he'd have Lyn again, he vowed as he clubbed his hair back into a neat queue. She was a treasure worth claiming far more than once.

After all, the secret passage was all that separated them. And nightfall was a scant day away. Even with a loveless marriage looming, he'd still have Lyn. He just had to convince her such an arrangement would work.

Whistling through his teeth, he descended the stairs to face his day.

The pandemonium in the breakfast room was his first inkling that things might not go his way. He heard her voice before he saw her, quivering with righteous indignation.

"Mr. Meriwether! What on earth are you doing?" Jacquelyn demanded stridently. "What is the meaning of this?"

Gabriel stopped under the lintel to survey the scene. His nieces were all on their hands and knees, scrub brushes, mops and pails of soapy water scattered about them on the flagstones. Hyacinth was whining incoherently. The twins were fighting back tears, and Lily seemed to have swallowed some soap, because a bubble formed on her lips every time she opened her mouth to howl. Only Daisy seemed to be enjoying herself, splashing and leaning on the brush to make long, messy strokes across the floor.

Mr. Meriwether drew himself up to his full height and favored Jacquelyn with a sharp salute.

"One of the little angels got herself in a spot of trouble last night, did she not?" the old man said. "When one o' the crew makes a mistake, the whole crew faces discipline. Best way to keep it from happening again, mark my words."

"These are wellborn girls. Not your pirate crew," Jacquelyn argued. "No one gave you leave to impose your brand of punishment on them."

"Mr. Meriwether hasn't been my first mate for all these years for naught. His authority comes from mine," Gabriel said from behind her. "And you must admit my nieces are sadly in want of discipline."

When Jacquelyn rounded on him with a look of fury in her gray eyes, he wished he could unsay the words. All trace of the willing, pliable Lyn was gone. Mistress Wren was back with a vengeance.

"I will not have them treated like . . . like a press-gang," she said with ice in her tone.

"It's not so bad," Daisy said cheerfully. "Playing pirate is fun. Mr. Meriwether said we have to swab the decks because otherwise the planks will shrink and the ship'll be taking on water before we know it. Isn't that right, Meri?"

"Right you are, Miss Daisy," the old salt said with a grin. Then he sobered and looked askance at Gabriel. "I didn't wish to overstep ye, Cap'n, but ye weren't up and about yet and it's the code I was after keepin'. 'Die all, die merrily,' ye know."

"These are children, not buccaneers. And I'll not have them treated so," Jacquelyn said, a frown marring her brow. "Die all, die merrily—what's that supposed to mean?"

"It means we share all things. Plenty and want, reward and punishment," Gabriel explained. "If a crew member knows his actions will affect his mates, he'll think twice before he brings retribution down on all of them. It's a valid principle, and Meri is correct in applying it to the girls."

Jacquelyn stared at him as if he'd suddenly sprouted another head.

"Come, children," she said scooping Lily into her arms. "It's time for your Latin lessons. You've had enough pirate nonsense for one day."

"Belay that," Gabriel countermanded. "These are my nieces and I'll see to their education. Right now, improving their behavior is more important than conjugating verbs. Hyacinth, stand up, girl."

"Really, my lord—" Jacquelyn began as she set Lily down to gird herself for battle.

"That will be all, mistress," he said with an upraised hand. "Pray, do not interfere again."

Her mouth opened wordlessly, then clamped shut. But the set of her jaw spoke volumes.

Why was Jacquelyn fighting him? He hated giving her a dressing down in so public a fashion, but she wouldn't listen to him otherwise. Now she merely folded her arms across her chest and stepped back a pace. If he looked closely, he suspected he might find steam leaking from her ears. Gabriel turned back to his nieces.

"Hyacinth?"

Sniffling, the girl rose to her feet.

"Has Mr. Meriwether laid into you with the back of his hand?"

"No, Uncle." She blanched at the thought.

"Then Meri is more merciful than I, for you committed an error worthy of corporal punishment," he said.

Gabriel's father had always believed a warm bottom was the best insurance of future good behavior. Lord knows, Gabe had eaten his supper standing because he couldn't sit more often than not. From the corner of his eye, he saw Jacquelyn glaring daggers at him.

Didn't she want him to take more interest in his brother's girls? How better than to see to their safety by disciplining them now, before they could get themselves into more trouble than he could get them out of?

"Do you recollect your mistake of last evening?" he asked Hyacinth, softening his tone.

Her gaze darted to Jacquelyn and then, when no help seemed to be coming from that quarter, Hy's watering eyes shifted back to him. "Yes, sir. I'm not likely to forget."

"Good. See to it that the incident is never repeated," he said. Her chin quivered so, he didn't feel the need to lecture her further. It was much easier to deliver a tongue-lashing to a bosun's mate who grimly withstood the verbal blistering than dress down a slip of a girl who looked ready to dissolve into tears any moment. "And don't you think it were best if your sisters avoid the same mistake?"

"Yes, sir."

"And you too, Daisy." Gabriel turned his attention to her. "You willfully sneaked into the ball without permission, did you not?"

"Well, if you want to put it so baldly. Yes, Uncle, I suppose I did," Daisy said, her eyes wide with surprise at being included in the reprimand. "But if I hadn't—"

"Your helpfulness later does not change the fact that you disobeyed a direct order to begin with," Gabriel said, forcing himself to glare at her with sternness. Fear of him might save the girls from folly later. He was willing to be the false villain today to keep them from a real one tomorrow. "Both you and Hyacinth are responsible for making your little sisters share in your punishment."

The twins shot Daisy and Hyacinth accusatory glares.

Lily stuck her little tongue out at them and then dumped a pail of soapy water on the floor.

"Very well. I don't want this detail dismissed until every stone in the chamber sparkles," Gabriel said. "Carry on, Mr. Meriwether."

"Aye-aye, Cap'n." Meri saluted, then his tone went soft as mush as he knelt beside the littlest Drake. "Oh, now Miss Lily, don't take on so. When we're finished here, we'll hie ourselves to the kitchen to see if Mrs. Beadle has any more of them cherry pies."

Gabriel rubbed his hands together, satisfied the issue was summarily dealt with. "Now what must a man do in order to be served breakfast around here?"

"For a start, he might rise before noon," Jacquelyn observed tartly.

Was the day really so far gone? He'd slept far better than one burdened with his sins ought. No doubt the romp with Lyn was responsible, but she didn't appear nearly as rested. He was about to say as much when Mrs. Beadle's appearance in the doorway saved him from a comment he might later regret.

"Beggin' your pardon, my lord." Mrs. B. dipped in a bulky curtsey. "The Lady Harlowe has arrived. I took the liberty of escorting her to the solar to wait your pleasure."

"Lady Harlowe?" he asked, groaning inwardly. The woman could hardly help her unfortunate likeness to a fish, but her cold personality had left Gabriel just as flaccid. "Millicent Harlowe?"

"The very same, in all her glory," Jacquelyn said as she began to lead the way toward the solar. He followed like a lamb to the slaughter. "The opportunity to wed a viscount's daughter is not so lightly dismissed. You needn't act surprised. I told you there would be further interviews today with your prospective brides."

"And you had to start with Lady Harlowe?"

"A baron cannot afford to choose a bride merely with his eyes." She turned around to face him, hands on her hips.

"If it's the Drake lineage we're trying to further, it would certainly help if the lady's appearance didn't curdle milk."

"Her attractive dowry should be sufficient to make up for any other deficiencies," Jacquelyn said. "But fear not, my lord. Miss Elisheba Thatcher is scheduled to visit on the morrow. I suspect a pretty face is more to your liking."

He leaned into her, pinning her against the wall between his long arms. "You know very well what's to my liking."

She pressed herself against the stone at her back and wouldn't meet his gaze. "Unfortunately, we cannot demand the ladies line up to see how well they bed you before you make your selection."

"That's not what I meant," he said. "Lyn—"

"Please," she hissed. "Please do not call me by that name, my lord."

"I liked it better when you called me Gabriel."

She closed her eyes, a thin line of anguish appearing between her even brows.

"Are we to pretend it never happened?" He inhaled her fresh scent and narrowly resisted the urge to kiss her. "You're all I can think of."

She trembled.

He nuzzled her temple, brushing her smooth skin with his lips. Even though Lady Harlowe was waiting, he'd like nothing better than to raise Lyn's skirts and take her again right there in the hall.

Or better still, to carry her back up to his chamber. The rest of the day would be none too long for love play with the bewitching Lyn. His body cheered this line of thinking with an aching cock-stand. He was ready to scoop her into his arms, Devil take the hindermost, when Jacquelyn opened her eyes and looked up at him.

The ice in her gray gaze froze his rising ardor.

"Hyacinth is not the only one who was guilty of an error last night. You and I committed a grievous one. An error that could hurt all of Dragon Caern. One that I shall take pains to see we do not repeat." She ducked under his arm and escaped down the hall toward the solar.

"You were free enough with punishment for the girls, my lord. Time to do your penance with Lady Harlowe. After all," she said over her shoulder, "die all, die merrily."

Chapter Nineteen

Jacquelyn flopped over onto her belly and pounded her pillow with her fist. She'd heard the chapel bell chime midnight hours ago and still sleep eluded her. Resting her cheek on the freshly subdued eiderdown, she forced her eyes closed and tried not to think.

Nothing would banish Gabriel Drake's form and face from her mind.

Bloody pirate, she thought crossly. He'd not only stolen her maidenhead, he'd stolen her ability to sleep as well.

No, that was not quite fair. She'd willingly surrendered her virginity to him. Then her innocence had fled completely in their wild night of passion. If she were brutally honest, she admitted she hadn't been forced into any of it. In fact, she'd all but seduced *him* the second time.

But he rose each morning looking as if he'd slept the sleep of the just, while she grew more haggard by the day. Truly, there was no justice in the world.

Perhaps it was the nightly round of drinking Gabriel and Mr. Meriwether still indulged in that allowed him to rest. She often heard them, singing their heathen pirate songs and laughing at ribald jokes. Once she'd crept out onto the landing and listened, shocked to her curled toes at some of the lyrics, but as soon as she heard his booted tread on the stairs, she'd scurried back to the safety of her chamber.

Jacquelyn had done a bit of rearranging in there to guard against future trysts. She'd had Timothy move her heavy armoire so it was in front of where the secret panel opened into the passageway. She thought she'd heard Gabriel's muffled curse behind the wall one night as he tried in vain to force the door open.

But only once.

Bother the man. She rolled over onto her back, tugging at her nightshift. The blasted thing kept riding up to bunch at her waist, leaving her legs and crotch to brush against the bed linens. Her body started its nightly mutinous complaint, the dull ache that kept her from sleep. She rubbed herself with the heel of her hand before she even realized she was doing it. Shocked, she pulled her hand away.

No, I will not turn into a spineless wanton.

She threw back the coverlet and swung her legs out of bed. Jacquelyn began pacing.

A league or two around the room should do the trick.

She wondered afresh if this was how her mother became a courtesan. Had there been a man who so ignited a fire in her, Isabella had been powerless to contain it?

"But I am not my mother," she mumbled as she shrugged on a robe over her nightshift. *Good Lord! Now he has me talking to myself!*

Who could say what other lows the man might reduce her to?

Isabella always maintained that her life as a woman of pleasure was a merry one, filled with endless parties and frivolity and song. But all Jacquelyn knew was that once her mother's protector had abandoned her, Jacquelyn was summarily evicted from her posh school and forced to make her own way in the world. Her mother's lover provided a pension for Isabella, but it wasn't sufficient to keep a "bird of paradise" in the style to which she was accustomed *and* support her grown daughter.

Mother has always been weak, Jacquelyn decided with a grim nod. Just as firmly, she decided she would not be. She wouldn't put her needs above the girls' futures.

Her body might clamor for more of Gabriel Drake, but she would not jeopardize the estate for the sake of her own pleasure.

Now if she could only be certain her will was stronger than her body.

She had to see Gabriel suitably wed. Anything that distracted him from that purpose had to be discarded.

Even if it was her.

A knock at her door stopped her midstride. She lit the candle at her bedside and padded to the door.

"Who is it?"

"Me."

Gabriel—confound the man—Drake. She sighed. Had she somehow summoned him with all her muttering and pacing? Perhaps the man was like a stallion that could catch wind of the mare in heat one paddock over.

She threw the bolt and opened the door only enough to glare at him through the narrow slit.

"What are you doing here?" she hissed through the crack. "Someone may see you."

"Then you'd better let me in quickly before they do."

Blast the man, he made sense. Propriety would not be served by engaging in a whispered argument in public, so she stepped back and let the door fall open.

He entered without a sound, but Jacquelyn regretted allowing him in already. He seemed to fill the room, not just with his muscular frame, but with his unique masculine scent as well—a fresh mix of clean male skin with the barest hint of a sea breeze. Jacquelyn threw the bolt behind him, hardly daring to breathe.

"Thank you for letting me in," he said softly. "You didn't have to, you know. It's not as if I'd force you."

No need, since her body was already his willing ally. Wasn't this how Lucifer wormed his way into the garden? With silver-tongued persuasion and a reasonable tone?

"What do you want?" she asked, then wished she'd bitten her tongue in two. The bold look of desire on his face was answer without need of words. She cinched the sash at her waist and folded her arms across her chest.

She willed him to see the GO AWAY stamped on her face. Surely there was no way the man could know how he made her insides caper about.

"You're not sleeping," he said.

"How can I when you come banging at my door in the dead of night?"

"Even before that." He looked around the room and nodded grimly when he saw she had strategically moved the armoire. "Every day, you look less like yourself."

She drew herself up to her full height, which admittedly wasn't much. "My apologies if my appearance distresses you, my lord."

"I didn't mean it like that," he said. "I've been worried about you."

Not too worried to stop dancing attendance on the women who came to tea and hoped to stay as his wife. There had been a veritable parade of eligible ladies in and out of the solar each day since the night of the ball.

Jacquelyn could discern no favorite among them yet. Gabriel was equally polite and charming to them all, even the unfortunate Lady Harlowe, but he did take Elisheba Thatcher riding when she asked to see more of the estate.

Grasping little witch, Jacquelyn almost blurted out before she caught herself. She shoved the unworthy thought aside.

"I trust my service to this estate by day has been sufficient," she said icily. "My nocturnal habits are none of your affair."

"I suspect they are precisely my affair. *Our* affair."

He leaned on one of the stout bedposts and looked askance at her.

She couldn't deny it. Her involvement with this pirate robbed her of all peace. He didn't try to force himself on her, but she feared he wouldn't have to. At the rumbling sound of his voice, something dark flared to life in her belly.

"Why are you . . . what brings you to . . ." She stopped. There was no way to ask a question to which she already knew the answer.

He was here for her.

She swallowed hard. Blood roared in her ears. He wasn't married yet, not even betrothed. If she bedded him again, no one would suffer betrayal. It wasn't as if she were his light-o'-love. In fact, no words of promise had passed between them, but just looking at him, her body grew tender and achy in all her secret places.

Didn't she deserve some happiness, even if it was only temporary? Men did it all the time, separating the needs of their body from other demands on them without a second thought. Why couldn't a woman take pleasure where she pleased? Who would be hurt if she took her ease with this completely willing man?

She would, she realized.

When it ended—and it must end, there was no question about that, for Jacquelyn would not defraud the future mistress of Dragon Caern—she would be the one bereft.

"My lord—"

"Gabriel," he corrected softly as he moved to shorten the distance between them.

"Gabriel." His name passed her lips fervent as a whispered prayer.

He advanced on her steadily, but she seemed to have misplaced the will to move. When his hands found her waist and tugged her close, she went without protest. Was there anything finer than the broad hard planes of his body and his even harder cock pressed tight against her?

Self-respect, a small voice said in the back of her mind. It was hard to hear over the throb in her groin. She felt herself softening, melting like a spring snow. Couldn't she just bed him and not let her heart get in the way?

When he bent to take her lips, she turned her head. It pained her to do so. "Please," she whispered, forcing the word out. "I . . . I can't."

"You're angry with me over the way I've let Meri discipline and train my nieces," he guessed.

"No, it's not that." She tried to pull away, but he wouldn't lessen his grip. "You were right. They did need a firmer hand. The girls are much better behaved and happier since Mr. Meriwether put them to useful occupation for part of the day."

"Then what is it?" He looked down at her with something like hurt in his dark eyes. "You don't want me?"

"Lord, no, that's not it." She sagged against him, every ounce of her body screaming at her. "Believe me when I tell you I do want you."

It wouldn't take much for her to throw herself on the bed, spread her thighs and beg him to take her. In fact, if she let herself remember any more of the way his mouth claimed her sensitive flesh, she'd be pulling him down with her.

Instead, she pushed against his shoulders and, thank heaven, he released her.

"I just . . . can't," she said.

Please God, may he not demand any more. She could give no more explanation and she didn't think she could stand up to a determined seduction.

He turned from her and stood still. Mastering himself, she realized. The thought of his need sent a fresh answering ache pounding between her legs. When he faced her again, she read resignation on his features.

"Well, then," he said. "I doubt sleep will come for either of us soon."

She nodded in agreement.

"Then we need action," he said as he crossed to the armoire and shoved it away from the secret passage. The huge piece grated over the floor.

"No, no, someone will hear you," she said.

"And they'll think Mistress Wren is rearranging her furniture when she ought to be sleeping." His grin was contagious. "But in fact, you'll be exploring the keep with me. We went up last time. This time, I propose we take the passages down. Are you game, Lyn?"

He pried open the hidden doorway.

She looked back at the rumpled linens in her bed. If she lay down, she'd only be bunching them further. Besides, he looked so hopeful, she didn't have the heart to tell him no again. "I suppose you're right. Very well. I'll come."

Maybe a vigorous tramp up and down the keep through the serpentine passages would settle the twitch between her legs. She picked up her candlestick and followed him through the hole in the wall.

Chapter Twenty

Light from her candle danced along the uneven outer walls. As she and Gabriel descended, the passageway widened so that in some places, they were able to walk side by side.

"That opening leads to the library," Gabriel said when they passed one of the secret doors. He raised his candle to show her the faint outline in the wall. "Rupert and I managed to escape our tutor more than once this way."

"Do you know where all the doorways lead?"

"No, not even when I was a child," he said. "There are so many doors, Rupert and I didn't have time to find them all. Besides, it's not as if we could explore them openly. Once we knew of their existence, we searched each room for signs of an opening—a scuff on the floor here, a nick on the wainscoting there—but we had to be cautious. If anyone else found out about them, the game would have been up. It was a great secret between my brother and me."

She heard both the smile and the sorrow in his voice.

"You must have been good friends as well as brothers," she said, wondering for the first time what her life would have been like if she'd had a sibling. Of course, she'd never wish Isabella on anyone else. La Belle Wren wasn't cut out to be anyone's mother.

Passing the library meant they'd reached a less-inhabited part of the Caern. They'd traveled far enough downward, she doubted any of the chambers they passed were occupied. It was safe to speak normally.

"It must have been nice, having a brother."

"It was. Sometimes we fought like tigers, but most of the time Rupert was a fine partner in crime," Gabriel said. "He was the elder, of course, but I usually ended up leading whenever there was skullduggery afoot."

"You weren't joking when you said the pirate was always there inside you waiting to come out," she said with a laugh.

He stopped and put a hand on her shoulder to make her turn to look at him.

"The pirate is still here, Lyn." His dark eyes were hooded. "You've dressed me as a lord and presented me to the world as a gentleman. I'll play the part since you seem to want it, but beneath the velvet frock coat and Brussels lace, you of all people know what I really am."

Her mouth went dry. She knew him all right. Deeply. Intimately. The man was an admitted scoundrel.

And still she wanted him. His body called to hers in the hot, silent language of lovers. It was all she could do not to answer.

She had to turn the conversation to safer ground.

"I can well believe you led your brother into trouble, then." She stepped away from him and continued down the corridor.

"Aye, though Rupert usually managed to squeak through our adventures without taint, while I got caught."

"You sound like Daisy," she said with a grin. "That child's main complaint is that she gets blamed for everything she does."

Gabriel chuckled. "No wonder she's my favorite."

He stopped and put a shoulder to a spot in the wall where a faint indentation made a hidden opening likely. He shoved with a grunt. The secret door grated against the stone floor and stopped after only giving a quarter inch.

"There are some doors we couldn't open at all, even when I was a boy," he said. "You're not the first to shove a heavy piece of furniture across the threshold, you know. But some of it is that the castle is so deucedly old and determined to keep its secrets. The Caern has settled and the doorways don't line up plumb any longer."

The air grew colder as they continued to descend. Moisture condensed on the walls.

"How far down do you think we are?" Jacquelyn asked. Even though she spoke softly, her voice seemed to echo from the dark ahead of them.

"Don't know. Rupert got cold feet some turns back and wouldn't ever come this far down with me. None of this looks familiar."

"That's small comfort."

"Come now, where's your sense of adventure?" He spied a pitch-daubed torch wedged into the wall and held his candle to it. The flame sputtered then flared, lighting much further down the passageway. A whole string of torches lined the corridor, waiting to be lit. Gabriel strode to the next one and fired it. The reek of burning tar tainted the damp, musty air. It may have been in the distant past, but this corridor had once seen heavy use. The rock face around the torch was grimy with soot.

"I think we should turn back," Jacquelyn said.

"Don't tell me the intrepid Mistress Wren is afraid. If I can pilot a ship to the Caribbean and back, I think I ought to be able to find your chamber again." Then he turned back to face her and waggled his brows. "Unless you have something in mind that would lure me to return to your bed sooner?"

A warm bed sounded like heaven, but she wasn't up to facing one with him in it. Not without losing her resolve. A cold tramp through a dark tunnel would be better for controlling the flutter in her loins.

"Lead on, my lord," she said as she blew out her candle and shoved her hands into her sleeves to warm them.

"Gabriel," he corrected. "We can't have an exploration

together if you insist on calling me by title. Here, let me warm your hands. They're cold as ice."

He gathered them between his and lowered his lips to blow his warm breath on them. Her fingertips tingled and a shiver that had nothing to do with being cold raced up her arm.

"Better?"

"Yes, much." She tugged her hands away, not trusting herself to let him touch her so.

"Your lips are blue," he said with a frown. He shrugged out of his shirt and draped it over her shoulders. "Here, put this on."

"But then you'll be cold."

"I'll make do," he assured her.

"But this is most unseemly."

"Gallivanting about the castle at midnight is unseemly enough. My being shirtless won't make matters worse. I only want to warm you. It's not often I play the gentleman in earnest, Lyn," he said. "Perhaps you'd better let me."

With her teeth threatening to chatter, she couldn't bring herself to protest too much. The unbleached lawn fabric still retained his body heat.

And his undeniably male scent.

And now she was treated to the sight of his muscular chest and bare arms. His brown nipples puckered, but his skin remained unmarred by gooseflesh.

"Here let me help you," he offered. He reached over and fastened the buttons that ran down her chest. He fingered the one that nestled in the hollow between her breasts.

Her nipples tingled at the nearness of his fingers, but he kept his promise to behave as a gentleman ought. Once the last button was done up, he caught up her hand and held it tightly.

"Don't want to get separated down here," he explained as he led her on. "Suppose the torches went out."

"Do you think it likely?"

"No, but it's the best excuse I can think of to keep holding your hand."

His warm hand was a comfort and his boyish admission struck her as innocent enough. She nodded and his eyes lit with triumph.

"Onward then, me hearty," he said in a rough imitation of Mr. Meriwether. "There be treasure waiting for them what is not afeard to chance the journey."

When he screwed his face into an approximation of Meri's evil-eyed squint, she laughed. "Treasure, my lord? Then by all means, let's push on."

They crept down the curving passageway, fingers entwined. Jacquelyn was mindful of her footing when the floor became uneven. Gabriel stopped long enough to light each torch. Finally they came to a set of winding steps that led downward into the dark. Gabriel pulled the last torch from its sconce and swiped it through the air. A pit yawned before them with no discernable bottom and only a curving flight of narrow stairs with no railings edging the open space.

"Do you smell that?" Gabriel asked.

The torch's flame wavered for an instant and the air freshened with a sharp salt tang.

"The sea?" Jacquelyn asked. The castle perched on a rocky point, but the surf was a dizzying fall below it. Had they really traveled so far beneath the weathered stone of the Caern?

"Put your hand on my shoulder," he ordered. "Keep to the right."

She pressed a palm to his shoulder blade, marveling at the warmth of his smooth, bare skin. With Gabriel's torch leading the way, they descended carefully. Moisture pooled in the slight indentations on the stone steps, mute testimony to thousands of pairs of feet wearing against the rock in the dim past. A low rumble, like an advancing thunderstorm, reverberated through the chamber.

Jacquelyn lost her footing on the slick steps and Gabriel caught her before she fell. He pulled her to his chest.

"You're trembling," he said.

"I'm still cold." She was afraid as well. The torchlight didn't shine far enough to reveal the black bottom of the pit. If she'd tumbled off the slick steps, she might be falling yet.

As she was now falling into the black depths of his eyes.

She shook herself and pulled back from him. "I fear I'm not much help on a treasure hunt."

"Bah! That was just a figure of speech," Gabriel admitted. "Uncle Eustace used to fill us boys' heads with tales of a treasure hidden in Dragon Caern, but it was all smoke and oakum." He tugged her closer. "You're the only treasure in this old castle."

He leaned toward her, but she turned her head. She was painfully aware of his member, thick and hard against her thigh. "Might someone else have heard the rumors of treasure?"

"It's possible," Gabriel said ignoring her rebuff. "I've been puzzling over why you were sent the message that I needed to be waylaid before I could make it home. Perhaps the rumor of a treasure is why someone wanted to make sure there are no more Drakes. Devil of a thing, to be cut down for a treasure that doesn't exist."

"But if someone believes it does, it makes sense to want the Drake barony extinct," she finished his thought for him. Her shoulders slumped. "It is imperative that you marry. Soon."

He raked a hand through his hair, his mouth set in a determined grimace. She knew her duty, and by heaven, she'd see him wed as soon as possible. But the way his bare skin glowed in the torchlight, all Jacquelyn could think was how glorious it would be to have this man in her bed.

And if she could only have him for a little while, did it make sense to waste one moment of it?

Chapter Twenty-one

"You're chilled to the bone. We'd best find your bed." His eyes gleamed as he looked at her.

Did everything she thought show so plainly on her face? If so, the sooner she was out of his sight altogether, the better for both of them. She might want to bed him, but all the reasons not to have him still held good.

"Aye, a warm bed sounds lovely right now." Jacquelyn rubbed her arms against the chill, purposely trying to misunderstand him. Better to let him think she pined for her coverlet than for his hot body between her bed linens. Besides, she was certain her nose must be blue and she hadn't been able to feel her feet since they'd started down the curving steps. She turned and began the climb back up. "I am freezing."

He followed after her as if she'd issued an invitation.

"I can help with that," he said folding his arms around her, pressing her spine to his chest.

His bare skin was warm, almost feverish. She turned in his arms to face him and pushed her palms against him both to draw out his heat and to separate from him by a finger's width. She didn't think she could bear the hard length of his body against hers for long.

He shivered involuntarily. "Your fingers are like icicles."

"I'm sorry." She tried to draw back further, but he held her firm.

"No need. You'll warm up soon enough." He cupped her hands in his again and brought them to his lips to send his warm breath over them.

A tingle of desire washed over her.

"You're more chilled than I thought," he said. "This may call for drastic measures. Come. We need to get you back into your bed."

She nodded and let him lead her back up the winding stairs.

"No doubt the fire in my chamber is out by now," she said softly. "My bed will be cold as a tomb."

"There's a remedy for that."

"Not one we should avail ourselves of."

"You disappoint me, mistress," he said as he swiped away a draping cobweb. "You are determined to think the worst of me. My sole aim is your comfort. I didn't ask anything improper of you. I merely said I could mend the problem of a cold bed. Any untoward ideas in this exchange are coming from you, not me."

She swallowed her surprise. Did he not want her after all?

"So this is the thanks I get after I handed over my shirt and refrained from any ungentlemanly advances this night," he said as he slogged up the steps. "Keep your hand on my shoulder so we don't become separated."

She tried to reach his shoulder, but between his height and going up the stairs, her palm kept slipping down to the broad expanse of his ribs.

"I'll swear your hands are getting colder," he said. "Perhaps you'd like to reach around and slip them into my pockets."

"You only want my hand close to your—" she stopped herself.

"Mistress! The entirely naughty direction of your thoughts amazes me."

"Do you deny that you want my hand on your . . . gentlemanly parts?" she said in frustration.

"No, I'll not deny it," he said with a chuckle. "But it still amazes me that your thoughts are running in tandem with mine."

She sighed in exasperation.

"Kindly lead me back to my chamber and I'll deal with a cold bed on my own. This subject is closed."

They climbed in silence. Then they came to the long corridor of rock where they'd left torches still burning. Gabriel rubbed each one out as they passed, letting the pathway behind them fall into darkness.

"The wind off water can be especially bitter. Seafaring folk have long had methods for dealing with the cold," he said, technically not ignoring her request to end the discussion, but coming damnably close to it. They came to the last torch sconce, retrieved their candles, lit them and continued their upward climb. "Meri told me once of the way the old Vikings used to keep warm on a long sea voyage."

"How was that?" she asked, despite herself. They were whispering now in the narrow space and hearing an occasional cough or snore from the far side of the wall.

"Body heat. At night, the Vikings climbed into two-man sleeping sacks."

"Two-*man*?"

"Only for warmth," he explained. "They generally left their womenfolk behind when they went off on raids and the old sea wolves didn't hold much with buggery."

"So is that what pirates do as well?"

"No, but then the Caribbee is much balmier than the northern seas. Here we are."

He pushed open the secret door into her chamber. The return trip took less time than she'd expected. Strangely bereft that their adventure was at an end, she stepped back into her familiar room. The full moon was framed in her window, washing the chamber in shades of gray. As she foretold, the fire in the grate was dead ash.

"Thank you for seeing me back," she said. "Good night."

"Aren't you forgetting something?"

"What?"

"My shirt." His smile glinted silver in the soft light.

"Oh! Yes, of course."

"If your fingers are too cold and stiff, I'll be happy to do the unbuttoning for you," he offered. "Anything for a lady, you know."

"Somehow, I don't think being unbuttoned by you will be conducive to my remaining a lady." Her fingers flew down the front of the shirt, tugging at the horn toggles lest he step in to help. She peeled the shirt off and held it out to him at arm's length. "Thank you."

"And is that what you really want, Lyn?"

She frowned quizzically at him, rubbing her arms with her palms for warmth.

"To remain a lady?" he asked.

"Of course," she said. "Just because we've tumbled into bed together in the past, there's no need to repeat the error."

"It didn't seem an error to me," he said his tone growing ragged. "Mayhap not a seemly pastime for a gentleman and a lady, but for a man and a woman, I can't imagine a better occupation."

"I assure you I do not want to bed you," she said, trying to remember whether Father Eustace had named lying as one of the seven deadly sins.

"Well, then you won't mind putting that notion to the test. Lie down with me."

"What?"

"You're still shivering. Your bed is cold, and I'm throwing off heat like a galley fire. Dragon Caern will certainly suffer if you catch your death of cold," he said. "Let us climb beneath your covers long enough to put the old Vikings' example to good use. As shipmates, as friends, we'll share my body heat."

"That's prepost—"

He covered her mouth with his hand. "Then once you're

warm, I'll rise and leave you, if that's still your wish. I give you my word."

"Your word as a pirate?" she scoffed.

Gabriel shook his head. "My word as a gentleman."

"All right," she said warily. "But only until the bed is warm."

His wide grin did not give her comfort. Neither did the fact that he began to unfasten the drop front of his breeches.

"What are you doing?"

"Undressing. It's a well-established scientific fact that bare bodies warm together faster than clothed ones."

"Did Mr. Meriwether tell you that, too?"

His sensual smile was evil incarnate. "No, experience taught me that."

A fizz of irritation sizzled through her. Jacquelyn knew the man was no monk, but the thought of him in bed with another woman made her feel prickly all over. She supposed she should thank him. His artless comment was what she needed to stiffen her spine enough to withstand whatever seduction he might be planning.

And he was no doubt planning one.

No matter. She would use his heat and then toss the lout out of bed on his ear. She pulled back the coverlet and began to climb in.

"If you're still clothed this will take longer," he warned.

"Do you believe me simple?"

"No, I believe you cold." He lowered his breeches, but she forced her gaze to remain riveted to his dark eyes. "Trust me, Lyn. I only want to warm you."

She glanced southward on his big frame. His body told a different tale.

"If you want me gone sooner, you need to strip, too." Gabriel pushed past her and climbed onto the fluffy feather tick. He settled on his side, propping his head on his hand.

It would serve him right, she reasoned. If she was able to lie naked beside him and still order him away, it would settle once and for all that their misbegotten entanglement—she wouldn't use a more tender description, even to herself—was irrevocably at an end.

"Very well," she said. "Turn your face to the far wall."

"Now where's the fun in that? It's not as if I haven't already seen—"

"Would you like to leave right n-now?" The chill caused her to stammer.

With an incoherent grumble under his breath, he rolled over, making the whole bed shake. She swept the room with a quick assessing glance to make sure there were no more strategically placed looking glasses as she toed off her slippers. Satisfied he couldn't see her this time, she peeled out of her robe and nightshift and climbed under the coverlet with him.

She settled into the mattress, the sheets cool and smooth on her bare skin. Gabriel didn't move.

"I'm here," she said in a small voice.

"Believe me, I know."

Jacquelyn trembled, whether from cold or something darker she wasn't sure. He still didn't move.

"How will this warm me?" she finally asked.

"Well, we can let my body heat make its way slowly over to your side of the bed," he said without the twitch of a single muscle. "Of course, that will probably take the rest of the night. . . ."

"What's the other option?" A shiver raced through her.

He rolled over and raised himself on one elbow. "Or you can allow me to warm you in a more active manner."

"And when I tell you to stop?"

"I stop."

"And when I'm thoroughly warm?"

"I will quit your sheets upon your command, mistress."

"Very well," she said.

"Uh-uh." He made a soft negative sound. "You haven't said please."

"What?"

"Aren't you always telling me that politeness is a thing to be cultivated? Lord knows you've corrected my manners often enough." He cocked an eyebrow at her. "Ask me nicely."

"I will do no such thing."

"Then I wish you joy of your exceedingly cold bed," he said as he threw the coverlet back.

The fresh wave of night air sent her into a spasm of shivering. "Oh, all right. Please."

He pulled the bed linens back up over them and leaned on his elbow again. "Please, Gabriel," he prompted.

She drew her lips together in a tight line.

He lifted the linens and started to ease out of the bed once more.

"Please . . . Gabriel," she said softly.

A smile spread across his face. "That is my every intention, Lyn. I shall not rest until you are . . . pleased."

Chapter Twenty-two

Jacquelyn had the sinking feeling she'd just made a deal with the devil.

Gabriel pulled her close, tucking one arm under her neck and draping the other across her waist. He hooked a leg over hers, the small hairs on his legs tickling her in a pleasant way. Every inch of his skin was warm, but his enraged cock at her hip was like a live coal encased in smooth, hard, male flesh. Her shivering stopped as his warmth enveloped her.

"Better?" he asked.

She nodded, not trusting her voice.

"Of course, for a deep chill friction is best." He rocked his hips in a slow knock against hers as his leg moved up and down. His splay-fingered hand wandered over her belly in a languid circle.

Against her will, she shuddered with desire.

"Now if friction doesn't work, more intense measures are warranted," he said before he disappeared beneath her bed linens.

"What are doing?"

"Warming you," he said. "Lie still, Lyn."

He didn't touch her, but his breath slid over her breasts, hot and moist. Her nipples tightened and she fisted the bed linens, fighting against the urge to arch them into his mouth.

Lie still, the man said, she reminded herself. She could do this. She could accept his heat without succumbing to his wiles. It was merely an exercise of her will over her wayward body.

She squeezed her eyes shut, trying to feel nothing but the blessed warmth of his exhalation.

The linens shifted around her as he moved down her body. His breath slid over her ribs and hovered near her navel. His open mouth had to be mere finger widths away and yet he never grazed her prickling skin once. Her entire body thrummed like a plucked string, but—drat the man!— he wouldn't pick up the bow and play the whole tune.

It was positively maddening.

The short curly hairs over her sex swayed in his hot breeze and she shifted, opening to him almost without conscious thought.

Almost.

The ache between her thighs was back with a vengeance. Pounding, relentless, the throb in her womb demanded surrender.

With supreme effort, she pulled her legs together and crossed her ankles.

A muffled snort came from under the linens.

"Something vexes you?" she asked.

"Only you, Lyn," his voice rumbled up to her. "Only you."

Undeterred, he continued his trek downward. He spread the warmth of his breath over her tightly clamped thighs and lingered at her kneecaps.

His heat swirled around her, his essence engulfing her.

"You know, only last week Father Eustace was regaling me with a bit of academe I thought I'd never have use for," he said, his voice ragged.

"What's that?" she whispered.

"He says the ancient words for breath and spirit are virtually the same. Maybe that's because our breath comes from deep inside us. Sharing it is like giving life." Gabriel chuckled. "Imagine he didn't have this sort of sharing in mind."

As Gabriel poured out his spirit on her, her spirit struggled to answer him.

Along with her thoroughly roused body, which she fought with every ounce of her battered will.

Because her feet were so cold, he rubbed them with his hands as well as caressing them with his breath. Life roared painfully back into them, then for a blessedly long while, her feet basked in the tender ministrations of his hands. He massaged the balls of her feet and rolled her toes between his fingers one by one. He caressed the delicate bones of her ankles. Gently, he uncrossed them and spread her legs wide.

She was too blissfully relaxed to care.

When he took her toe into his mouth and sucked, a streak of desire shot up her leg to quiver in her groin.

Her breath caught in a gasp.

And he heard it.

Pressing his advantage, he moved between her splayed legs. He trailed his mouth up along the inside of her leg, pausing to dally with the crease behind her knee. Jacquelyn knew she ought to protest, but for the life of her, she couldn't bear to stop the shivers of ecstasy that replaced her shivers of cold.

His warm breath was on her crotch now, her secret folds moist and hungry for him. He nuzzled her with his nose and lips, softly, tentatively.

Then he devoured her.

Had it been possible, she'd have died of pure, white-hot pleasure.

She moaned. She writhed. She twisted her fingers in his hair and whispered incoherent encouragement to him.

The world was bunched in a tight fist and threatened to shatter at any moment.

Gabriel moved up her body, leaving her throbbing mound. She arched herself against him, pressing a wet trail down his chest and flat belly. His mouth was at her breasts, paying skillful homage to her aching nipples.

Just the tip of him teased her wet folds.

All thought of restraint fled. Need crowded reason to a dark corner of her mind and Jacquelyn eased herself down, trying to impale herself on his hard shaft.

His head popped from under the linens and the full length of his body covered hers. A mere inch of him pressed through her swollen vulva and stopped. Frustration tore at her throat, but she resisted the urge to squirm under him as he gazed down at her.

"I believe I've warmed you thoroughly," he said. "Shall I take my leave?"

"Do you think you can?" she asked incredulously.

"No," he said with a wicked smile as he slid his full length into her.

He held perfectly still and she reveled in the sweet sensation of fullness. Jacquelyn groaned and draped her arms over his shoulders. She tipped her chin up and offered him her lips.

He took them.

And took them. The joining of their mouths was less a kiss and more a conquest. She put up only the slightest of defenses, which he battered away with heart-stopping sweetness. Then she began a campaign of her own, teasing him with her tongue and stealing the breath from his lungs.

Then his hips began to move.

She arched into each thrust, raising her hips to meet him. Tension clenched her gut. Just as she neared a point of collapse, he held her tightly and rolled so that she was on top of him.

"Sit up straight," he urged.

She did, the blood coursing through her body rendering her suddenly oblivious to the room's chill. One of his hands teased her breasts. The other found the exquisite little point of pleasure between her folds and played a lover's game with that quivering bit of flesh. Jacquelyn threw her head back and growled with pleasure, astounded at the sounds coming from her own throat, but powerless to stop them.

Then Gabriel grasped her hips and pressed her down hard on his groin. His body stiffened and shuddered. She felt him pulse like a fountain inside her and she answered his release with her own shattering completion.

Body convulsing in waves of pleasure, she collapsed onto his chest. His heart pounded beneath her ear like a battering ram slamming against a castle's stout oak doors.

That's it exactly, she thought drowsily.

He was driving himself into her heart through her body. And she'd just proven she was powerless to stop him.

Strangely enough, Mistress Wren didn't give a tinker's damn.

Oh, she was vaguely sure she'd care most vehemently later, but for now, she'd sooner have lopped off her right hand than sever the sweet connection of their flesh and the warmth of his breath on her crown.

Her breathing grew slow and even. Gabriel felt the last knot of tension slip from her as her hand went slack on his shoulder. Lyn was as boneless as a cat lying on his chest.

A beautiful, naked cat.

Gradually, his erection settled and he slipped from her moist cleft. He sighed. For a few blinding moments, they shared one heartbeat, one breath. No longer. They were separate beings once again.

This woman was the closest to heaven a pirate like him was ever likely to come. Who knew when, or if, he'd ever breach her defenses again?

One of the muscles in his calves spasmed in a cramp, but he didn't want to move for fear of waking her. He pointed and flexed his foot to work it out.

He inhaled her sweet, well-satisfied, womanly scent.

There were other things he needed to work out as well. Like how in hell he'd be able to marry another when Jacquelyn was all he craved.

He chanced a kiss on her tousled crown and was pleased when the rhythm of her breathing didn't change.

The future was a fog. Whenever he'd run up against a moist gray curtain while he captained his pirate corsair, he'd felt his way through the low-lying cloud. He'd sounded the depth at regular intervals, trimmed his canvas and run silent, hoping for a break in the miasma.

Somehow, there was a way through this mist that would keep Jacquelyn by his side.

He'd just have to find it.

Chapter Twenty-three

A ray of sunlight shafted through the window and teased Jacquelyn's eyes open. Her first conscious thought was how wonderful her bed felt this fine morning, all toasty and comfortable with the linens and coverlet bunched perfectly. Her second thought was how splendid a thing it was to wake beside a gloriously naked man.

She sat bolt upright.

"What are you still doing here?"

Gabriel stretched his limbs and yawned hugely. "Sleeping. Trying to, at any rate." He laced his fingers behind his head and cast her a lopsided grin.

Their lovemaking rushed back into her with a brush of remembered passion. A low drumbeat in her belly thumped once or twice.

"Well, you can't stay here," she said, frustrated that she must force him from her bed. "You must be gone, and quickly."

"Really, Lyn, you need to stop ordering me about." He made a *tsk* of disapproval while giving her a mock-stern look. "Did I miss something or am I no longer Lord of Dragon Caern?"

"You are yet lord." She rolled her eyes at him. "But that doesn't give you leave to sleep in my bed."

"No, seems to me last night *you* gave me leave to sleep in your bed." He ran his fingers up her arm and past her shoulder to slide his hand around the nape of her neck. "Along with certain other liberties."

"Gabriel, please . . ."

His smile grew more wicked by the moment. "Those are

the magic words, Lyn." He pulled her down and kissed her thoroughly.

Gasping, she tore her mouth from his, her fingers splayed on his bare chest. His smooth skin felt so good beneath her palms, but she forced herself not to dwell on it.

"What if someone goes to your chamber and finds you missing?"

"They'll think I'm someplace else?" he suggested unhelpfully.

"No, they'll start looking for you from one end of Dragon Caern to the other," she said, "and it won't do for us to be found naked in my chamber."

"The secret passageway is still open. How about if we're found naked in *my* chamber?"

She swatted his shoulder. "Why do you insist on making things so difficult?"

"Oh, Lyn, give it a rest. This early in the morning, I'll wager none are about but Mrs. Beadle, who's more interested in making my breakfast than where I make my bed." He drew her beside him in a way that brooked no refusal. "Don't spoil a perfectly lovely interlude by borrowing trouble. Can we not enjoy a moment's peace?"

With her body flush against his, peace was not the first thing that leaped to her mind. But she laid her head in the crook of his shoulder and let his warm masculine scent wash over her. She didn't have the will to fight him any longer. In fact, last night had proven she had very little will at all.

Come disaster, come calamity, come a rabble at the door bearing certain ruin, she wouldn't leave this man's side.

He stroked her spine and let his fingers draw lazy circles around the dimples above her buttocks. A tingle of arousal fizzed through her, but she was satisfied for the moment just to let him hold her.

Last night's passion was still fresh in her senses. Her whole body ached in a loose-jointed way, but it was a pleasant ache. It was as though her every knot had been untied, every kink pressed smooth. She was content as she had never been in her whole life.

"I've been thinking," Gabriel said as his hand crept around to cup one of her breasts.

It didn't take a gypsy fortune-teller to divine the direction of his thoughts, but she felt bound to ask, "What about?"

"That treasure," Gabriel said, absently thrumming her nipple with his thumb. "If it did exist, seems to me there'd be a way to turn it to our advantage."

"Well, of course," she said, wishing if he were going to make love to her he'd get on with it. After last night, she didn't know how much teasing her body could bear before she was reduced to pleading. "We could use the treasure to buy new livestock and help your tenants improve their houses. There wouldn't be old thatch on any roof on your whole estate by the time we'd finished."

"That's not exactly—"

Thinking of the possibilities presented by the mythical dragon's hoard of gold, Jacquelyn pushed awareness of her growing arousal aside. "We could build a school, a new infirmary. Oh, there are any number of things that treasure could do."

"I meant something more personal." Gabriel slid a finger under her chin and tipped her face up to his. "We both know I must marry. You are the one I want, Lyn."

He wanted her! It wasn't exactly a declaration of undying love, but her heart still did a jig against her ribs. Then reality lashed her and her brows knit together. The treasure was a fantasy. He'd said so himself. There was no way for him to take her to wife.

"You must marry a well-moneyed lady. I am the bastard

girl-child of a courtesan." She rolled over to give him her back. "Besides, even if there was a treasure to be found, no amount of money would render my birth noble."

"I don't see why the circumstances of your birth matters," he said, raising himself on one elbow and running his other hand from her shoulder down past her waist. He edged closer to her, leaving a proprietary palm on her hip.

"Believe me, it does," she said. "All my life, I've known I was different. The headmistress at Lundgrim's Academy for Young Ladies of Good Family tried to insulate me from slights, much good it did. I believe she even circulated the tale that my mother was the widow of some minor French nobleman who'd retaken her English name upon his death and then died herself, but the rumors persisted. And when all the rest of the girls went home for Christmas, I stayed at school."

The old hurt throbbed in her chest, but when Gabriel pressed a kiss against her temple, it eased a bit.

"Isabella didn't have either the time or the space for me. She rarely visited the school and when she did, the headmistress was clever enough to keep her out of sight of the rest of the students." Jacquelyn bit her lip. "My mother is . . . not an inconspicuous person."

"You say you didn't spend much time with her as you grew up, and yet it seems you knew her well. Probably better than I knew my father."

"Isabella was a great letter writer," Jacquelyn said with a sigh.

Whenever one of her mother's missives arrived at the school, Jacquelyn was summoned to the headmistress's office, where she was expected to read the letter and then surrender it immediately. The headmistress always burned them in her sight. Unlike the other students, Jacquelyn wasn't allowed to keep the letters to pore over later, lest any of her mother's "less-than-salubrious" correspondence fall into the hands of "impressionable minds" and corrupt any of the other students with "worldly vice." The immediate loss of her mother's letters probably led Jacquelyn to absorb and remember more of Isabella's words than she might have if she'd been allowed to keep them.

But destroying the missives was probably a wise course of action, especially since Isabella took it upon herself to fully educate Jacquelyn about what passed between a man and a woman through several detailed letters. Ears tinted scarlet as she read silently under the headmistress's watchful eyes, Jacquelyn learned about the passions of the flesh from one who might be considered a true expert.

Ignorance, her mother had written, *is not always conducive to bliss.*

"She wrote to me faithfully," Jacquelyn said. "Isabella always said she filled her days with maintaining her correspondence because her nights were filled with . . . other things."

And now Jacquelyn was intimately acquainted with those "other things." She understood Isabella better, but Jacquelyn still resented her mother for placing her own needs above her child's.

Gabriel spooned his body around hers and whispered in her ear. "There must be a way to induce your father to wed your mother and claim you. Surely that would settle the question of your legitimacy sufficiently for those who care about such things."

He spoke with the unintentional callousness of one whose birth held no taint.

"First of all, I don't know who my father is," she said testily, trying to ignore his erection pressing against her bottom. "Perhaps Isabella doesn't either. Not for certain. And second, even if she does know who he is, he's no doubt already married. I don't think my mother ever took a lover who wasn't. In that respect, she was very particular. She always said married men were more generous and less complicated, whatever that means."

"Well, then we'll use the rumor of the treasure to lure some other titled gentleman to wed her and claim you." He planted a wet kiss behind her ear. "Lord knows, men have done far worse to gain a fortune."

"Even an imaginary one? We'd have to spend money we don't have traveling to London." She noted with surprise that his body stiffened slightly at this. "Then I'd have to try to convince Isabella to go along with the scheme. I doubt she would."

"Why not? Don't most women want marriage more than anything?"

"My mother is not most women," she said, grinding her teeth. Gabriel had slid his arm around her and started teasing a nipple with one hand while he traced her ear with the other. "She's what French philosophers call a free spirit. She says marriage is a brand of female slavery. The only way a woman can maintain her dignity is to belong to herself."

"Well, that's an original view," he said. "Though I gather she didn't mind accepting gifts from men."

"Oh, no, that was never an issue. 'Take money from a man,' she'd say. 'Jewels and carriages, a house if you can manage it, but don't take his name.'"

Jacquelyn sighed.

Gabriel stopped teasing her breast and tightened his grip around her, but said nothing. She was grateful for his wordless understanding.

"Even if my mother gave consent to the ruse, we'd have to find an agreeable gentleman she'd be willing to settle on." Jacquelyn sighed. "And it would accomplish nothing. The treasure isn't real. It makes no difference in the long scheme of things whether I'm ever acknowledged by my sire." Her voice dropped to a whisper. "You must wed soon."

"Only if we stay here," he said.

"What?" She rolled back to face him.

"If there's one thing my stint at piracy taught me, it's that the world is wider than I ever imagined," he said. "We could leave England, Lyn, and settle ourselves anywhere in the world."

The possibilities dazzled her speechless.

"Think of the places we could go. Some of the islands in the Caribbee are beautiful beyond belief—green and blue jewels rising from the turquoise sea," he said wistfully. "And there are even a few dots of land left there where I haven't outstayed my welcome. Or if island life isn't to your taste, we might make for the Colonies."

"I can't picture you hacking out a homestead in the wilderness when our own little war party of savages has already bested you here," she said, stifling a giggle as she remembered the girls' farcical rendition of aboriginal Americans.

"No need. We could settle in Boston or Charleston," he said, warming to the idea. "I'm still a better-than-fair nautical man. I could turn respectable and captain a legitimate vessel."

"From pirate to honest merchantman?"

"A shorter step than pirate to titled gentleman, believe me. But to have you by my side, I'd even return to piracy," he said, planting a kiss on her cheek.

She decided to put scripture to practice and turned the other one to him as well. He complied and then moved up to kiss first one closed eyelid, then the other.

"To hear Mr. Meriwether tell it, that would be no sacrifice at all," she said as pleasure washed over her. " 'A merry life and a short one' is how he described piracy. But a pirate vessel is no place for your nieces. Would you abandon them to some boarding school?"

"No, we'll take them with us wherever we go," Gabriel

said with a grin. "So piracy is out then, though I suspect Daisy has an aptitude for it."

She swallowed a laugh. "You may be right." Then her face grew serious. "And what of Mrs. B.?"

"She could come, too," he conceded. "Meri would insist upon it if only to insure the continued flow of cherry pies to his belly. Besides, we'll need Mrs. B. to ride herd on the girls."

"And what about Timothy? And Father Eustace?" she said pensively. "And all your tenants and crofters? With you gone, the Crown will have an excuse to appoint a protector of the estate. A new lord who cares nothing for the old families here might well raise their rents so high, they'd be forced off the land to starve."

"Seems to me I was once almost murdered to avoid that very calamity," he said, trying to lighten the mood. "Surely a new lord wouldn't be such a disaster."

She didn't find this convincing.

"It's not a chance you can take. Like it or not, you are no longer the second son of a gentleman, who may pick and choose a life for himself. You are Lord of Dragon Caern," she said softly. "Nobility has its privileges, but it also comes with duties. It is your obligation to care for these people."

"Even if I will it otherwise?"

"Especially if you will it otherwise." She palmed both his cheeks, the rough stubble of his beard pricking her skin. The truth pricked her heart even deeper. "If you do only what pleases yourself, you're no better than a tyrant."

"Remember whom you're talking to, mistress." He turned his head and pressed a soft kiss into her palm. "A pirate has no rule but his own wishes."

"You are no longer a pirate," she said, willing it to be true.

"And neither am I a lord by any measure but name," he said. "Not yet."

"But you will be," she said with assurance.

Gabriel tipped her face toward him and she thought he was going to kiss her. Instead he just looked at her as if he were trying to burn her features into his mind.

"Do you ever tire of being right all the time?" he finally said.

"Frequently," she admitted. "But only since I met you."

He lowered his mouth to hers in a kiss of bittersweet regret. It wasn't the flame of passion they'd shared in the night, but the connection between them in the gentle brush of their lips was even more real. When he pulled back, she blinked back the tears that threatened to salt her cheeks.

"Kiss me again," she urged.

"That might lead to another. You've a naked man in your bed who generally wakes in a friendly frame of mind even without the benefit of a beautiful naked woman beside him." A wry grin tugged at his mouth. "Don't make promises you don't intend to keep."

"I never do."

He took her mouth again and she melted into him.

And for quite some time, neither of them made any promises at all.

Save the promise of pleasure, given and received.

Chapter Twenty-four

"If I want anything done right, I must do it myself," Catherine Curtmantle muttered under her breath as her coach breasted Dragon Caern's drawbridge. "As usual."

Hugh was of no use whatsoever. The worthless twit couldn't even manage to debauch a virgin and get himself decently killed over the debacle. Instead he'd muffed the ravishing, lost a sword fight to Gabriel Drake and been humiliated before the nobility of a dozen shires by that horrid, unruly gaggle of Drake children. If Hugh couldn't oust Lord Drake from the Caern, whether by guile or by force, Catherine decided she would prefer widowhood.

A weak husband was decidedly worse than no husband.

So now it was up to her to make certain Gabriel Drake never married.

The obvious choice was to seduce him.

Catherine patted her new wig with feline smugness, enjoying the irony. Tightfisted Hugh had to part with some of his carefully hoarded coin to outfit her in the latest fashion so she could seduce the man her husband hadn't been able to kill.

Not that Hugh was privy to her plans, of course. He didn't have the intelligence to appreciate the subtleties of their situation. He was perfectly willing to commit adultery himself. But Catherine knew Hugh would be far less sanguine about his wife doing the very same thing.

"At least I'm not seducing a child," Catherine said, basking in the glow of moral superiority. Then she reached into her bodice and hitched her breasts up a bit. She looked down to admire the effect. She was sure it wouldn't be visible straight on, but from this angle, one pink nipple peeped from behind a froth of lace at her bodice. If it weren't daytime, she'd have dabbed a bit of rouge on it, to make sure the alluring little nub stood out. But the real trick to artifice was that it should seem not to be so.

A seduction should proceed naturally, at least as far as the man knew. They might own everything and think they held all the power, but a wise woman could control every encounter. Catherine knew that, with the right motivation, a woman could turn a man's head as neatly as she directed the biddable gelding she rode for pleasure. He just needed a tug on his bit and the judicious use of spurs.

It shouldn't be too hard to arrange for Gabriel to view her from above. After all, he was a tall man.

If she could manage to meet with him in his library, she might open one of his many tomes and invite him to peek over her shoulder at some fascinating passage. If she held the book just so, he'd not be reading very long.

Men were so blessedly predictable about such things.

She thought about inching the other nipple up as well, but decided that while one might be taken for an innocent error in her toilette, two would be a tad too fast, even for a seduction. Satisfied with her preparations and slightly excited by the sight of her own tight nipple, she drew a deep breath as the coach rumbled to a stop.

The door opened and she allowed the gawky stable boy to hand her down from her seat. When she murmured her thanks, he blushed dark enough to fade his freckles.

Must have caught a peek, she thought smugly.

The round housekeeper met her at the tall, arched entry and escorted her to the solar with instructions to wait there upon "the master's pleasure."

Yes, indeed, the master's pleasure was her chief aim. Not

only would she keep Gabriel from marrying, she'd enjoy the process.

He was still as darkly handsome as the day she'd jilted him for Hugh Curtmantle. And if Catherine did say so herself, she was still considered the local beauty. Two such pretty people would doubtless find mutual attraction undeniable. She'd long since lost interest in Hugh's grunting attentions, but the chase was always the most delicious part of any affair.

She was determined to lead Gabriel Drake a merry one. And once she'd seduced him into bed, she was even prepared with one those cunning "French letters" to protect herself against another confinement or some horrid disease. Even though Gabriel Drake looked the picture of health, who knew where a pirate might have dipped his wick?

Catherine was determined that any "votary of Venus" who breached her defenses would find himself sheathed in the little lamb's bladder she had secreted in her reticule. She'd even imagined the naughty game she might play when she drew the pink ribbons of the condom tight on Gabriel's erection.

All in all, this was shaping up to be a capital plan.

"Oh, Baroness Curtmantle! There you are."

It was the chatelaine who breezed into the solar, out of breath and flushing prettily. She ducked a quick curtsey. Catherine had met her at the ball. What *was* her name?

No matter.

"I'm here to see Lord Drake," Catherine informed her loftily. "The housekeeper was supposed to deliver the message that I've come calling, but perhaps you might see to His Lordship's whereabouts and apprise him of my presence. I cannot believe he'd keep me waiting longer than a snatched breath."

"Actually, Lord Drake sent me to fetch you with his

compliments," the chit said. "He is elsewhere engaged at present, but wonders if you'd be pleased to join his party in the garden."

Catherine pursed her lips. "Why? Are his nieces producing another play?"

The young woman had the grace to look chagrined. After all, it was not often one had to endure the sight of one's husband being nearly roasted alive. Catherine would have been thoroughly humiliated had not most of the ball guests chosen to believe Hugh was a willing participant in the charade. He was declared a "damned good sport" by one and all. Catherine wanted to sink into the very earth.

"Actually, yes," the young woman said. "Some families sing. Others recite bad poetry. The Drake children seem to be gifted in the thespian arts. The girls are performing for Lord Drake's guests this very moment."

"How droll!" Catherine waved her fan languidly before her. "And whom are the little darlings threatening to immolate this day?"

The woman—Miss Lark? Sparrow? No, Wren, that was it!—Mistress Wren had the effrontery to frown at her briefly.

"Lady Curtmantle, none here hold you responsible for your husband's reprehensible behavior," she said in clipped tones. "But perhaps you should be thankful that Lord Drake chose an unconventional method to teach your husband humility rather than render you a widow."

Catherine's jaw dropped. No servant—and what was this woman if not merely a servant who carried heavier responsibility than most?—no servant should speak to her in such a manner.

"Shall I deliver your regrets to Lord Drake or would you care to follow me?" Miss Wren asked.

"I know my way to the garden," Catherine said, narrowing her eyes at the cheeky Miss Wren. "Perhaps you are unaware, but Lord Drake and I were once close friends, exceedingly close friends. I am certain he would not condone your insolent tone."

"Forgive me if my tone offends you, my lady." The chatelaine cocked her head. "Close friends, you say? It was my understanding that you were once Lord Drake's betrothed, but perhaps I've been misinformed."

Catherine lifted her chin. "Servants' gossip is not always to be trusted."

She rose majestically and swept past Miss Wren.

"Oh, then you must not have betrayed Lord Drake with Baron Curtmantle, after all," she said. "The play will be over if we tarry long, so I'll leave you now. But may I suggest, Lady Curtmantle, that you step aside into an alcove to adjust your bodice before making your way to the garden? Your abigail seems to have been . . . singularly negligent in your toilette this morning."

The insufferable little bitch had the audacity to stare pointedly at Catherine's bosom. Her nipple was still winking behind the thin veil of lace, pert as ever, but now the pale skin around it flushed crimson with embarrassment. It was one thing to plan a seduction. It was quite another to be caught at it.

Catherine stepped behind one of the curtains and shoved her breast back down. Once Hugh managed to get himself named protector of this pile of rocks, Catherine decided her first demand would be that the sharp-eyed Mistress Wren be released from service. Without good character.

The Drake children's play was in full swing when Catherine slipped into the garden. A makeshift stage was set up on one side of the central fountain with chairs arranged in neat rows for viewing. Catherine took quick stock of Gabriel's other guests. She recognized Millicent Harlowe and several other hopeful young ladies along with their chaperones leaning forward in their seats in an effort to look interested in the farce being presented.

On stage, four of the girls had what appeared to be large papier-mâché boats attached to their hips, with rope rigging slung over their shoulders to hold the vessels in place and ridiculous tall hats designed to simulate a mast and sail on their heads.

"On July 12, 1588, a fleet of one hundred and thirty warships set sail from Spain to attack our beloved England."

The speaker was that dreadful Hyacinth, the eldest of Gabriel's nieces, the one Hugh tried unsuccessfully to deflower. She gave her narration from a podium at stage right.

To Catherine's surprise, Gabriel, a priest and a scruffy, thoroughly disreputable-looking fellow who she'd wager hadn't bathed in months, appeared on the stage. Like the children, they too "wore" ships, but Spanish flags flapped from their absurd headgear.

"The frigates and galleons of the Spanish Armada were bigger than the English schooners, but the English were more swift and agile," Hyacinth informed them.

In demonstration, the little "schooners" darted about between the larger "frigates and galleons" to the delight of the fawning ladies in the audience. The scruffy character tried to turn circles along with the children and only succeeded in making himself dizzy enough to weave like a drunkard before he sank to the floor. One Spanish galleon sent to the seabed by the gallant English.

Catherine tried to smile and chuckle along with the others, but her face felt brittle. Once Hugh controlled the destinies of these spoiled children, she'd see to it they were fostered out as far away as possible. Or perhaps they could be sent to a nunnery to insure no furtherance of the Drake line. Yes, that would probably be best.

"The English chased the Armada up the channel and set a fire ship adrift toward them," Hyacinth read from her script.

One of the Drake children stepped out of her ship costume and produced a flint and steel from her pockets.

"Daisy," Gabriel's tone held a stern warning. "What did I tell you about using real fire?"

Daisy rolled her eyes and shoved the flint and steel back into her pocket.

Perhaps a nunnery on the Continent for that one, Catherine mused.

Then Daisy raced to the side of the stage and came back with a length of fiery cloth. She wrapped her little sister, the smallest ship, with the simulated blaze and gave the tyke a shove toward the Armada. The Spanish frigates tried to evade her, but the priest became tangled in the child's trailing "flames" and went down in a blaze of orange muslin.

"The Spanish didn't dare try to run the English gauntlet by sailing back through the channel, so they traveled north, trying to escape around Scotland," Hyacinth explained.

Gabriel, the only remaining Spanish frigate, began to sail away from the harrying English.

Catherine glanced over to see Mistress Wren lean against the wall, her features going soft and drowsy as a cat on a windowsill while she gazed on the Lord of Dragon Caern. The chatelaine looked as if she might break into a full-throated purr at any moment.

Well, that explains much, Catherine thought. *The trollop fancies herself in love with Gabriel.*

"But as you know, the weather in Scotland is generally not felicitous to any, not even the Scots," Hyacinth continued. "Terrible storms rose up to meet the Spaniards and many ships were lost."

Upon this dire pronouncement, the four youngest of

Gabriel's nieces fell upon him with arms flailing, simulating foul weather. The Lord of Dragon Caern put up a valiant effort, but in the end, he was ignominiously rolling on the floor under a tangle of giggling children. Unlike the true history, none of these Spanish ships escaped English courage and craftiness. Or foul Scottish weather.

The audience applauded politely when Gabriel stood with his littlest niece straddling his shoulders, demanding a pony ride. As the players took their bows amid general hilarity, Catherine noticed that Gabriel tossed a glance toward Mistress Wren, his face flushed and beaming.

It was a fleeting unguarded moment, but she recognized a look of utter captivity when she saw it.

Catherine heaved a deep sigh. Seduction was no longer a viable plan. Gabriel Drake had already been seduced.

She ground her teeth together, wondering how best to make use of this new development. The goal was still the same, of course. To make certain Gabriel didn't wed.

Unfortunately, Catherine would have less joy of the enterprise than she'd hoped. No matter. The Viscount Linley would be visiting later in the fall to stag hunt with Hugh. She'd always been sizzlingly aware of him in a way that made her body hum. She'd find another use for the lamb bladder in her reticule.

Gabriel's gaze slanted toward Mistress Wren again. Catherine caught another unspoken message zinging from him to his chatelaine. Men were so transparent sometimes. Or perhaps, Catherine was more perceptive than most.

Yes, indeed. Gabriel was a lamb she could lead to slaughter. And he'd just shown her the best way to go about it.

Chapter Twenty-five

*J*acquelyn pushed through the kitchen door and recoiled immediately, bringing a scented hanky to her nose. "Mrs. Beadle, what on earth is that stench?"

"Whatever do you mean, mistress?" Mrs. B. didn't bother looking up from the ham-sized mound of dough she was kneading into submission.

"That." Jacquelyn waved an arm toward the offending crock bubbling on the hearth. "What are you cooking there?"

"Why, that's naught but a couple of hens I've set to boiling along with some herbs and an onion or two." She paused to flour her hands and the rolling pin and began flattening a ball of the dough into a perfect circle. "We'll have the broth with bread for luncheon and the meat for supper, I'm thinking."

Jacquelyn's stomach roiled in protest. "Why are you using old rotten meat?"

"Old? Rotten?" Mrs. Beadle bristled under the accusation. "For shame, mistress! As if I'd ever set bad flesh on the table at Dragon Caern. These hens are freshly killed. Twisted their necks for them myself, I did. Had the devil's own time with it, too, let me tell you. Lively ones, they were. Nothing a bit wrong with these biddies." She gave an injured sniff.

Jacquelyn lowered the hanky and took another tentative sniff. She quickly recovered her nose. If she hadn't already emptied her stomach twice that morning, she was sure she'd leave her breakfast on the clean stone pavings of Mrs. B.'s immaculate kitchen.

"What ails you, mistress?" Mrs. Beadle's round face puckered into a sympathetic frown.

"I don't know," Jacquelyn said into the heavily perfumed

hanky. Even the rosewater scent she loved now had a metallic tang to it. "Nothing smells right."

Mrs. Beadle rounded the stout table and laid the back of her floury hand against Jacquelyn's cheek.

"You've a touch of the ague, like as not," she pronounced as she waddled back to her work. "No fever, though. A garlic poultice will fix you right up. Soon as I'm done with these pies, I'll make you one."

Jacquelyn doubted the strong scent of garlic would settle her uneasy stomach, but she perched on one of the chairs to wait. She hoped it wouldn't be necessary to make another dash to a chamber pot. The need to void her bladder was so urgent; she'd barely made it the last time.

Whatever was wrong with her, she feared it wasn't the ague.

"You're making pies again?" Jacquelyn asked, trying to distract herself from the scent of boiling poultry.

"Aye, gooseberry this time," Mrs. B. confided. "Mr. Meriwether picked them himself, or so he told me. Actually, I think the children did most of the work. With the tall tales he fills their noggins with, that old scallywag can make any chore an adventure." Mrs. Beadle shook her head in mock reprimand, but a chuckle escaped her lips.

Could Mrs. Beadle actually harbor tender feelings for Gabriel's old first mate? Jacquelyn wouldn't have thought so, but the odd little smile on the housekeeper's face made her wonder.

"So, you're making pies for Meri again," Jacquelyn said. "That's the third time this week unless I'm mistook. Some might say you're spoiling the man. Do I detect a romance in bloom?"

Mrs. Beadle's brows lowered in a frown. "Certainly not! This is but a business arrangement."

"A business arrangement?"

"Aye," she said, pounding the crust with more enthusiasm than the task warranted. "We've reached an agreement, that old salt and me. I make him a pie and he takes a bath. And there's an end to it!"

Mrs. Beadle dusted the excess flour from her hands and looked up at Jacquelyn, concern making her clamp her lips tight for a moment.

"Mistress, you've gone pale as a chicken breast. The kettle's boiling. Let me get you some tea."

"Thank you," Jacquelyn said when Mrs. B. set the cup and saucer before her, then she waved the housekeeper off. "No, no cream or sugar."

"But you always take your tea with a bit o' milk and a lump or two."

"Not today," Jacquelyn said, gratefully letting the warm tea slide down her throat. "Nothing tastes right, either."

"Sickness will do that to a body," Mrs. Beadle said philosophically, then she chuckled. "Lady Helen was like that when she was bearing Miss Lily. If you was a married lady, I'd say you were breeding instead of down with the ague. 'Course Lady Helen also had a weak bladder and nipples so tender she could hardly bear to dress. Couldn't keep down her breakfast if her hope of heaven depended upon it for the first six months."

Sensitive nose, weak bladder, tender nipples, queasy stomach—Jacquelyn ticked off her symptoms one by one. To make matters worse, she was late for her monthly woman's trial. Mrs. B's words confirmed Jacquelyn's worst fear.

She was either carrying Gabriel's child or she was dying.

Jacquelyn wasn't sure which would be worse.

By day, Gabriel served admirably as Lord of Dragon Caern. He meted out justice, advised his tenants and paid court to the ladies who hoped to become his baroness. He even made time to play with his nieces or oversee some of their lessons. Jacquelyn found reasons to avoid him during the sunlit hours and he didn't seek her out.

But by night, Gabriel was either in Jacquelyn's bed or she was in his, finding new ways to drive each other to exhausted completion. And when they were utterly spent, they talked. He regaled her with tales of piracy and she told him of the doings at the Caern he'd missed while he sailed the Spanish Main. Sometimes, they recovered enough to make love a second time, with unhurried thoroughness. Sometimes, they sank into satisfied slumber, their bodies fitting together with the natural unselfconsciousness of lovers.

By tacit agreement, they didn't discuss his impending nuptials or what it would mean to their nightly trysts. They reveled in the eternal now.

The odor of the roasting chickens made Jacquelyn retch silently.

Now was irretrievably gone.

When Mrs. Beadle's back was turned, Jacquelyn fled the aromatic kitchen and bolted up the stairs to her chamber. She shoved a rug under the door to stop up the crack beneath it—anything to get away from the stench of roasting flesh.

Nothing would allow her to escape the inconvenient truth growing in her belly.

"Mistress Wren." Timothy's voice pleaded through her shut door, his consternation evident in the uneven breaks and squeaks in his tone. "Are you there, mistress?"

"Yes, Timothy, I'm here," Jacquelyn said wearily. She'd stripped off her dress and lain down in her shift across her bed, willing the nausea to pass. "What is it?"

"It's Lady Curtmantle. She's in the solar and she says it's urgent."

"Tell her Lord Drake is otherwise occupied," Jacquelyn said. She thought Gabriel was planning to ride over to inspect the site where a new mill might be built for his tenant's grain. Once he wed, the mill was first on the list of improvements his bride's dowry would pay for. Jacquelyn had helped him draw up the plans herself, heart aching that another woman's money would be needed to bring the mill from dream to reality.

"The lady doesn't wish to see Lord Drake," Timothy explained. "She's asking for you, mistress."

"Botheration," Jacquelyn muttered. The first time she laid eyes on the woman, something inside her twitched with the knowledge that this person meant the folk of Dragon Caern no good. She couldn't point to any particular behavior on the lady's part that gave her that irritated tingle on her spine, but she couldn't shake the feeling, either.

Lady Curtmantle had been the soul of proper behavior, confessing to Jacquelyn on her most recent visit her disgust over her husband's attempt at Hyacinth's ruination. Of course, there was that exposed nipple incident. But Jacquelyn had it on good authority that some grand ladies were now appearing in London with not one but both pink nubs rouged and powdered and proudly on display. A show of ankle was deemed shockingly fast, but exposed nipples as part of a lady's décolletage was not considered particularly risqué for an evening fete. Lady Curtmantle might conceivably have made an honest mistake.

But Jacquelyn doubted it.

And lately, Catherine Curtmantle had been calling with maddening regularity. Just social visits, and if Gabriel was unavailable, the baroness seemed just as pleased to bore Jacquelyn with inane pleasantries. Her conversation was mindless drivel for which Jacquelyn had little patience and less time, but she bore it in the interest of keeping peace with their neighbor to the north.

"Tell her I'll be down directly," Jacquelyn said through

the door as she stepped into her panniers. Her empty stomach rumbled. Jacquelyn hadn't taken any nourishment since her lost breakfast, but now her nausea was fading. "Oh! And see if Mrs. Beadle's gooseberry pie is ready to serve."

If her mouth was full of pie, Lady Curtmantle couldn't talk so much. Jacquelyn would figure out a way to rid herself of the baroness. Then she'd deal with the stickier problem of how to tell Gabriel she was bearing his child.

At least, we know he's capable of getting an heir, Jacquelyn thought wryly, remembering the way she'd baited him that first day. At the time, she'd meant to bully Gabriel into doing what was necessary for the estate.

Now she wished with all her heart he was free to do what was necessary by her.

"Ah, mistress," the baroness said as Jacquelyn entered the solar. "How lovely to see you—oh! Perhaps I've come at a bad time. You don't look at all yourself. So pale. I do hope you're quite well."

Jacquelyn parried the woman's pointed inquisition and steered the conversation to safer ground. They made small talk over a cup of excellent tea and Lady Curtmantle pushed her gooseberry pie around her plate a few times while Jacquelyn told her of Gabriel's plans for the new mill.

"You know, Jacquelyn—may I call you Jacquelyn?" the baroness asked and then hurried on without waiting for a reply. "One of the reasons I've been calling so often of late is that I care deeply about Lord Drake's happiness. I must tell you, I'm frightfully concerned."

"Really?" Jacquelyn set her teacup down and leveled her gaze on Lady Curtmantle. "Given your history with him, I find your concern difficult to accept."

"Yes, well. Touché, mistress. He has confided in you, I see." The baroness had the grace to blush slightly. "I admit it. I was young and lusty and in retrospect, unbelievably stupid. Alas for the past. I could not change it even if I would, but given your present with him, I doubt you're in a position to sling stones."

"What?"

"You heard me," she said. "Anyone with eyes can see that you and Gabriel are . . . having an *affaire de coeur*, playing hide the sausage, whatever you like to call it."

Jacquelyn was glad she'd abandoned her tea. She'd have choked on it by now.

The baroness sighed. "He's a fine figure of a man, Gabriel Drake. I can't fault you for succumbing to him."

Jacquelyn rose shakily to her feet. After catching them in the armory, Father Eustace might suspect their relationship had grown, but he'd not say a word to anyone. If Lady Curtmantle knew, who else had noticed the irresistible attraction between her and Gabriel?

"Sit down, my dear. We are not finished. Now, it is no shocking thing for a man in Gabriel's position to keep a mistress," Lady Curtmantle went on. "But it really is more than society can bear for him to keep one under the very roof he intends for his bride. Have you decided how you'll handle things once he weds?"

The baroness took a delicate sip of her tea. Her pointed tongue laved her top lip as she lowered her cup, like a cat licking cream from its whiskers.

Jacquelyn sank back onto the settee. She moved her mouth, but no sound would come out.

"No discreet love nest in your future? Well, then," she said. "I see I shall have to take matters into my own hands then."

"Whatever do you mean?" Jacquelyn sputtered.

"A word in the right ear, my dear." She arched a powdered brow. "If you intend to remain here after Gabriel weds, I shall find it incumbent upon myself to apprise his future bride of the true nature of your relationship to Baron Drake. Don't think for a moment your presence will be tolerated beyond the wedding vows."

Lady Curtmantle cocked her head. "My husband keeps his mistress in Bath. I've no objection to him having one, you see, but I've no great need to see the doxy every day, either. No doubt the future baroness of Dragon Caern will hold a similar view." She took another sip from her cup. "Excellent tea, this."

"Why are you involving yourself—"

"In your affairs?" the baroness finished for her. "Because, as I told you, I care about Gabriel's happiness. No man can please two women if they reside under the same roof, not even a veritable stallion like your Gabriel. Honestly, now. I find mistresses seldom consider any but their own wishes, but think of his position for once. For all that he's a pirate, Gabriel Drake does not possess a heart of stone. He's a man of deep feeling. After all, he drove himself to the sea over me once." She preened, patting her wig. "He's dreadfully single-minded in matters of the heart. Do you suppose he'll be likely to find contentment with the mother of his children with you down the hall?"

Jacquelyn felt as though she'd been punched in the gut. Gabriel had said something very near to Lady Curtmantle's remark more than once.

The baroness was right, damn her eyes.

When she allowed herself to think of Gabriel's impending marriage, all Jacquelyn considered was how she'd bear the fact that he'd take another woman to wife. She'd never considered how difficult it might be for Gabriel.

And now with her belly threatening to grow, Jacquelyn's position was impossible.

"I have to leave," she said woodenly.

Lady Curtmantle nodded sagely. "I knew you were a reasonable sort. You may actually care for the man, after all. Where will you go?"

Jacquelyn sat still as stone. There was really no help for it. She had no other option. "My mother lives in London."

"London! How lovely for you," Lady Curtmantle said as if Jacquelyn were going off on holiday. "I've heard of your mother, the infamous Isabella Wren. Still a celebrated woman of pleasure, is she not? No doubt with her connections among the demimonde, she'll help you find a suitable position in no time."

The baroness's lips twitched in a smirk.

"I will not become a courtesan," Jacquelyn said firmly, narrowing her eyes at her unwelcome guest.

Lady Curtmantle's brows lifted in amusement. "Oh, my dear. Such resolve is too little, too late. Whether you will it or no, you are already a member of the Cyprian corps." The baroness lifted her teacup in a mock toast. "Just a singularly ill-paid one."

Chapter Twenty-six

*O*nce night fell, Jacquelyn couldn't bear to wait for Gabriel to come to her. For one thing, she didn't want him to spy the trunk she'd packed and start asking questions. She'd already told Timothy that she'd be leaving with the gig an hour before dawn. The stable lad was to have her mare hitched to the small, two-wheeled vehicle and come to haul her luggage down for her before anyone else stirred. If anyone inquired, Timothy was to say Jacquelyn was off to Bath to inspect a new shipment of silks that had recently arrived. The girls would need new dresses for their uncle's wedding, after all.

Of course, Lady Curtmantle knew Jacquelyn's true destination. She'd cursed herself a dozen times for letting her plans slip. But she doubted the baroness would tell Gabriel where she was headed, not when Lady Curtmantle so obviously approved her actions.

As caustic as Lady Curtmantle was, Jacquelyn decided the woman had actually done her a favor. Her snide cuts forced Jacquelyn to evaluate her position in the cold, hard light of logic instead of the haze of passion. After weeks of deliberate indecision, Jacquelyn knew what she must do.

She'd kissed the girls goodnight as usual, complaining of an eyelash in her eye when Daisy noticed the unshed tears threatening to spill over her lids. She loved them fiercely, but she had to leave them for their own good.

She just didn't have the strength of will to leave without seeing Gabriel once more.

As soon as the Caern settled into gentle quiet, she lit a candle and slipped into the secret passageway. Had she really thought she could somehow continue with their secret trysts once a new Lady Drake was installed?

Evidently her body had been doing the thinking. And still was. Already, her whole being thrummed in anticipation of his strong arms about her, his mouth searching out her secrets, his hard shaft pounding between her thighs. The moist warmth of arousal pooled in her groin.

Oh, God! What will I do without him? Jacquelyn nearly sobbed in despair. She stopped walking for a moment and closed her eyes, willing herself to shove aside all thought of the morrow. If she had only this one night, let her have it.

All of it.

She turned a corner in the narrow space and almost ran headlong into him. Gabriel gathered her into an embrace and a kiss that nearly stole her soul. It certainly made her drop the candle.

He stooped and pinched off the wick with a rumbling chuckle. They were plunged into total darkness, but as long as Gabriel held her, Jacquelyn decided she wouldn't care if she was cast into perdition itself.

"I can think of better ways to set the place ablaze. Oh, Lyn, the day's been so long," he breathed into her ear as his hands roamed her curves. "I've had the taste of you in my mouth all day, but it's never enough. Come, love. Let us take our fill."

She sagged against him and he led her back to his chamber.

Let me not think, she pleaded silently. *For this last time, let me only feel.*

She didn't let him speak after he pushed the secret doorway closed behind them. She hurled herself toward him, pressing feverish kisses to his neck and down his bare chest. The salty sweetness of his skin made her soft palate ache. She nipped his taut brown nipple and reveled in his low groan. Her hands found the drop front of his breeches and plunged in to claim his engorged cock.

He was so warm.

A single pearl of fluid formed at his tip and she bent to take him into her mouth.

"Lyn," he chanted her name softly as she knelt to pull his breeches past his heavily muscled calves. "You drive a man beyond reason. If you keep that up, I . . . I fear I cannot be as gentle as I want to be with you."

She straightened and looked him in the eye. "Don't be gentle."

Gabriel had warned her the first time they met that there was a beast in every man, but she hadn't believed it. She had no doubts now.

In rutting glory, there was no finer specimen than the beast who now bent her over and slammed himself into her. He rode her savagely. He bruised her inner thighs with his thrusts, drew blood when he claimed her flesh with his love bites, and marked her body and soul with his total possession.

Somewhere amid the madness she thought she heard a voice that sounded like hers. It kept saying the same thing over and over.

"Harder. For God's sake, harder."

Much later, Jacquelyn lay beneath him, fighting to draw a breath. His body still trembled with spent passion, but he raised himself on his elbows to look down at her.

"Lyn, I'm sorry for using so—"

She pressed her fingertips to his lips. "I wanted you to, just like that."

Every joint ached and she suspected she'd be sore for a week, but she needed him to take her, to ravish her. She couldn't have borne tenderness.

But now she pulled his head down to her breasts. He nuzzled her nipples for a moment before he laid his rough cheek in the hollow between them. His warm breath slid over her charged skin, sending a final burst of longing racing through her veins.

In the years to come, this was how she'd remember him, lying between her breasts, his body heavy on hers, their raging need finally stilled. Only a quiet yearning left to shudder in the wake of their fire.

"Gabriel?"

"Hmm?" His body jerked and she realized he'd drifted into light sleep.

"Have you decided which one?"

"Which one what?" his voice was rough and slurred.

"Which woman you'll wed?"

"Oh." He drew a heavy sigh and rolled off her. "I'm thinking Lady Harlowe."

"You're joking." The lady came with a hefty dowry, but to call her plain would have been high praise.

"No, I'm serious." He propped himself on one elbow and looked down at her. "She is the daughter of a viscount, after all."

"I didn't think that sort of thing mattered to you."

"It doesn't." He traced circles around her areola. When her nipple rose into a stiff peak, he lowered his mouth and gave it a nip. "I thought Lady Harlowe would be the easiest choice for you."

"For me?" Jacquelyn pressed her palm against her breast to still the ache he'd started.

He flopped back on the bolsters and covered his eyes with his muscular forearm. "Well, for one thing, you'd never have to wonder if I sought her bed for anything other than an heir. I thought Lady Harlowe might keep things simple between you and me."

Now Jacquelyn raised herself to look at him. "How do you mean?"

"The woman I wed may have my name, my house and lands," Gabriel said as he cupped her cheek. "But you have me."

It was the nearest he'd ever come to a declaration of love. And just when Jacquelyn needed to hear it least.

She couldn't bear to look at him, so she snugged herself next to him and laid her head on his shoulder.

"I think," she said, willing her voice to stay even, "that you should choose Elisheba Thatcher."

Her wealthy, but title-bare father promised a generous dowry for her. Pretty and vivacious, young Miss Thatcher was Gabriel's best chance at someone who could bring him the heir Dragon Caern needed and whom he wouldn't mind making one with in the least. In time, who knew? It might even grow into a love match.

Gabriel said nothing. Jacquelyn could barely stand to breathe.

"Did you hear me?" she finally asked.

"Aye, I heard you," he said testily. "But can we please talk about it tomorrow? I don't mind losing sleep when you keep me awake rutting you blind. Talking me to death is another thing altogether."

He pulled her close again and she let him. She needed to feel him next to her, to feel his tense muscles go slack in relaxation.

Once his breathing fell into the steady rhythm that told her he slept, she rose from his side. Jacquelyn disappeared into the secret passage, hand covering her mouth to stifle her sobs.

Chapter Twenty-seven

"Yes, my lady, I'm quite sure," Catherine Curtmantle's abigail said for the third time.

Her name was Jane, but Catherine didn't use it often. She referred to her servant as "girl" or "you there." Usually Catherine found the girl's biddable ignorance irritating, but Jane had her uses. Gathering up juicy tidbits of gossip from surrounding estates without being clever enough to guess at her mistress's need for the information was foremost on Jane's very short list of accomplishments.

"Mrs. Beadle was quite keen on that point," Jane said with a hopeful expression. In an effort to please her mistress, the girl had been known to tell her only what she thought Catherine wanted to hear. But Catherine had a heavy hand, so she'd only done it once. "Mistress Wren has taken herself to Bath, so Mrs. B. says, to buy some new silks for the little misses." Jane sighed. "Silk be ever such a lovely fabric, ain't it?"

"Never mind that. What else did Mrs. Beadle say about Mistress Wren?"

"She's expected back any day now. In fact," Jane's face brightened as she recalled more of her conversation with Dragon Caern's housekeeper, "Lord Drake is restless as a penned stallion, Mrs. B. says, and may take himself to Bath to see did she have trouble if she don't return soon. Oh, and Mrs. Beadle thanks you kindly for the rosemary. She was nearly out and—"

"Keep to the point, girl," Catherine cut in. "When did she say Lord Drake might leave?"

Jane's cornflower blue eyes slid up and to the right. "I

don't recollect her naming a day in particular. She just said soon."

"And Lord Drake hasn't settled on any of the young ladies he's been courting?" Catherine asked. "No proposal of marriage to any of them?"

"No, and don't that beat all?" Jane's eyes went round as a fledgling owl's. "Seems he won't even pay court to them hardly without Mistress Wren to arrange matters. Makes a body wonder, don't it? Mrs. Beadle says it don't hardly make sense for Mistress Wren to run all over creation for dresses for a wedding what ain't even certain yet. 'Course, it's not for the likes o' me to question what turns about in His Lordship's mind, but—"

"Certainly not! In fact, there's little enough room in that small brain of yours for your own thoughts. Don't even attempt to understand your betters, girl," she said, looking down her nose at the girl. "That will be all."

Catherine waved her away and turned her attention back to the thick ledger book. Hugh had understated their income again by a substantial amount. Yet another thing she'd have to handle.

"Oh, you there," she called Jane back before the servant had time to scuttle away. "Find Lord Curtmantle and tell him I wish to see him immediately."

At any other time, the sorry condition of their financial affairs would have sent Catherine into a tizzy, but she felt confident that positive changes were in the Curtmantle's immediate future. Still it wouldn't hurt to let Hugh think she was stewing over them. She didn't look up when she heard his booted tread on the threshold of her morning room.

"What is it—oh, Catherine, not again. What did I tell you about troubling your head over such things?"

"It seems to me that someone needs to trouble over them,"

she said primly. "However, our ledgers are not what I wish to discuss with you. Did you send that note to Cecil Oddbody as I told you?"

"Yes, but I still don't see why he'd need to keep an eye on an aging whore's house."

"Isabella Wren is not a whore. She's a courtesan," Catherine said. "Not that someone with your lack of discernment would know the difference. Any woman can spread her legs, but few can dazzle a man outside the boudoir as well. But be that as it may, it's not Isabella Wren we are concerned with. It's Gabriel Drake. I happen to know that he will be on La Belle Wren's doorstep within days."

"In London?" Hugh threw himself into a side chair and hooked a booted foot over the opposite knee. "Drake's not so daft as that. You know what Oddbody said. If Gabriel Drake sets foot within the city limits, he'll be fitted with a hemp necktie before he knows it. London is a death sentence to him."

"Nevertheless," Catherine said, "he will be there, mark my words. Now, you need to ride immediately to Oddbody's side so you can be there when the arrest is made. You bungled the last assignment he gave you. We certainly don't need that little worm to think he's accomplished this all by himself. If you are there when Gabriel hangs, Mr. Oddbody will be hard put to deny you your due. I've ordered your horse saddled and provisioned. You leave within the hour."

Hugh's lip curled in displeasure. "I can't leave now. Linley's due tomorrow for our annual sport. The game is thick this season and a magnificent stag has been sighted near our southern border."

"Viscount Linley is coming?" She all but purred, thinking of the lamb's bladder condom still in her reticule. "Don't

trouble yourself about him. I believe I can keep His Lordship entertained until your return."

After a week on the road, Jacquelyn finally saw the spires of
London ahead. She was satisfied her ruse had worked. Even
if Gabriel became suspicious that her trip to Bath was taking
too long, he'd be heading the wrong way if he went looking
for her.

In time, he'd come to see this was for the best.

Her head might reason so, but her heart still rebelled. She
lifted her chin. What was it her mother had said once? Like
most of her sayings, it had made little sense at the time, but
now the words came back to Jacquelyn with crystalline
clarity: *a heart is something that might be ignored long enough for
it to cease to matter.*

Her mother was a self-confessed pragmatist. Jacquelyn
squared her shoulders. Isabella's daughter could be practical
as well.

Isabella Wren lived in Charles Court, a block off the
Strand. It wasn't exactly Mayfair, the fashionable new
neighborhood that was home to members of parliament and
courtiers alike, but it was certainly several steps up from the
sturdy tradesmen's quarter of Cheapside. It had been years
since Jacquelyn had visited Isabella, well before she took the
position at Dragon Caern. Jacquelyn was forced to ask directions more than once as she drove the gig down the
crooked streets.

Unfortunately, she received different answers each time.
Apparently there were several ways to reach her mother's
home. None of them direct.

When she heard the chimes of Westminster sound, she was
able to orient herself. Daylight was waning. Linkboys raced
to light the way for well-heeled pedestrians, and householders
hung the required lanterns outside their doors. Jacquelyn

turned the cart down a cobbled lane, lined with three-storey houses in the Palladian style. The red-brick exteriors were brightened with white trim and twin chimneys smoked merrily from opposite ends of each rooftop, like a row of proper English gentlemen settling in with their evening pipes.

Jacquelyn reined her mare to a stop before a house with a green door and an intricate stained glass creation spreading fanlike above it. Because of the unique ornamentation, Isabella had christened her home Peacock House—also a sly reference to the string of dandies and gallants who came and went with astonishing regularity through that green door.

"Ah, Mademoiselle Jacquelyn, it is you, is it not?" Nanette, her mother's French maid, greeted her warmly at the tall front door. "So long it has been, *cherie*. Madame will be overjoyed to see you. Leave the gig. Jerome will see to your things. This way, *s'il vous plaît*."

Clutching her satchel, Jacquelyn followed Nanette into her mother's parlor. Isabella was seated at her writing desk, quill in hand, peering at the missive before her through a set of pince-nez Jacquelyn had never seen her wear before.

Her mother's bone-deep beauty was still there, her cheekbones and delicate jaw seemingly sculpted by a master, but her skin looked paler by the candlelight than Jacquelyn remembered, though she was sure her mother wore no rice powder. She sported no wig. Her own hair was pulled into a thin bun with tight ringlets laced with silver dangling by either of her lovely cheekbones. Obviously, there was no ball or opera this night. Isabella was dressed *en déshabillé* for an evening in. Tiny blue veins could be seen through the thin skin at her temple. Her long neck, once the envy of feminine London, sported the tiniest hint of a wattle.

As if sensing eyes on her, Isabella looked up. Her vibrant smile erased any notion of advancing years.

"Jacquelyn, darling! What a delightful surprise!" Isabella

stood and rushed to her, hands extended. She kissed the air beside each of Jacquelyn's cheeks in the French manner and then drew back to look at her. "A bit road weary, I see, but my! How lovely you've grown."

"Thank you, Mother."

"Oh, we can't have that. What if someone overhears you and realizes that I'm old enough to have a daughter your age?" Isabella said with a twinkle in her violet eyes. "Call me Isabella, dearest."

"As you wish, Isabella," Jacquelyn said, feeling every bone-jarring league of the road she'd traveled. She didn't want to talk. She didn't want to think. She wanted nothing more than a hot bath, a hot meal and a clean bed, in that order, but the news that brought her to her mother's door was not likely to improve with keeping. "Just think what people will say in a few months when they realize you're old enough to be a grandmother, as well."

Isabella cocked her head like a bright-eyed robin, and swept Jacquelyn's form speculatively with her penetrating gaze. "I don't suppose you've a husband stashed in that satchel, do you, darling?"

Jacquelyn shook her head. She was past tears. Her mother would not hurl recriminations at her. Isabella was fond of saying that folk found it most easy to forgive those sins that strongly resembled their own. But that didn't stop Jacquelyn from mentally flaying herself for allowing her passion to lead her to this predicament.

Isabella sighed and pulled her into a warm embrace. "In that case, lovie, perhaps you'd best call me Mother."

Chapter Twenty-eight

A walk along the beach usually helped Gabriel put his thoughts in better order. The long roll of the breakers, the cries of gulls and kittiwakes, the sight of a sail disappearing over the horizon all soothed him, helped him see things in a new light. He preferred the fresh snap of a sea breeze, but it was a steep climb down the cliffs from Dragon Caern to the rocky beach below, and he'd already wasted enough time.

As he adjusted the saddle forward on his gelding's withers, he decided the scent of warm horseflesh and old leather had much to commend it for settling a man's spirit as well. But his mood was still three points west of foul. Mostly because he couldn't get his last conversation with Lyn out of his head.

He'd settled on Millicent Harlowe for a number of sensible reasons, none of them to do with his personal comfort or wishes. But Lyn wanted him to marry Elisheba Thatcher. And he'd cut her off in a tone more surly than he intended. It had been due to more than tiredness. He couldn't bear the thought of wedding anyone but Lyn, let alone someone pretty enough to cause her additional pain.

Then when he'd roused in the morning, she was gone. Oh, she'd left the message with Timothy about shopping in Bath, but he should have known she didn't mean to return. He shouldn't have waited a day.

At least now he was finally doing something about it. No matter what anyone said, he wasn't going to marry anyone but Lyn, and there was an end to it. He stooped to catch the girth under his horse's belly and cinched it tight.

"Goin' somewheres, are ye, Cap'n?"

Meri's gravelly voice at the stable door startled him. He'd hoped to slip away unnoticed, but trust Meriwether to sense he was about to jump ship.

"To Bath," Gabriel said, setting his jaw. He didn't owe anyone an explanation for his actions. Not even his old shipmate.

"Are ye thinkin' that's the wisest course?"

"Mayhap not, but I can't seem to steer clear of it, Meri," Gabriel said, suddenly deeply absorbed by the need to adjust his horse's bridle.

"Want company on the road?"

"I'd rather you stay here and look after things for me till I return."

If I return, Gabriel amended silently. He was done with the whole charade, the endless parade of hopeful misses in his parlor. He could no longer step to the farce of this mating dance. Lyn would just have to listen to reason. And if she wouldn't, well . . . he was still a pirate at heart. She'd look good slung bottom to the sky over his saddle.

"No, Meri, it's best you bide here," Gabriel said. "Besides, the girls would miss you."

"Aye, and I'd miss the wee heathens right back, come to that," Meri admitted. "Cap'n, ye know I'd never try to tell ye where to drop anchor—"

"Then don't," Gabriel cut him off.

"I'm a simple sailing man. I know what I know and it's generally not much. Ye take the lead and I'll follow ye to hell, singing all the way. Mutiny is not in me," Meriwether said. "But I've got to ask ye, have ye thought this through with something other than yer cock?"

Gabriel rounded on him and grabbed him by his greasy lapels.

"If you weren't my friend, you'd be a dead man."

"If I weren't yer friend, I'd not bother to say it." Meri screwed his face into a horrible scowl. "When ye were at the helm of the *Revenge*, ye never put yerself before the crew. Ye were ever the first into a melee, last to withdraw. Now ye run from yer duties. I can't think Miss Jack would approve of the change in your character."

"Leave her out of this," Gabriel growled.

"Can't. Not when she's at the heart of the trouble," Meri said. "I never thought to care much about these landlubbers, but the people here have wrapped their hands around me old heart. I wonder that ye now seem ready to desert the folk in this snug cove who depend upon ye."

Gabriel released the older man and rummaged through his saddlebag. There was an empty water flask he needed to fill, and even though food was the last thing on his mind, prudence dictated he should probably raid Mrs. Beadle's larder before he left.

"Who said anything about deserting?"

"Ye're the one saddling his horse," Meri observed.

"I'll be back," Gabriel said, wondering if it would be true. "As soon as I find her."

It was a measure of their friendship that Meri didn't back down.

"Truth is, seems to me the lass has made the right choice," Meriwether said. "Ye're expected to wed, lad. Like it or not, it seems the one ye want won't do for yer wife. I'm not sure what ye're intending, but unless ye enjoy living in the center of an unending squall, ye'd best not have two women with a claim on ye under the same roof."

"Since when did you become such an expert on women?"

"Never said that, Cap'n. But it don't take much learning to see ye're bound for mighty shallow shoals if ye keep to this heading. Mrs. B. says—"

"Mrs. B.? Who else have you been talking with about this?" Gabriel demanded. "Is everyone in the Caern privy to my personal doings, then?"

"The way you mooned about whenever the lass should chance to pass ye by? Only the ones with eyes," Meriwether said. "Which might be a smaller number than ye might think, most folk being so interested in their own troubles they've not much time for anyone else's."

A carriage rattled past the open stable door. Gabriel recognized the Curtmantle crest embossed on its side, twin lions rampant—a bastardized version of the ancient Tudor coat of arms, which Hugh claimed as his heritage.

Gabriel left his mount and walked to the doorway to watch the carriage make a sharp turn. Dust swirled in its wake as it came to a halt before the sturdy oak entrance to Dragon Caern. A lad dressed in threadbare livery leaped down from his perch on the back and opened the passenger door with a proper obeisance to the occupant.

Catherine Curtmantle stepped lightly from her equipage, her dainty shoes and more than a quick glimpse of her delicate ankles leading the way.

"No doubt you're right, Meri. Most folk are more worried for their own troubles," Gabriel said. "Then there are those who bring fresh trouble with them wherever they go."

Good breeding warred with Gabriel's wishes. More than anything, he wanted to mount his horse and ride, but his sense of duty won out. He strode toward the carriage. At the very least, he might cut this unwelcome visit short.

"Good morning, Lord Drake," Catherine said, extending her gloved hand.

He ignored it. Good breeding will only goad a man so far. This woman had once ripped out his heart. He wouldn't touch so much as her fingertip if he could help it. He gave her a curt nod. "Lady Curtmantle."

Her plucked brows lifted. Miffed, she withdrew her hand. "I'm calling to see—"

"I regret I am unable to oblige you at present," Gabriel said. "A pressing matter requires me to leave at once."

She narrowed her eyes at him and pursed her lips. She looked like a cat trying to decide whether to devour her wounded prey here or drag it back to her lair. "And might that pressing matter be taking you to Bath?"

"If it did, it's hardly your concern, madam."

"You're quite right," Catherine said airily. "Why should I care if you waste your time?"

"It's mine to waste," he said, forcing a tight-lipped smile. "Now if you will excuse me . . ."

"By all means, though you'll not find what you seek in Bath." She waved her hand airily. "I'm sure Mrs. Beadle can tell me enough to satisfy Mistress Wren of the children's well-being."

She flounced through the tall front door, with Gabriel in her wake. When she turned aside into the solar, he grabbed her shoulders and spun her around.

"What do you mean?" he demanded. "You've heard from Jacquelyn?"

"I received a letter from Mistress Wren requesting I visit to ascertain if your nieces are well," Catherine said. "I mean to do just that."

"Let me see the letter," he demanded.

"I burned it as she requested. Evidently, your chatelaine values her privacy."

He remembered Lyn telling how she'd watched as the headmistress of her school burned her mother's letters. She might have made such a request. Still, Lady Curtmantle seemed an odd choice for a confidant. "Why would she write you?"

"She and I have more in common than one might believe." Catherine shot him a mirthless grin. "You, for one thing. What in the world do you think we talked about while you danced attendance on your fawning debutantes?"

Gabriel frowned. He had noticed Lyn and Lady Curtmantle in earnest discussion more than once, but never considered that they might form an uneasy alliance. He should have asked Lyn about it. He'd always been too busy trying to figure out the quickest way to get Jacquelyn into his bed to waste time over trivialities. "Is she well?"

"You mean she hasn't written to you? Oh dear, it is as I feared." Lady Curtmantle popped open her fan and fluttered it vigorously before her deep décolletage. "She obviously doesn't want you to know where she is."

"Since you brought it up, if she's not in Bath, then where is she?"

Catherine closed her fan and fingered its lace edge. She made *tsk* noises with her teeth and tongue. "Why should I betray her trust?"

Gabriel scoffed. "Madam, when it comes to trust I fear you are out of your depth."

"As are you. Will you hold my past sins against me forever?" She lowered her gaze. Her lips parted softly, the perfect penitent. "You can run off to play the pirate as it suits you and then return as lord of the manor with barely a break in your stride. How is it you can change, but no one else is allowed that luxury?"

"Catherine." It was a mistake to speak her name. Boyishly stupid or not, he'd loved her once and the dead embers of remembered longing stirred briefly. Lady Curtmantle was still beautiful, but hers was a cold beauty. And she wasn't his Lyn. "If ever you cared for me in the slightest, tell me where she is."

"It's not that simple—"

"Then let me simplify matters for you, madam." Gabriel pressed her against the stone wall. His hand closed over her white throat. "If Jacquelyn complains you betrayed her confidence, you may tell her you were forced to reveal her whereabouts. And you needn't worry about being convincing, because it will be true."

"You wouldn't hurt m—" Catherine's mouth gaped as he cut off her wind.

"I've killed my share of men," Gabriel admitted conversationally. "Not that I didn't avoid it whenever possible, of course. We pirates follow the path of least resistance, you know. If we can make off with the goods without committing a mortal sin, we will. But sometimes murder and mayhem is inevitable when someone won't acquiesce to our demands. Some folk just want killing, Meriwether always says."

The whites showed all around Catherine's pale blue eyes as she struggled to free herself. When his grip tightened, she stopped kicking and clawing, focusing all her energy on trying to squeeze a breath through the narrow passageway he left her.

"Never have killed a woman. Though I suppose it's not much different than dispatching a man," he said philosophically. "Probably easier in some ways, so long as the woman isn't trying to kill me back."

She blanched pale as parchment and he lessened his grip enough to give her a little air. She gasped like a trout flopping on a riverbank.

"You really came to see about my nieces?"

Her head moved in a barely discernable nod.

"You aren't trying to do me or Jacquelyn any harm, are you, Catherine?"

Her lips moved in a silent *no*.

He eased his grip further. "Good. Now where is she?"

"London," Catherine wheezed. "The letter came from London."

Damnation. Of all the bolt-holes Lyn might have made

for, why did she have to choose that one? He was sure he'd never told her that he couldn't set foot in the city without threat of hanging. Or had he let it slip and she was counting on him not following her there?

When Gabriel released Catherine, she sagged to her knees. "I know London well enough to know a person can disappear into its rabbit warrens and never be seen again. Where is she staying?"

"With her mother, I think. Where else would she go? Isabella Wren is not a person who shuns attention. She should not be too difficult to locate," Catherine said, her voice wispy and crackling. She massaged the bruised skin of her throat.

Remorse coalesced into a cold lump of guilt in his belly. He'd always despised men who brutalized women and now he'd become one. Meri was right. He wasn't thinking clearly at all.

"I ask your pardon, Catherine," he said softly as he reached down to raise her to her feet. "I should not have used you so."

She swallowed hard and huffed out a sigh.

"You are forgiven, Gabriel," she said as she smoothed her dress with both hands. "I know you're a man of great feeling and such men are prone to rash action. After all, your love for me made you run away to the sea."

"You think I went to sea pining for you?" He tipped her chin up to force her to meet his gaze. "I was a boy and I'd been betrayed by two people I trusted implicitly. I was more angry than hurt. The thoughts of murder rampaging through my heart scared me spitless. I ran away to keep from killing Hugh, though in hindsight, that may have been a mistake."

"Gabriel, if you're planning to run off with her, I can only wonder at your sanity," Catherine said. "You can't desert your home again. You'll be throwing away everything. You can't really tell me this chatelaine, this nobody, means so much to you."

"I'm no longer a boy who fears his own rage. I'm a man who's not afraid to unleash it, if necessary. And I'm not running away." He turned and stomped to the door. Now that he was heading for London instead of Bath, he had a few things to square with Meriwether, but no matter what his friend said, he was still going. "I'm running toward the only home I'll ever know. If someone tries to get between me and Jacquelyn, God have mercy on them." He stopped and leveled a glare at her. "For I won't."

Chapter Twenty-nine

$\mathcal{D}$aisy crept through the dark corridor, light-footed as a cat. She'd been upset when Uncle Gabriel left without a word of good-bye, but then she found something that sent all thought of her uncle skittering away.

Before Miss Jack left, one night she thought she heard the steady, furtive sound of someone moving behind the wall. Hyacinth called her a rude name when she told her about it. It was probably just a mouse behind the lath and plaster, but Daisy was certain she wasn't mistaken. Someone, someone much bigger than a mouse, was creeping around behind the walls.

If someone else was behind the walls, there must be a way for Daisy to get in there, too. She launched into an exhaustive search, crawling on her hands and knees, looking along the baseboards, hoping to feel a draft of air. Daisy skinned both elbows and braved Mrs. B.'s wrath over the dirt she ground into the front of her skirts at the knees, but her search proved fruitful.

When she had first discovered the secret door in the unused upstairs maid's room a week ago, she forced Hyacinth to eat her words and bullied her into exploring with her. But then a long cobweb had trailed across Hyacinth's face when she wasn't expecting it and the little ninny had bolted back to the safety of their shared room.

"No, Daisy," Hy said. "I won't come. It's just not . . . dignified to go poking around in the dark like that."

Which meant Hyacinth was afraid.

But Daisy wasn't frightened. She was curious. So each

night, after she was sure Hy was sleeping soundly, Daisy lit a candle and slipped into the dark maze behind the walls.

It was rather like working a large puzzle, trying to figure out where she was in the keep. She listened for sounds coming from the other side of the walls: half-overheard arguments between Mr. Meriwether and Father Eustace in the parlor and Mrs. Beadle barking orders to the scullery maids in the kitchen. She located Timothy's room by the sound of his voice and made the astonishing discovery that he was sharing his little chamber with Mary, the dairymaid. Judging from all the grunting and panting Daisy heard through the wall, whatever they were doing together seemed to require a great deal of effort.

As Daisy explored, she constructed a map of the place in her head. By the third night, she was able to find her way to a little balcony looking out over the top of the battlements and back again without getting turned around once.

But she really wanted to go farther down.

She'd tiptoed as far as the unused dungeons and managed to creep past the empty cells and unusual implements. She thought she'd reached the bottom of the maze, but beyond those misery-encrusted rooms, there was another corridor. It was lined with torches that, judging from the soot on the walls, had seen hard use in the distant past.

This place was different from the rest of the secret passages. There was no sense of people living on the other side of these walls. The passage had been hewn from the rock beneath the Caern itself and it led downward into darkness.

A pixie of fear danced along Daisy's spine.

She wondered suddenly how Dragon Caern had earned its name. Had she stumbled upon the entrance to some beast's lair? A low rumble from the dark sent her flying back to safety.

But that black corridor kept calling to her. She wanted desperately to answer the summons, but she couldn't go alone. She needed someone who wouldn't be afraid of whatever they might find at the end of that dank hole. Wouldn't be afraid of a dragon, even. She needed . . . a pirate!

Of course! Pirates were the most fearsome folk on earth, weren't they? How lucky that she happened to have one right there.

After much coaxing and cajoling, she managed to drag Mr. Meriwether out of his bed and into the secret corridor.

"And I was after having a perfectly good dream about this little island where the girls swim out to the ships wearing— oh, hang it all, Miss Daisy!" Meri scratched his beard. "Are ye sure this can't wait till morning?"

"No, we have to find out if there's a real dragon under the Caern," Daisy said. "I'm sure I couldn't sleep a wink if we don't."

"Ye'd be the only one," Meri grumbled, but he kept pace with her through the dark maze.

"Oh, no!" Daisy exclaimed when they reached the level of the dungeons. "You forgot your sword. How will you fight the dragon without one?"

"Me frog sticker will have to do for whatever dragons there be here," Meri said, smothering his yawn.

When they reached the rock-walled passageway and Meri lit the first torch, he perked up a bit. "This be a different sort of place."

"I think the dragon lives down there. Shh! Listen." She grabbed the old pirate's hand for safety.

That same low rumble came again, this time with an answering hiss.

"What's that?" Daisy asked.

"Sounds like me mistress calling," Meri said with a smile. He sniffed the air. "Smell that? The sea, lass. Come."

Mr. Meriwether carried a lit torch and Daisy trotted to keep up with him now as he lengthened his stride. They made their way down a circular stone staircase where the hiss–boom sound was even louder.

"You sure that isn't a dragon?"

"Nay, child. Just the tide coming in," he said as they neared the bottom step. The pathway narrowed, forcing them to go single file. It led sharply to the right. Meriwether ducked to enter the new corridor.

The smell of the sea was stronger now. When Daisy's fingertips brushed the walls, she found them cold and slick.

Meri straightened his arthritic back ahead of her and light from his torch shot skyward into a large vault. Daisy peered around him.

At one side of the stone chamber, the sea boiled in through a low opening, eddying in a heaving pool. But on the landward side, every place she looked was piled high with crates and chests. One of them had been turned on its side and its contents were dumped on the ground. A sparkle of gold caught the light of Meri's torch. Coins spilled onto the wet stone, glistening like fallen stars.

"We didn't find your dragon, Miss Daisy," Meriwether whispered in awe. "But we surely found his hoard."

"What is this place?" Her voice returned to her several times in receding echoes.

"A smuggler's hole." Meri lit another torch wedged into the rock face and the room brightened. "When the tide is out, a crew brings its cargo in through the sea cave. When the tide comes in." Meri clapped his hands once. "Slick as snot, the door is closed."

"I didn't know there was a sea cave near Dragon Caern."

"No, likely few ever knew of it," he said. "The entrance must be curved behind the rocks, unhandy-like. Makes it nigh invisible unless you know where it is."

"Do you suppose someone is still using this as his hidey-hole?"

Meri knelt and swiped a hand across the top of one of the chests. He held up his finger to show her the thick layer of grime. "No one has been here in ages."

When he pried the chest open, more gold greeted Daisy's dazzled eyes. Meriwether held a coin aloft, inspecting the inscription.

"Spanish," he said. "And old beyond counting. I've never seen its like, and I've seen me share of doubloons. Lord knows there are still plenty of them swirling about the Caribbee."

Meriwether opened another chest and found gold ingots wrapped in decaying velvet. Daisy picked up a long crowbar and jimmied open another crate. There was no treasure in this one, but she found a stash of ancient weapons, a rusted arquebus and a pouch of rounds, several crossbows and bolts and a melon-shaped helmet. She lifted the helmet, the bronze green with age.

"That belonged to one o' them Spaniards, or I'm mis-took," Meriwether said.

"A conquistador," Daisy supplied. She'd studied pictures of the Spanish conquerors in one of the books in Uncle Gabriel's library. "But what's it doing here?"

"Waiting to be found," he said softly. "Ye know what this means, don't ye?"

She shook her head.

"It means your Uncle Gabriel was not the first pirate on the Drake family tree." One corner of his mouth jinked up and his old eyes glittered with pleasure. "Father Eustace was telling me that Gabriel's great-great—oh, I don't know how many times—great grandfather was a privateer for Queen Elizabeth."

"Do you mean Sir Francis Drake?"

"No, don't think this fellow had a *Sir* afore his name. This is Phineas Drake we're speaking of, the lone black sheep amongst the spotless Drake herd, to hear the good father tell it. Or perhaps lone wolf is more likely. Eustace said his brother always denied the tales of treasure in Dragon Caern." Meri's gaze swept the cave. "He musta never saw it."

"Someone must have known it was here," Daisy argued. "How could you forget something like this?"

"Ye'd be surprised how much treasure is hidden in this funny ol' world and none among the living knows of it." He flipped a coin up to watch it sparkle in the torchlight. "A pirate crew will bury a cache and next thing ye know, up comes a squall and the ship goes down with all hands. And the sea takes the secret with them."

"But this treasure is right under our feet," Daisy said, remembering the times Miss Jack pinched and scraped to make sure the estate would have enough to make it through a thin season when the wealth of Midas rested here unspent. "How could it be lost?"

"Expect a place like Dragon Caern keeps its own secrets. Take the passageways ye led me down tonight, for example. Does anyone else know they're there?"

"Only Hyacinth, and she's too afraid."

Meri pocketed one of the shining coins. "Well, there'll be no livin' with Father Eustace now that we've proved him right about this." His smile faded. "A treasure like this is dangerous for all who know of it. Gold does funny things to a man's mind, ye ken. Makes him think things. Do things. I can see why someone let the knowing of it die with them."

"Well, we know about it now," Daisy said with a shiver. Now that she knew there was no dragon, she'd gone from being afraid to being cold.

"Aye, lass, that we do," Meri said. "But until we know what that uncle of yours wants to do with it, I think it were best the treasure stayed a secret."

Daisy agreed and held up her little finger to him. When he screwed his face into a puzzled frown, she sighed. "Adults. They think they know so much."

Before she let him escort her back to her chamber, in order to keep the whereabouts of the treasure safe, Daisy led a mystified Meriwether through the ritual of the "pinky swear."

"There," she said satisfied. "That settles that."

Chapter Thirty

"Why, this is utterly ridiculous!" Isabella scowled down at the scandal sheet beside her plate of buttered eggs and toast.

"What is?" Jacquelyn asked from her place at the far end of the long dining table. Ordinarily gentle folk ate the first meal of the day in a small breakfast room instead of a larger dining room, but Isabella was never one to settle for ordinary. Since she rarely rose before noon, purists might insist the meal was nearly dinner in any case.

"This theater critic is being purposely thick." Isabella pushed the sheet aside and peeled an orange slice, carefully removing all traces of the white pulp. "Anyone with eyes knows the real play at the theater last night was going on in the Duke of Kent's private box when his wife came at intermission and surprised him with his mistress."

"How awful for her," Jacquelyn said as she chased a fig around her plate with her spoon. The elegant sideboard behind her fairly groaned under the weight of choices Nanette set out to tempt Jacquelyn's fickle appetite. Food still held little fascination for her. "And yet it amuses you. Don't you care about the wife's pain?"

"She felt no pain, I assure you. The wife had brought her exceedingly handsome 'cousin' from York to the theater with her." Isabella laid a finger aside of her nose and gave a sly wink.

Jacquelyn frowned in puzzlement.

"The duchess has no familial relations from that region of which I'm aware. The young man was *her* light-o'-love, you see. Oh, you should have been there, dearest, but then we'd have had to share my opera glasses and I fear I wouldn't have relinquished them for worlds. The duke turned the most charming shade of purple," Isabella said with a laugh. "And now he's known before the world for what he is."

"An adulterous husband with a choleric temper?"

"Worse. A hypocrite," Isabella said. "Society will wink at a gentleman's indiscretions, even secretly cheer them, but it will not abide a fraud. I'm afraid His Grace's theatrics over-shadowed the poor players on the stage by several leagues."

Isabella sipped her tea. "I wonder if that was precisely the reaction the duchess was hoping for. She must have known he'd be there. Oh, brava!" Isabella clapped her hands together soundlessly. "Do you suppose she might have arranged the confrontation on purpose?"

"Why on earth would she do that?"

"To put the cheeky bastard on notice, I imagine," Isabella said, lifting her cup in a mock toast. "I give you the Duchess of Kent. Well played, madam."

"You speak as if marriage were some sort of chess match."

"Aptly put, dearest. I suspect matters of the heart always are a game on some levels. Heaven knows, a mistress must use strategy when dealing with her lover. But it's a rare wife who shows such initiative. I suspect the duke's mistress will be in want of a patron very shortly," Isabella predicted. "Who knows? He might actually love his wife and not have realized it until that moment."

Jacquelyn shook her head. If she lived to be a hundred, she'd never understand her mother's way of thinking. "Love hurts badly enough without trying to cause each other additional pain on purpose."

Her mother tossed her a sympathetic smile. "Sometimes, I forget how very young you are, lovie."

"I don't think I'll ever feel young again," she murmured.

Isabella sighed. "Actually, my pity goes to the mistress."

"There's a surprise," Jacquelyn muttered to the cooling porridge she couldn't bring herself to try.

"Well, I hope the girl was sensible enough to arrange for a pension in her contract at least," Isabella said.

"A pension?"

"Of course, love. A woman of pleasure must look to her own future, for no one else will see to it for her," Isabella explained. She waved a hand around the sumptuously appointed dining room, glittering with silver and fine glassware. "As you can see, I did. When one is young and beautiful, it's easy to be sidetracked by romance and passion. However, as the years pass, I'm more comforted by jewels and banknotes than an admirer's love sonnets in praise of my charms. Besides, they are invariably poorly written and at this stage in my career," her shoulders bunched in a self-deprecating shrug, "patently false."

Despite her age, which she worked tirelessly to keep at bay, Isabella was still much in demand. She accompanied gentlemen to soirees and sporting occasions, acting not only as an ornament to her partner's arm, but also as a sparkling wit to draw others to her companion. Isabella counted many famous artists and philosophers, both in London and on the Continent, as her intimate friends. An invitation to one of Isabella Wren's dinner parties was cause for rejoicing among the city's demimonde.

"I do wish you'd come with me this evening. The opera is a new one and is said to be utterly charming," Isabella coaxed. "An Italian castrato is singing. Abominable practice, of course, but what a sublime sound. Have you ever heard one?"

Jacquelyn shook her head and mentally shuddered at the mutilation involved in producing those musical wonders.

"Imagine the purity and sweetness of a boy soprano and the strength of a man's chest and breath capacity. Not much of interest lower down, *bien sûr*, but the music makes up for other deficiencies, I'm told. Do say you'll come. We have a lovely box reserved."

"I'm sorry, Mother. I'm not exactly feeling up to socializing."

"Why ever not? Your belly is still flatter than my own. No one would guess that you're bearing, child. Why not enjoy yourself for once?"

"Ah!" Jacquelyn cast her a wry smile. "I believe enjoying myself is what got me into this predicament."

"No, never say that. If you loved the man, do not regret the joy you gave each other." Isabella fluttered down the length of the table, teacup in hand. She settled beside Jacquelyn and leaned toward her confidingly. "Did you love Gabriel Drake?"

More than words, Jacquelyn thought, but didn't dare say. To admit it aloud would be to bare her heart and its only safety lay in staying as hidden as the imaginary treasure of Dragon Caern. She turned the question back on her mother. "Did you love all your men?"

"All your men," Isabella mimicked. "Listen to you. Anyone would think I was a two-penny prostitute who turned tricks in the alley. I have been the soul of discernment. I'll have you know, my dear, that while I've had a coterie of admirers, the number of men I've actually taken to my bed over the years may be counted on one hand."

Jacquelyn digested this astounding fact.

"But the answer to your question is yes," Isabella said, her voice wistful. "In my own way, I loved them all."

Isabella finished her tea in silence, the only sound the soft clink of the bone china cup settling into its gilt-edged saucer.

"My dear, you know you are welcome to live with me for as long as you wish," she finally said. "However, with the odd hours I keep, my mode of life is hardly conducive to child rearing."

"Is that why you abandoned me to Lundgrim's Academy for Young Ladies of Good Family?" Jacquelyn asked. "I always imagined you were simply too busy for me."

"Oh, lovie, is that what you thought?" Isabella placed a hand on Jacquelyn's forearm. "If only you knew how often I wanted you here. But however much I enjoy my life, there are certain . . . disadvantages. I wanted you to be a lady, to make a brilliant match someday. That's why I insisted you be educated."

"You're too smart a woman to believe in fairy tales," Jacquelyn said. "You must have known without proper familial connections there would be no grand marriage for me. All I might hope for was a position as a governess. And it seems I've bungled that in spectacular fashion."

Jacquelyn had been gone from Dragons Caern a little more than a fortnight, but she still was unsure what she was going to do. She'd had no plan beyond reaching her mother's home when she rode off. Now a sense of lethargy stole over her, robbing her of the will to act. She knew she had some decisions to make, but she resisted the attempt. After all, her choices were responsible for her present. How could she trust herself to do any better for her future? Especially now that she had another little life to consider as well.

"Actually, I've been meaning to speak to you about your future, and this seems the perfect opportunity," Isabella said as if she'd read Jacquelyn's mind. "You're pretty enough to do well as a top-tier courtesan. Your French is excellent, and when you put your mind to it, you can be charming. I'm assuming you are fairly well acquainted with various methods of pleasuring a man."

"Your letters were most explicit on those points, Mother," she said.

"A mother must share what she knows," Isabella said. "However, experience is always the best teacher."

"And the hardest," Jacquelyn said.

"Admittedly," Isabella agreed. "After the child is born, you will have limited options before you. With my connections, I should be able to launch you into demirep society as my protégé."

Horror must have shown on Jacquelyn's face.

"Not to your taste? Well, gay society, late hours and hedonistic pleasure aren't for everyone, but I want you to consider your choices," her mother said without rancor. "Still, your aristocratic education need not go to waste. If you're prepared to wed quickly—quickly enough that society will allow itself to believe your babe premature—there may yet be a way for you to make a grand match. How would you fancy being a countess?"

"From courtesan to countess?" Jacquelyn swallowed hard. "That's quite a leap."

"Not as far as you might think," Isabella said.

Jacquelyn choked out a laugh. "Mother, are you sure that's just tea you've been sipping? I'm bearing another man's child. I'd be surprised if a ditch digger would wed me in this state."

"And yet, my dear friend Lord Geoffrey Haversham, heir to the Earl of Wexford, is prepared to do just that," Isabella said.

"How could you discuss my situation with a stranger?" Jacquelyn demanded indignantly.

"Geoffrey is no stranger. I count him one of my closest companions. He is the soul of discretion and I trust him implicitly," Isabella explained. "He and I have been keeping company for over a year now. The man is charming, witty and wealthy enough in his own right for it not to matter that you are without either pedigree or substantial dowry."

"Mother, I—"

"In fact, I didn't ask. He *offered* to wed you," Isabella went on. "Geoffrey assured me he will welcome and cherish your child as if it were his own. You will both want for nothing. None will ever have cause to doubt that Geoff is the sire by any action or word of his."

"Mother, you're making no sense," Jacquelyn said, the bare thought of wedding some stranger making her stomach curdle. "Why would Lord Haversham do such a thing?"

"What I'm about to tell you is in the strictest of confidence, you understand." The tip of Isabella's tongue slipped between her lips for a moment as she gnawed it thoughtfully. "Because Geoffrey . . . well, there's no way to state the facts less baldly and still be clear. You see, Geoffrey likes men."

Jacquelyn blinked. Her education, it seemed, was not as complete as she thought.

"You'd never guess it to look at him—an avid sportsman, tall, attractive, sings like a bird and dances like an angel. He's the perfect gallant. Bless his heart, Geoffrey's been hard put to keep it secret, but he manages," Isabella said. "Says his father would die of apoplexy if he ever found out, so Geoff's been very circumspect. Never visited a molly house in his life and swears he never will. In fact, he's only had one lover—his Italian valet, you see. He's been with him for years. I believe they quite dote upon one another in absolute secrecy, you understand. But as a future earl, Geoffrey desperately needs a wife and—"

"And I need a husband to give my child a name," Jacquelyn finished for her, unconsciously resting one hand on her abdomen.

"Actually, this could work to both your advantages," Isabella said. "Geoffrey is enlightened enough to realize that you have needs which he's unable to meet. He said he wouldn't even care if you took a lover—discreetly, of course—and bore other children, whom he would happily acknowledge, because a man can never have too many heirs."

Jacquelyn covered her face with both hands.

"He'd be good to you. Generous and grateful, exceedingly useful qualities in a husband," Isabella urged. "Think of the child."

A life of privilege. Wealth. The blessings of an education. An earldom, if her child should turn out to be a boy. Cosseted protection and a prominent match, if a girl. As the offspring of an earl, Jacquelyn and Gabriel's child would be welcome at court. And Jacquelyn would finally be what she'd longed to be all her life.

A lady.

And a total bald-faced lie. Nothing in the life her mother tempted her with would be real.

"I can't," she said.

"Don't decide now," Isabella said. "Come with me to the opera tonight and meet him. Honestly, the man could charm the birds from the sky."

"Mother, I have to go." Jacquelyn pushed back from the table and stood.

"Where?"

"To answer an advertisement. There's a dressmaker on Close Street who's looking for an assistant."

"Doing what?"

"Needlework—mending, alterations, that sort of thing. I'm no tailor, but perhaps with training—"

"You'll be treated like a servant and paid even less. All that sewing will ruin your eyes," Isabella predicted. "And what kind of life will that give your child?"

"I don't know," Jacquelyn admitted in frustration. "But at least it will be something true."

"And what about the fact that the father of your child has left you and the babe to fend for yourselves?" Isabella said, her tone becoming strident. "A man should be held responsible for his get. At the very least, he should provide for your living until the child comes of age. That's also true."

Jacquelyn stopped at the door and looked back at her mother over her shoulder. "He doesn't know. And he never will."

Chapter Thirty-one

Gabriel wasn't sure what he expected from Jacquelyn's mother. His experience with women who sold their favors was limited to the whores Meri had frequented in Port Royal. He certainly didn't anticipate a lady of such obvious refinement and dignity as Isabella Wren.

"Lord Drake, what an unexpected pleasure," Isabella said, her slender fingers lifted gracefully in greeting. "My daughter has told me so much about you."

Gabriel digested that mildly disturbing fact. He recognized echoes of Lyn's fine features in her mother's lovely face as he bowed over Isabella's hand. Jacquelyn had told him her mother was fluent in five languages. Gabe decided Isabella Wren could still bring a man to his knees in each of them.

"And she has told me much of you as well," he said circumspectly.

Ever the coquette, Isabella cocked her head, her astonishing violet eyes twinkling. "All of it true, alas! Pray, be seated."

Gabriel was still covered with dust and muck from his helter-skelter ride from Cornwall, but his quest to find Jacquelyn would brook no delay for niceties like a bed in a roadside inn or a hot bath. He'd slept only when he could go no further, hobbling his mount and catching a few hours under an accommodating oak. He traded horses at almost every stop and rode one nearly to exhausted collapse. Even so, the trip had taken him three days.

Then once he'd reached the outskirts of London, Gabe was forced to take circuitous routes through the city, avoiding all official-looking personages. His time as the Cornish Dragon had earned him a good bit of notoriety, and there was even a broadsheet written about his exploits with an eerily accurate picture of his likeness. He'd hang if he was caught in London. It was a sticky end he'd just as soon avoid, so he couldn't stop at a bathhouse to make himself presentable, lest someone recognize him. He knew he looked like hell on a plate and yet this elegant woman insisted he sit and make small talk while her servants prepared finger sandwiches and biscuits.

"Is Jacquelyn here?" he asked.

"No, since my daughter left your employ, she is seeking another post. She went to see about a very unsuitable position with a milliner, of all things," Isabella said, making a moue of distaste. "Still, it could be worse, I suppose. I do hope she'd not expected to try her hand at hat making. I believe they generally go quite batty."

"Why is she doing this?" Gabriel was unable to remain seated. He stood and paced Isabella's parlor. "She doesn't need to support herself. Doesn't she realize I'd give her everything I have?"

"I'm gratified to hear it," Isabella said primly.

"Besides, Jacquelyn's far too accomplished for a position like that," Gabriel said, trying to make sense of Lyn's actions. "She's run a large estate, nearly single-handed. At the very least, she might be looking for a post as a governess in a fine house, not working in a shabby little shop somewhere."

"I agree. You know, Jacquelyn didn't tell me how very attractive you are, Lord Drake. A nice hot bath and a quick trip to a gifted tailor and I've no doubt you'd cut quite a figure." Isabella smiled at him as she poured out his tea and dropped a large lump of sugar in without asking his preference. "Unfortunately, she also neglected to mention that you're not terribly bright."

Gabriel jerked back in surprise.

"If a thoroughly capable young woman does not seek a position for which she is eminently qualified, what does that suggest to you?" Isabella asked pleasantly.

"That . . . something has happened that disqualifies her in some way?"

"Ah! There may yet be hope for you," Isabella said. "Now, what do you suppose might have happened?"

"Well, I suppose— Oh!" The wonder and the horror of it hit Gabriel's chest with the force of nine-pound round. He sank so heavily into one of Isabella Wren's low chauffeuses, he feared the stubby cabriole legs might give way under his weight. "She's . . . she's with child, isn't she?"

"Now then, that was an exceeding short walk, wasn't it?" Isabella's pleasant smile faded. "If she asks, and I'm certain she will, you must tell her that I did not divulge her secret, since she would not appreciate any interference from me in this matter, however well-meant. But since *you* broached the subject and since this is *your* child we're discussing, what do *you* propose to do about it?"

"What I've wanted to do for some time now, but Jacquelyn wouldn't let me," Gabriel said. "One way or another, I intend to make her my wife."

"Well, my estimation of your intelligence grows by leaps and bounds, Lord Drake," Isabella said as she handed him a steaming cup and saucer. "I don't give my friendship lightly, but I believe I've decided to like you very much indeed." A brisk clicking of heels sounded in the hall and stopped at the doorway to the parlor. "Ah! Here comes Nanette with our repast."

The French maid dropped a quick curtsey.

"Alas, *non*, madame," she said briskly. "There is a small party of gendarmes at the front door. Jerome is trying to reason with them, to delay them enough to give you time to decide how to handle this delicate situation."

"What do they want?" Nonplussed, Isabella sipped her tea as if the arrival of the authorities was either a trivial annoyance or a regular occurrence.

Gabriel hadn't noticed anyone suspicious when he barreled down the cobbled block, but someone must have been watching. Waiting for him to turn up on Isabella Wren's doorstep.

"They want me," Gabriel said dully.

"Why?" Her expressive brows arched in interest.

"Because it was a condition of my pardon," Gabriel explained. "If I'm arrested in London, I'm to be hanged."

"Hmph! My estimate of your intelligence has just plummeted again, Lord Drake. It's a good thing I've already decided to like you. Besides, the tale about what you've been pardoned for is bound to be a long and diverting one and I shall wish to hear it as soon as we've time," she said coolly before turning back to her servant. "What about the back door?"

"A guard, he is already posted," Nanette said, fingering the lace on her apron in nervousness.

"Stop fidgeting, Nanette. It makes people think you've something to hide. Well, there's nothing for it." Isabella rose majestically. "Let them in."

"What?" Gabriel nearly doused himself with the contents of his teacup.

"Let them in *slowly*," Isabella amended. "Invite them to search the house starting with the cellar. Lord Drake and I will avail ourselves of the back staircase."

When Isabella swept from the room, Gabriel was obliged to follow. As they tiptoed up the servants' stairs, he heard the tramp of heavy boots and several shouted orders as the constables invaded La Belle Wren's home. At the sound of broken crockery, Isabella didn't panic, though she did quicken her pace. He marveled at the woman's poise.

"Where are we going?" he whispered.

"My boudoir. It's a good place to think . . . among other things," she added throatily.

It wasn't intentional, he didn't think. Since she must know he loved her daughter, he couldn't imagine Jacquelyn's mother was actually flirting with him. He suspected sly innuendo was simply her native tongue and she couldn't resist speaking it with every man she met.

Isabella pushed open the ornate gilt doors to reveal an opulent chamber, draped with silks and dominated by a massive, thick bed.

"I don't think this is a good place to hide," Gabriel said.

"Careful, Lord Drake. We've already established that thinking is not your strong suit."

"They're sure to look under the bed."

"I'm certain of it." One of Isabella's brows arched and a smile lifted her mouth. "But they aren't likely to look *in* it, are they?"

The muttered curses and sounds of shattering gewgaws told Isabella the searchers were nearing her inner sanctum. She drew her chemise over her head and draped it on the chaise before climbing naked into the big tester bed.

"Oof!" said the large lump by her left hip.

"Not another peep out of you, sir, no matter what you may feel or hear," she ordered, giving the lump a stinging swat. "Or I shall reconsider our very tentative friendship."

When she helped Gabriel Drake wedge his large frame between her second and third feather ticks, she hoped he'd sink further into the lower mattresses. Instead Lord Drake created an unsightly and damnably noticeable hump in her bed. So she ordered him out to quickly undo her laces and then back into hiding while she stripped.

Now she plumped some of her extra pillows by her right side in an effort to balance the bump formed by Gabriel on her left and draped her thick counterpane across both. She tucked the sheet under each armpit and waited as the search party drew nearer. To her surprise, Jacquelyn burst through her bedroom door instead.

"Mother!" Jacquelyn flew to her bedside and plopped down. It was a good thing it was on Isabella's right, or Gabriel Drake might have had all the wind knocked out of him. "There are men dismantling your home."

"I know, dear."

"Nanette says they are looking for Gabriel." Jacquelyn lowered her voice to a whisper.

"Yes, dear, that's true."

"But he's far from London."

The lump shifted and Isabella eyed it pointedly. "He may be closer than you think."

Jacquelyn's jaw dropped. "What are you thinking? They'll find him for certain."

"Not if we're clever, lovie," Isabella said. "Exceedingly clever. Now's the time to put that education I paid so much for to good use."

Isabella had done little enough for Jacquelyn over the years. Saving the father of her future grandchild might go a long way toward expunging Isabella's past sins of omission.

"What are we going to do?" her daughter asked. The lump that was Gabriel moved again and Jacquelyn reached over and gave him a sharp rap. "For heaven's sake, be still."

"We are going to be charming, lovie. Now put on that little mobcap and prepare to be my upstairs lady's maid."

To her relief, Jacquelyn scurried to do her bidding. Isabella's palms were damp and she wiped them on her coverlet as the constables battered down the door. They tumbled into the room in a rush and then stopped dead at the sight of her as if frozen in quicklime. She had only a moment to size up her audience, but it was enough.

They were men. How hard could it be?

To her surprise, Jacquelyn jumped in ahead of her.

"For shame, gentlemen, how shall Madam ever get her beauty sleep with all this racket?" Jacquelyn asked them with a mock stern frown followed by a coquettish wink.

Not to be outdone, Isabella gave a languorous stretch that caused several jaws to drop. "All the doorknobs in my home are fully operational and I rarely lock them unless I'm . . . entertaining someone. So you see, there's no need to ruin my perfectly good latches."

Jacquelyn arranged a few pillows behind Isabella so she could recline gracefully. The sheet slipped down far enough to expose the tops of her bare breasts. When Jacquelyn would have pulled it back up, Isabella stopped her with a slight shake of her head. Distraction was her chief weapon at present and she silently thanked God that men were so predictably susceptible to it. Once she settled herself, she drew her knees up under the coverlet to form a further camouflaging tent and fixed her gaze on the man she singled out as the leader.

"Now then, Captain," Isabella said, purposely overstating his rank. "How may we be of service to you?"

"It's Lieutenant, ma'am. Lieutenant Hathcock."

"Really? Well." She let her tone drift lower, deep into seductress range. "That's quite a name to live up to."

His face went red as a ripe tomato, but she could sense he was pleased by her teasing. He squared his shoulders and stood a bit straighter. "We're looking for a man—"

"My, what a coincidence!" Jacquelyn giggled and arched a suggestive brow. "Looking for a man, you say? That's Madam's usual occupation as well."

The men laughed, but the lieutenant silenced them with frown.

"We're looking for a particular gentleman."

"Believe me, sir," Isabella quipped. "I'm also quite particular about my gentlemen."

One or two of them were biting their lips to keep quiet.

"The man we want is Lord Gabriel Drake," Hathcock said. "He was reported entering this house."

"Lord Drake? Hmm. Doesn't sound familiar. I don't suppose you'd know his full title. That might jog my memory," she suggested, casting a surreptitious glance at Jacquelyn to see how she reacted to hearing her lover named as the fugitive these men sought. A forced smile lifted her daughter's lips.

Keep it light and ribald, she willed Jacquelyn to understand. That's how Isabella had decided to play things, broad strokes for the masses, but with a hint of the unattainable these yokels would find classy.

"The gentleman's a baron, I believe," Hathcock said.

"A baron, you say." Jacquelyn peered up at him from under her lashes with feigned innocence. "I should think not. To my certain knowledge, Madam has never taken anything less than a viscount to her bed."

Bravo, lovie! But a shade too close to the mark. Isabella felt the lump to her left wiggle a little. "A woman in my profession has standards to maintain, you understand," Isabella purred.

Another round of snorting and stifled grunts greeted this sally.

"Of course, I was tempted once by a divine tenor on tour from Rome." Isabella decided a naughty little story might divert their attention, even if Gabriel Drake should take it into his head to move again. "I'm terribly devoted to the opera, you see. All those lightning-fast runs and trills—the man sang like a god for four mortal hours. If he could keep his voice up that long, just imagine what he might be able to do with his . . ." Isabella paused to let them finish her racy thought. "But to my sorrow, I soon learned why he was able to hit those glorious high notes so easily."

"Ah! What I 'eard is true then," one of the men said. "Them light tenors hain't got no balls."

"None at all," Isabella confirmed with a knowing grin that sent them into snickers. She had them now. "However, I have it on good authority that lyric tenors do, in fact, possess one."

Their laughter advanced to full-throated guffaws.

"And I'm told that dramatic tenors with those tight, forced high notes are actually the proud owners of two jewels," Isabella said confidingly. "But while they sing, someone is hidden beneath their costume squeezing the life out of them."

Uproarious hilarity greeted this pronouncement. Even Lieutenant Hathcock was wiping tears of mirth from his eyes.

"Lieutenant, would you allow me to send Jacquelyn down to the kitchen to ask Nanette to prepare some refreshment for you and your men? You must be hungry after your hard work dismantling my home." She slanted her gaze at him and let her sheet drift down another inch, showing her still impressive décolletage. "As you can see, I'm in no position to do it myself."

Two hours later, she was still holding court, still naked under her sheets, and they were all still lounging about her boudoir. Jacquelyn had plied them with sandwiches and tea while Isabella composed little kiss-and-tell stories of love and lust among the upper crust, with all the names changed to protect the guilty, and charmed them from her tester bed with naughty banter. They'd stopped their active search, but she was beginning to worry that they'd never leave.

Once or twice, the left lump on her bed shifted restlessly and she dug a sharp elbow into it as a surreptitious warning. A couple of times, Jacquelyn actually sat down on top of him, artfully arranging her skirts to disguise his movement. Then once he settled, she hopped up to refresh the constables' tea cups.

Gabriel hadn't twitched in the last hour and Isabella wondered if he'd suffocated under all those feathers.

Death by hanging or death by poultry—dead was still dead.

Chapter Thirty-two

"Well, Lieutenant Hathcock, I can't tell you how I've enjoyed your visit, but actually I do have an assignation this evening—no, no, I can't give you the gentleman's name, but please be advised, he is at least a viscount," Isabella assured him.

"Madam really must begin her toilette," Jacquelyn chimed in. "Beauty does require a certain amount of homage if she is to be coaxed out."

The men began protesting that she was lovely just as she was—or perhaps especially as she was. Men did generally prefer women without clothing.

It occurred to Isabella that she was probably much older than any of their wives or sweethearts and yet her soft life of luxury had spared her many of time's ravages. But while she might cheat Father Time for a bit, he would not be held off indefinitely.

She tried to tell herself that her bed was usually empty now by her own choice, since she was heavily involved in helping Lord Haversham maintain his illusion of a sexual liaison with her, but her heart damned her for a liar. Even if Geoffrey weren't lavishing her with public attention, she might still be privately alone.

She wondered occasionally what it might have been like to have lain beside the same man since her youth, to have given him many children, to have nursed him through illness or struggled with adversity by his side, to have loved once and loved well?

She'd never know.

God must be a man, Isabella had often said to her philosopher friends, *for He has arranged things so a woman must take what she wants. And then He makes her pay for it twice.*

So Isabella had decided to take soft fabric to drape over her milk-smooth skin and hard jewels to adorn her throat in a winking crescent and to surround herself with fine things.

And an abundance of pleasure.

Of course, the pleasure was a bit wanting of late, but she believed a little loneliness was the payment demanded for her opulent life. When she thought of the discomforts of poverty, the hazards of multiple pregnancies and her distaste for sickness in general, she decided she'd made a fair trade.

Now if she could only trade for a few moments' privacy so she could somehow spirit Gabriel Drake safely out of her house, Isabella promised herself she'd stop making deals with the Almighty and never barter with Him for more ever again.

"Really, gentlemen," she said in her gayest tone, "I must be—"

"What's going on here?" a diminutive man with a voice out of all proportion to his smallness demanded from her bedchamber doorway.

Isabella narrowed her eyes at him. She'd seen him at court during the last masked ball. Yes, she knew him by his slimy reputation as well as his name—Sir Cecil Oddbody, Keeper of the King's Privy Seal. She didn't recognize the strapping fellow at his side, but the new man's murderous frown did not commend him to her. Jacquelyn sidled to a corner of the room and kept her eyes downcast, letting the mobcap obscure her face.

Sir Cecil glared at the constabulary and, to a man, they cringed.

"My dear friend Lord Curtmantle," Oddbody lifted a palm to indicate his companion, "sent word that—"

"Welcome, my lord. My name is Isabella Wren," she said

to Curtmantle with far more dignity than a naked woman in a room full of men should possess. "Whence do you hail?"

Oddbody scowled afresh at her interruption, but she'd always found conversational niceties like introductions useful rudders for steering an unpleasant interview to friendlier waters.

"I have a tidy barony in Cornwall," Curtmantle said.

"Just a baron, worse luck for 'im, eh?" one of the men whispered, and several of them sputtered with mirth. "Reckon she'll throw 'im out?"

Sir Oddbody's eyes bulged, clearly irritated at the inappropriate snickers. "*Baron* Curtmantle sent word that the fugitive we seek was seen entering this house. I came expecting to find the pirate already in irons. At the very least, Lieutenant, you and your men might be engaged in an exhaustive search of the premises. Instead, I find you enjoying tea and crumpets with a naked whore."

"Well, Your Worship," the unfortunate lieutenant said, "it hain't exactly the lady's fault she's naked. We sort of stumbled in on her unannounced, you might say. But Gorblimey! If she hain't been pleasant as she can be about it and since she's stayed fair covered up the whole time, I don't see how you can rightly call her naked." Finding more courage the longer he spoke, he lifted his chin in defiance. "Why, I'll lay me teeth she hain't no whore. She's what you might call a . . . a . . . well, I don't know the word for it proper-like, but—"

"Never mind, Lieutenant," Isabella said. "I appreciate your chivalry, but I fear Sir Oddbody's mind is made up about me. Some minds are so narrow, you see, it's quite impossible to fit a new idea into them."

Humor was still her best defense and the men showed their appreciation with a rumbling chuckle. Encouraged, she continued, "And you couldn't squeeze an original thought out of them if you put them into a coffee grinder."

Sir Cecil turned his steely, ratlike gaze on her.

Yes, indeed. A few turns in a very large grinder would improve Oddbody out of all knowing.

"That's quite enough from you, madam," he said with a delicate twitch of his nose that reminded Isabella even more forcefully of the rodent he resembled. "Or I shall have you removed forthwith and detained for questioning."

"I'd tread lightly, sir, if I were you." Isabella had been reclining on her pillows. Now she drew herself upright, careful to keep the sheets high across her chest now. "This is my home and you are an unwelcome visitor. I have some very dear friends at court who would find your actions most distressing."

"You have no idea who you're dealing with," Oddbody said.

"And it's obvious you have no idea just how highly placed my friends may be," Isabella countered.

He waffled a bit, clearly unsure how well connected she was. Isabella would hate to call in favors, but she did hold markers from some exceptionally prominent persons.

What was the point of notoriety if it didn't protect one's silk-clad behind from time to time?

Isabella saw the sizzle of disappointment in his eyes, signaling that he was preparing to concede this skirmish to her. Then she noticed Baron Curtmantle eyeing Jacquelyn with interest.

"You, girl," he said. "Let me see your face."

She peered at him from under the floppy cap.

"That's her." Lord Curtmantle pointed an accusing finger. "Jacquelyn Wren. The woman he came to London for."

The lump that was Gabriel shifted at the mention of Jacquelyn's name and Isabella lolled to her left side to cover the slight movement.

"What are you talking about?" Jacquelyn said, determined to brazen it out.

"Mistress Wren, we can conclude our business here quickly and easily or we can move it to another location where the whole sorry affair becomes much more protracted and . . . not at all easy," Sir Cecil said, his face contorted with suppressed impatience. "To avoid such an unfortunate occurrence you only need answer one question. Where is Gabriel Drake?"

Jacquelyn stepped back a pace. "Why do you want him?"

"That is none of your concern," he said. "We know he's in London. All we need to know is where he's hiding."

"Lord Drake is in Cornwall," Jacquelyn said. Isabella wished she could whisper to her to stop fidgeting with her hands. Her daughter was evidently not an accomplished liar. "He has no reason to come to London."

Sir Cecil chucked her chin and emitted a noise that Isabella might have called a giggle if it hadn't sounded so sinister. "Oh, I can think of at least one. Now where is he?"

"I . . . I . . ." Jacquelyn stammered, unable to mask a shiver of distaste. Then she raised her eyes and met his gaze squarely. "I haven't seen him since I left Dragon Caern nearly three weeks ago."

"Liar," Oddbody hissed.

"If she says she hasn't seen him, you may believe her," Isabella said. After all, Jacquelyn was telling the truth this time. She hadn't seen him. She'd only sat on him a time or two. "And you, sir, will not insult my daughter in my own home."

"Quite right," he turned and shot her a leering smile. Isabella knew she'd made a tactical blunder. "I have more potent methods of interrogation at my disposal elsewhere. Lieutenant Hathcock, arrest this young woman on the charge of harboring and concealing a condemned felon."

"No!" Isabella said, but before she could gather the sheets about her to rise in protest, the mattress beneath her began bucking like a stallion. Gabriel Drake threw off his place of concealment, sending Isabella to the floor in a tangle of bed-clothes.

"Belay that!" he roared. Drenched with sweat from his long concealment between her mattresses, anger roiled off him as if he were a vengeful Poseidon rising from the waves. "I'm the one you want. Leave her out of it and I'll go with-out a fight. Otherwise, you have my solemn promise I'll make my capture very costly for you. A condemned man has little to lose."

Jacquelyn broke free of the men who held her and ran to Lord Drake. She threw her arms around him. "What are you doing here?"

"I had to come, Lyn," he said as he allowed the constable to bind his hands behind him in a heavy shackle. "You know why."

"Oh, Gabriel." Jacquelyn's face crumpled before she pressed it against his chest.

Her daughter's despair lanced Isabella's heart. She could do nothing more for Gabriel Drake, but she could make cer-tain that that little weasel, Cecil Oddbody, didn't leave with more than one captive. Isabella hitched her sheet around her body and tucked a trailing end over her breasts. She rose and hurried to Jacquelyn, gently disengaging her from Lord Drake.

"Come away, lovie," she whispered urgently. Jacquelyn allowed Isabella to lead her to one side.

"Well, madam," Oddbody said, stopping her in her tracks. "What have to say for yourself? Hiding a felon between your mattresses. No matter that he's a baron, Lord Drake is still a criminal. Aiding a fugitive from the Crown is a hanging of-fense in its own right. No matter how well-placed your friends may be, I doubt they can save you from this!"

"I invaded this house and hid on my own initiative," Gabriel said. "The lady knew nothing of my presence between her mattresses."

"Beggin' your pardon, Your Worship," Lieutenant Hathcock said with a squeak, "but I expect that's about the size of it. After all, Lord Drake's just a baron. Everyone knows Isabella Wren don't take no one to her bed, 'less he be a viscount at the least. We'll all swear to it, won't we?"

The constables nodded vigorously.

"Very well," Cecil Oddbody said with a huff. "But mind how you go in the future, madam, and rest assured I shall be watching you. Take him away."

As Gabriel was led away, he passed Lord Curtmantle. Quick as lightning, Lord Drake swept his leg at the baron's knees, bringing him crashing to the floor. Before the constables could muscle him away, Gabriel had planted his foot squarely on Curtmantle's chest.

"I should have killed you when I had the chance, Hugh," Gabriel spat. "You've traveled a long way to play Judas."

Several billy clubs pounded his shoulders and the constables pulled him off the downed man.

"Don't flatter yourself," Curtmantle said. "You're a far cry from a spotless lamb and you know it." A flat smile spread across his face. "But you're right. You should have killed me. Just think how much it's going to pain you when you see me doing a jig at your hanging."

Jacquelyn tried to tear herself from Isabella's arms, but she wouldn't let her go.

"Hush, child. Not now," Isabella whispered fiercely. Then she raised her voice. "I assume you're taking him to the Tower. When might we bring food and other necessities?"

Oddbody sneered at her. "Do you imagine I'll see him in the comfortable chamber Raleigh languished in? Not for a moment, madam. For the likes of Gabriel Drake, a more suitable lodging is required."

Now that Gabriel was shackled and a welt was rising from his cheek where one of the constables had clubbed him, Oddbody was feeling braver. He strutted a step or two.

"You see, a pirate has the blackest of hearts—cold, unfeeling and utterly beyond redemption," Oddbody explained. "His prison should reflect that. If there was a darker hole than Newgate, rest assured I'd make use of it. However, since this is the worst we can do until his appointment with Madame Gallows, Newgate Prison will have to suffice. Come along."

Two men dragged Gabriel away and the rest filed after them.

When the room was empty, Jacquelyn collapsed in a heap. "Oh, Mother, what happened? Gabriel was pardoned for his piracy."

"So he really was a pirate? That *is* a tale I shall want to hear." Isabella sank down beside her. "Evidently, one of the conditions of his pardon was that he not be found in London ever again. I take it he failed to mention that tidbit of information to you."

"I had no idea." Jacquelyn stared at her upturned palms in seeming fascination. "Then it's my fault he's been taken."

"Don't be ridiculous," Isabella said. "Lord Drake is not a child. He knew the risk in coming here and he was willing to take it. You can't blame yourself for his actions. You can only accept responsibility for your own decisions, which for most people is quite burden enough without assuming anyone else's."

"But they're going to hang him!"

"Not until the end of the month, so that gives us a little time," Isabella said. "They'll wait until then because the populace expects it. London likes a good hanging day. You'd think it was a holiday instead of just a chance to watch some poor fellow dance the hempen jig."

Jacquelyn erupted in sobs.

"Go ahead and cry, dear," Isabella said, running a motherly hand over Jacquelyn's head. "It's best to get such things out of your system, but when you're finished, dry your eyes. We have work to do."

Jacquelyn sniffed and shook her head slowly. "What can we do?"

Isabella took her daughter's chin in her hand and kissed her. "Oh, my dear. Even as a child, you were so grave and proper. You always knew the right thing to do." Something inside her was pleased that she could finally be a help to Jacquelyn. "Well, for starters, you should go down to the kitchen with Nanette and make up a food basket. By all accounts, prison meals are both scanty and unpalatable. The man is still alive. If he's alive, he needs to eat."

Jacquelyn wiped her face with her skirt and nodded.

"Once we've spoken to your Lord Drake, we'll know what else he needs. Send Jerome to fetch me when you're ready to go to Newgate and I'll come with you. We'll need something to take for a bribe," she said. "I hope those oxen didn't steal all my silver."

Jacquelyn started for the door. "What will you be doing?"

Isabella forced a smile. "What I always do this time of day—catching up on my correspondence."

And writing the most important letter of my life, she added silently.

Chapter Thirty-three

*O*ch! Me big toe aches something fierce!" Meriwether pulled off his boot and stared at the toe protruding from the hole in his striped stocking. The nail was cracked and blackened, but that was not related to the pain. It was because he hadn't seen fit to wash more than strictly necessary the last time Mrs. B. required him to bathe.

"You've got the gout, old man," Mrs. Beadle said without looking up from the chicken she was denuding of its feathers. "The rich man's disease. It's all them sauces and pies you've been eating. And you've been making a sizable dent in the meat larder around here. Too much time as a trencherman and not enough in useful employment. It's the gout."

"No, it ain't gout," Meri said, trying to wiggle the stiff joint. "And if it were any but yourself blaming your fine cookin' for me misery, he'd be looking for his ears afore long."

"Hmph!" Despite her snort, Mrs. Beadle's lips spread in a brief smile at his praise. "Try less gravy on your potatoes and see if it don't improve."

"No, this has happened afore," Meriwether said, rubbing his foot. "It does this from time to time and what I've put in me belly or not don't signify in the slightest. I remember once . . ."

He stopped in midsentence. A niggling suspicion chewed at his brain like a terrier worrying a rat.

"Well, go on," Mrs. Beadle said as she laid the chicken out on her chopping block.

"It don't happen but what the Cap'n ain't in some spot o' trouble or other," Meri said. "The first time was the night before we sank the *Defiant* and I fished him out of the deep." Meri went on to describe several incidents where his toe had warned of impending calamity.

"Then there was that time off St. Thomas when this French captain was after hanging 'im. Even had him locked up in the jail there in Charlotte Amalie, but we sent a volley of nine pounders through the walls and broke him out. Replenished the crew with the other prisoners in one stroke so it turned out for the best, ye see, but if the Cap'n had only listened to me big toe afore he went ashore that night—"

Meri stopped abruptly and pulled his boot back on. "I've got to hie meself to London town and no mistake."

Meriwether explained what he knew of the captain and Mistress Wren's whereabouts.

"Well, I thought she was overlong at choosing silks in Bath," Mrs. Beadle said.

"It ain't only that they're not in Bath." When Meri told her of the condition placed on Gabriel's pardon, Mrs. Beadle was mad as a kettle at full boil. Meriwether tried to placate her, but Mrs. B. wouldn't even listen to him. He decided to let her rant.

A woman wielding a meat cleaver is not to be trifled with.

"And you stood there and watched him ride off knowin' the trouble he could be getting himself into," she accused. "Of all the slack-brained, puddin'-headed—"

"Well, I can either let ye talk me to death or chop off me head, but I've one sure way to shut ye up for a mite."

Meri grabbed Mrs. B. by the waist and swung her into his arms for a smacking kiss right on the lips.

"Oh!" she said. "Oh, my goodness!"

"I hope not, old woman," Meriwether said. "Generally when a man kisses a woman, her goodness is the last thing on his mind."

The meat cleaver clattered to the floor. The sharp blade missed Meri's foot, but the thick maple handle whacked his big toe a good clout. He yowled and hopped on his good foot, cradling his throbbing one with both hands.

"Well, I can let you scream your fool head off or I can shut you up, old man," Mrs. Beadle said. She grabbed both of his ears and pulled his face to hers for another resounding kiss.

The fact that he even had a big toe was momentarily forgotten.

"I suppose this means you'll be callin' me Joseph," he said when their lips finally parted.

"I suppose I'd better."

"And what might I call ye, *Mrs. Beadle* being rather long and unhandy. And the way ye make me feel like a young buck, *old woman* don't seem to fit exactly, do it?"

"Well, my Christian name is Hagitha."

"Hagitha, hmm? Don't suppose ye have an un-Christian one to use as a spare?"

She swatted him, but he wrapped his arms around her ample middle and gave her a squeeze.

"Now then, how about we compromise and I call ye Mrs. Meriwether?" He drew her into another whiskey-tinged kiss.

Neither of them called anyone anything for a good long while.

Of course, Meriwether still had to go to London. He couldn't ignore the warning of his big toe. Mrs. Beadle wasn't one to be left out of such an important journey. She insisted that she should go with him in case Miss Jack needed her. And in truth, Meriwether was loath to leave Mrs. B. after discovering that her lips were soft as her ample hips.

And sweet as her cherry pies.

But then there were the children to consider, and Father

Eustace didn't feel up to the task of keeping track of the little dears by himself. By midafternoon when the heavily provisioned wagon rolled over Dragon Caern's drawbridge, Mrs. Beadle was driving the pair of matched bays with the girls chattering in the back. Loping along as outriders, Meri was mounted on his piebald cob and Father Eustace rode what he assured everyone was a steady, reliable mule.

Before the first five-mile marker, Hyacinth was cross with everyone. The twins were refusing to speak, even to each other. Lily seemed only able to ask "Are we there yet?" and Daisy bedeviled Mrs. Beadle at every other rise in the road to be allowed to take a turn driving the wagon.

"I've never been to London except by ship," Meri said to Father Eustace as they plodded along keeping pace with the wagon. "Is it a far journey by land?"

"If we're fortunate, it'll take a week," Father Eustace said morosely. "If we see foul weather, or a broken axle, or a horse goes lame or highwaymen . . ."

"I take yer meaning, Father," Meri said with a sigh. "God help us."

"Amen to that," the priest agreed. "Amen to that in spades."

Chapter Thirty-four

There had been a prison on the same site, hard against the ruins of an old Roman wall, since the time of Henry I. Its reputation for cruelty and hideous torments made Newgate a byword for suffering. The prison had been torn down or burned countless times, always resurfacing in the same spot like a festering carbuncle on London's backside.

Jacquelyn was surprised to see that Newgate's latest incarnation was an impressive stone edifice complete with statuary, a place of unlikely tranquility. A small candle of hope glimmered in her chest.

But once inside the gate, Jacquelyn and Isabella were assaulted by the stench of ancient misery, a potent mix of urine, vomit and excrement. Jacquelyn raised a scented hanky to her nose and bit the inside of her cheek to keep from adding to the miasma.

Only slightly less offensive than the smell was the din. Shouted obscenities, piteous wails and even a few growls Jacquelyn was sure couldn't be human pierced her ear. It was like the choir of the damned warming up.

Mr. Pinckney, the current warden, drove a hard bargain for the favor he was about to grant, even though Isabella turned her considerable charm on him. Coin of the realm seemed to be the only inducement Mr. Pinckney was disposed to respect.

It was customary for prisoners to pay not only for their keep, but also for food and whatever niceties they requested, like soap or a warm blanket. Even once an inmate served his sentence, release was not assured. Until he'd paid Mr. Pinckney for his stay, he wasn't going anywhere. Most unfortunates condemned to Newgate were there for life.

And it generally wasn't that long a stay.

After Isabella parted with an exorbitant bribe, the warden escorted them to see Gabriel. Pinckney led them to a large common room in the central hall, enclosed with iron bars on all sides with a narrow walkway for the jailers and any visitors who might dare to bring sustenance to the inmates. Scores of prisoners—men, women, children, entire families along with a few farm animals—were penned in the large space, the stone floor of which served as bed, dining table and latrine for all.

"I don't see him here," Jacquelyn said.

Mr. Pinckney consulted his ledger. "Drake, Gabriel. Condemned pirate. Central Holding. He's here all right. Look closely. People are not generally at their best here in Newgate. You may find him somewhat . . . altered."

"There," Isabella whispered as she pointed to a figure chained near the far wall of bars. "This will absolutely not do." She handed Jacquelyn the basket of food and bedding and turned a falsely bright smile on the warden. "Good sir, perhaps you and I can return to your office where we might discuss a change of accommodations for Lord Drake."

Isabella took the man's arm as if he were one of her opera-loving friends. In truth he was a money-grubbing leech who prospered through lessening the suffering of others by only the smallest of degrees. She led him away chattering as she went, her tone as gay as if she were in a fine salon.

If her mother could put a brave face on things, Jacquelyn decided she could, too. She squared her shoulders and marched around the pen, trying not to notice the pitiful cries of the other prisoners who had no one to bring them needful things. She promised herself she'd bring two baskets next time.

She managed to control her rising panic, but when she drew near to Gabriel, a scream clawed at her throat. She swallowed it back. She'd be no comfort to him if she allowed herself to crumble.

He was manacled at the ankles and wrists, the heavy chains tethering him to a ring in the floor. Gabriel was sitting slumped down, faced away from her. The back of his jacket was streaked with brown stains and a small pool of red was spreading by his left hip. He'd been caned or whipped and the jacket forced back on him, blood caking on his open wounds.

A sob escaped her throat.

He turned at her voice. With a clank of iron, he rose unsteadily to his feet. "Lyn, you shouldn't be here."

She extended a hand through the bars. "My heart is here. Where else would I be?"

He strained toward her as far as his bonds allowed. With effort, he was able to brush her fingertips with his.

"Mother's arranging for you to be moved from here." *First things first*, she ordered herself. If she concentrated on improving his conditions now, she could shove away the thought of him hanging later.

"Seems Cecil Oddbody swings a bigger stick than I imagined," he said. "I don't think your mother has enough money to tempt Pinckney to change his orders."

"You underestimate Isabella Wren's powers of persuasion," she said, forcing a tremulous smile.

"It doesn't matter. Tell your mother to save her coin." He shook his head. "Whether I sleep on fine linens for the next fortnight or on cold stone, in the end, I'll hang just the same."

"No, I refuse to believe it," she said. "There must be something we can do. Mother can convince one of her well-placed friends to appeal to the king."

"My pardon was specific on that point. If I should be taken in London, 'said pardon shall be void and the standing sentence shall be administered without trial and without further clemency on the part of His Royal Highness,'" he quoted. "The service I did His Majesty only extends my credit so far, you see."

"You knew what would happen and yet you came," she said. "In God's name, why?"

"My heart was here," he said with a slow smile. "Where else would I be? I had to see you, Lyn. You left before I could tell you how much I love you."

She covered her mouth with her hand to stifle the sob. Then she lowered it. Her lips moved, forming the words, *I love you, too,* but she couldn't force enough air out to make a sound.

"I just couldn't go forward with the farce of marrying someone else," he said. "And before you get angry with me—"

"Gabriel, I'll never be angry with you again," she said, finding her voice.

"Wish I was going to live long enough to hold you to that." A corner of his mouth turned up. "Then this would be almost worth it. But I wanted to tell you not to worry about Dragon Caern. I haven't neglected my duty. Meri is looking after the girls. If I don't return—when I don't return—"

"Don't even say it."

"Listen to me. I knew the risks. Meri promised me he'll see to you and the girls for the rest of his life. You'll not likely live in style, but that old pirate will make certain you don't starve. If the worst happens, I gave him orders to sell off all the stock and everything that isn't nailed down. Meri will divvy out profits among my tenants and crofters. They can do what they please with it, but I told him to make sure they cleared out before the Crown names a protector or they might be forced to surrender it."

"The pirate who gives away his wealth," she said softly. "You are a lord, after all. Your father would be proud of you, Gabriel."

He shrugged and then winced at the pain the gesture caused him. "I was hoping to make *you* proud."

"I always am. Never think otherwise," she said fiercely. "Gabriel, there's something I need to tell you as well—"

"Drake!" Pinckney's foghorn of a voice interrupted. He and Isabella reappeared, flanked by three burly guards. The warden tossed a long key at Gabriel. "Unshackle yourself and make your way to the door. This lady has paid for an easement of your burden."

Isabella hurried to Jacquelyn's side and flashed Gabriel a toothsome smile. "I stand by my initial assessment of you, Lord Drake. A nice hot bath, a gifted tailor, and you'll cut a fine figure."

"Pity the next lady on his dance card is Madame Gallows," Pinckney said, laughing obscenely at his own wit. "But provided you have the coin, madam, we can clean him up well enough to suit that Gray Lady."

Pinckney ordered the three guards to mind Gabriel as he was transferred to one of the solitary cells. If Gabriel were in fighting trim, he'd easily have been a match for these three. But now he moved with such stiffness and obvious pain, Jacquelyn ached for him. He'd been badly beaten before being dumped in Newgate.

The solitary cells were reserved for those who could afford to escape the squalor of Central Holding. Gabriel's new home was the size of a glorified butler's pantry, but it did boast a narrow string bed and a barred window the size of his hand.

He sank onto the creaking bed. Jacquelyn suspected he couldn't lie down with the wounds on his back, but he seemed more comfortable seated. Compared to Central Holding, this cell was a guest suite in Windsor Castle.

"We shall require a hipbath, filled with water—hot water, mind you," Isabella told Pinckney. "Some good-quality soap and medicinal salve. Something from a reputable herbalist, now. I'll stand for none of your bear grease and soot."

Her mother had noticed the bloodstains on Gabriel's jacket as well. As Isabella emptied more of her purse into Pinckney's grasping hand, Jacquelyn reflected that God had been especially kind to her in her choice of mothers, after all.

"Now, then," Isabella said as soon as the bath was ready and the jailers left them with several rude, ribald comments. "Off with those rags, Lord Drake."

"I'm accustomed to bathing in private," he said testily.

"And are you accustomed to washing and doctoring your own back?" Jacquelyn said. When she and her mother stood united, no man could gainsay them, but Gabriel seemed determined to try.

"Come now, love," Jacquelyn said, easing his jacket off with gentleness. "There's nothing here I haven't already seen and if Mother sees something that surprises her, you'll be the first to know."

"All right, ladies," he said, rising from the bed. "I hope it comforts you to know that you are the first to force me to hoist the white flag."

Jacquelyn and her mother helped him undress and to her sorrow, there was something Jacquelyn hadn't seen before. She was prepared for angry welts on Gabe's back, maybe a few lashes that had drawn blood. She didn't anticipate the crisscross pattern of shredded flesh. Jacquelyn felt the blood drain from her face and her vision tunneled for a moment.

"Well," Isabella said, looking him up and down as he lowered himself into the steaming hipbath. "I can certainly see why you like him, daughter."

"Mother!"

"Just using the eyes God gave me," Isabella said, then she leaned over and whispered into Jacquelyn's ear. "Smile, dearest. He needs it."

Gabriel sat stone-still as Jacquelyn sponged his wounds, but occasionally the muscles beneath his lacerated skin twitched like horseflesh quivering to rid itself of a fly. She bathed him in silence, letting her fingertips remember every bit of him. To Isabella's credit, she busied herself with tearing muslin into strips, her eyes averted to give them the illusion of privacy.

"Isn't it enough that they arrested you?" Jacquelyn said. "Why did they do this to you?"

"Somehow, Oddbody has heard the rumor of the Dragon Caern treasure and is convinced it exists." Gabriel stood, the soapy water sluicing over his form. "He wanted to know more and thought I should be able to tell him."

Jacquelyn blotted his back dry, trying not to injure him further. She applied the salve and wound the clean muslin around his ribs. "You should have made something up."

"I was tempted," Gabriel admitted as he slipped an arm into the fresh shirt Isabella had brought.

"Found it in my boudoir. Can't remember whose it is," her mother said with a wicked grin. "Occupational hazard."

Jacquelyn helped him with the other sleeve.

"But I figured out about halfway into the beating that if I told him anything, I wouldn't even make it as far as Newgate," Gabriel said as he stepped into some buff-colored breeches that were a snug fit.

"Hmm. Misjudged that a bit," Isabella said as she eyed his lower half. "We'll bring you another pair tomorrow. Now, see if you can do something with his hair, lovie. The man looks like a wild savage."

By the time Pinckney returned with his lackeys to retrieve the hipbath, Gabriel was as well-turned out as they could make him with borrowed clothing and not a razor in sight. He still looked every inch the gentleman he was.

"Mr. Pinckney," he said. "I wonder if I could trouble you to send the priest straight away."

"Ah, yes. A certain date with death turns a man's thoughts to God, don't it?" the warden said. "You'll wish to be shriven, of course."

Gabriel shook his head. "I'm due to hang at month's end. There isn't time enough to confess my sins." He reached for Jacquelyn's hand. "No, I need to make this lady my wife. I was hoping the priest would consent to marry us. That is," he turned to look askance at her, "if the lady consents first."

"Yes, Gabriel, with my whole heart, yes." She could deny him nothing. If he'd asked her to fly, she'd have taken a leap from any battlement he chose.

The brief ceremony had the fuzzy-edged feel of a dream. Jacquelyn repeated her vows but the words were unnecessary. Her heart was so bound together with this man's, they shared the same rhythm. This crude rite could only acknowledge the sacred joining that had already occurred. The kiss at the end was the only part of the proceedings that seemed real.

And its bittersweet tang made her weep.

Chapter Thirty-five

The days fled past like dry leaves scuttling over the cobbles. Jacquelyn visited Gabriel on each of them, bringing food and wine and fresh linen, determined to keep his spirits up as she prayed for a miracle. The wounds on his back were healing without infection thanks to her attentions. She saw to it that he had books to read and worked tirelessly to keep the general misery that was Newgate from leeching into his cell. When she discovered the straw tick he slept on was crawling with lice, she had it burned and replaced.

That was the day he put his foot down.

"That's it. Go away!" he commanded. "No matter how much you try to fix this place, you put yourself at risk every time you come. I can't bear to see you here."

"And where else are you likely to see me?" she countered with sauciness that would have done her mother credit. She tried so hard to put up a brave front, she couldn't allow herself to feel the hurt of his rejection. She took refuge in anger. "Do you think you're the only one suffering?"

"No, but I'm the only one who'll hang," he said, giving voice to the stuff of her nightmares.

When tears threatened to spill over her lids, he sighed deeply and took both her hands in his. Her left forefinger was heavy with his father's signet ring. He'd given it to her because he had no other with which to seal their vows.

"Lyn, listen to me. I have but two days left. As you love me, here's what I want you to do. Take a coach back to Dragon Caern. Leave today. Live."

"But I—"

"I know you intend to stand by me to the end, and I love

you for your courage," he said in a gentler tone. "But it will give me no comfort to see you at Execution Dock."

Mention of the public gallows made her knees weak. Though the populace greeted hanging days as if they were a festival, hanging was a grim business for those who provided the entertainment. At Tyburn, the usual place of execution for felons, the condemned might be lucky enough to have his neck snap in the drop, though the body inevitably twitched and voided itself in a macabre dance. But at Execution Dock, the gallows reserved especially for pirates, the ropes used were far too short to offer the slim chance of instant oblivion. Gabriel could look forward to fifteen or twenty minutes of strangulation while the crowd made catcalls and laid odds on how long he'd last. His body would be left to be covered by three tides, then tarred and hung on display in a gibbet as a warning to other seafaring men who might be tempted to piracy.

"Hanging is no sight for a woman who's bearing." He slid his hand warmly over her abdomen and splayed his fingers protectively over the tiny life that grew there. "Think of the child."

"I'd rather think of his father."

"Then think of me as I was. Think of me at Dragon Caern," he urged. "I can bear dying knowing that you carry part of me with you. I can even bear hanging. But I can't bear for you to see it."

Gabriel had his way in the end. She agreed not to come again. She promised not to see him hanged. He seemed satisfied, his spirit more settled, as they parted for the last time. Gabriel even promised her in return that he would let the priest hear his confession.

"As much as we've time for at any rate," he said with the wicked grin she'd come to love.

She found herself outside the prison gates without knowing how she got there, but she supposed she must have put one foot before the other in a stunned trance. The world had a thin veil draped over it, all the sharp edges blurred and indistinct. As Jacquelyn bounced along in her mother's barouche, she wondered if the numbness would ever go away.

Somehow, she doubted it.

"Well, there she is, children." Meriwether's croaking voice greeted Jacquelyn when she pushed open her mother's front door. In a flurry of arms and legs and excited greetings, the girls surrounded her, hugging and kissing and nearly knocking her off her feet. Father Eustace was right behind them, offering a consoling hand.

"Come, now, that'll quite do, ye wee heathens," Mrs. Beadle said, borrowing Meri's pet name for the girls. "Let Miss Jack catch her breath."

"In fact, dears," Isabella said, "I wish you'd all come with me into the garden for a bit. Nanette has prepared a delightful tea, just for us. It will give Jacquelyn a chance to visit with the boring adults while we youngsters have some fun. You can see her later." She added a wink to the invitation and the children trooped happily in her wake.

Once again, Jacquelyn thanked God for her mother. She couldn't bear to cry in front of the girls. Fortunately, Mrs. B., Meri and Father Eustace were willing to let her weep as long as she needed without interruption.

When her tears subsided into moist hiccups, they began gently quizzing her about the situation.

Yes, her mother had written for help from her highly placed friends, but no, they'd received no word, and Isabella couldn't be sure the party in question was even in the country at present.

"Why did you come to London?" Jacquelyn asked Meri. "I sent no word."

"Blame me big toe. It hasn't failed me yet." Meri went on to explain the prescient nature of that digit and wonder of wonders, the discovery of the legendary Dragon Caern treasure. "I figured Cap'n was in trouble and so I brung two of them chests filled with gold. Do ye not think we could bribe the jailers into letting him wander off?"

"Gold isn't worth much if you're too dead to spend it," Father Eustace said. "The warden would no doubt be taking Gabriel's place at the gallows if he allowed such an escape."

"Besides, if it were a question of money, my mother would already have paid a ransom. How did you manage to bring so much?" Jacquelyn asked.

"Well, we started overland," Mrs. Beadle said. "Then Joseph here remembered that the *Revenge* was tied up at Plymouth. We turned around and made for there since the girls weren't such good travelers on the road, but they were charmed by the idea of sailing on their uncle's old pirate ship. Joseph's shipmates were disposed to take on passengers and we halted to retrieve as much of the treasure as Joseph thought needful to help Lord Drake."

Jacquelyn first digested the astonishing fact that Mrs. B. was calling Meri by his Christian name, and then something else clicked in her brain.

"Is the *Revenge* still in port?"

"Aye," Meri said. "I convinced 'em we'd be needing a way to return to Cornwall, so Cap'n Helmsby is givin' his crew a bit o' shore leave, so to speak. Since the pardon, they've been hauling cargo for one ship line or other. They're mortal tired of honest work and need a bit of diversion."

"Do you think your old crew would still be loyal to Gabriel?" Jacquelyn asked.

"Only every man jack of them," Meri affirmed.

"And do you think they could be enticed into a little 'dishonest' work?" A plan began to form in Jacquelyn's mind. It was dicey and by no means foolproof, but she had to try.

"What bee have ye buzzing in yer brain, missy?" Meriwether slanted an assessing look at her.

"I promised Gabriel I wouldn't see him hang," she said, hope sputtering to life for the first time since he'd been taken. "Before God, I mean to keep my word."

Chapter Thirty-six

*H*er skin was satin and fire at once, smooth to his touch and flame to his senses. He took her rosy nipple in his mouth and tasted a bit of heaven. Oh, that little sound she made as he pleasured her. He'd give anything to hear it again.

A bell tolled in the distance.

She arched into him and he gathered her close. She spread herself to receive him, making those helpless little noises of urgency that threatened to shred his control.

Someone was still ringing that damn bell.

He dove into her, home at last. He—

Opened his eyes. The bell was real. Slow and measured, it tolled a relentless message.

"They always ring the bell on hanging days. Gives folks cause to reflect and repent if they've considered taking up evil ways," Pinckney had told him. "And time enough to nip down to Execution Dock. The good spots go fast."

Gabriel sighed and rose from his bed. He'd slept remarkably well for someone who knew it was his last night on earth. And his dreams . . . well, Lyn had been with him all night, alternately passionate and tender. His cock still throbbed. It was a pity he hadn't been able to finish the last dream.

He scraped the dark stubble from his chin and dressed carefully in the new suit of clothing Isabella Wren had thoughtfully ordered for him. A condemned man was expected to appear in his finery and thanks to Jacquelyn's mother, Gabriel would be turned out well enough to appear before King George himself. He ignored the full-bottomed wig she'd sent over, clubbing his own hair back into a queue. He never liked wearing a wig in life. He doubted death would improve the experience.

Gabriel waved off Pinckney's offer of breakfast. Not only was the gruel unpalatable, Gabriel didn't want to burden his belly with something it would only purge later. To this end, he'd shunned food since Lyn left him for the last time. If he was bound to die, he'd make it a good death. The thought of his own shite streaming down his kicking legs was almost worse than hanging itself.

As he was led out into the autumn sunshine, he experienced a strange sense of well-being, a lightness of spirit that surprised him. He stepped up into the oxcart that would bear him to Execution Dock, feeling oddly thankful that it wasn't raining. If a man had to die, why not die on one of those rare bright days when the world was fresh and bright and full of promise?

The cart rattled away from Newgate, squeezing through the twisting lanes and past the Tower. It must have rained in the night. Puddles collected in some of the sunken cobbles, shimmering on the old streets like pools of liquid silver. Why had he never noticed how astonishingly beautiful everything was?

Crowds were beginning to follow him. A few jeered. One or two bowed their heads in prayer for his mortal soul. A little boy hurled a rotten cabbage at him. It struck him squarely on the chest, leaving a patch of muck on Gabe's brocade waistcoat. Gabriel smiled at the lad.

"Well thrown," he called.

"Thanks, mate," the urchin replied, hefting a second cabbage and then deciding against it.

Gabriel had faced death before in countless skirmishes and battles and hadn't flinched. But when the pirates fished him from the deep and gave him a choice, he'd been afraid to choose death. Now that the choice was made for him, he felt only calm resignation.

And more than a little curiosity. If, as Shakespeare said, death was the "undiscovered country," he would look upon this day as the start of a new adventure. Despite what he'd told Lyn, he did talk with the priest and was assured that his sins, though they were many, were forgiven. Gabriel wondered if his father would be there to greet him when he stepped through death's portal.

The oxcart turned a sharp corner and the gallows of Execution Dock came into view.

Please, God, he prayed for the first time in years, *let me not arrive in that strange new land with shite on my breeches.*

There were hundreds of people jostling on the wharf. He could hear dozens of conversations going on around him, all sharp and distinct. He grasped the rough wood of the oxcart's rails and felt each splintered indentation in the grain. All his senses were on high alert as he looked out over the crowd that had come to see him hang. He almost expected to smell the color of the harlot's red dress as she shoved her way to the front for a better view, or the muddy brown smock and apron of the tanner's apprentice who'd enterprisingly climbed a light pole.

The gallows at Wapping's Execution Dock were built low on the bank of the Thames, so that once a prisoner was hung at low tide, his body might be covered over by the prescribed three tides as a warning to others. Gabriel descended the stairs to the dock and mounted the scaffold without assistance. To please the crowd, Gabriel turned to the hangman and made a leg to him, as elegantly as possible for one whose hands were bound. The executioner nodded a silent acknowledgment behind his bizarre leather mask. The gathering cheered Gabriel's bravado.

He gave the same obeisance to the stoop-shouldered official who regarded him through a raised lorgnette. When Gabriel passed the hooded priest, he was surprised to hear the man whisper, "Courage," instead of intoning a blessing.

The official wheezed through a lengthy recitation of Gabriel's crimes. Flashes of his life scrolled past his vision, the blue-green water of the Caribbean as vivid and fresh as if he were actually there again. The official droned on and the crowd began shifting restlessly, emitting a low growl of warning not to try its patience indefinitely.

Wind whipped up a whiff of the Thames, a brackish stink of dying shellfish laced with tar. Gabriel shut out the vision of that sludgy water washing over his corpse. Instead, he conjured Lyn.

He had no regrets, save her. He should have married her in Cornwall, taken her against her will if necessary and the Devil take the rest. But he'd never have made her happy that way, and with a start he realized that making her happy was more important to him than anything. Even his life. So he couldn't have done anything differently, and the thought gave him a certain amount of peace.

Suddenly, the official and the crowd fell silent and he realized he was expected to speak.

"Of the crimes listed, I am guilty," Gabriel said, his voice ringing against the row of buildings that hugged the waterfront. Onlookers even leaned from the second-storey windows. "And of sins unlisted, I am also guilty. So I go to a just punishment without resentment. Of my life, I will say only that I was blessed to have loved once and loved well. My one regret is that I was unable to love long."

The crowd chuckled at his attempt at gallows humor. He noticed one wag scribbling furiously on a portable writing desk. Gabriel's death speech would find its way into one of London's ubiquitous newspapers.

He didn't have time to wonder if the speech would be

judged good or not, for his attention was riveted on the hangman. The noose was slipped around Gabe's neck and the knot
by his left ear cinched tight. Gabriel took a deep breath.

Any moment now.

"Gold," someone shouted. "Gorblimey! It's rainin' gold!"

The onlookers turned as one and over their heads, Gabe saw
a shower of glittering coins tumble from the upstairs windows
of one of the houses by the wharf. He caught a glimpse of
someone who looked like Lyn leaning out the window, a
bright smile pasted on her lips as she shoveled more gold onto
the crowd. And was that Hyacinth and Daisy beside her? Mrs.
Beadle, the twins and Lily were dumping treasure from the
other window as quickly as they could.

I'm seeing things, Gabriel thought, as the trap door opened
beneath his feet and the noose cut off his wind. The rope bit
his neck. No one was even looking his way now as he frog-
kicked the air beneath his feet, hoping in vain for something
to push up on. As he twisted, he saw that the guards who'd
accompanied him in the oxcart from Newgate had deserted
their posts. Even the hangman and the official were edging
away, eager to join the crowd scooping up doubloons. He
was going to die utterly alone.

Except for the priest. The holy man threw back his hood
and as Gabe's vision tunneled, he looked into the eyes of his
favorite uncle. Eustace whipped out a dirk and sliced the rope.
Gabriel dropped a mere two feet and landed in the squishy
muck of low tide.

"Come on, man," Eustace said, reaching a hand down to
haul Gabriel back up onto the scaffold. "Before they run
out of coin."

Even though his hands were still bound before him, Gabriel
ripped the noose from his neck and dragged in a lungful of air.
The stink of London never smelled so sweet. Eustace grabbed

him, and together they splashed into the brackish water of the Thames.

"You save me from hanging to drown me, Uncle?" Gabe said when they reached deeper water. Then a punt pulled alongside with Meriwether at the oars.

"I give ye leave to come aboard, Cap'n."

Gabe and Eustace hauled themselves over the side of the shallow-drafting craft just as the crowd ashore realized they'd missed something. Hurrying back to the edge of Execution Dock, the mob roared like a single feral animal robbed of its prey.

"Better let me row," Gabe said, holding out his hands so Eustace could free them.

"Naw, even you ain't fast enough," Meri said, pointing to the small flotilla of boats being launched. The authorities were headed their way.

Gabriel fingered the rope burns on his neck. Now that he'd had a taste of Madam Gallows' embrace, he was not eager to return willingly. "What now?"

"Hold fast," Meri warned as Gabe saw the *Revenge* nose its way around a bend in the river. A long cable, submerged in the brown muck of the Thames, now rose dripping from the water suspended between the prow of Meri's punt and running up to the *Revenge's* windlass. The punt jerked forward, stopped, then nearly lifted from the water, shooting over the surface as the *Revenge* reeled in the small craft like a harpooned whale. They left the officials' vessels bobbing in their wake.

Once they were near enough, Gabe, Meri and Eustace climbed up the lowered rope ladder and stepped gratefully onto the deck of Gabe's old pirate ship.

"Permission to come aboard?" Gabriel asked belatedly of the new captain, Helmsby.

"Granted," his old shipmate said. "And I surrender the vessel to ye as well, Cap'n. Welcome 'ome."

The crew cheered him roundly, but he pressed himself to the rail, watching Execution Dock grow smaller as the *Revenge* came about to sail out to sea.

"What of Jacquelyn and the children?" he asked Meri.

"Oh, the womenfolk will make their way back to Cornwall and we'll pick 'em up there. Though I don't reckon it'll be a pleasant trip. Them nieces o' yers aren't ones to suffer in silence," Meriwether said. "We figure to load up the rest o' the treasure then."

"It's real?"

"Real as the deck ye stand upon, but Miss Jack promised half of it to the crew for their help in yer rescue, ye see."

The only thing Gabriel could see was a long phalanx of beefeaters marching along the riverside from the Tower toward Wapping.

Toward Lyn.

Then he saw two women and a gaggle of children being prodded into the oxcart that had drawn him from Newgate. They hadn't gotten away cleanly after diverting the crowd's attention. The guards held back the crowd, but the mob surged around the cart. With their bloodlust cheated, they'd be in an ugly mood.

"Make sail!" Helmsby bellowed.

"Belay that," Gabriel said. "Lower the boat. I have to go back."

Chapter Thirty-seven

For the first time in Gabriel's command, his crew mutinied. Instead of lowering the jolly boat as ordered, they sailed the *Revenge* farther up the Thames, risking running aground until the tide rushed back into the waterway. They hoisted both the Jolly Roger and a red flag, signaling that they would give no quarter. Only once they had their guns trained on the beefeaters swarming Execution Dock did they consent to lower the boat for Gabriel to return to land under a flag of truce.

"If the worst should happen, run before the wind and get the ship out of here," Gabriel told Helmsby before he went over the side.

"If the worst should 'appen, rest assured we'll be in the thick of it, Cap'n," Helmsby said. "We ain't enjoyin' bein' respectable all that much in any case. Remember the code. Die all, die merrily."

Gabriel and Meriwether rowed back to the dock and stopped a few feet from the pilings. Lyn and Mrs. B. held his nieces close in the back of the oxcart, trying to shield them but unequal to the task. Cecil Oddbody, flanked by the stiff-ruffed beefeaters, stood before the cart that held all the treasure Gabriel valued in this world. Since the *Revenge's* guns had rolled out of the gun ports, the crowd had fallen back, but they still hovered in the fringes intent on the drama being played out before them. This was undoubtedly the best hanging of the season.

"Well, Drake," Oddbody said. "Looks like you'll dance the hempen jig this day after all."

"Only if you're disposed to negotiate the release of the

women and children you're unlawfully holding," Gabriel said.

Meri cocked his pistol and balanced it across his forearm. "I think I can drop 'im if ye wish it, Cap'n."

Oddbody reached into the cart and pulled out a squealing Lily to hold before him as a shield.

"No, no, don't take her." Jacquelyn reached after the child, but Oddbody wouldn't release her.

But Lily wasn't willing to stay without a fight. She squirmed and kicked and finally clamped her little teeth down on Oddbody's arm. He gave a girlish scream and released her. Lily ran toward Gabriel, made a running leap off the end of the dock and into her uncle's arms. He caught her and deposited her beside Meri, where she burst into tears.

"I had to bite him, Meri," she said between wails. "Don't let Mrs. B. tan my bottom."

"Don't ye fret, missy," Meri assured her without lowering his pistol. "I'll square things with Mrs. B."

"Well, at least we know what you are, Oddbody," Gabriel said. "Any man who hides behind a little girl is the most pitiful coward alive."

The crowd jeered, hissing at Sir Cecil. The scowls on some of the beefeaters' faces said they agreed, but they kept their muskets trained on the oxcart.

"These women and children may look like innocents, but they were caught red-handed aiding and abetting the escape of a convicted pirate," Oddbody said, trying to rally support. "They'll be duly executed for their crimes."

"And yet you won't be able to hang me this day," Gabriel said. "And while I live, I'm still Lord of Dragon Caern. You won't be able to get your thieving hands on my barony, unless I allow it."

"What are you proposing?"

"Release them now," Gabriel said as he rowed the boat

closer to the dock and slipped a rope over one of the posts. "Let them get into the boat with Mr. Meriwether, and you may have me."

"And watch you all sail away? I think not."

"I give you my word."

"The word of a pirate." Sir Cecil spat the words.

Gabriel stepped onto the dock and made a graceful leg. "No, the word of a gentleman. A bond, I believe, you are not able to return."

The crowd cheered.

Sensing the momentum shifting, Oddbody relented. "Very well. Release the prisoners."

Mrs. B. and Jacquelyn shepherded the girls into the waiting boat. Gabriel wished he could take a moment to speak to Lyn, but he felt he must stand at the ready, glaring at Oddbody to keep the man from changing his mind. Then at the last moment, Jacquelyn untied the boat and gave it a shove. Meri started rowing.

"Lyn, get in the boat," Gabriel ordered.

"No, I won't leave you again."

"You'll die here."

"Die all, die merrily." She shot him a quick smile and slipped her hand in his. They turned together to face Oddbody and his guards. He squeezed her hand, knowing he didn't deserve the love of such a woman, but grateful beyond words for it.

The crowd fell to hushed expectancy. This little drama had more turns and twists than a play at the Rose.

"Seize them," Sir Cecil screamed.

But before the guards could follow his command, a coach rattled into the dock area, the crowd making way for it like the Red Sea parting before Moses. The glittering crest of the Elector of Hanover was emblazoned on the side of the grand conveyance. When the matched quartet of white horses were reined to a halt and a footman leaped down to open the door, King George himself stepped majestically from the coach, followed by . . . Isabella Wren.

The crowd, the beefeaters, Jacquelyn and Gabriel, even Oddbody, fell to their knees in deep curtseys and bows, not rising until they heard His Majesty speak.

Of course, it was in German since King George spoke no English, but they all assumed they'd been given permission to rise.

The king spoke again, and Isabella answered him in flaw-less *Deutsch*. His Majesty cast an assessing glance at Gabriel and then turned back to Oddbody.

"His Royal Highness wishes to know why you are trying to hang a man who did him the service of rescuing his royal cousin from French pirates?" Isabella translated.

"Be that as it may, sire," Sir Cecil said with a wheedling tone, "this man has violated the terms of his pardon by ap-pearing in London."

Isabella relayed this information. "The king did not con-sent to any such restriction. When our gracious sovereign pardons a man, he remains pardoned. You have overstepped your authority, Sir Cecil. His Majesty suspects this is not the first such instance." She swept toward the courtier and held out her hand. "The king orders you to surrender his privy seal immediately."

Visibly shaken, Oddbody complied, placing the heavy signet ring in the center of Isabella's palm.

The king leaped into the fray, gesticulating wildly to the beefeaters and then pointing to Oddbody. It was so clearly an order for his arrest, no interpreter was needed. The captain of the beefeaters took obvious delight in manacling Cecil to the oxcart and driving it away with the erstwhile official forced to trot along behind it lest he be dragged to Newgate Prison.

The crowd jeered its contempt for Oddbody and found

good use for the rotten vegetables it had decided not to toss at Gabriel.

King George turned his piercing dark eyes on Jacquelyn and strode over to inspect her, lifting her chin with one finger. Then he raised a questioning brow to Isabella.

Isabella's lips lifted in an enigmatic smile.

"Majesty," Gabriel said. "As your humble vassal, I may not marry without your blessing. However, I find this woman," he cast a loving look at Lyn, "who cannot claim noble blood, is the only one I want. We have already secretly wed. I beg your indulgence in this matter."

Isabella relayed his message and the king spoke at length.

"His Majesty says that sometimes one is obligated to wed outside the dictates of one's heart," Isabella said, a real blush kissing her cheeks. "But in your case, Lord Drake, he sees no such impediment. He is delighted for you, but he cautions that noble blood is of no use if it does not flow through a noble heart."

The king spoke again.

"His Majesty is not surprised that even without his favor, you have done as your heart inclines you, but he forgives your impulsiveness," Isabella related. "And now, he orders you to get that bloody pirate ship out of his harbor before you have another impulse, or he'll change his royal mind."

Epilogue

"Is it normal for it to take this long?" Gabriel asked as he made his tenth circuit of the solar.

"Ye're asking the wrong person," Meri said. "But don't ye fret, me wee Hagitha will see yer babe into the world safe and sound. Here, have another dram. Best whiskey I ever tasted. Who knew Curtmantle had such a good collection of spirits?"

Once Cecil Oddbody was pressed, he informed the Crown that Baron Curtmantle was his minion in the plot to relieve Gabriel of his barony. In fact, Lord Curtmantle was accused of engineering the death of Rhys Drake in what was supposed a hunting accident. So King George saw fit to relieve Hugh Curtmantle of his lands and title. He declared Curtmantle's barony extinct and ordered Hugh and Catherine transported to the Colonies to labor as indentured servants for the rest of their sad lives.

Along with Cecil Oddbody.

Then, as a favor to Lord Drake, His Majesty installed the unlikely personage of Joseph Meriwether as the new baron to the north of Dragon Caern. Meri was mostly pleased to have inherited such a fine wine cellar, but Hagitha Beadle, the new Mrs. Meriwether, was delighted to be known as "my lady."

And there had been another wedding in the family. Isabella Wren finally took a man's name. The new Lady Haversham wrote from Rome that she and "dear Geoffrey" had decided to wed while gallivanting about the Continent.

Isabella was sorry to miss the birth of her first grandchild, but she had never been much use in a sick room and had absolutely no interest in changing a newborn's napkins. She promised to visit once Jacquelyn and Gabriel's child reached a "more interesting age."

Gabriel stopped pacing the solar. "Meri, I can't wait any longer."

"Them women are like to have yer balls for breakin' in on 'em during a birthin'," his friend said cheerfully.

"Well, since my balls caused the problem in the first place, they might not be wrong." Gabriel left Meri to his whiskey and took the curving stairs two at a time.

When he reached his chamber, he hesitated. After nearly hanging, he didn't fear much, but the last few hours spent wondering what was happening to Lyn had reacquainted him with terror. There was no sound coming from beyond the portal, but he didn't think that was a good sign. He pushed the door open slowly.

Lyn was reclining on a mound of pillows, her lovely hair streaming past her shoulders. Even from across the room, he could see that her locks were damp with sweat. One breast was partially exposed and she was looking down at it. No, he realized, she was looking at the wadded bundle in her arms.

"What are you doing here?" Lady Meriwether exclaimed. "We haven't had time to clean the babe or—"

"No, it's all right," Lyn said with a tired smile. "Come in, Gabriel. There's someone who wants to meet you."

He tiptoed toward the bed, feeling like an intruder in his own chamber. Gabe eased a hip down on the side of the bed as Lyn pulled back the blankets to show him a little head, dark hair plastered to the tiny skull.

"Meet your daughter," Lyn said. "I know you were hoping for a son but—"

"Who wants an ugly old boy when I can have the two most beautiful women in the world?" he said as he cradled the baby's delicate head and leaned forward to kiss first Lyn, then the pulsing soft spot on his daughter's crown. "I never believed it was possible to love two people with my whole heart, but I do."

Lyn put a hand to his cheek as the baby rooted at her breast. "We can try again for a boy."

"Ah! The trying is my favorite part, but after all this, I won't rush you. When you're feeling ready, tip me the eye," he said, as he helped guide his daughter's lips to his wife's swollen nipple. "But once you've given me the word, be forewarned, my lady."

She arched a questioning brow at him.

He kissed her again, slowly and deeply. "What a pirate wants, a pirate takes."

Author's Note

Pleasuring the Pirate is a work of fiction, but an actual historical person makes a brief cameo appearance in the story—King George I. First of the Hanoverian kings, he neither spoke English nor spent much time in his island nation, a fact which may explain the relative peace and prosperity of his reign. In his personal life, he was a man of his age. He kept a number of mistresses and reportedly sired children by some of them—so, hinting that my heroine is one of his by-blows is not too far a stretch. It is worth noting however, that though George I was rather cavalier about his own bed partners, he had his wife imprisoned for thirty-two years after he caught *her* with a lover.

The scene in *Pleasuring the Pirate* in which Jacquelyn and Isabella hide Gabriel between feather mattresses to avoid arrest is borrowed from a real-life account. Grace Elliott, a famous English courtesan, saved the Marquis de Champcenetz from a date with Madame Guillotine during the bloody days of the French Revolution in the exact same manner. Miss Elliott was imprisoned, but later escaped France with her lovely head still attached to her shoulders. Her heroism during a dark time is a testament to character that has nothing to do with how she secured her living.

I hope you enjoyed *Pleasuring the Pirate*. Please do stop by my Web site at www.emilybryan.com for a peek at what's coming next!

Happy reading,

Emily

Coming March 2009:

Vexing the Viscount
by Emily Bryan

Read ahead for a sneak peak.

Item: One clay lamp
after the fashion of an erect phallus
—from the Manifest of Roman Oddities,
found near London, England
3rd July, in the Year of Our Lord 1731

"Hmph! I wonder if that's life-sized," Miss Daisy Drake murmured as she leaned down to inspect the ancient lamp. Talking to herself was a bad habit, she knew, but since none of her friends shared her interest in antiquities, she often found herself without companions on this sort of outing.

"Of course, it would be on the most inaccessible shelf in the display case." Solely to vex her, she suspected. Daisy scrunched down to get a better look at it. The clay lamp was only about four inches long, but in other respects, so far as Daisy knew, was perfectly life-like. She opened her small valise and drew out paper, quill and inkpot in order to take a few notes. "Where *does* the flame come out?"

"Right where one would expect," a masculine voice sounded near her. Daisy's spine snapped suddenly upright.

The crown of her head clipped his chin with a *thwack* and she bit her tongue.

"Oh!" One of her hands flew to her throbbing mouth, the other to the top of her head where her cunning little hat was smashed beyond recognition. Her sheaf of papers fluttered to the polished oak floor like maple leaves. The small inkwell flew into the air and landed squarely on the white lawn of his shirtfront.

"Oh, I'm so dreadfully sorry." Daisy dabbed at the stain with her hanky and only succeeded in spreading it down his waistcoat. A black blob dribbled onto his fawn-colored breeches. At least, thank Heaven, plastering the man with ink covered her unmaidenly interest in that lewd little lamp. "How clumsy of me!"

Then she made the additional mistake of looking up at him. Her mouth gaped like a cod for a moment. She forced it closed by sheer strength of will.

He'd grown into himself since she'd seen him last. His fine straight nose was no longer out of proportion to the rest of his face. As he rubbed his square jaw, Daisy saw that the little scar on his chin was still visible, a neat triangle of pale, smooth skin. She'd recognize that anywhere.

After all, she'd given it to him.

His curly dark hair was hidden beneath a dandy's wig. Oh, she hoped to heaven he hadn't taken to shaving his head as some fops did. Uncle Gabriel was a dogged opponent of the fashion. Said it was nothing but French foppery. Since Uncle Gabriel's opinions were only slightly less authoritative than a papal bull, the aversion to wigs had rubbed off. Besides, hiding a head of hair like Lucian's was almost sacrilege.

An ebony wisp escaped near his left ear.

Good. Daisy breathed a sigh of relief. His dark mane was one of Lucian's finest points, after all. Not that there weren't plenty of others.

His full lips twitched in a half smile.

"An interesting piece, isn't it?" He was still the same old

Lucian. Still direct, even at the expense of propriety. He wasn't going to play the gentleman and pretend he hadn't caught her ogling that Roman phallus.

"Indeed." Surely he understood her interest was purely intellectual. "Obviously a cultic object of some sort. It is certainly a curiosity."

"It is gratifying to meet a young lady who is...curious," he drawled.

Daisy lifted her chin in what she hoped was a confident manner. "Antiquities give us but a glimpse into the lives of the ancients. That lamp merely poses new questions."

"Ah, yes, and you raised some intriguing ones," he agreed, one of his dark brows arched. "I'd be happy to help you discover the answers."

Was he suggesting something improper? If he was, it would serve him right if she gave him another scar. Daisy might be innocent yet, but thanks to Isabella she was not wholly ignorant of men.

"You owe me no further assistance. Not after I ruined your shirt. And your waistcoat. And your—" She shouldn't have allowed her gaze to travel the ink's path down the front of his breeches. To cover her embarrassment, she sank to the floor to retrieve her scattered notes.

"Think nothing of it." His voice was now a deep rumble instead of the adolescent squeak she remembered. "I should be more careful where I put my jaw. I do hope you have not suffered an injury to your head."

His eyes were even darker and more beguiling than she remembered. The fact that she even had a head temporarily escaped her notice.

"Please, allow me." Lucian knelt beside her and helped her reassemble her pages. Then he offered his hand to help her up and she took it.

Had someone loosed a jar of Junebugs in her belly?

"Thank you, my lord," she murmured, for lord he was.

Lucian Ignacio de Castenello Beaumont. Son and heir of Ellory Beaumont, Earl of Helmsby. Daisy assumed Lucian was now styling himself Viscount Rutland, one of his father's lesser titles, since the earl was still very much alive.

But Daisy remembered him as Iggy.

His ears had turned an alarming shade of red when she called him that. He complained Iggy was not dignified, as though a skinny, dirty-kneed twelve-year-old was capable of anything remotely like dignity.

But he was no longer twelve. Lucian must be two and twenty by now. The last time Daisy had heard his name bandied about in Polite Society, the sober matron doing the talking lowered her voice, but the words "rake" and "wastrel" were unmistakably used.

Neither of which did anything to slow her racing heart, Daisy admitted with a sigh.

She accepted the stack of papers from him, casting about in her mind for the right thing to say. "There's no salvaging your ensemble. I'll have a new suit of clothing made for you."

She could afford to be generous. After all, she'd discovered the family fortune beneath the stones of Dragon Caern just when other members of the nobility were losing theirs in the South Sea stock swindle.

"I wouldn't hear of it," he assured her smoothly, though she'd heard his father had invested heavily in the failed company. Perhaps his mother's family was still solvent. She'd been a *contessa* in her own right in her homeland. All vestiges of Lucian's Italian accent were gone, erased by a few years at Oxford, no doubt. Daisy thought that a terrible shame.

"I've been meaning to retire this suit in any case," he

informed her. "The style is *tres passé, n'est ce pas?*"

That would be a pity since the cut of that green frockcoat does wonderful things for his shoulders and as for those bree— Daisy caught herself before her thoughts completely ran away with her, but lost her fight with the urge to gape at the way his breeches molded to his thighs.

His smile broadened.

"I see my lord has become an avid rider," she said because no other coherent thought would form in her mind.

Only the regular exercise of squeezing a horse between his legs could account for his musculature. She was glad he'd finally learned. He certainly had no aptitude for it on his first and only visit to Dragon Caern.

"Indeed, I ride daily," he said, flashing a fine set of teeth. "But how could you 'see' that?"

Her mouth formed a silent 'oh' and she mentally cursed herself. She was acting like some pudding-headed debutant.

"Riding improves a man's…posture." Daisy bit her lip to keep from babbling further. A guilty blush heated her cheeks. She sidled away from the case where the phallic lamp was on display.

Lucian looked around the nearly deserted exhibit hall. "It seems there is no way for us to be properly introduced, but perhaps you will allow me the honor of giving you my name."

He doesn't recognize me!

How was it possible that she could carry about his image in her head for all these years and he should have completely forgotten that Daisy Elizabeth Drake even existed? Bristling with indignation, she took another step backward to put more distance between them.

Before she could remind him that he should know her

name quite well, the door behind her swung open and whacked her soundly on the bottom.

"There you are, Rutland." A monocled gentleman waved Lucian in with urgency. "We've been waiting for you."

Daisy recognized him as Sir Alestair Murray, head of the Society of Antiquaries. She'd petitioned for admission several times only to have Sir Alestair black-ball her membership on account of her gender. The man cast a quick dismissive gaze over her and turned back to Lord Rutland.

Murray's eye-piece dangled from its silver chain when he noticed the ink stain marring the viscount's finery. "Good God, man, what's happened to you?"

"It was—" she began.

"My fault entirely," Lucian finished for her. "I will be in directly, Murray."

Lucian turned back to Daisy. "Perhaps once I've delivered my presentation, we may continue our discussion. I'd enjoy learning what such a charming young lady finds so…curious in these dry halls." He made an elegant leg and shot her a wicked grin. "And for your information, the answer is no."

"No?" Her brows nearly met in a puzzled frown.

"It's not life-sized."

Alissa Johnson

As Luck Would Have It

A WOMAN OF THE WORLD...

After years of wild adventures overseas, Miss Sophie Everton is in no hurry to return home to the boring strictures of the ton. But she's determined to reclaim her family's fortune—even if she has to become a spy for the Prince Regent to do it.

A MAN ON A MISSION...

Before she can get her first assignment, she lands right in the lap of the dark and dashing Duke of Rockeforte. She's faced hungry tigers that didn't look nearly as predatory. Somehow the blasted man manages to foil her at every turn—and make her pulse thrum with something more than just the thrill of danger.

AND THE FICKLE FINGER OF FATE

To make a true love match, they'll have to learn to trust in each other...and, of course, a little bit of luck.

Available October 2008!   ISBN 13: 978-0-8439-6155-3

☐ **YES!**

Sign me up for the Historical Romance Book Club and send my FREE BOOKS! If I choose to stay in the club, I will pay only $8.50* each month, a savings of $6.48!

NAME: _____

ADDRESS: _____

TELEPHONE: _____

EMAIL: _____

☐ I want to pay by credit card.

☐ **VISA**   ☐ **MasterCard.**   ☐ **DISCOVER**

ACCOUNT #: _____

EXPIRATION DATE: _____

SIGNATURE: _____

Mail this page along with $2.00 shipping and handling to:
Historical Romance Book Club
PO Box 6640
Wayne, PA 19087
Or fax (must include credit card information) to:
610-995-9274
You can also sign up online at **www.dorchesterpub.com**.
*Plus $2.00 for shipping. Offer open to residents of the U.S. and Canada only. Canadian residents please call 1-800-481-9191 for pricing information.
If under 18, a parent or guardian must sign. Terms, prices and conditions subject to change. Subscription subject to acceptance. Dorchester Publishing reserves the right to reject any order or cancel any subscription.